WHAT MATTERS
BLOOD

BY
TOM WALLACE

PUBLICATIONS

California

Behler Publications
California

What Matters Blood
A Behler Publications Book

Copyright by Tom Wallace 2004
Author Photograph by David Coyle
Cover design by Sun Son – www.sunsondesigns.com

Library of Congress Cataloging-in-Publication Data is available
Control Number: 2004094877

FIRST EDITION

ISBN 1-933016-08-6
Published by Behler Publications, LLC
Lake Forest, California
www.behlerpublications.com

Manufactured in the United States of America

To Marilyn Underwood

Acknowledgments

The author wishes to thank the following people for their help, advice, faith and support: Louise Wallace, Julie Watson, Ed Watson, Bobbie Watkins, Wanda Underwood, Denny Slinker, Scott Boggs, Brooks Downing and Doug Barnes. Also, a special thanks to Lorna Lynch and Karen Novak whose magical editing skills helped shape and improve this book.

Author's Note:

The Lexington, Kentucky, of this novel is, as Kristofferson would say, partly truth and partly fiction.

PROLOGUE

Killing women was much easier than writing a novel.

Eldon uncovered this truth two years ago, on that cold, blustery February night when he claimed his first victim. The first of the Chosen Ones. That night, as bullets of ice peppered the windows, he stepped out of the darkness and into the light. Into illumination. He had ascended, moving into a world that had long awaited his arrival.

Eldon murdered Allison Parker, strangling her with a belt, in her own apartment. From beginning to end, it had taken him less than two minutes to extinguish her life. In contrast, it had taken him six years to write his first novel, seven to write the second. He hardly broke a sweat killing Allison; he sweated blood penning those two books.

Of course, time wasn't the issue here. It wouldn't have mattered if it had taken him two hours to kill Allison Parker. Or two days. The crucial point was this: it had been *easy*. No more difficult a task than taking out the garbage. No more of a challenge than stepping on a cockroach.

Killing Allison—and, later Becky Adams—had been... effortless.

Eldon's thoughts were interrupted by a crack of thunder so close it seemed to come from inside the car. Then another crack, this one louder. Very close, he whispered to himself. *Too* close. To his right, a zigzag spear of lightning creased the night sky. Then another boom of thunder. He jumped, shivered, felt goose bumps crawl up his arms. Thunder frightened him. Ever since he was a kid. Lightning was okay, but thunder—that was a different matter.

Seconds later, as Eldon turned right off Harrodsburg Road onto Lane Allen, there were two more blasts of thunder. Then the clouds unleased a deluge. Relentless sheets of rain, driven by a savage wind, slapped hard against his windshield. His wipers, though working double time, fought a losing battle against the torrent of rain cascading down from the sky. Visibility went from poor to worse.

Jesus...this rain. It's a monsoon. We're not supposed to get crappy weather like this. Not in Lexington, Kentucky.

Take it slow, he mumbled to himself. Be cautious.

But wasn't he always cautious? More careful than a surgeon? More disciplined than a monk? Yes, most assuredly, he was. He had killed twice, yet he would be the last person on earth anyone would suspect. Caution and discipline—the foundation of his success.

Eldon turned right, pulled into the Commonwealth Plaza parking lot, then slowly circled until his car faced the row of shopping center buildings. Taking his handkerchief from his coat pocket, he wiped the windshield and looked out, squinting hard to see. The parking lot, as best he could make out, was empty. Not a single car. Certainly no human beings. Just pools of water growing deeper by the minute. No one, sane or crazy, would be foolish enough to brave this nonsense. This was enough rain to douse the fires of hell.

He looked at his watch: 8:10. No need to move, he decided. Better to stay here, relax, let the storm pass, wait until thunder's cannons were silent. Rain like this can't last much longer.

The irony of seeking refuge here, less than one hundred feet from the dance academy owned by—*her*, wasn't lost on Eldon. Thinking of her now—and that other scorpion—the two who should have given him refuge all his life but hadn't sent a wave of revulsion coursing through his body. Refuge was the last thing he would get from them. Refuge...or love.

God, I hate them. Hate them for what they think they are. For their superiority attitude.

No, I will not allow them to intrude upon tonight. I shan't be that weak. I shall cast them back into the oblivion they deserve.

A smile crept across his face.

Soon, I shall cast that evil pair from this earth.

Closing his eyes, listening to the rain hammer his car with ever-increasing force, he sent his thoughts in other directions. Allison Parker and Becky Adams. How easy it was to take a human life. Why he was able to kill without remorse. Without guilt. Eldon had always known he would become a killer. He'd known it since he was a young boy, living in hell with those twin devils, his life ruled by misery. But why had it taken so long for the inevitable to happen? Why had he delayed his destiny? He was, after all, in his mid-thirties when he killed for the first time. That's late for a first-time killer, especially one who knew from an early age that it was never a matter of if, only when. Why had the dam that held back his river of hate taken so long to collapse? He had no answers for these questions, nor did he particularly care if those answers forever eluded him. He was beyond mysteries, beyond answers. Beyond judgment.

Then there was the most fundamental question of all: why kill in the first place? Why take another's life? Murder dated back to the very beginning—according to scripture, the first act between two men resulted in a homicide—yet the sanctity of life is now, and has always been, the one constant in all civilized societies. To kill was to look the Creator, the giver of life, squarely in the eye and say, "fuck off." What would possess a sane man—and Eldon certainly considered himself sane—to follow such a path?

But Eldon had no time to spend considering these matters. They were irrelevant to him. Pointless. To ponder them for a minute, to search for cause and effect, to use, as Camus had said, "the acrobatics of logic" in an attempt to give reason or meaning to the act of murder was a colossal waste of time and energy. He would not submit to such folly, involve his intellect in such a futile undertaking. Besides, there were no answers out there, waiting to be uncovered like bones at an archeological dig. Camus had called it when he'd said, "the worm is in man's heart." Let that stand as the final testament. Let the search begin and end there.

That Allison Parker had been the catalyst for his breakthrough was certainly no mystery. He had killed her because she was so aloof, so arrogant, so smug—*so much like them*—and because she had dismissed him as though he were an insect. Hadn't he been kind to her? Hadn't he helped her on at least two occasions? Hadn't he treated her with respect and dignity? Yes. And, yet, when he dared to ask her to lunch—a harmless mid-day outing, not even a real date—she had laughed in his face, turned and strolled away.

At that moment, Eldon knew he had at last come face to face with his destiny. There could be no more putting it off. No more procrastinating. He would kill Allison Parker. He would dim forever those eyes that had showed such condescension, repugnance, and superiority toward him. He would silence that laughter.

He would rid the world of one more woman who doubted his masculinity. *How dare they question that?* In death, she would discover his manhood.

Sitting in his car, fighting sleep, Eldon saw a light flicker inside the dance academy. Seconds later, he saw a woman step outside, holding a raincoat over her head, looking up at the sky. He knew it wasn't *her*—it couldn't be; her car wasn't in the lot. Had to be that young dance instructor. Abby something. He'd seen her once, briefly, from a distance, not more than two weeks ago. A real looker. Resembled Allison Parker and Becky Adams.

Resembled *them*.

He'd made eye contact with her that afternoon, nodded, smiled. Her eyes met his, then moved on. Like he wasn't present in the room. Invisible. In that instant, he knew she was destined to be his next Chosen One. For her arrogance, she would pay the ultimate price.

Eldon smiled. He hadn't planned on killing her tonight. Indeed, he had yet to put together a plan or establish a time in which he would act. He'd figured on at least another week, maybe two. There was never a need to hurry or take unnecessary risks. Better to be methodical than impulsive.

Caution and discipline—never leave home without them.

And yet, much to his surprise, he felt no fear, no apprehension. No self-doubting. Why not tonight? he asked himself. Why put it off? The situation couldn't be more conducive to success. The Chosen One was alone. He also knew from recent research that she lived by herself. There was no one else in sight. No potential witnesses. In this rain and darkness, no one would see him pick her up or leave the parking lot. His black car would be little more than a shadow moving through the night.

The voice in his head whispered, "go."

Eldon drove slowly through the rain-drenched parking lot, pulling up next to the curb in front of the dance academy. He lowered the window on the passenger side, leaned across the seat, said, "Stranded?"

"Seems that way."

"What time was your ride supposed to be here?"

"Eight."

"I'm sure this rain is the cause of his delay."

"Probably so. But it would've been nice if he'd called, let me know he was running late."

"Have you tried to contact him?"

"Called his cell phone. No answer." She came closer to the car, looked inside. "Haven't I seen you somewhere before? Aren't you—"

"I have been many places, my dear, so it's very possible that our paths have indeed crossed."

"No...I've seen you somewhere. Recently."

"The bookstore, perhaps?"

"That's right. The bookstore. Last week, I believe. By the way, I'm Abby. Abby Kaplan."

"Would you care for a ride home, Abby? No sense staying here alone."

"I probably should wait. Give him a few more minutes."

"Nonsense," Eldon said. "In this weather, it could be an hour or more before he shows up. Better let me give you a lift."

"I live on Bellefonte."

"That's no problem."

"You sure? I don't want you going out of your way."

"I am not so noble as to do that which is problematic. It would be no trouble at all to give you a lift."

Abby nodded. "Let me turn off the lights and lock up."

"Take your time, my dear. Your chariot awaits."

CHAPTER 1

Seventeen years as a homicide detective had taught Jack Dantzler one thing: All killers fuck up.

Dantzler reminded himself of this as he sat in his car, stuck in traffic, waiting for the light to change: *All killers fuck up.* It was inevitable. Like the Yankees winning another World Series, or Hollywood turning out more and more cinematic crap. It wasn't going to change either, not unless there was a sudden increase in criminal intelligence. And the odds of that happening were seriously slim.

Planning the perfect crime was easy; it was the carrying it out that proved the tricky part. Dantzler had built his reputation on discovering the miscalculations of murderers. His reputation, for the past seventeen years, had been flawless. Thirty-three homicides; thirty-three perps caught, convicted, and sentenced. *Perfect—like God's soul.* Until now.

Dantzler parked, climbed out of his Forester and headed toward the small brick house, with yet another murder investigation staring him in the face. He felt a million light years away from perfection. A dull, throbbing pain stabbed at his temples and his stomach churned a mad alchemist's mixture of bile, anger, and frustration. He steeled himself against a cop's worst nightmare—the ever-present fear of failure—by doing what he'd always done in moments like this. He silently whispered his own private mantra: *I'm smarter than you, goddammit.*

Standing on the wet sidewalk outside the house, Dantzler viewed the all-too-familiar scene. Yellow tape ringing the yard, uniformed cops stationed like sentries guarding the royal palace, medical personnel, C.S.I.'s coming and going, and rubbernecking neighbors speaking in whispers, wondering what could possibly have happened.

Just this, Dantzler could have *told them. A nice house in a secure neighborhood—your neighborhood—has been visited by evil. Norman Rockwell meet Norman Bates. Now go home, folks, hug your kids and be thankful it wasn't your house.* Dantzler lifted the yellow tape and ducked under it. A young patrolman, his face stone-like and serious, raised his eyes and said, "Bad scene inside, sir."

Dantzler nodded. He didn't need to be told what was awaiting him. He knew. The way he knew that tomorrow's dawn would bring with it another beautiful sunrise. The way he knew that men and women and children everywhere would wake and rise and go about living their lives, finding joy and happiness in a world that had become dark and dangerous and treacherous. Man's continuing faith in the future was the last great miracle.

He knew that waiting for him inside was a beautiful young dark-haired woman, naked, dead on the sofa, surrounded by various "friends."

Just like the other two. Allison Parker and Becky Adams.

If he was right—and all his cop's instincts said he was—then there could be but one conclusion: This was the work of a serial killer.

He'd said so after Becky Adams was murdered, but his was the lone voice within the Homicide Department. Others argued against him, citing the lengthy time period between the two murders—seventeen months—and the fact that the killer used a belt to strangle Allison and a silk scarf in Becky's case. Legitimate points, Dantzler admitted, then and now...but—absolutely dead wrong. There were too many aspects being overlooked by his colleagues, most notably the calling cards left by the killer on the victims' body, and the fact that the killer had chosen out-of-town victims, thus greatly increasing his chances of eluding capture. Dantzler knew with certainty after the second murder that this was the work of a single person, and nothing was going to change his mind. Not the atypical time frame, not the different instruments of strangulation. And certainly not a chorus of dissident voices coming at him from within the department. He hadn't earned his reputation by being a blind follower.

No, this trio of deadly dramas was the work of the same director. Dantzler knew something else as well: confirmation of that conclusion lay just inside the front door he would enter within seconds. Dantzler took a deep breath, ran his fingers through his long, brown hair, then slowly walked up the steps onto the porch. *I'm smarter than you, goddammit.*

Dantzler entered the house and surveyed the scene. Instantly, he realized two things: the same killer had indeed committed this crime; and there were far too many people milling around. The crime scene would soon be royally fucked up, if it hadn't already been. He walked past one of the uniformed officers and approached a young woman he recognized but didn't know.

"Officer." Dantzler looked for her nametag, couldn't see it. "Officer..."

"It's Sergeant, sir," she said. "Sergeant Dunn."

"Are you in charge here, Sergeant Dunn?"

"Yes, sir."

"You fond of big crowds?"

"I'm not sure I understand the question, sir."

"Simple. Do you like big crowds?"

"Not particularly. No."

"Neither do I, especially at one of my crime scenes." Dantzler waved toward the room. "Get everyone out of here who is not absolutely essential to the investigation."

"Yes, sir."

As she turned to leave, he said, "Do you know who discovered the body?"

"Yes, sir. A neighbor from across the street. Kenneth Bradley."

"Did anyone talk to him?"

"I did."

"And what's his story?"

"He was delivering a cake his wife had baked for the victim. He said he didn't think anyone was home—there was no car in the driveway—but since there was a light on inside, he decided to knock anyway. When he didn't get a response, he looked in the window and saw the body. He then ran home and called the police."

"Little late to be delivering a cake, isn't it?"

"His wife insisted."

"Wives will do that."

"Yes, sir."

"How well did he know the victim?"

"Not all that well. Apparently, his wife knew her better than he did."

"Did you speak with her?"

"Tried to, but she's so shaken they had to sedate her. I told her that someone would meet with her again later. But I really don't think she's gonna have much to offer."

"You never know."

She nodded. "Oh, and I also had Johnson and Havens do a quick canvass of the neighbors on the block. Came up with a big fat zero there, too. No one heard or saw anything out of the ordinary last night. None of them really knew the victim. They were familiar with her mainly because they'd seen her jogging, usually very early in the morning."

"Make sure I get their names. They'll all need to be re-interviewed."

"Yes, sir."

Dantzler was silent for a moment, then said, "Do you know what kind of car the victim drove?"

"Blue BMW. I'm not sure of the year or model."

"Any idea where it is?"

"No, sir."

"Should be easy to get that information." Dantzler nodded toward the living room. "Make that herd disappear."

"Yes, sir."

She started to walk away.

"Sergeant Dunn."

"Yes, sir."

"Good work."

***

For the next thirty minutes, as the C.S.U. personnel went about their business of collecting potential evidence and processing the crime scene, Dantzler moved around the room, careful not to intrude upon the work being done. He jotted notes, sketched several rudimentary drawings of the area surrounding the body, then called the photographer back and told him to take several close-up shots of the wound on the victim's neck. He also ordered more photos of the bloody carpet next to the victim's head.

"You get good ones of the postcard and the medal?" Dantzler asked, pointing at the victim. "Tight, up close?"

The photographer, whose name was Barnes, nodded. "Yeah, at least a half-dozen of each. Want me to take some more?"

"You'd better. Just to be on the safe side. The scarf, too."

Barnes snapped away from several angles, then looked up at Dantzler. "Damn, I've never seen anything like this before," he muttered.

"I have," Dantzler answered.

Two hours later, at a little past midnight, Dantzler finished his preliminary investigation. It hadn't yielded much, and he hadn't expected it to. No prints, no blood spatters, no signs of a struggle, no witnesses. Nothing. Just another victim, another statistic, another senseless theft of human life.

Whoever committed this crime—and the other two—was a sharp cookie, a definite big-leaguer. He had no intention of getting caught, and, thus far in the game, he had demonstrated the skills and intelligence to stay free of the noose. No slip-ups, no oversights. Just ruthless efficiency.

Mac Tinsley, a smallish man with dark owl-rim glasses, walked in front of Dantzler. He pointed at the body lying on the couch.

"Can I have it?" he said. Like ordering a sandwich at the deli.

"Got an approximate time of death for me, Mac?"

"Judging by the absence of rigor, I'd say she's been dead a good twenty-four hours, possibly longer. Won't know that until later. Any further questions?"

"No."

"Then can I take her?"

"Yeah. She's yours."

"I'll get you some preliminary results late tomorrow," Mac said. "But if this is anything like the other two..."

"This is *exactly* like the other two."

"Well, then, don't expect much."

At 12:22 a.m., Dantzler watched as the ambulance carrying the body of Abigail Lynn Kaplan, of New York City, 23, daughter of Rachel and Eli Kaplan, made its way to the morgue, the first stop on a final journey that would end in Brooklyn's Beth Israel Cemetery.

Dantzler's cell phone went off. He removed it from his jacket pocket and flipped it open. The call was from Captain Richard Bird.

"I understand we've got number three on our hands," Bird said.

"What we've got is a serial killer, Rich," Dantzler said. "Which is exactly what I tried to tell you after the Adams girl was killed."

"Any reason for me to hope otherwise?"

"Nope. Same scene, different victim."

"Fuck."

"That's what I like about you, Rich. You're so damn eloquent. Profound, too."

"You're the one with a degree in philosophy—you be profound. Me, I'll stick with crude and vulgar."

Dantzler laughed.

"Listen, Jack," Bird said, "who's there with you?"

"A couple of unnies, Walters from the C. S.U., Sally from latents, and the new kid. I think she said her name is Dunn."

"Laurie Dunn. What's your take on her?"

"She did a damn good job tonight. I was impressed."

"This was her first homicide."

"Even more impressive."

"I'm putting together a task force, which you'll head, and I want her on the team. We've got to catch this maniac and I think she can help us."

"She's awfully young, Rich."

"Jack, how old were you when you worked your first homicide case?"

"Twenty-four."

"She's older than that. She can handle it."

"What makes you so sure she's ready for something this big?"

"Remember the Zeldin case? The one where the father abducted his kid, kept her locked up in the cellar for a couple of weeks?"

"I remember—what's that got to do with Dunn?"

"She broke it. Got the father to admit what he'd done and where the kid was."

"I didn't know that."

"Of course not. Douglas, being the publicity hound he is, took all the credit. Never once mentioned Dunn's contribution. But it was Dunn's work that saved the kid. She came through like a seasoned pro. Charlie Bolton said she's got more natural talent for police work than anyone who's come along since you first joined the force. Coming from Charlie, that's damn high praise. I wouldn't send you a dud, Jack. Not at a time like this. Trust me, she can help."

"Okay, she's on the team."

"Why don't you bring her up to speed tonight? Give her a crash course on the first two murders."

"It's past midnight, Rich. Little late for a crash course, don't you think?"

"That's what coffee and all-night diners are for, my friend. Prep her as best you can tonight, then let's meet in my office tomorrow morning at nine."

"You mean '*this*' morning at 9."

"Details, details…it's always the picky details with you, isn't it, Jack. Yes, *this* morning. Be there."

Dantzler punched off, then went into the kitchen. Laurie Dunn, her back to him, was watching Gene Walters collect samples of a dark stain from the floor.

"Sergeant Dunn," Dantzler said.

Startled, Laurie turned quickly, her right hand instinctively dropping toward her .38.

"Easy there, Dirty Harry," Dantzler said, holding up both hands. "Shooting me is only going to cause you a mountain's worth of paper work. You don't want that."

"Sorry, I didn't hear you," Laurie said, clearly embarrassed.

Gene Walters stood and smiled. "Jack's like the wind—present but invisible."

"Why, Geno, I had no idea you were a mystic."

"The extent of what you don't know would fill volumes, Jack."

"You got that right." Dantzler looked at Laurie. "Come with me."

"Where are we going?" she asked.

"School."

CHAPTER 2

Coyle's All-Night Diner, one of Lexington's last remaining downtown treasures, was especially busy, even for one o'clock on a Saturday morning. The reason for tonight's population surge was a large group of black-clad Goth types, fresh from a midnight showing of Kubrick's *A Clockwork Orange* at the Kentucky Theater. They commandeered two tables and three booths in the rear of the diner, huddled together like cabalists, whispering secrets in their own unique language, and oblivious to the rest of the world.

Dissecting the world of Alex and his fellow Droogs. Dantzler observed the group with interest. It consisted mainly of high school kids, although a couple of the boys were clearly older, probably students at the University of Kentucky. The male-female breakdown was about even, with the boys winning easily in the tattoo department and the girls coming out on top in the area of body piercing. Although their intent was to affect a scary, sinister look, most of them, boys included, came off looking like Winona Ryder in *Beetlejuice*. Despite their best efforts at nonconformity and anti-social appearance, these kids didn't fool Dantzler. He'd bet his next two paychecks that they were bright as hell, fairly insightful, and probably pretty nice to boot. A little lost, sure, and a major worry to their parents, but nothing to be overly concerned with. He didn't see a Dylan Klebold in the bunch.

Laurie glanced over her shoulder and studied the group for several seconds. "Think they'll lead the next big revolution?" she said, turning back to face Dantzler.

"You kidding? Ten years from now, they'll all be working on Wall Street and driving Beemers." Dantzler clasped his hands behind his head and leaned back. "You're wondering what this meeting is all about. Right? "

Well, yeah, you could say that. Laurie picked up her half-empty mug of hot chocolate and took a sip. After nearly thirty minutes of silence wrapped around about five minutes of small talk, she still had no real clue why she was sitting in an all-night diner at such an ungodly hour of the morning when she could be home in bed catching a few much-needed winks. If that weren't perplexing enough, the fact that she had practically been ordered here by a legendary homicide detective, a man she had never spoken to in her life before tonight, sent her sense of curiosity off the charts. It had to do with Abby Kaplan's murder, that much she was sure of. But why here? Why now? Why her?

She nodded. "What is it all about?"

"How do you feel about working Homicide?" Dantzler asked, breaking nearly a minute of silence.

"It's been my goal from the day I first joined the force. It's everyone's goal, isn't it?"

"Do you think you're ready for it?

"Yes."

"It can be tough," he said. "Physically and emotionally. It requires a special mentality to do it and not go nuts. You have to burn inside to succeed...to speak for the dead. And yet you have to somehow keep yourself at a safe distance, to not get too close to the victims. It's a delicate balancing act, and not everyone can do it. I've seen this job get the best of good, earnest, hard-working cops."

"I can handle it, sir. I've spent the past two years with the Missing and Exploited Children's Unit, so I know something about 'burning inside to succeed while keeping a safe distance.' I can't imagine that speaking for the dead could be any more difficult than speaking for kids."

"You worked with Charlie Bolton over there, didn't you?"

"For the first year. Until he retired."

"Charlie's a good man. You couldn't have had a better rabbi."

"Am I being assigned to Homicide, sir? To work this murder?"

"Murders."

She raised her eyebrows. "How many we talking about?"

"Three." Dantzler lifted the water pitcher and refilled his glass. "I'm including the Parker and Adams murders as well."

"The three cases are connected?"

"Yeah. Seems we have a serial killer on our hands, Laurie."

"So...the rumors are true."

Dantzler nodded. "Captain Bird is forming a task force and he wants you on it. So do I."

"Yes... sure. Of course, I definitely want to be part of it."

"What have you heard about any of this?"

"Whispers, here and there," Laurie said, shrugging. "You know, break room chatter, mostly. The vics were strangled, something about a postcard and a religious medallion. Pretty bizarre stuff. After what I saw tonight, I guess the rumors were true."

"Unfortunately, yes."

"Something like this—a serial killer with such a twisted M.O.—is usually all over the TV and newspapers. They make TV movies about those folks before the case is even solved. You guys have done a helluva job keeping the lid on it. How'd you manage it?"

"We've been lucky so far."

"Luck always helps," she said.

"Yeah, maybe so. Only trouble is, luck's a lot like a teenager. You can't always count on it."

"Meaning?"

"Meaning, I have a hunch our luck's run out, that the shit is about to hit the fan."

"You're talking about the press, right?"

"What else? The vulture corps. There's no way something like this stays a secret for long. It's just a matter of time until someone connects the dots and figures it out. When that happens, our job becomes about a hundred times tougher to do."

Laurie pushed her mug aside and leaned forward. "Tell me how you've been lucky."

"Well, for starters, the timing of the murders has certainly worked to our advantage," Dantzler said. "The first two were seventeen months apart, this one nine months later. I suppose we should be thankful he hasn't been more voracious. And up till now, we've been able to keep certain facts away from the press.

Particular details of the crimes that make it clear this is the work of a single killer."

"Are you absolutely certain that it is?"

"Yeah."

"How do you know that? I mean, why are you so positive?"

"The way he kills them. What he leaves on the bodies."

"So what *do* the media folks know?"

"Essentially that the two—three—victims died as a result of asphyxiation. Period."

Dantzler took a napkin off the table. He folded it in half, then into quarters. After wadding it into a ball, he tossed it against the wall and watched it bounce back onto the table. "This is one careful bastard that we're after, Laurie," he said. "This guy's not going to be easy to catch."

"What makes you so sure it's a male?"

"History, mainly. Although the number of violent homicides committed by women in this country is rising at an alarming rate, there are still very few known instances of female serial killers."

Laurie shook her head. "That's a Criminology 101 lecture, not an answer to my question."

Dantzler grinned.

"What's so amusing?"

"I usually get by with answers like that. It's good to know that you'll keep me on my toes." He motioned to the waitress. "Marcy, could I get another cup of coffee?"

Marcy Coleman grabbed the coffee pot and filled Dantzler's cup. "Would you care for more hot chocolate?" she said to Laurie.

"No, thanks," Laurie said.

After watching her walk away, Dantzler dumped a spoonful of sugar into the cup. "Without looking at Marcy, tell me how you would describe her to a complete stranger," he said, stirring cream into the coffee.

"What are you doing, testing my skills?"

"Don't be a wise guy," Dantzler said. "Just humor me, okay?"

"Female, Caucasian, approximately five-nine, one-thirty to one-forty pounds, auburn hair, twenty or twenty-one, green eyes, dark complexion, a slight overbite, two small circular moles on her left cheek, a four-to-six-inch scar, probably the result of arthroscopic surgery, on her right knee, a..."

"Enough, already," Dantzler said. "No need to show off."

"What was that all about?"

"Marcy Coleman is an almost-identical replica of the three murdered girls. To put it even more bluntly, the resemblance is scary. If she's a student at UK, my advice to her would be don't go out alone until we find this guy."

"Want to know something else?" Laurie said.

"What?"

"She also looks a lot like me."

CHAPTER 3

Jack Dantzler lived alone in a small ranch-style house on Lakeshore Drive. He loved the place, which he purchased in the early 1990s after years as an apartment dweller. It was an average-looking house with three bedrooms, two full baths, den, living room, kitchen, basement, and a screened-in back porch. What made it special was the large lake that bumped up against his backyard. Dantzler loved the water, and although this was a long way from the ocean, until the day came when he could hang up his shield and move to the beach, this would do just fine.

He had not always lived alone in the house. For almost a decade, he shared the place with Beth Robinson and a chubby yellow cat named Dylan. Beth, or "BR" to her colleagues, was a forensics whiz whose extraordinary skills put her on a fast climb up the career ladder. Everyone knew that it was only a matter of time before she would move up, so when the FBI came calling with a job offer, she and Dantzler agreed that the opportunity was too good to pass up.

Beth moved in August 2001, exactly one month before 9-11. The parting had been painful for both of them, but more so for Dantzler, who always suspected—as did most everyone else—that his feelings ran deeper than hers. Initially, they'd tried to keep the relationship going, getting together whenever their heavy workloads permitted. But the effort necessary to keep the fires burning eventually wore them down, and they decided it was best to make a clean break.

Beth left for Quantico, taking Dylan with her. Dantzler had dated several women since the split, but nothing even remotely resembling a serious relationship had flourished. Beth, he knew, would be a hard act for anyone to follow. The same went for Dylan, which explained why Dantzler was in no hurry to bring in another pet.

Dantzler lay on a recliner, a tall glass of Pernod and orange juice in his right hand, staring out at the moon's reflection dancing on the water. The CD player was on, the volume down. Leonard Cohen, his all-time favorite, was singing "The Future," a grim, apocalyptic epic that Dantzler felt came as close to accurately reflecting the sad state of world affairs as anything he'd read, seen, or heard in the past twenty years.

"I have seen the future, baby, it is murder."

You got that right, Leonard. And the present ain't so hot, either, Dantzler thought.

Oh, for the good old days when even the worst evil had a certain amount of reason—even logic—connected to it.

Dantzler sipped at the drink, his third, and felt the effects of the alcohol kick in. He wanted distance from the death and madness Leonard Cohen so accurately chronicled. Distance from the death and madness that had descended on the Kaplan family. The Parker and Adams families. All the families that had loved ones stolen from them in such brutal fashion. Yet, he knew that no amount of Pernod could make it happen. He understood this better than most. Death was his business. Death never went away.

Death always has the last laugh.

Next to him, on a small metal table, was an 8x10 picture in a gold frame. He picked it up and brushed a thin layer of dust off the top. It was his favorite picture, taken in Florida when he was six years old. In the photo, he was standing between his parents. Sarah and Johnny Dantzler.

They were on a pier, arms wrapped around each other, the blue ocean water behind them. Mom in a red two-piece bathing suit, hair pulled back in a ponytail, smiling as only she could. Her face beautiful and radiant and full of life. His dad's eyes fixed on her, soaking in that radiance like rays of sunlight. And loving her with all his heart.

His dad was only twenty-eight when the picture was taken. Tall, muscular, proud, more handsome than a movie star. Johnny Dantzler was a man who seemingly had everything within reach.

Everything, that is, except time.

Even now, Dantzler could remember with perfect clarity that Saturday afternoon, September 19, 1970, when the two Army officers came to the house to deliver the news that his father had been killed. They told the family that he was walking point when his squad had been ambushed by Viet Cong snipers. The rest of what the officers said came out as one long run-on sentence: bullet to the chest...died instantly...died a hero in the service of his country...burial with full military honors...you have our condolences.

Dantzler could still hear his mother's high-pitched, animal scream. Could still see the uncertain, dazed look on the faces of his grandparents and his mother's younger brother, Tommy. Could still see the neighbors rushing in to offer support and sympathy. He remembered thinking at the time how news of death seemed to cause everyone to speak low and move quickly. People whispered; people rushed.

He was barely six then, yet he'd felt a depth of sadness and hurt that he doubted could ever be rivaled. But he had been wrong. He would feel it again. Eight years later when his beloved mother was murdered.

Death always has the last laugh.

He brought the picture to his lips and kissed it. Tears filled his eyes, overflowed, and trickled down the sides of his face. There were some nights when the dam that held back his tears was even weaker than whatever faith he had left.

God, he still loved them. And missed them.

God? Where was this so-called gentle and loving and protecting God on the night Sarah Dantzler was strangled to death? How could God look away while one of his loveliest, most precious flowers was being crushed? Why didn't this God of love and mercy intervene on Sarah Dantzler's behalf?

Because, Dantzler had long ago concluded, God is the supreme master of indifference, that's why.

Dantzler gently put the picture back where it had been. He took another drink and stared out at the shimmering water. His thoughts immediately went to the three dead girls. The brutality, the senselessness, the violence...

Somewhere in this city a madman was walking free, no doubt planning his next murder.

Dantzler leaned back and closed his eyes.

I'm smarter than you, goddammit.

CHAPTER 4

The old house at 431 Sycamore Street was a two-story wooden structure fronted by four round columns on the porch. It had been built in the early 1920s, and save for minor touchups after World War II and again in 1965, little about it had changed. The rooms were huge, the floors were wood, the ceilings high. The centerpiece of the house was a winding stairway, made of oak, located in the dining room. There was a spacious kitchen, a screened-in back porch, a good-size backyard, and a wine cellar. This was the way houses used to be, long before post-war Eisenhower America raced to the suburbs to fill those cheap pre-fab replicas that now lined the streets with monotony.

When it was built, the house cost less than four thousand dollars. In today's market, with all those aging Yuppie-type baby-boomers dying to "get back to the basics," it could easily bring in excess of three hundred thousand. Location was another plus. The Chevy Chase area was one of the last remaining Lexington neighborhoods still considered to have old-fashioned character and charm. In a city sprawling toward permanent blandness, here was a reminder of the beauty and simplicity of yesteryear.

Eldon Wessell loved this house. He always had. Indeed, he never for a second in his life lived anywhere else. Even when he attended the University of Kentucky, he chose to live at home. The thought of living in a dorm, or renting from someone else, never entered his mind.

This was more than home to Eldon. This was his castle, his refuge.

Eldon stood at his bedroom window and looked out at the ancient elm tree. How old was the tree, he often wondered. How long had it been there before he came into this cruel world thirty-nine Februarys ago? He couldn't even begin to guess. It didn't matter, really. Regardless of its age, the tree, whose branches scratched against his window when whipped by a strong wind, was his oldest companion, his closest confidant. Many times, in moments of supreme anger or frustration, when he had no one else to turn to—and he rarely did—he had opened the window and shared his feelings with the old elm tree.

His bedroom, located at the top right of the stairs, was one of four on the second floor. Next to it, connected by a door, was a guest bedroom he had long ago claimed as his (why not? he couldn't remember a single guest ever staying overnight in that room), and in the corner on the right side of the hallway was a large bathroom. Across the hall were two more bedrooms—his mother Ginger's (Gee, to friends) and his sister Rose's. Directly across from his bedroom was a sewing room.

Eldon's bedroom was almost as barren as a monk's. Its furnishings consisted of the huge four-poster bed that was topped by a white lace canopy, and two medium-size dressers. There was a large walk-in closet, an oval mirror to the left of the bed, and in one corner a PC rested on a small table. Next to the table was a laser printer. With the exception of a small cross directly above the head of the bed, the walls were bare.

It had long ago been established that his bedroom and the guest bedroom, which he considered one unit, were off limits to his mother and sister. They were never to set foot in either. Not as long as he was alive.

Eldon Wessell hated his mother and sister, and couldn't recall a day when he didn't. It was as if that hate had accompanied him from the womb like a twin brother. From his earliest days of childhood, it had always been them against him. They never once sided with him on anything. Every vote went against him; every idea he put on the table was quickly shot down. In his world, the math couldn't have been simpler: two against one. He was an outsider even in his own house.

Always.

Eldon had long ago given up any hope of making a connection. He hated them because they acted so aloof, so superior. And because they never took him seriously. The reason for this, he knew, was because of his appearance, which was decidedly different from theirs. Gee and Rose were thin and tall—nearly five-ten—and had been blessed with classical bone structure, firm, tight skin, and a regal bearing. Indeed, both women conducted themselves in a manner befitting royalty, which was something else that got under his craw. To him, they were just a pair of aging queens—high-strung, distant, smug. Gee, now sixty-four, was still a remarkably handsome woman. Even Eldon, though he choked on the thought, had to admit as much. To look at her was to see a woman who gave every indication of easing into old age with the grace and dignity of someone like Katherine Hepburn. If Gee were so inclined to fix herself up, which she rarely did, she could easily pass for a woman of fifty.

Rose was forty-two and her mother's clone. The elegance and beauty had clearly passed from mother to daughter. Yet, despite her good looks and impressive body, she had never married. Over the years there had been a series of potential candidates, none of whom were successful in getting her to the altar. A gifted pianist, she had been a music teacher at Lafayette High School until she was thirty-two. Then late one night, following play rehearsal, she was attacked in the parking lot by two former students. Badly shaken by the incident, she left teaching and opened Rose's Dance Academy, which had turned out to be enormously successful and profitable.

Eldon, by contrast, stood just five-five, and he drifted between one-sixty and one-seventy. He had a round, moon face, pale skin, large blue eyes, and thinning blonde hair. Even though he lifted weights religiously and considered himself a strong man, he was cursed with a genetic makeup that denied him the muscle definition he so desperately sought. Although he preferred to think of himself as stocky, more often than not, he heard himself referred to as "roly-poly" or "the chubby type."

Once, when he was eight and Rose was eleven, they were sitting with a gang of neighborhood friends in a movie theater watching a Bugs Bunny cartoon. Rose had turned to him and said in a loud voice, "You know, Eldon, you look like Elmer Fudd."

It was then—and it remained so today—the most humiliating moment of Eldon Wessell's life. The echo of their laughter still rang in his ears.

It was also a moment with a touch of irony. In truth, he was an Elmer. Elmer Donald Wessell, to be exact. However, thanks to his mother's rapid pronunciation of Elmer Donald when he was still a young boy, it had blessedly been shortened to Eldon. Thank God for small favors.

Eldon Wessell had once looked at himself in a full-length mirror and wondered if some people develop a body type to match their name. He was convinced they did. No way Robert Mitchum could have ever been short and overweight.

Or maybe he owed his looks to his father. More than likely he did, and yet that was something he would never know. His father left the family when Eldon was three months old and had never been heard from again. There wasn't a single picture of the man in the house, and Gee never mentioned him. When Eldon asked questions, she responded with silence and a cold stare. He remained the biggest mystery in Eldon's life.

Eldon had often looked at tall, angular Rose and asked himself how it was possible that they could be the product of the same father. How could two people, so different, spring forth from the seed of one man? How could the mystery of the genetic code have run so amuck?

God, he hated Rose. Loathed her. More than once he had visualized killing her. Her death, as he imagined it, always came in the most brutal, violent way possible. Death wasn't enough—she had to suffer.

He often cursed the two clumsy young students for their failure to cause her more than fear and psychological harm. He wished they had been able to finish what they started—to rape her, then kill her. That was certainly what she deserved.

But Rose, always the lucky one, was rescued before any real damage could be inflicted. The attackers had torn her clothes and bruised her slightly before being chased away by several school officials. She was left shaken but unharmed.

Eldon was especially disappointed that the rape hadn't been completed. It would have been fitting, he felt, for prim and proper Rose to lose her virginity in such an ugly, degrading manner. With her arrogance and her perfect bone structure and her demeaning, condescending attitude.

How he despised that creature. Yet, different as they were, Eldon did share one thing in common with his sister—he, too, was a virgin. However, that's where the similarity ended. His virginity was by choice; Rose's wasn't. Hers was decreed by that goddamn Catholic Church that dominated her—and Gee's—life. They were slaves to two thousand years of dogma and psychological browbeating. Not him. No, if he wanted to lose his virginity, he could. At any time, without guilt or shame. But he didn't. He chose not to. There were other ways to satisfy oneself sexually without having to perform the grotesque act of intercourse.

Rose, burdened by that pure-as-Virgin-Mary malarkey, couldn't allow a man other than her husband to enter her. No doubt, Eldon reckoned, it was Rose's insistence on remaining chaste that had driven away her stream of suitors. They weren't about to sign a lifetime contract without first sampling the goods. He couldn't blame them, either. And Rose, that shining symbol of purity, wasn't about to let anyone touch her or see her before the wedding night.

Oh, if she only knew.

If Eldon's bedroom was a monument to austerity, the guest bedroom was a glorification of the world of art. Every inch of the walls was covered by prints of the greatest art treasures. Some were framed; others were taped or stapled to the wall. Da Vinci's *Last Supper* adorned the wall above the bed. A Rembrandt self-portrait hung on the wall next to the door. There were reproductions of works by Raphael, Blake, Picasso, Cezanne, van Gogh. The bust of Homer rested on a table next to an antique rocking chair. On the dresser, Durer's Praying Hands were clasped together.

Eldon cherished them all, and even if they were only reproductions, he valued them as if they were originals.

The unframed picture on the left wall was his favorite. The *Pietà*, Michelangelo's magnificent sculpture depicting Mary holding the mortally wounded body of Christ. If perfection existed in this world, Eldon had long ago concluded that it existed in this single work of art.

It was his oldest artistic possession (he purchased it when he was eleven), and the one he treasured above all others. Even though he had little use for Jesus or his message of meekness and forgiveness, he did envy Christ for one thing: He had a mother who loved him.

Eldon treasured the *Pietà* not because of its stunning beauty or its artistic meaning; he treasured it because it had always been his window into the forbidden.

The picture, which was only a 9x12, dangled from a six-inch string wrapped around a nail. It was suspended at eye level, and could easily be swung from side to side. Behind the picture there was a two-inch hole in the wall.

Eldon discovered the hole when he was eight. At first, it meant nothing to him—just a flaw in an old house. However, as he grew older, as he became aware of certain feelings within his own body, the hole became a telescope that took him on a dark journey into a world of endless sexual pleasure.

Looking through the hole, he could see the bathroom. He could see it all: clear, unobstructed. The huge bathtub, with no shower stall or curtain to block his view of the bather, was straight in front of him. The toilet and lavatory were to the right, the full-length mirror on the left. The entire room lay right before his eyes, almost begging him to bear witness to the activity taking place within. And all he had to do was to silently move sad Mary and dead Jesus out of the way.

Eldon spent endless hours peering through that hole into his own world of private pleasure. He had watched his mother's still-proud body ease into old age, even as his sister's youthful body was blossoming into full womanhood. He had seen his mother expertly fondle her large breasts before letting her hand slide down into the mysterious dark forest between her legs. He had watched her hand move, slowly, in circular movements; seen her head tilt forward, eyes closed; heard the deep moan.

He had seen thirteen-year-old Rose discover herself, seen her slide forward in the tub, spread her legs and let the water run directly onto her clitoris. Three years later he had watched as she took the peculiar, oblong-shaped piece of plastic and eased it inside her vagina. He heard the painful grunt, watched as she removed it, seen the blood. He stood spellbound as she again worked it inside her, this time with more assurance, moving it up and down, slowly, until her head, like Gee's had done, slumped forward, eyes closed. He heard the rapid breathing, the quick gasps for air, then that same deep moan. Thanks to his mother and sister, Eldon Wessell had no reason to lose his virginity. In his mind, he lost it every night, spying on those two most-hated women. Gee and Rose...two withering saints. They would never know the pleasure they had provided. Whether bathing, urinating, or masturbating, they had been unknowing stars in his live-action peep show.

Of course, he was not allowed his own deep moan when his head fell forward. No, his moment of pleasure had to be silent, and he had long ago disciplined himself to remain quiet when his orgasm overtook him. He was immensely proud of this control. He was equally proud of his ability—even at age thirty-nine—to climax twice within a twenty-minute period.

Once, when he was much younger, he climaxed twice within eight minutes. The first climax came while watching his mother bathe; the second when Rose and a girlfriend, after bathing, danced around the bathroom dripping wet. That orgasm had been especially intense, and had tested to the limits his ability to remain silent as the semen spurted from his penis.

As Eldon stood at the window and looked at the old elm tree, the familiar feeling of hatred boiled inside him. His mother and sister had belittled him all his life. Treated him as a second-class citizen, when, in truth, he was far more intelligent than either of them. He had known this since he was a child. Rose received all the praise and glory ("Oh, Eldon, your sister will someday be a famous concert pianist," Gee said time and time again), but he, roly-poly Elmer Fudd, had the better brain.

Intelligence, he reminded himself, takes many forms. There's intellectual intelligence—which he had in abundance—street intelligence, common sense intelligence.

There was yet another type of intelligence, more specialized, hidden. It's the intelligence that belongs to the holder of secrets. And when it came to secrets, he possessed more than anyone could imagine.

CHAPTER 5

Dantzler entered the police station at 7:40 a.m. to find that the shit had officially hit the fan. Richard Bird stood with his back against the wall facing a bank of camera lights, looking every bit like Clint Eastwood or Harrison Ford surrounded by adoring fans at the Cannes Film Festival. Only in Bird's case it was a media herd rather than screaming women that had him bunched in. They wanted information not autographs.

The mob surrounding Bird included all four of the city's TV stations, two each from Louisville and Cincinnati, five local radio stations, three newspaper reporters, a reporter from the college rag, one from the Associated Press, and three other reporters that Dantzler didn't recognize but presumed were from the national print media.

The mob had certainly changed in the twenty-plus years he'd been on the job. Most of the faces now belonged to thirty-something women who dressed a lot like men, had blonde hair, perfect teeth, and were, for now at least, holding their own in the battle against the bulge. All seemed deadly earnest and very polite, almost school-like in the way they raised a hand and waited to be acknowledged before posing their questions. Not at all like what Dantzler remembered in the old days. A snarling pack of grizzled men who would cut your throat one minute then buy you a drink an hour later. Bourbon drinkers. Straight. Mixed was for sissies.

Dantzler did see one familiar face in the crowd: Andy Waters, a fifteen-year *Herald* veteran. Waters folded his reporter's notebook, crammed it into the back pocket of his Levis, and walked toward Dantzler, a huge grin covering his face.

"Well, well, the dark prince," Waters said. "This early on a Saturday morning. Must be something pretty important to get

you down here today." Waters extended a hand, which Dantzler
accepted. "You working, or just a guy in love with his job?"
"Somewhere in between," Dantzler said.
"I doubt that." Waters smiled. "Talk to me, Jack. As the
kids like to say, whussup? Off the record, if you like."
"I don't know *whussup*, Andy. My hunch is, right now you
know more about this situation than I do."
"When has anyone ever known more than you?"
"Flattery won't earn you a penny with me, Andy. You know
that. By the way, who leaked today's story to the *Herald*?"
Waters put his hand over his heart, feigning indignation.
"You know I can't tell you that."
"Had to ask. Listen, Andy. In the future, if you get
something hot, would you run it by me first? As a favor."
"Sure. But if it's big-time stuff, I gotta go with it. *You* know
that. We both have rules that have to be followed."
"Just promise me that I hear about it first. You do that and
I'll take care of you in the end. Deal?"
"Deal."
"Thanks, Andy."
Dantzler walked toward the stairs and glanced over his
shoulder. Bird looked less like Clint or Harrison and more like
Karloff's Frankenstein monster a few seconds before the
villagers began tossing those burning torches. Bird, who at six-
six was at least a head taller than any of his inquisitors,
alternately listened, nodded, and spoke, his eyes rapidly moving
from side to side in response to the battery of questions being
fired his way. He was good at this part of the job. Always had
been. Bird, Dantzler knew, was a much better administrator than
investigator. Better at headquarters than in the trenches.
Dantzler made quick eye contact with Bird, smiled,
shrugged, then strolled unnoticed past the crowd and up the
marble steps. That was another big difference from the old days.
Back then, upon seeing Dantzler and knowing that something
important was in the wind, the media mob would have
descended on him like vultures to road kill.
Bird's office was on the second floor, across the hall from
the Chief's office, and three doors down from the Homicide

Division that had been Dantzler's home for nearly twenty years. Dantzler stopped at a water fountain for a quick drink, then continued down the hall. A uniformed officer, still in his early twenties, came out of the men's room and walked toward Dantzler.

"Heard about last night, sir," the young officer said. "Sounded pretty nasty."

"You could say that."

Darleen McCormick, Bird's personal secretary, sat behind her desk in the outer office. Known as "Dynamite," she was a fixture in the department and a favorite of everyone. No taller than five-one, even with frosted hair piled high on her head, Dynamite was tougher than wet rawhide—three times divorced, a two-fisted drinker, and the owner of a vocabulary that would make Richard Pryor blush. She was thought to be in her early sixties, but no one, not even a detective as skilled as Dantzler, had been able—or willing—to discern her true age. Better to question Manson about his crimes than to question Dynamite about her age. Some areas of inquiry are better left alone.

The only known date associated with Dynamite was November 26, 1963. Her first day on the job. The day after JFK's funeral. Beyond that, all data was strictly off-limits.

When she looked up and saw Dantzler, a smile flew across her face. Her hazel eyes sparkled. "Goddamn, look what the cat dragged in," she chuckled. Her voice, ravaged by a lifetime of cigarettes, was low and scratchy. "I can't recall the last time I saw you here this early on a Saturday morning."

"Neither can I." Dantzler pointed at the stack of messages on the desk. "So, tell me, Dynamite, how bad has it been?"

She rolled her eyes upward. "Honey, this is absolutely the worst I've ever seen. Nothing in the past begins to compare to this. Nothing. And I'm afraid it's only going to get worse. The phone has been ringing off the hook. I've got a shit load of e-mails. Just this morning I've had calls from CNN, MSNBC, USA Today, and believe it or not, the Los Angeles *Times*. I mean, how did they hear about it? And what time is it out there, anyway? A little past 4 a.m, right? Don't those West Coast buzzards ever sleep? It's crazy."

"You know the media. They take to something like this the way a hot-blooded man takes to you."

"I say screw 'em all. We'd all be better off if they didn't sensationalize everything the way they do. Next thing you know, Geraldo will be here."

"You're looking at it all wrong, Dynamite. You have to use the media to your advantage. Play them like a musical instrument. Let them work for you. Only don't let them know they're being played."

She put her arms around his neck, pulled him down, and kissed him on the cheek. "I'm glad you're on our side, Jack. I'd hate to think what things would be like if you were a bad guy."

"Truth is, Dynamite, I'd be a lousy criminal. Having a conscience doesn't serve the bad guys very well. Now you..." Dantzler smiled. "You would've been an A-one criminal. Smart, shrewed, fearless. You would've put Bonnie Parker and Ma Barker to shame."

"Exactly what are you sayin' about me, Jack? That I have a criminal's personality?"

"I'm saying you have a one-in-a-million personality. That you would be at the top of the list, no matter which direction you took."

"There are times, Jack, when I don't know whether to kiss you or kick you in the balls."

"I vote for kiss."

"I don't know. After that assessment of me, I'm leaning toward a punt."

Dantzler pulled her close and gave her a bear hug. "This place would crumble like the Roman Coliseum if it weren't for you. You're special, Dynamite. That's all I'm really trying to say."

"A national treasure," she said, smiling. "A true work of art. Right?"

"Just like the *Pietà*," he said.

Dynamite sat behind her desk and began pecking away on her keyboard. She typed two sentences, stopped, and looked up at Dantzler. "What do you make of that?" she said.

"Hard to say. Obviously, the *Pietà*, its meaning, is somehow tied in with the message the killer leaves."

"'Please, deliver me from my torment.'" Dynamite shook her head. "Weird."

"Our boy is clearly in a great deal of agony. He's pleading for us to stop him."

"Why doesn't he come forward and give himself up?"

"It doesn't work that way. This guy is tortured, tormented, living in his own private hell. He wants to escape. But in his mind he'll never do that unless someone else stops him."

"Save us all a lot of time and trouble if he'd stop himself."

"Has to be an outsider," Dantzler said. "Someone else who does the cleansing. You still go to confession, Dynamite?"

"Are you kidding? You think I'd have any shot at heaven if I didn't look for a break in the old sin department? I mean, I gotta have someone with clout plead my case for me."

"Well, basically it's the same principal here. But for our guy, forgiveness can't be attained through prayer. Or by pleading his case to a priest, rabbi, or minister. That wouldn't be good enough for him. Wouldn't stroke his ego. He'd never see his name in the headlines, which is what he ultimately wants. That's what all these serial killers really want—to have their names added to the list. Bundy, Gacy, Ramirez, and…fill in the blank. No, his salvation can only be attained by being caught."

Dantzler went to the door to Bird's office and started to open it.

"Hey, Jack," Dynamite said.

He turned to face her.

"Catch this bastard, will you?"

Dantzler always felt a great sense of comfort every time he stepped inside Bird's office. Nothing had changed for the past ten years, and that was fine with him. He liked consistency, even when others found it boring and depressing. Bird's office had the same gray walls, same desk, same pictures that had been there for more than a decade. An ancient brown rug covered the floor beneath the desk, and a battered leather couch sat in the corner. There was an empty fish tank that still had rocks at the bottom, and a stuffed skunk mounted on one wall stared down into the office. A former mayor once said he wasn't sure if he'd ever seen a more depressing office in his life, adding, "the place must've been decorated by a color-blind Sing Sing inmate."

Dantzler went past the desk and opened a door that led into the conference room. It wasn't exactly a festive-looking room, but when compared with Bird's office, it was the Taj Mahal. In the center there was a rectangular table surrounded by eight wooden chairs. To the left, side by side, there was a bulletin board and a green chalkboard. To the right, near the end of the table, there was a small stand that was home to a silver coffee pot and a stack of plastic cups.

Eric Gamble sat at the table, his tired eyes fixed straight ahead. The highest-ranking black working homicide, Gamble was exceptionally handsome by any standards, a strong, athletic man in his late twenties with short hair and a thick, neatly trimmed mustache. Although Dantzler seldom worked with a partner, he had on a couple of occasions been paired with Eric. Both cases involved domestic violence disputes that resulted in gunshot deaths. It was textbook stuff, easily solved. Dantzler liked the kid, and considered him to be a sharp young detective with a bright future.

Eric quickly rose when Dantzler entered the room. He wore tan slacks, a blue shirt open at the collar, a navy blazer, brown loafers, and no socks. His sartorial splendor, easily the finest and most expensive in the department, had earned him the nickname of Mr. GQ.

Dantzler extended his hand. "Morning, Eric," he said.

Eric shook Dantzler's hand firmly. "I notice you didn't say 'good morning.' Any particular reason why?"

"Good morning—that's an oxymoron in my book."

"This early, I'd have to concur with you on that."

"Late night with the ladies, Eric?"

"Lady."

"Ah." Dantzler reached out and touched the sleeve of Eric's blazer. "Wish I could afford threads like this. I'm curious. How do you do it? I make bigger bucks than you and I can't afford them."

"Creative money management."

Dantzler laughed. "You must be damn good at it."

"Yeah, I know a few tricks." Eric returned to his seat and leaned back. "Word is, Captain Bird is forming a task force. How many detectives does he plan to assign?"

"Don't know. The fewer the better if I have anything to say about it."

Eric chuckled. "You like that lone wolf shit, don't you, Lieutenant? Arnold Schwarzenegger killin' a hundred bad dudes by himself."

"Please, Eric. If you're gonna compare me to an actor, at least make it one who can act. De Niro, Pacino, Freeman—one of those guys."

"Somehow I can't see those guys kickin' the Terminator's ass."

"I've got a bulletin for you, Eric. Arnold *was* the Terminator."

"Oh, well, all you white dudes look the same to me."

"So I've heard." Dantzler tossed a folder onto the table and sat across from Eric. "What do you know about Laurie Dunn?"

"Single, sexy, beautiful, cocky, raunchy sense of humor..."

"Jesus, Eric, who are you, Larry fuckin' Flynt? I want to know what kind of a cop she is, not whether she's a centerfold candidate."

"The best. Outstanding."

"You've worked with her?"

Eric nodded. "Once. Must've been about a year ago. A couple was going through an explosive divorce and child custody was the powder keg. Anyway, the mom got custody. About ten days later, the kid, a little girl, was taken from school by the father. Just grabbed her off the playground one day during recess, took her to his place, and practically held her hostage. It got pretty intense. He threatened to kill himself and the kid if the court didn't give him joint custody. He had a gun and I knew he was willing to use it. Well, Dunn managed to convince the guy to let her come inside and talk to him. She went in—without her weapon or a vest—and about ten minutes later, the little girl comes running out. Then about fifteen minutes after that, Dunn and the guy come out. And *she's* holding *his* gun. She's got guts."

"Looks like she'll be working with us on this."

"I second that motion." Eric rubbed his eyes and yawned.

"Will Larraby be working with us?"

"Unfortunately, yes."

"Why unfortunately?"

"The man couldn't find a Jew in Tel Aviv."

"What's the story with you guys, anyway?"

"Let's just say we never bonded."

"What about Matthews and Costello?"

"Top-flight detectives, both of them. But that fuckin' Larraby…"

"*Who's* fucking Larraby?" Laurie Dunn said, opening the door. "Whoever she is, give her my sympathy."

She extended her hand to Eric. "Nice to see you again, Eric."

"Ditto," Eric said, taking her hand.

She looked at Dantzler. "Seems like ages since I last saw you. When was it, about three hours ago in Coyle's?"

"More like five."

"Short night either way."

"And until we stop this guy, I'm afraid we're looking at a lot more short nights."

Dantzler watched as she filled a cup with coffee and took the chair next to Gamble. Eric had been right—Laurie Dunn was definitely an attention-getter. Maybe not a classic beauty, but certainly better than average in the looks department. She was wearing dark blue slacks, a white blouse, suede jacket, and brown loafers. There was a small gold stud in each ear, and a gold cross around her neck. If she was wearing make-up, he couldn't spot it. Not that she needed make-up.

Dantzler guessed at her age. Late twenties, he judged. Possibly thirty. He couldn't help but wonder why a woman this attractive would ever become a cop. She could have easily parlayed those looks into a bigger paycheck than a cop gets. Lots of women with much less to offer certainly had. Why hadn't she?

He made a mental note to find out why.

CHAPTER 6

At precisely nine o'clock, Richard Bird bolted through the door, went straight to the coffee pot, picked up a Styrofoam cup, filled it with steaming coffee, and sipped. He took another sip before sitting at the head of the table. "Jesus, what a morning," he said. "If I never see another microphone or hear another question, I'll be..." He looked at Dantzler. "They're all over this story like flies on a garbage can."

"They'll have to be handled," Dantzler said. "Controlled, at least to some degree."

"It won't be easy, but you're absolutely right...it has to be done." Bird turned toward Eric and Laurie. "Eric, Laurie."

"Captain," they said in unison.

Bird looked at his watch. "Matthews and Costello should be here anytime," he said. "Larraby's in court this morning, so he won't be joining us. I know that breaks your heart, Jack."

"Any day without Dale Larraby adds a month to my life," Dantzler said.

"Be nice. I know that's a stretch, but you can do it. For the sake of *esprit de corps.*"

The door opened and Dan Matthews and Milt Costello, two of the most-senior detectives on the force, walked into the room. Both were Vietnam veterans; both were highly respected within the department. Costello, 55, was two years older and a good fifteen pounds heavier than his partner. Matthews, who stood four inches taller than Costello, was considered second only to Dantzler when it came to detective skills. Partners for more than a decade, they were known within the department as Bud and Lou. The two men, almost in unison, grabbed a chair, flipped open a notepad, and took out a pen.

Bird stood and pointed toward Laurie. "Dan, Milt, this is Laurie Dunn," he said. "She's going to be working with us on this." He emptied a packet of sugar into his coffee. "We've borrowed her from Missing and Exploited Children until we get this situation resolved."

"Sounds like a solid idea to me," Matthews said.

"I agree," Costello chimed in.

"Judging from the scene downstairs, I'd say we now have the media to contend with," Matthews said.

Bird stirred his coffee, sipped, then said, "Yes…and that's not gonna make things any easier. I was hoping we could keep them in the dark a little while longer, but obviously that hope's been flushed down the toilet."

"What happened?" Matthews asked.

Bird sighed deeply. "The same thing that always happens. Some bastard leaked something to a reporter. The guy called me at home last night, wanting to play twenty questions. Naturally, I told him as little as I could possibly get away with. But it was clear from the questions that he knows more than he should."

"Was it Andy Waters?" Dantzler said.

"We should be so lucky. If it had been Andy, I could've maybe worked something out. He's a reasonable guy. But it wasn't Andy. It was one of those eager young Turks who dreams of becoming the next Woodward or Bernstein."

"Did you try to get him to sit on it for a couple of days?" Dantzler said.

"Of course. And you can imagine his response to that suggestion."

"He told you to piss off."

"He didn't say those precise words, but that's how it translated."

"How much does he know?" Dantzler asked.

"Fortunately, not as much as we do. He thinks the killer used a blue silk scarf on all three victims. That's not true. Only the last two were killed with a scarf. For the first victim, the killer used a belt. Hopefully, I can use that little discrepancy to downplay the serial-killer angle. At least for a while."

"I doubt it," Dantzler said, scratching his chin.

"I do, too," Bird admitted.

"Any idea who leaked the information?"

"No. But I intend to find out. And when I do, I will personally kill him." Bird opened a manilla folder, took out a stack of 8x10 photos, and began passing them around. "The victims," he said. "Name and date of death are on the back." "Jesus," Costello said. "They could easily pass for sisters." Taking a piece of chalk, Bird began writing on the board.

1. Allison Parker, 21, Atlanta, Ga., 2/7/03
2. Becky Adams, 19, Hamilton, Ohio, 7/13/04
3. Abby Kaplan, 23, New York, N.Y., 4/19/05

"Ladies and gentlemen, these are our victims," Bird said, pointing to the green board. "All killed in the same manner, all killed, presumably, by the same perp. Since Jack is heading up the investigation, I'll let him fill you in on the details. You can bring Larraby up to speed later on." He looked at Dantzler and shrugged. "The floor's yours, Jack."

Dantzler sipped at his coffee, then slowly placed the cup back on the table. Standing, he said, "Our killer is a real sicko, folks. A certified loony. Probably some kind of a religious wacko to boot."

"What's his M.O.?" Costello said.

Dantzler nodded toward Laurie. "You were there, Sergeant Dunn. Tell them what you found."

Without hesitation, Laurie stood, cleared her throat, said, "He strangles the girls, always from behind, according to Mac, undresses them, lays them on the bed, spreads their legs and, inserts a gold St. Jude medal into their vagina. That's been the M.O. with all three victims."

"Like I said, a blue-ribbon fruitcake," Dantzler said.

"Does he have sex with them?" Eric said.

"Never."

"You sure?"

"Positive. Semen was found inside one of the victims, but she'd had sex earlier that night with her boyfriend. He confirmed it, and tests proved he was telling the truth."

"Maybe our boy uses a condom," Matthews said.

Dantzler shook his head. "Nope. No sexual penetration at all. Just the St. Jude medal."

"Patron saint of hopeless causes," Costello whispered.

"This nutso is a hopeless cause, that's for sure."

"You're positive he kills them before he undresses them?" Matthews said.

Dantzler frowned, letting the question hang in the air for several seconds. Finally, he said, "Maybe not one hundred percent positive, but it sure looks that way. The clothes are never torn, never damaged in any way. I figure if these girls are being made to undress while they're still alive, at least one of them would have been so shit-nervous she would have damaged some article of clothing by accident. Hell, I know I would."

"And the press knows nothing about the St. Jude medal?" Eric said.

"God, I hope not."

"And we've got to make sure they don't," Costello said. "We need at least one card that only we know about."

"Well, there are a couple more little items that the press doesn't know about," Dantzler said.

"What?" Costello said.

"Are you familiar with the *Pietà*?"

"Michelangelo's *Pietà*?" Matthews said.

"Yeah."

"Sure, I'm familiar with it."

"I'm not," Costello said. "What is it?"

"A famous sculpture of Mary cradling the body of Jesus."

"Why are you telling us about the *Pietà*?" Matthews asked.

"Because our fruitcake friend always leaves a five-by-seven color picture of the *Pietà* just above the victim's pubic hair. More of a self-made postcard than a photo, really."

"And a message, no doubt," Matthews said. "A guy like this always leaves a message."

"Yeah," Dantzler said, "His says, 'Please, deliver me from my torment.' And it's always signed, 'Mike L. Angelo.'"

"Naturally," Matthews said. "You said there were a couple of things. What's the second one?"

"He cuts them, probably with a small pocket knife, and he always does it at exactly the same place on the victim's body."

"Let me guess. One of the breasts," Costello said.

"Nope. The jugular. And he does it *after* the victim is dead."

"You're sure the cuts are postmortem?" Matthews said.

"Absolutely. And so is Mac. There's minimum blood loss. Almost none, in fact. If those girls were still alive when they had their jugulars sliced and diced, they'd bleed like stuck hogs."

Matthews shook his head and ran his fingers through his silver hair. "Damn, what's the point of that?"

"What matters blood?" Dantzler said softly.

"What?"

"Something Nietzsche wrote."

"Any relevance here?" Matthews said.

"Probably not."

"Good," Matthews said, chuckling. "I'd hate to think we've been reduced to relying on that crazy German bastard to solve our homicides."

Laurie pointed to the chalkboard. "What about the three women?" she said. "Anything at all that ties them together?"

"Only that they were killed by the same man, they were students at the University, and they all were from out of town. Our guy never offs local women, which, of course, means that he's cagey."

"It also means that it'll be that much harder for us to catch the bastard," Bird said.

"How so?" Laurie said.

"It's more difficult to investigate out-of-state victims," Dantzler said. "Family, close friends, potential suspects...the farther away they are, the tougher it is to get to them. It's a logistical thing. Distance increases the degree of difficulty, that's all. If they were from this city, or even this state, the whole process would be easier for us."

"Which brings up the next question," Costello said. "What about the feds? Are they—"

"Chomping at the bit," Bird said. "Can't wait to get the call, then come charging in and 'save our ass.' Typical. They've offered us Glenn Rigby, and, of course, he's eager to get involved."

"Rigby *is* an ace profiler," Matthews said.

"Jack's a much better profiler than any of those jerks, and they all know it," Bird countered. "I'll remind 'em, in case they forgot. Maybe I'll hurt their precious feelings and they'll stay in the shadows where they belong."

"Don't piss 'em off, Rich," Dantzler said. "We may need them before this thing is over."

Bird groaned. "A guy can dream, can't he?"

Dantzler looked around the table, then said, "Study these case files today and tomorrow. *Really* study them. By Monday morning, I want every detail, no matter how remote, to be as familiar to you as your birthday. Dan, I'll leave it to you to enlighten Larraby. I know that's a challenge, but do the best you can. You're all gonna see that we simply don't have much to go on right now. No prints, no obvious motive, no link among the victims, no consistent time pattern. Nothing. Our killer is one neat and careful guy. He's not gonna be easy to catch. That means we've really got to dig in."

"And fast," Bird interjected. "The last thing we need is panic among the masses, which is exactly what we'll get if we don't solve this thing pronto."

"We'll catch him," Dantzler said.

"Am I mistaken, Jack, or didn't you just say that he wasn't going to be easy to catch?"

"He won't be easy to catch, Rich. But we have one thing working in our favor."

"Which is?" Bird said.

"He's begging to be caught." Dantzler looked at Laurie. "Laurie, since you're the most familiar with the Kaplan case, I want you to begin looking for any connection she may have had with the first two victims. Were they friends? Did they have classes together? Did they have the same major? Were they in the same sorority? Really dig on this. Dan, Milt, you guys take another look at the forensics and the physical evidence from the first two murders. See if anything at all was overlooked. Eric, I want you to talk to instructors, classmates, and counselors, anyone who might be able to provide a link with any of the three women. If there's even the slightest connection, we've got to find it. So far we've treated this as three separate cases. That changes, starting right now. Now we treat them as the work of a single killer."

Dantzler closed his folder and stood. "Let's get together again on Tuesday morning at seven-thirty. No one misses unless it's cleared by me. Got that?"

Head nods all around the table.

"Another thing," Dantzler said, "and this is critical. What we say in this room stays in this room. No exceptions. I mean, you don't talk to anyone. Friends on the force, family, priest, rabbi… I don't give a shit. Nothing leaves this room. As for the media, all questions from them will be routed to Rich. He'll handle that end of it. Okay?"

More head nods.

"All right," Dantzler said. "In the words of Gary Gilmore, 'Let's do it.'"

CHAPTER 7

Dantzler spent the next three hours alone in his office, reviewing the case files for the Parker and Adams murders. He hoped some bit of overlooked information would jump out and slap him in the face, but it didn't. It never did. But this case—these cases—yielded even less than normal. There was nothing new, nothing overlooked. Nothing.

I'm smarter than you, goddammit.

Scooping up the Kaplan file, he left the office and drove to Saint Joseph Hospital. He needed to see Mac Tinsley, the medical examiner. Twenty minutes later he pulled into the hospital parking lot. The lot was virtually empty, typical for a Saturday afternoon. Had it been a weekday, finding a place to park would have been nearly impossible. After securing a spot in the rear lot, Dantzler went through the back entrance of the hospital, then down the steps to the morgue area. Mac was the first person he saw. The little bird-like man had just finished the Kaplan autopsy and was walking back to his office when Dantzler caught up with him in the hallway.

"Jackie boy, I sincerely hope you're not here looking for nuggets, 'cause if you are, you're gonna be sorely disappointed," Mac said, opening the door to his office. "If you want to know what I found today, just read the file on the other two girls. It's practically identical in every way."

"Practically?"

"My mistake—make that *exactly* identical."

Dantzler laid the file on the table and looked around the office. "How come you don't have coffee in here?" he said, sitting.

"'Cause I never drink the stuff, that's why." Mac removed his white lab coat, tossed it on the floor, then settled into the big leather chair behind his desk. "Next question?"

"What did the tox screen turn up?"

"The girl was on Lisinopril—for her blood pressure. Low dosage, which means it probably wasn't too bad. Stomach contents consisted of broccoli, carrots, and cauliflower. The classic California medley. There were no recreational drugs, no alcohol, nothing. The girl was cleaner than my grandmother."

"Sex?"

"Not a single sperm to be found. I'd say she's been celibate for at least ten days."

"But she wasn't a virgin?"

"Jack, how many twenty-three-year-old virgins are left on this planet? None, that's how many. They're all apparently up in Heaven awaiting the arrival of all these crazy terrorist who blow themselves and everybody else to smithereens for the sake of Allah."

"Cause of death?"

"Jack, didn't you hear what I said? Abby Kaplan's death was a carbon copy of the other two. She was strangled from behind by someone, most likely a male, using a silk scarf. I say male, because the killer had enough strength to crush her windpipe. He then went through his crazy rituals of placing the medal and the postcard in their proper places. And at some point along the way, for God knows what reason, he used a knife, a very small one, to lacerate the jugular on the right side of her neck."

"Is there any chance he does the cutting before he kills them, then somehow manages to control the bleeding? Maybe using the scarf as a kind of tourniquet?"

"I've never seen you reach like this before, Jack."

"I've never had three unsolved murders before."

"Well, the answer to your question is no. It's not possible. You've been a cop a long time, seen more than your share of dead bodies. You know what happens when the jugular—when any main artery—is cut. There's enough blood to fill a bathtub. Abby Kaplan was lying on her right side, meaning that the flow of blood from the wound would have been downward. If she'd been cut before she died, the area around her head would have been drenched in blood. And the killer, unless he could fly, also would have been drenched."

"And he would have left footprints."

"Precisely. There would have been blood on the walls, ceiling, floor, everywhere. And there wasn't. No, Jack, this sick bastard cuts these girls *after* he kills them."

"How long after?"

"Excellent question—your first of the day, by the way. Judging by the small amount of blood loss, I'd say several minutes after death. Anywhere from ten minutes to half an hour. He's certainly in no hurry."

"So he kills them, undresses them, decorates them with postcard and medal, then cuts them?"

"That's how I see it," Mac said.

"Jesus, why?"

"You're the hot-shot cop, Jack. And you're the one who studied philosophy. I'll leave answering the heavy questions to you."

Dantzler stood, grabbed the file, went to the door, then turned back toward Mac. "Funny, but I don't recall Kierkegaard ever talking about shit like this."

It had just begun to sprinkle when Dantzler drove past the Landsdowne Country Club. He turned right off of Landsdowne onto Bellefonte, drove another hundred yards, then turned into the empty driveway next to Abby Kaplan's house. He cut the engine, jumped out of the Forester, and darted toward the porch.

He beat the heavy stuff by five seconds.

Dantzler unlocked the door, ducked under the yellow crime scene tape, and slipped inside. The empty house seemed—felt— much larger than it had last night when a legion of people were milling around. In fact, the place was spacious—three bedrooms, three bathrooms, den, kitchen, plenty of closet space. Full basement, screened-in patio. Green carpet, beige walls, a ceiling fan in every room. Plush in every respect. He scribbled "owned/rented?" in his notepad, closed it, and put it in his coat pocket. It didn't matter, really. Either way, digs like this didn't come cheap. He figured at least twelve-fifty a month plus utilities. Throw in cable and the phone and you were talking well over fifteen hundred bucks a month. Too expensive for the average college kid living alone. But an average college kid didn't live in this house. Abby Kaplan's old man was a prominent heart surgeon in Manhattan. Money for her was no problem; her family's pockets were deep.

Not that Abby flaunted her affluence. The furnishings were nice but not overly expensive. Certainly nothing boasting extravagance. Judging by the interior decorating, Dantzler summed Abby up as classy and slightly conservative, maybe even frugal.

He picked up a framed picture off the entertainment center. It showed Abby, dressed in cut-off Levis and a halter top, smiling broadly, and standing next to a tall, distinguished-looking man. Her father obviously. Dantzler could tell by their resemblance, and by the pride registered on the man's face. His eyes were swimming with joy.

True love is always best expressed in the eyes. So is the deepest pain and sorrow.

After carefully setting the picture back on the shelf, he turned and looked at himself in the mirror. His face was drawn, almost gaunt. The eyes dark, desolate. A dead man's eyes. His brown hair, always longer than departmental regulation, was uncombed and fell below his collar. The stubble on his face was no more than a day away from being classified as a beard. He again looked at his eyes. Zombie eyes.

He looked at the picture of Abby's father and knew those eyes would never again be that happy. The joy and sparkle that were in them when this picture was taken had been stolen by a senseless act of violence. The same way joy had been stolen from him those many years ago.

Noise from the porch snapped Dantzler out of his trance. He turned and saw a man standing at the door. Medium height, stocky, balding, and dressed in a blue suit with his shirt collar open. He had a beard sprinkled with liberal amounts of gray, and an expression that registered both distress and panic.

"I'm James Winstead," he said, his voice quivering. He stepped inside and closed the door. "I own the house."

"That answers one question for me," Dantzler said.

"What's that?" Winstead's voice registered the same distress as the look on his face.

"Whether Abby owned or rented." Dantzler took out his notepad and a pen. "How long had she lived here?"

"Mind if I sit?" Winstead said, hanging his raincoat on a rack. "I'm feeling a little rocky right now. Abby was...well, aside from being one of the best students I ever had, I was also quite fond of her."

"Please." Dantzler motioned to the sofa. He waited until Winstead settled in. "You and Abby were involved?"

"Involved? You mean romantically? Oh, good heavens no. I'm fifty-one, Abby is—was—twenty-three. Look at me, Detective. Middle-aged, balding, overweight. Even if I'd wanted to, what chances do you think I would've had with a woman who looked like Abby?"

"Older teacher, younger student—it's happened before."

"No, we weren't involved. If I recall correctly, she did have a boyfriend. I don't know his name, though. Sorry"

"Russ Steinberg."

"Yes, that sounds right. A pre-med student. Goes to school somewhere up north. Ohio or Illinois, I believe."

"How long had Abby lived here?"

"*Had.* Speaking of her in the past tense seems so..." He wiped his face with a handkerchief, neatly folded it, and put it in his coat pocket. "A little over two years."

Dantzler looked around the room. "Place like this—rent must've been fairly steep. What'd she pay?"

"A thousand dollars a month, plus utilities."

"Pretty sweet deal. You could easily get fifteen hundred, maybe more."

"The money wasn't important to me, Detective. I was only too happy to help her out. Not that I'm wealthy or anything like that. Far from it. But I am a tenured professor, and I do have some other rental property. So I do okay. When I got divorced four years ago, I decided to downsize. I bought a condo at The Oaks and rented the house to Abby. She was such a sweet girl...I was—"

"How long have you known Abby?"

"Well, I was her adviser from the first day she arrived on campus. That was more than five years ago. I had her in a couple of classes, too. A wonderful student, an even better human being."

"She was studying dance?"

"Music and dance, yes. She was working on her masters. She would have finished next month."

"How did she pay for this place?"

"She worked. Taught dance at Rose's Dance Academy. She also gave private lessons to some of the more gifted young students. Abby was a talented dancer. Worked professionally a couple of summers while she was still in high school. Two summers ago, she toured in *Fosse*. That's big time, Detective. But Abby hated the rat-race aspect of being a professional performer. The endless auditions, the rejections, the constant selling of yourself to people with little or no real talent. She had no taste for that part of it. That's why she decided to become a teacher."

"You seem to know a great deal about her."

"Well, we did have a couple of fairly lengthy conversations over the years, and she told me a few things about herself and her background. And, of course, I had her in class, so I picked up some things there, too."

Winstead seemed exhausted from speaking. He lowered his head and took several slow, deep breaths. When he looked up, his eyes were filled with tears. "It's my fault, you know. What happened to Abby. It's all my fault."

"How so?" Dantzler said.

"I was supposed to pick her up that night. The night she was killed. From Rose's Dance Academy on Lane Allen. But with all the rain, traffic was backed up everywhere. I didn't get there until eight fifty."

"And Abby was already gone?"

Winstead nodded.

"Did you see anyone? Any cars?"

"No. The parking lot was deserted. There weren't even any cars parked in front of the restaurant at the other end of the shopping center. And at eight o'clock, that place is almost always packed."

"Why were you picking her up?"

"Her car is in the shop being worked on."

"Where?"

"The place on High Street that works exclusively on foreign cars. Abby drove a 2000 BMW. A blue one."

"I have to tell you, Mr. Winstead, I'm getting the feeling that you aren't being entirely forthcoming about your relationship with Abby. That perhaps it was more than you're admitting. Would you like to revise your assessment of that relationship?"

Winstead's eyes widened. "No, no, Detective, I'm being completely honest with you. We were friends, that's all. I was her landlord, her teacher, her adviser. She could trust me. That's why she asked me to give her a ride home. There's nothing more to it."

"Did you try to call her once you realized you missed her?" Dantzler said.

Winstead shook his head. "I figured she must've caught a ride with someone else. Rose, maybe. Or one of the parents. I really didn't think it was important to call her. Now, I'd give anything if I had."

Dantzler looked at his watch. "It's four ten—why'd it take you so long to come forward with this information?"

"I just heard about it an hour ago. I wasn't feeling well when I awoke this morning, so I unplugged the phone, took a couple of pills, and went back to bed. One of the professors in the department came by and told me. I came here straight away."

"Can you think of anyone who might want to do something like this to Abby?"

"No. Not to Abby or anyone else. It's horrific. Sick."

"You'll need to come to the station sometime Monday and give a full statement." Dantzler took a card from his shirt pocket and handed it to Winstead. "In the meantime, if you happen to think of anything that might help, I can be reached at any of those numbers."

The two men stood just as Dantzler's cell phone buzzed. "Dantzler," he said. Dynamite passed along the news of Dr. Kaplan's arrival. "Tell him I'll be there in fifteen minutes." "Sounded important," Winstead said, opening the front door. "Abby's father is here." "I thank God I'm not in your shoes right now, Detective." "Yeah."

Less than an hour later, Dantzler walked into Richard Bird's office and found himself staring into a pair of familiar eyes. Only this time, they were joyless. Just as he knew they would be. Dantzler had never learned to like being right all the time. "Come in, Jack, and have a seat," Bird said. "Care for some coffee?" "No, thanks." Dantzler eased to his left and sat on the couch next to the wall. Bird motioned to the man sitting across from him. "Jack, this is Doctor Eli Kaplan. Doctor Kaplan, Jack Dantzler. Jack's the lead investigator on this case." The two men acknowledged each other with a silent nod. Dr. Eli Kaplan sat deathly still, hands clasped together in his lap. More distinguished looking in person than in the photo, he was in his late forties, slender, not as tall as Dantzler had surmised from the picture, with thick black hair highlighted by sideburns that had gone completely white. He wore an expensive gray suit, white shirt, blue tie, gold cuff links, red suspenders, and a pair of black Italian loafers. Dantzler studied the man with great interest, focusing mainly on his eyes. They were moist and red. How many hours had this man already wept for a daughter he would never see again? No matter, Dantzler knew, for the tears already shed were just the beginning of what was still to come. "I'm very sorry about what happened to your daughter," Dantzler said. "I know how you feel." Dr. Kaplan turned his head slightly to the left. "I doubt that very seriously, Detective Dantzler," he whispered. "Unless you've had a loved one taken from you in such a brutal and senseless manner, you can't possibly comprehend the pain my family and I are feeling."

"My mother was murdered twenty-five years ago," Dantzler said softly. "When I was fourteen. The circumstances surrounding her death bear some similarity to your daughter's."

"Sorry. I…"

"No need to apologize. You couldn't have known."

"Doctor Kaplan would like to know if you have any objection to his taking some things from his daughter's house," Bird said. "Will that be a problem?"

"No. Take what you need," Dantzler said. He leaned closer to Dr. Kaplan. "I know this is a difficult time for you, Doctor, but it would be a great help to me if I could ask you a couple of questions about your daughter. Is that okay with you?"

Dr. Kaplan nodded.

"Were you aware of any problems Abby might be having with a boyfriend?" Dantzler said.

"You mean here at the University of Kentucky?"

"Yes."

"Abby had no boyfriend here."

"I take it she did have one."

"Russ Steinberg. He and Abby have been going together for three years. They planned to be married next year."

"Where does Russ live?"

"He attends Harvard. He's a second-year medical student there."

"Did Abby ever mention problems of any type?"

"What kind of problems?"

"Regarding men."

"There was only one man in her life. Russ."

"What about former boyfriends?"

"Abby was a popular, attractive young woman. Sure, she had a few boyfriends when she was younger, but none that I'd consider serious. It was your typical teenage romance kind of thing. Puppy love, nothing more."

"Maybe there was a guy she'd rejected somewhere along the way. Someone with an obsession for her."

"No, I don't think so."

"Did she ever talk about problems in the classroom? A professor with a romantic interest in her?"

"No."

"Have you ever met James Winstead?"

"Sure. Several times. He was one of her instructors, and her current landlord. Why do you ask?"

"Did Abby ever have problems with him?"

"On the contrary, she thought very highly of him."

"What about a student who wouldn't leave her alone? Someone in administration who was bothering her? Was there anything at all that might indicate trouble?"

Dr. Kaplan shook his head. "No. Abby loved it here. The location, Lexington, the people. She wanted to make her home here after she graduated. Maybe buy a small farm—own some horses. So did Russ, for that matter."

"Is it possible that Abby might have had a problem and wouldn't have told you about it?"

"Abby and I were extremely close, Detective Dantzler. We always have been. If she had a problem, believe me, I would have heard about it."

"Perhaps she spoke to your wife. You know, daughter to mother."

"We are not a family of secrets, Detective. If she'd told one of us about a problem, she would've told us both."

"Is your wife in town? If she is, perhaps…"

"My wife did not accompany me to Lexington. She has cancer. Now this. And the rabbis say God never gives us more than we can bear."

Dr. Kaplan lowered his head and began to sob. Tears streamed down his face and dripped to the floor. Dantzler started to say something, to offer his sympathy, but he didn't. He'd been where Dr. Kaplan was now. He knew that nothing anyone could say would ease the pain and suffering.

"I'm terribly sorry," Dr. Kaplan said. He took his handkerchief from his pocket and wiped his eyes. "It's just that…She was still a child. She hadn't even really begun to live. Now this…this…act of madness."

He swallowed hard and fought off a new wave of tears. "I've spent my entire adult life trying to help people by fighting off death," he said. "Most of the time I succeed. But sometimes I don't. Sometimes the patient dies. Death is something I am forced to accept. But this…this is something I can't…" Dr. Kaplan folded the handkerchief and blew his nose. He stood, straightened his shoulders and looked Dantzler and Bird. "Anything else?" he asked.

Dantzler looked at Bird and shrugged.

"No, that'll be all," Bird said. "If you'd rather not go to your daughter's house, just tell us what you need and I'll send someone to get it for you. Might make it a little easier."

"Nothing is going to make it easier," Dr. Kaplan replied. "I do appreciate your offer, but there are things—personal things—I'd rather not have strangers rummaging through. I hope you understand."

"Completely," Bird said.

Dr. Kaplan walked to the door. "You know, it's funny, but I really don't care if you catch Abby's killer or not. If you do or if you don't, it's not going to bring her back. And that's all I—my wife and I—really want."

"Believe me, Doctor Kaplan, we want to catch him," Bird said.

Dr. Kaplan nodded and opened the door. Before leaving, he turned back to Dantzler. "Out of curiosity, Detective, how was your mother killed?" he said.

"Strangled."

"Was her murderer caught?"

"No."

"Would it have made any difference to you if he had been?"

"No."

CHAPTER 8

Laurie drove out Tates Creek Road, hooked a left onto Cooper Drive, went two more blocks, then made another left onto Duke Drive. The route took her past the post office and toward Christ the King Catholic Church. She slowed to a crawl on Duke, straining to read the house numbers, before eventually coming to a stop in front of 424.

The small, white wooden house sat several yards off the street and was fronted by a pool-table green manicured lawn. There were two huge, trimmed bushes and a small bed of roses. On the front porch there was a swing and two chairs. Next to the steps leading up to the porch was a concrete handicap ramp flanked on both sides by two metal handrails.

Laurie went around to the backyard, which was a carbon copy of what she'd seen in the front—small, neat. The yard, which was enclosed by a green wooden fence, extended out to an alley. Beyond the alley, she could see the back of a two-story duplex. She took out her notepad and drew a quick diagram of the scene. Satisfied with her rendering, she walked back around to the front of the house.

She rang the doorbell and waited for nearly a minute. When no one answered, she rang it again, this time pushing harder, as if the extra pressure would somehow make the noise louder inside. Finally, after another minute of waiting, a young girl, maybe sixteen, yanked the door open. She wore cut-off Levis, sports bra, no shoes. Deep tan, rings on every finger, pierced belly button. Youthful sex appeal advertised for all to see. It was a look, Laurie knew, that she had worked overtime to achieve.

"Yes, who are you?" she asked. Her tone was a mixture of boredom and indifference.

Laurie held up her ID shield. "Sergeant Dunn," she said.

Unimpressed, the young girl cocked her head and glared at Laurie through ice-blue eyes. "So...you're a cop? Big deal. I haven't done anything wrong."

"You sure of that?"

"Yeah."

"Betcha if I looked hard enough, I could prove you wrong."

"Go ahead and kill yourself. It's your time, not mine. I really couldn't care less."

"Good thing bad manners aren't a crime or I'd have to bring you in."

"Ha, ha. That's real funny. Maybe you should be a comedian."

Laurie fought the urge to slap her. "What's your name?" she asked, trying not to show her anger.

"Amber."

"Well, Amber, does Grace Kinkade live here?"

"She's my grandmother."

"Does she live here was my question?"

"Yeah, she lives here. What do you think, that I own this place?"

"Would you please inform Mrs. Kinkade that I'd like to speak with her?"

Without answering, Amber spun around and marched away. Laurie toyed with the idea of cutting the kid some slack—it's just a phase, she reminded herself—but for some reason she wasn't in a slack-cutting mood. Not for Amber. Not with an attitude like that. Slack had to be earned.

Two minutes later, Laurie heard the familiar sound of a wheelchair rolling across a wooden floor. The woman in the wheelchair had snow-white hair and wasn't much bigger than a small child. Grace Kinkade wheeled herself into the living room and waved Laurie in. Laurie smiled, stepped inside, closed the door, and followed Grace into the living room.

"My granddaughter tells me you're with the police," Grace said. "Since I haven't committed any crimes lately, I will be more than happy to talk to you. Now, if I were guilty of something, I would've said no. Told you to get a warrant, then come back. While that was happening, I would lawyer up. That's how they do it on TV."

"Well, cops on TV…"

"I watch all the police shows," Grace said. "Always have, going back to the old 'Dragnet.' But my favorite is 'NYPD Blue.' The language is a little raw, and they show too many naked bodies, but I just love that chubby detective. Sipowicz. You know, they even showed his butt, which I really didn't need to see. But I just love him. He's so contrary."

"If I behaved like he does, I'd be in jail."

"Yes, he does go a little overboard at times, doesn't he?" Grace said. "He says certain criminals need to be tuned up. Did you ever tune anyone up?"

"Not yet."

"Would you like something to drink? Iced tea or Coke? Juice? I'll have my granddaughter get it for you."

Laurie shuddered at the thought. "I'm fine, thanks. Now..."

"Don't you just think it's scandalous the way these young girls dress today?" Grace asked, shaking her head. "Those pants Amber has on—they look like they're three sizes too small. And exposing her stomach like that. Just scandalous, I'm telling you. Young girls should take more pride in their appearance. In my day, if a girl dressed like that, she'd get a bad reputation fast. Well, at least she doesn't have one of those awful tattoos. I hate those things."

"Mrs. Kinkade..."

"My husband Earl had one on his forearm. A dagger with a snake wrapped around it." Grace sighed loudly. "He got it when he was in the Marines. A lot of the boys came back from World War Two with tattoos. They'd get drunk, dare each other, and the next thing you knew, they'd sober up and wonder why on earth they did it. I don't think a day went by that Earl didn't regret having it."

Laurie pointed to a picture on the wall. "Is that your husband?" she said.

"That's Earl. He was just about the best husband a woman could ask for. He's been gone thirteen years now. Lung cancer—he was a heavy smoker."

"I'm sorry."

"I sure miss the old coot, tattoo and all."

"Mrs. Kinkade, I'm investigating the murder of Allison Parker and I know you spoke…"

"Allison Parker?" Grace, obviously confused, took a few seconds to let Laurie's words sink in. Finally, her face lit up. "Oh, yes, the pretty dark-haired girl. I used to see her emptying the trash behind her building. Terrible what happened to her. She was murdered, you know?"

"What can you remember about the night you saw her in the car?"

"It was very cold. Snowing, I think. No, that's not right. Ice—we were having an ice storm. Turned out to be a nasty couple of days."

"Exactly where were you when you saw Allison?"

"I was standing at the kitchen sink, looking out the window. This was about three months before the MS got so bad that I finally had to get this wheelchair. It was pretty late—nine or ten, if I'm not mistaken. It's rare to see a car back there, so that's what got my attention. At first I didn't know anyone was in the car. It was too dark to see much of anything. There's supposed to be a light back there, but some of the neighbors complained that it kept them awake, so the city people removed it about a year ago. Anyway, I was looking out the window when the car door opens and I see the two people in the car."

"How long did the light stay on?"

"Oh, five, ten seconds, maybe. I don't know for sure. Long enough for me to tell that it was Allison Parker."

"You told the investigating detective that Allison was with a man."

"Yes, that's right. He was in the car with her."

"Can you remember anything about him?"

"He was bald, I do remember that. But that's about all I remember. Ten seconds isn't a lot of time."

"What was their demeanor?"

"Demeanor? I don't understand."

"What were they doing? What was their body language? Were they speaking, not speaking?"

"I really can't tell you about any of those things. The light wasn't on long enough for me to see what their demeanor was."

"Did the light come on because someone opened the door, or because someone turned on the interior light?"

"Allison opened the door. That I do remember."

"But she didn't get out."

"No, she stayed in the car."

"Any idea what kind of car it was?"

"No, sorry. Now if Earl was here, he could tell you make, model, year, size of the engine, and how much it cost. He knew everything about automobiles."

"Back to the man. I know you only got a quick glimpse, but if you saw him again, do think you might recognize him?"

"No, I don't think so. He was just a normal-looking chubby bald man."

"Chubby? The man was heavy-set?"

"Stocky—I think that might be a better description."

Amber came into the room eating a Baby Ruth candy bar. She strolled between Laurie and Grace, plopped down on the couch, stretched out, and took another bite. Laurie looked at her eyes—slightly unfocused and ringed with dark circles—and immediately suspected her of using drugs. Pot most likely, and judging by her behavior, she had probably used within the past hour.

"I'm bored, Granny," Amber said, bouncing off the couch. "When's Mom gonna be here?"

"She said it would be around ten-thirty. After her meeting." Grace looked at Laurie. "Her mother, my daughter Betsy, is on the city council."

"Then I suppose in a way I work for your daughter," Laurie said, standing. She took out a card and handed it to Grace. "Thank you for taking the time to speak with me, Mrs. Kinkade. You've been a big help. If you happen to think of anything else that might be important, you can reach me at that number."

"I don't think I've been all that much of a help," Grace said, looking at the card.

"I know more now than I did when I got here," Laurie said. "That means you've been a help."

Grace smiled. "Amber, would you be kind enough to walk the nice detective to the door?"

Amber led the way with Laurie three steps behind. When they reached the door, Amber opened it and stepped aside. Then in the grand manner of a Waldorf-Astoria doorman, she bowed and waved Laurie through. "Goodnight, Miss Nice Detective," she whispered.

Laurie drew herself to within inches of Amber's face. "Tell me, Amber. How would your mother, a city councilwoman, react if I informed her that her daughter smoked pot?"

"You wouldn't," Amber snapped. "I mean, I don't do drugs. Drugs are for losers."

Laurie started down the steps, then turned back. "You know what, Amber? I think maybe I will get that search warrant after all. Come back here and see if your story checks out. Yeah, I think I'll do just that."

Laurie silently chuckled on the way to her car. When she got in, she saw Amber standing, frozen on the porch, a look of fear on her once-cocky face. Laurie knew that in a matter of seconds Granny Kincade was going to hear the sound of a toilet being flushed.

Laurie laughed out loud as she drove away.

Sitting in the Baskins-Robbins on Tates Creek Road, Dantzler watched as across from him, six-foot-six-inch Richard Bird, hopelessly wedged between table and chair, was finishing off three large scoops of chocolate almond ice cream. The pink plastic spoon moved at warp speed, little more than a blur as it attacked the paper cup. When Bird deemed further attacks useless, he dropped the cup and spoon into a trash basket next to the table, wiped the chocolate evidence from his mouth with a napkin, looked up and smiled like a contented five-year-old.

"What can I say?" he said, gleefully. "I'm a sucker for chocolate."

"Obviously," Dantzler said. "I don't know why you tossed the cup. It's so clean they could use it again."

Bird snorted. "My doctor would have a coronary if he knew how much ice cream I consume in a month's time. To hell with him. I don't smoke or drink, and I go easy on the fried food and red meat. My BP is fine and so is my cholesterol. Know what I say? Fuck him if he can't take a joke. Hell, I'm in ten times better shape than he is. Even on my bad days."

Bird stood, stretched, and motioned toward the door. "Let's split this joint before I get another urge," he said.

Dantzler held the door open as a dark-haired woman herded a young boy inside. The kid was maybe three, his eyes wide, anticipation and excitement written all over his young face. They were followed by a man carrying a baby wrapped in a blue blanket. Husband, wife, two kids. Bright, shining future in front of them. Dantzler's thoughts drifted to Allison Parker, Becky Adams, and Abby Kaplan.

Apparently Bird's thoughts had drifted in the same direction. "Tell me, Jack, were you able to find anything in the Kaplan girl's house?"

"Not really," he said, pulling his attention free from the scene inside. "Just that the killer knew her. He knew all the victims."

"You sure?"

"Can't be any other way. There's no forcible entry, no signs of a struggle. He's being allowed inside. Invited in is my guess."

"That's scary."

"He knows them, Rich. And they know him."

"Fuck." Bird leaned against his car. A woman with two small children walked past and shot him an angry look. He shrugged, gave her an "oops, I'm sorry" look, then waited until she was inside before continuing. "If the girls are letting him in, then there has to be a connection among the victims. A link of some sort."

"Maybe Laurie will come up with something."

"You don't sound very hopeful."

"My hunch is the killer is their only link."

"Then he has to be someone at the University."

"I agree."

"That's the best news I've had in two years," Bird said. "Because if you're right, we've automatically narrowed the list of suspects down to about twenty-five thousand."

"You can cut that number in half," Dantzler said. "No way our killer is a female."

"Which means we're now down to roughly twelve thousand suspects. I suppose we should thank God for small favors."

"I haven't sent God many thank-you cards lately. Not when shit like this continues to happen." Dantzler hesitated as the perfect all-American scene walked outside and past him, the young boy doing a number on a strawberry ice cream cone. "God's not exactly at the top of my favorites list these days."

An hour after leaving Amber standing frozen on the porch, Laurie walked into the police station. The desk sergeant, Bruce Rawlinson, saw her coming in and looked at his watch.

"You're working late hours these days, Dunn," he said, smiling. "What's the matter, your love life gone sour on you?"

"Love life—I've heard that term before," Laurie said. "I think maybe it was in a movie. Yeah, a movie with Bogie and Ingrid Bergman. But it's certainly not something I'm personally familiar with."

"You just haven't been looking in the right places," Rawlinson said. "You hook up with me and I'll show you what love is all about."

"Aren't you married, Bruce?"

"Sometimes. But what's that got to do with the price of eggs in China?"

"Don't take this personally, but if you were the only guy left in the world, I would become a lesbian faster than you could say Rosie O'Donnell."

Rawlingson cackled out loud. "That's what I like about you, Dunn. You ain't no Sally Subtle. And since I would hate to see you switch sides and play for the other team, I'm gonna deny you my love."

"Jeez, Bruce, that'll be tough for me, but I think I'll survive."

Rawlinson's cackle echoed off the marble walls as Laurie bounded up the steps. Although it was pushing midnight, she wanted to type up the Grace Kinkade interview notes while they were still fresh in her mind. She sat at her desk, turned the computer on, and waited for it to boot up.

Only now did she realize how wired she was. She'd gotten less than five hours sleep in the past two days, yet she was wide awake. It was the job, she knew, that had her so energized. Despite what she had told herself about the importance and excitement of working Missing Children, it didn't begin to compare with working Homicide. This was a completely different ballgame altogether, and it was the only one she wanted to be in.

Being picked for this job was the career break she needed. It didn't take an Oxford grad to know that. Laurie realized her good fortune the second Dantzler told her that she was being assigned to Homicide. She'd immediately called Charlie Bolton to tell him, waking the old bear at three in the morning.

Charlie couldn't have been happier. He told her to listen, work her ass off and, most of all, to be fearless. "You've got the smarts and you've got moxie," he said. "But so do a lot of people. Not everyone has bravery. The courage to be fearless. That's what separates the great from the near-great."

Now, sitting alone at midnight in the War Room—so christened by Eric—hearing Charlie's words echo in her mind, Laurie felt a rush of adrenaline surge through her body like a jolt of electricity. She also felt a wave of anxiety. What if she failed? What if she didn't have the bravery Charlie spoke about? What if she couldn't measure up to Dantzler's standards? What if she didn't have the chops to be a good homicide detective?

Laurie chased away her doubts with a silent tongue lashing. *You can do this job. No one can rise to Dantzler's level, least of all a rookie. So just listen and learn. Go with your instincts, your talent. Never question your talent.*

And most of all…be *fearless.*

Smiling, Laurie popped a Certs into her mouth, scooted her chair forward, and began typing.

CHAPTER 9

The dream was always the same:

Dantzler sees his father running down a busy city street, passing people whose faces are hidden behind masks. The harder his father runs, the slower he moves. Soon, despite his labored struggling, he can barely move his legs at all. The scene shifts. Now his father is standing on a riverbank. Maybe it's Vietnam. Dantzler isn't sure. Across the river, his mother stands alone, frantically waving her arms. It is raining hard, but she isn't wet. She is nude, and she's calling out Dantzler's name. Over and over, he hears his name. It echoes like the cry of a bird in the faraway distance. He stands frozen, eyes wide, as a dark cloud begins to close in behind her. Dantzler sees his father move to the waters' edge, ready to leap into the muddy river and swim to her. But just as he's ready to jump, there's a loud blast and then a bullet smashes into his chest, knocking him to the ground. Bright red blood pours from the wound. Standing alone, Dantzler watches helplessly as the dark cloud engulfs his mother, lifts her up, and carries her off into the night. He falls to his knees and covers his ears with his hands. Still, he continues to hear her voice calling out his name.

"Jack, Jack, please save me!"

Dantzler's eyes snapped open. He stared into the darkness for several seconds, then managed to pull himself into a sitting position. He looked at the alarm clock. 4:50 a.m. Yawning, he flopped back down and closed his eyes. The sound of his mother's haunting cry still echoed in his ears.

Some demons refuse to die.

At 7:15 on Tuesday morning, Laurie paced the floor, pausing every few seconds to look at her watch, then at the door. She was anxious to get started, to get on with things. To "relocate the bad guys to their habitat behind bars," as Charlie Bolton always said.

She had been in the War Room since seven. Wired by the challenge that lay in front of her, she had risen at five, jogged three miles, showered, dressed, grabbed a bowl of Corn Flakes, a small glass of cranberry juice, and a cup of coffee, and driven downtown to Police Headquarters.

She walked into the building at two minutes before seven.

At 7:30, she sat at the table, opened her notepad, and began refreshing her memory. Or tried to. But she couldn't. Her restlessness quickly got the better of her. She stood and began pacing the room, pausing occasionally to look at her watch. The feeling of anxiety swelled.

Waiting wasn't her cup of tea. *Come on, guys. Let's get this thing going.*

Two minutes later Dantzler walked in. His dark eyes were fixed straight ahead in a stare that Laurie found menacing. He greeted her with a nod and a grunt as he shot straight for the coffee pot. After filling his cup, he pulled out a chair across from her and sat down.

"Why the look?" he said, his voice scratchy as sandpaper. "Something on your mind?"

"Well, it's just that I've heard that you're a stickler for promptness."

"Forget what you've heard," Dantzler said. "In the first place, seventy-five percent of what you hear is bullshit and the rest is fiction, which I don't mind at all." He sipped the steaming coffee. "I'm sure you've also heard that I intimidate people. Right?"

"Right."

"Do you think I'm intimidating?"

"Well, you certainly are intense. I can see how that might intimidate someone."

"This is an intense business we're in. Never think otherwise."

"Yes, sir."

Dantzler brought his hands up and rubbed his eyes.

"You working with us—with me—will give you an edge," he said, rolling the cup in his hands. "People are bound to talk, to whisper. There will be rumors and conjecture. How'd *she* get that assignment? Who'd she have to sleep with to get it? A guy like Dale Larraby—he'll seethe inside because you're on this job. He's a caveman who thinks women on the force will lead to the downfall of mankind. His jealousy could make him difficult to deal with. If he causes you grief, ignore it. If it gets too bad to ignore, tell me and I'll handle it. Only two things matter in this job—putting away the killers, and bringing about justice for the victims' loved ones. That's it. Everything else—personality clashes, egos, pride, jealousy—should be flushed down the toilet. Remember...if it can't help you, fuck it."

"I'll keep that in mind."

"Listen to me, Laurie," Dantzler continued. "If you're going to succeed in this business, you've got to be cocky and arrogant. You have to believe deep down inside that no one is smarter than you. That's exactly what our killer thinks—that he's smarter than all of us. Arrogance and good instincts—in the final analysis, those may be the most important things you need to be a good cop. Understand?"

"Yes, sir."

"And cut the 'sir' crap. It makes me feel a hundred years old."

"You aren't?"

"Okay, good people, tell me what you've got," Richard Bird said. He stood at the end of the table, his eyes flashing from side to side. "You know how much I hate silence. Please, someone dazzle me."

Dale Larraby cleared his throat and scooted his chair forward. A solidly built man in his early fifties, Larraby had a reputation for being unflinching and extremely aggressive. It was a reputation that had followed him since his days as a national Golden Gloves boxing champ. He also had a reputation for being an average detective and a dismal human being.

"I spoke with Rose Wessell," Larraby said. "Or I tried to, anyway. She's pretty much a zombie right now—really out of it. What I did get from her was that she left the Academy sometime after eight, right when the heavy rain started coming down. She wanted Abby to come with her, but Abby declined, saying she'd rather wait for her ride. James Winstead was supposed to pick her up. He's her landlord. Anyway, Rose left. And that was the last time she saw Abby Kaplan."

"Do you plan to speak with Rose again?" Bird asked.

"At some point, yes," Larraby said. "But it would be a waste of time right now. The lady's a wreck."

"The problem is, we don't know how much time we have until he strikes again," Dantzler said. "What we do know is that we've got a maniac out there who's killed three women, and we don't have clue number one. Given that we don't know Jack shit at this point, I'd say no interview is a waste of time."

"Then why don't you go talk to her, Jack?" Larraby said, his right hand closing to a fist. "See what you can come up with."

"*Somebody* will have to interview her, that's for certain."

"Gentlemen, let's tone down the attitude," Bird snapped. "Did you ask Rose if Abby Kaplan was having problems with anyone? Did she seem concerned about anything? Was she worried, troubled?"

"Would've done no good asking those questions," Larraby answered. "Not now, anyway. The woman could barely give me her name, much less intricate details. I'll talk to her again in a week or so, when she's more up to it."

"You'll talk to her tomorrow, Dale," Bird said. "On this one, I agree with Jack. We can't afford to sit on our asses and wait."

"Let Laurie talk to her," Dantzler said.

Larraby almost flew out of his chair. "If anybody talks to her, Jack, it'll be me. Not some virgin."

"Tough guy like you threatened by a skirt," Dantzler said. "That's an embarrassment to Neanderthals everywhere."

"Fuck you, you arrogant prick."

"Come on, guys," Matthews said. "Cut the nonsense. We've got more important things to do than listen to this bullshit."

"Dan's right, fellas," Bird said. "It's either co-exist or else. And take my word for it, neither of you will like else."

"Just a friendly exchange between two colleagues," Dantzler said, smiling.

"Jack's idea does make sense, Dale," Bird said, looking at Larraby. "Letting Laurie do the interview. Woman to woman, you know? It might be easier for Rose to open up."

Larraby slumped back in his chair and glared at Dantzler. "You're the boss."

Bird looked at Matthews and Costello. "You guys come up with anything interesting?" he said.

The two men exchanged glances. "Go ahead, Dan," Costello said.

Matthews studied his notes for a brief moment, then said, "This James Winstead fella is definitely worth a closer look. He apparently used to beat up his wife—now ex-wife—on a fairly regular basis. There were four reported incidents within a two-year period. And as we all know, if there were four that were reported, who knows how many weren't? She never pressed charges, so the bastard got a free ride. At some point, I guess she got tired of being his punching bag and finally divorced him. That was about four years ago. She's out of town—won't be back until Friday—but we plan on talking to her then."

Matthews looked across the table at Dantzler. "I know you said the guy seemed kosher, Ace," he said. "But I don't think he is."

"Doesn't sound like it," Dantzler replied. "Can anyone corroborate his whereabouts for Thursday night?"

"Don't know. But finding out is first up on our to-do list."

"Anything on your part, Milt?" Bird said.

"Not really. I'm still studying the evidence from the first two murders, but so far I haven't found anything. I'll keep digging, though. Who knows? Maybe something will pop up."

"What about you, Laurie?" Bird said. "What've you got?"

"I went back to re-interview Grace Kinkade, and—"

"Wait," Bird interrupted. "Grace Kinkade? Refresh my memory."

"She's an elderly lady whose house backs up against the duplex where Allison Parker lived."

Bird nodded. "Yeah, I remember her. Go on."

"On the night Allison Parker was murdered, Grace remembers seeing Allison sitting in a car talking to a man. She can't remember the make or color of the car, but she did remember something about the man. He was bald and heavy-set. *Chubby* was the word she used to describe him."

"How could she see them if she lives behind the duplex?" Costello asked.

"There's an alley that separates the duplex from Grace's backyard. The car was parked in the alley. Grace just happened to be looking out the kitchen window that night."

"What's your gut feeling about the woman?" Dantzler said. "She a flake, a nut, sound, what?"

"Kinda eccentric, maybe. And definitely a talker. But she seemed pretty sharp for someone her age."

"Go see her again," Dantzler said. "Take a sketch artist with you and see if he can put something together. I know we did this before, but who knows—maybe she'll come up with something this time. Talk to this woman. Really press her. Make her see something. Anything. I don't care if she describes a cartoon character. We need a face to give us something to go on."

"I'll call her tomorrow," Laurie said.

Bird motioned to Eric. "Your turn, big guy."

"I still haven't found anything that connects the victims," he said. "Except, of course, that they all went to the same school. Far as I can tell, they didn't know each other or have any classes together."

"There may not be a connection," Bird said, adding, "but keep digging. Right now, anything would be more than we have."

Twenty minutes after the meeting broke up, Laurie sat alone in the break room, occasionally plucking a potato chip out of the small bag that lay on the table. She chewed slowly, her mind on what had transpired during the meeting. Specifically, what had transpired between Dantzler and Larraby. The two men clearly detested each other, but the venom was more than she expected.

Costello came into the room, quickly followed by Matthews. Bud and Lou, she thought, side by side. Partners. Two guys who do get along.

"So, what's the deal with Dantzler and Larraby?" she asked.

Costello leaned over and took a chip out of Laurie's bag. "Natural enemies—like a cobra and a mongoose." Costello popped the chip into his mouth and chewed vigorously. "Believe me, what you saw today was nothing."

Matthews pulled up a chair, turned it around, and sat, his arms resting on the back. "If one of those two found the Holy Grail, or proved the existence of God, the other one wouldn't acknowledge it. Those two are like the Jews and the Arabs— they just don't get along. And it's been that way from the day they first met."

"Why?" Laurie said, sipping from a bottle of Evian.

Matthews shrugged. "Attitude, personality, talent— everything. Look, Jack Dantzler is one great detective. I mean, the best. He's one very bright human being. Hell, he graduated college when he was barely twenty. Now, along with that intelligence and talent, there's a certain amount of arrogance. Maybe that just goes with the territory. As someone fated to live on a much lower intellectual level, I wouldn't know. But Jack can be unforgiving, especially toward those who don't come close to him in terms of ability and work ethic. Which is practically everyone. Jack respects effort, though, even if you are a dumb shit like me and Milt. That's why we all get along okay. But Jack sees Larraby as being dumb *and* lazy. That's a combo Jack can't tolerate."

"Something else, too," Costello said. "Jack's always been the department golden boy, which has pissed off a lot of people around here over the years. You saw an example today, when Jack said you, rather than Larraby, should talk to Rose Wessell. Personally, I agree with Jack—I think it's a good idea, makes a lot of sense. But looking at it from Larraby's angle, it's just one more example of Golden Boy Jack getting his way. Rich could've handled that situation in a better way."

"Keep your eye on the prize," Matthews said, "and that's catching the bad guys. Everything else, the politics, the personality clashes, the egos—all horseshit. Never allow that stuff to become a distraction. Don't get stuck in the muck"

"Fuck the muck," Costello said, taking the bag of chips from Laurie.

"Wasn't that the title of a famous song?"

"Damn straight," Costello said, chewing. "Biggest hit ever for Frankie Laine."

"Who's Frankie Laine?" Laurie asked.

"Just another old fart like Milt and me," Matthews said, laughing.

CHAPTER 10

Eldon Wessell awoke with an erection. He stumbled groggily to the window, opened it, and gulped in the cool, clean, damp April air. Beyond the ancient elm tree, he could see the brightening horizon. Eldon seldom missed a sunrise. Before retiring each evening, he always checked the newspaper or television for the official time for sunrise, then set his alarm clock accordingly. Usually twenty to thirty minutes before the sun came up. It was that half-hour before sunrise that he loved best, when the forces of the past and future were still locked in combat.

Eldon unbuttoned his pajama top and let the fresh air caress his hairless chest. For nearly twenty minutes he stood motionless, chill bumps covering his body, and watched with a child's awe as the sun broke free from the shackles of night and began its ascent toward the heavens.

Eldon worked his right hand down inside the pajamas and grasped his penis. He began working his hand up and down, slowly at first, then more rapidly, bringing himself to the brink of orgasm. At the crucial moment, when even the slightest movement would send him over the edge, he squeezed his penis tightly. Eyes closed, he stood perfectly still until the surge of pleasure that threatened to overtake him had passed.

This was a morning ritual for Eldon. An exercise in discipline. A test to make sure that his inner strength had not weakened, that he continued, as always, to control his own sexual destiny.

Discipline and patience—the two guiding principles in his life.

As he stripped off his pajamas, he reminded himself that there was no need to hurry. He was in control, and therefore knew exactly when he would experience his next orgasm. He knew when and where it would happen, and who would be the instrument of that pleasure.

He went into the bathroom, filled the huge tub with hot water, climbed in, and stayed there for close to forty minutes. Gee and Rose slept in on Saturdays—they always attended late-night Friday Mass—thus allowing him uninterrupted possession of the bathroom for an hour at a minimum. Plenty of time to constantly reheat the water, bringing it to a near-scalding temperature, and turning the bathroom into a virtual sauna.

As he lay there, rivulets of perspiration and water dripping from his pink skin, his thoughts were on the next Chosen One. Deborah Tucker. The most-beautiful one thus far. When he first met Deborah nearly two years ago, he knew instantly that she would one day fulfill his desires. She was a vision that spring morning. Tall, elegant, dark hair, marvelous smile—perfect in every respect.

Feeling himself harden again, Eldon began to masturbate. Again he brought himself to the precipice of orgasm, only to back away at the last second. Time, he told himself, there is plenty of time. In all matters, even those concerning pleasure (no, *especially* concerning pleasure), discipline is the single most important factor. A successful person must develop discipline, shape it, harden it like steel, and never allow the forces of weakness to chip away at it.

And Eldon considered himself a successful man. Why shouldn't he? The proof, as they say, is in the pudding. And he had more than enough proof to defend his claim.

Three were dead. Wasn't that sufficient evidence to silence anyone foolish enough to be critical or skeptical? What further proof could anyone possibly need?

"Three," he mumbled under his breath. "Count 'em, three."

Three was only a number. A cold, indifferent statistic, not at all unlike the ones you find on the stock index page in the newspaper. But as any true Wall Street analyst will tell you, statistics aren't always the best way to gauge success.

No, Eldon reasoned, the real measure of his success could best be found in another piece of information. The most critical piece of all.

Three were dead. And he was free.

Eldon counted himself among the few and the fortunate, that select group of Americans who happily march off every day to jobs they love. While most of his friends grumbled and complained bitterly about how much they hated what they were doing, Eldon went to his job each morning with eager anticipation. He felt great sorrow for those who were unhappy with their occupations. He could think of nothing worse than spending a lifetime working at a job that was unfulfilling and unsatisfying.

Eldon's normal schedule was 8 a.m. to 5 p.m., Monday through Friday, with an occasional Saturday thrown in. Eldon didn't mind the work or the hours; indeed, he often worked overtime, which he never reported on his time card. He often made a Saturday appearance, even if nothing was going on.

Which is precisely what he did on this Saturday. Entering the store, Eldon saw the two female employees sitting at their cash registers. Seeing them made his blood boil. One was asleep, the other yawning and stretching like a lazy cat. Showing no pride in themselves, or in their job. It was an example of the unprofessionalism he found so abhorrent in a growing majority of today's young people. It didn't matter that the doors had been open for barely ten minutes, or that no customers had arrived, or that the two girls had most likely been to a keg party lasting until the early morning hours. There were simply no excuses for behavior such as this. Never. Professionalism, like loyalty, was a constant. It was not to be taken for granted or taken lightly.

The yawner saw Eldon coming toward her, sat up, and cleared her throat loud enough to wake her sleeping friend. "Mr. Wessell," she said, "Didn't expect to see you here this early on a Saturday."

"I think that's quite obvious." Eldon looked at the sleeper, who snapped awake and began rubbing her eyes. "Late night, Bonnie?"

"Eh, yes, sir, pretty late."

"Party?"

"Not a formal party, no," Bonnie said. "Just a bunch of us got together at Two Keys."

"Ladies, your social life is your business," Eldon said, "but what you do here is my business. I will not tolerate unprofessional behavior. Sleeping, yawning, and slouching certainly qualify as unprofessional. Believe it or not, you are not indispensable to the operation of this bookstore. If you doubt that, follow me to my office. I have an entire drawer filled with nothing but resumes and applications that I will be more than happy to show you. So, my advice to both of you is this—behave in a professional manner. Otherwise, you will be replaced. Am I clear on this?"

"Yes, sir."

"Absolutely, sir. Won't happen again, sir."

"Good. See that it doesn't." Eldon pointed to the magazine stand. "I would appreciate it, Bonnie, if you would straightened the magazine stand. That area looks like it has been bombed. I know that should've been taken care of before closing last night, but as you can see, it wasn't. I will discuss that matter with Barbara on Monday."

"Yes, sir," Bonnie said, getting out of her chair. "I'll take care of it right now."

"Thank you."

Eldon was the first to admit that he was obsessed with his job. But it was a healthy obsession, he believed, one that truly successful people recognize as supreme dedication to responsibility. It was, Eldon had always felt, the kind of obsession that takes you to the top of your chosen profession.

Every great person, Eldon had long ago concluded, was obsessed. No one can rise to the top of the ladder unless he is driven to do so, even at the expense of sacrificing other aspects of his personal life.

There was an enormous responsibility being assistant manager of the University bookstore. It was a responsibility Eldon didn't take lightly. He accepted responsibility the way most people accept money.

And, of course, there was the pride factor. Pride in one's work, regardless of the profession, is a measure of that person's character. If you do top-quality work, if your performance level is consistently high, then you never have to feel inferior to anyone.

At work, Eldon was a king. An equal to anyone. Here, he'd made his mark. He was successful. There could be no denying that. He was well liked and well respected by everyone associated with the bookstore and the University. Hadn't they proved it by giving him the lion's share of responsibility for running the place? Hadn't they told him to take charge, to make sure things ran smoothly and professionally? Yes, yes, yes. They had, in essence, put the bookstore in his hands.

Although he was officially listed as the assistant manager, it was common knowledge that the manager, old Mr. Blakemore, was a figurehead and little else. It was Eldon who did the bulk of substantive work. It was Eldon who shouldered the heaviest burdens. More important, he made most of the key decisions. Nothing was purchased unless first okayed by him. Nothing was changed without his approval. Even most personnel matters were left to him. If you wanted a job in the University bookstore, Eldon Wessell was the man you had to impress.

Gee and Rose couldn't touch him here. Here, he was his own man. An equal to anyone, respected by everyone.

Eldon's reputation was built on more than two decades of solid performance. He had gone to work there part-time during his sophomore year at the school, and had never worked a day anywhere else. Friends often remarked about how unusual it was that he'd never received a paycheck from any place other than the University. They said it in a disbelieving way, as though it was something truly unique. In this day and age, when people jump from job to job, it might be. But not to Eldon. To him it was a source of great pride. To stay in one place, to successfully serve one master for a long period of time—that was a throwback to an era when loyalty meant something.

Eldon always reminded his friends that Joe DiMaggio and Mickey Mantle never received a paycheck from any franchise other than the New York Yankees. Sandy Koufax was a Dodger and only a Dodger. Bill Russell never wore any color other than Boston-Celtic green.

Eldon used this analogy to prove a simple fact: The really great ones don't get bounced around.

CHAPTER 11

Deborah Tucker was a native of St. Louis, and a junior theatre major at the University. She was a tall, angular woman with thick black hair that cascaded wildly onto her shoulders. She possessed a wonderfully ironic wit and a true gift for the art of acting. It was a gift that had not gone unnoticed by her drama instructors, who were quick to give her the best roles. By the end of her freshman year, she was already being touted as one of the finest actresses the theatre department had ever had. As a sophomore, she played Lady McBeth and Maggie the Cat. And two months ago, she scored a stunning triumph as Mary Tyrone in O'Neill's *Long Day's Journey Into Night.* No longer did anyone speak of Deborah Tucker in terms of potential; after her performance as Mary Tyrone she was being hailed as the real thing.

These were happy days for Deborah. She was in love with David Metzger, the first true love of her life. Her parents, after seeing her perform in O'Neill's classic tale of family tragedy, finally had accepted the reality of her future as an actress. What had once been reluctance on their part had, by the sheer force of her talent, been transformed into enthusiastic support.

Two days ago her father sent her a dozen red roses and a bottle of expensive French wine after learning that she had been accepted for a summer internship at Chicago's Goodman Theatre. On the card inside the box of flowers, he had written, "You have a marvelous talent. Now go reach for the stars. And break a leg. Love, Dad."

Deborah cried for half an hour after reading her father's words.

On this Saturday morning, Deborah crawled out of bed and fixed herself a glass of orange juice and a bagel. After eating, she spent twenty minutes on a stationary bike, and another ten minutes doing sit-ups. She then showered, dressed, and went outside.

As always, she greeted the morning with a cheery smile.

Deborah rented a garage apartment in the pricey Hartland Subdivision. She loved the place, which was small and cozy, and probably not unlike one of those SoHo lofts she hoped to someday live in. She felt safe there, too. And with all that had been going on lately, feeling safe was nothing to take for granted. The garage was attached to a large residential house that was owned by a prominent circuit judge. Deborah adored him. He was kind, wise, fatherly. She was also close to the judge's wife and three children. After nearly two years renting from them, she had come to be accepted as a member of the family.

She bounded down the steps and was about to get into her car when she remembered that she had a couple chores to attend to before taking off. The judge and his family had departed yesterday for a vacation in Florida. She had promised to feed Sylvia—an ancient cat that everyone agreed could stand to miss a meal or two—and water the plants. ("Let one plant die and you're dead," the judge's wife Nancy had jokingly threatened.)

Although she was already running late, Deborah knew she had to perform her tasks now rather than put them off. For her, procrastination invariably resulted in forgetting. She ran to the porch, found the house key under a brick, and went inside.

Fifteen minutes later, after spraying water on the plants and adding another pound to Sylvia's already tubby body, Deborah locked the house, slipped the key back under the brick, got in her car, and drove off. She had one stop to make—to mail her letter of acceptance to the Goodman Theatre—before hooking up with a group headed to Louisville to see the premier of a new play at the Actor's Theatre.

She smiled as she drove to the post office. These were great days, and they were only going to get better.

Eldon walked through the bookstore and went straight to his office. He wanted to make sure that a certain textbook to be used for a summer session economics class had been ordered. It had. Good thing, too, because publishers were notoriously slow about filling orders. After checking on several smaller matters, he turned his attention to next week's work schedule. Several employees were fighting the flu bug, and two others, members of the debate team, would be out of town for three days. He spent the next fifteen minutes jockeying with the work schedule, moving names around, filling the various holes that seemed to keep popping up. It became increasingly clear to him that several students were going to have to put in some extra hours. That meant he would have to hear their bitching and griping. But what else could he do?

Satisfied that he'd plugged all the holes well enough to ensure that things would run smoothly, he picked up the morning newspaper. The banner headline streaking across the top of the page nearly caused him to jump out of his chair.

DANTZLER TO HEAD SPECIAL TASK FORCE

Eldon's heart pounded like a jackhammer, sending blood rushing to his head. He felt weak, almost faint. He closed his eyes and took several slow, deep breaths. Once the dizziness passed, he looked up. Had anyone seen him? he wondered. Seen his moment of weakness?

No one had.

Eldon picked up the paper and began reading. He read swiftly, gulping in the words, silently mouthing each one. Only when he saw a certain name did he allow his eyes to linger.

Jack Dantzler.

DANTZLER TO HEAD SPECIAL TASK FORCE
By Julie Warren

LEXINGTON — Capt. Richard Bird, chief of detectives, announced on Friday that a special Homicide task force has been formed to investigate the murder of three University of Kentucky students.

Bird acknowledged for the first time the possibility that the three women were killed by the same person.

"At the present time, we're not prepared to rule that out," Bird said. "However, neither can it be confirmed. There are similarities, yes. But there are also differences."

Jack Dantzler, the department's top homicide investigator, will head up the task force, Bird said. Joining Dantzler are Dan Matthews, Dale Larraby, Milt Costello, Eric Gamble and Laurie Dunn.

"That's a heavyweight team of investigators," Bird said. "I have every confidence that they will identify and apprehend the person or persons responsible for these crimes."

The need for a special task force arose following the murder of Abby Kaplan, 23, Thursday, April 19. Miss Kaplan, a graduate student at the University, was found dead in her house on Bellefonte Friday morning by a neighbor. According to the medical examiner, Miss Kaplan died as a result of asphyxiation.

Miss Kaplan's death follows the earlier deaths of Allison Parker and Becky Adams.

Calling the killer—or killers—of the three women a classic "night owl predator," Bird said his department has followed up on dozens of leads, yet is "still no closer to apprehending a suspect now than they were this time last year."

"We're still out in left field on this one," Bird concluded.

Eldon giggled out loud, caught himself, and again looked up to make sure no one had seen him. He couldn't believe it. Jack Dantzler. The ace of aces, brought in for one specific purpose: To catch him. Insignificant, roly-poly Eldon Wessell.

Eldon giggled louder this time, not worrying about being heard. Let the whole universe hear. Let the heavens hear. He no longer cared.

He read the article again, more slowly this time, savoring the words the way he would savor a great poem. Most of all, he savored his own feeling of power. He, Eldon Wessell, had the whole town jumping. Eldon's round face was a mask of pure joy.

Me against the great Jack Dantzler.

He slapped the paper against his thigh, his eyes wide with delight.

Now the real fun was about to begin.

CHAPTER 12

At 7:30 that same Saturday morning, Dantzler sat at his desk, feeling bright-eyed, alert. He felt as though he'd slept ten hours rather than two. Multiple homicides were excellent energy source.

Milt Costello came into the room carrying a small white bag in his right hand. He laid the bag on Dantzler's desk, pulled up a chair, and sat. "Bagels. Plain, onion, and garlic. Take your pick. Cream cheese—low-fat, of course—is inside. Enjoy."

Dantzler pulled out an onion bagel, spread a thick layer of cream cheese on it, and took a huge bite. After taking a second bite, he held up the bagel and grinned. "For an old Kentucky goy boy, you do the Jewish race proud, Milt," Dantzler said, taking another bite. "*A dank.*"

"What's that mean?" Costello said.

"Yiddish for thanks."

"Oh." Costello stopped putting cream cheese on his bagel. "You're not Jewish, are you, Jack?"

"My grandfather on my dad's side was. But when he married my grandmother, a nice blonde Methodist *shiksa*, he pretty much got booted out of the tribe. So, yeah, I suppose there's a trace of Hebrew blood flowing in these veins."

"Hell, Ace, you might be descended from Moses or Solomon or David. You might be royalty. That'd be pretty cool."

"I kinda doubt that, Milt."

"Want to hear a great story, Jack?"

"Sure."

"My grandfather was just about the most anti-Semitic old fart who ever walked the face of the earth. I mean, he hated Jews. Blamed them for everything. He genuinely believed that every Jew who had lived for the past two-thousand years should be executed for killing Christ. And, of course, we're talking about a guy who probably never spoke to a Jew in his life. Well, one day we were watching TV together at his house. I must've been fourteen or fifteen at the time. It was just the two of us. Anyway, we were watching a documentary on the Holocaust. They started showing scenes of bodies in the ovens, prisoners executed by firing squads, people who couldn't have weighed seventy pounds, dead kids, babies, more bodies. Just really horrible, grisly stuff. My grandfather sat there, staring at the screen, not saying a single word. I figured he was loving every second of it. Then they showed a scene of a bulldozer pushing a pile of bodies into a deep pit. You could almost hear the bones cracking and snapping and breaking. Well, all of a sudden, my grandfather started to cry. The tears just flooded down his cheeks. And at that moment, I knew exactly what he was thinking: That it was the same kind of hatred inside him that led to this. Right then, right before my very eyes, I saw a man experience a life-altering moment. And, hell, he must've been eighty at the time. But from that day until he died, the man never said an unkind word about anyone, especially the Jews. It was pretty damn amazing, let me tell you."

Costello finished off a bottle of orange juice and smiled. "You don't get to hear stories like that every day, Jack. And all for the price of a bagel. You can't beat that."

"Nor would I even try, Milt."

"I think maybe I've got something," Eric Gamble said as he walked into the War Room. "A possible link between two of the victims."

Dantzler and Laurie were sitting at the table studying each other's notes. Matthews sat across from them, finishing off the last bite of an egg salad sandwich. Costello doodled on a napkin. It was early afternoon and all four detectives had been at work for more than four hours. They stopped what they were doing and looked at Eric, who stood by the door breathing hard. Matthews used his right foot to nudge a chair away from the table, then motioned for Eric to sit. Eric pulled the chair out further, sat down, and removed the notepad from his hip pocket.

Before he could speak, Richard Bird charged into the room. "Dynamite informs me that Eric might have some good news," he said. "It's been nine days since the last murder, folks. I *need* some good news."

Bird's outburst was followed by an equally loud silence. Eric seemed to be energized by Bird's enthusiasm, or by the sudden quiet that followed. His fingers scrambled through the pages of his notepad until he found the section he was looking for. He glanced up at the five detectives as if he was waiting for the green light to proceed.

"This is not the first grade, Eric," Bird said, breaking the silence. "You are not required to raise your hand before speaking. So, please, deliver your good news."

Eric looked at his notes. "Allison Parker and Becky Adams both did a great deal of modeling. Local stuff, mainly. Nothing big, far as I can tell. Department stores, a few of the trendy clothing boutiques, some sporting goods places, that sort of thing. Anyhow, both women had fairly thick portfolios. I did some checking on who took the photos. Allison's were taken at a now-defunct place called Sunshine Photography. Becky's were taken at Photos Par Excellance. The owner and photographer at both places is Casey Potter."

"Never heard of Casey Potter," Matthews said. "We have anything on him?"

"Yes and no," Eric said, shaking his head. "There's a lot of paper on him, but far as I can tell he's managed to keep his butt out of seriously hot water. That doesn't mean he's a choir boy, though."

"What *does* it mean?" Bird asked.

"That he has a knack for always being one step ahead of the posse."

"Okay, so bring us up to date on this posse-beating Casey Potter," Bird said.

"The only son of a prominent, super-wealthy Southern family. His great-grandfather invented a piece of farm machinery that made millions. The family is from Natchez, Mississippi. That's where Casey was born, and where he had his first photography studio. Since leaving Natchez in 1968, he's done a lot of moving around. Apparently, he's pretty good at what he does. From 1972 to 1978, he lived in Los Angeles and shot stills for the movies. After leaving California, he returned to the South. That's when his errant ways really began."

Eric paused, poured himself a glass of water, and drained it in one swallow. "Early in his career, Potter focused mainly on family or group pictures. Even did a few weddings. But before moving here six years ago, his specialty was children's portraits. It was..."

"Let me guess," Matthews interjected. "Good old Casey couldn't keep his hands off those darling young children he was photographing."

"You got it," Eric said.

"Was he ever arrested?"

"Never. Complaints were filed, but nothing went beyond that stage."

"Any particular age group?" Bird asked.

"Not really. In Mobile he was suspected of fondling a three-year-old girl after the mother found a scratch in the child's genital area. She couldn't prove that Casey was responsible, so it was dropped. In Atlanta the mother of a thirteen-year-old girl decided that Casey's hands were getting a little too friendly. She slapped him and walked out. There were similar instances in virtually every city where he's set up shop. Always with females, by the way. He doesn't care for boys."

"Jesus, how does a fuckin' scumbag like that escape the law?" Bird said. "You'd think someone would have nailed his nuts to the wall by now."

"There was never anything concrete," Eric said. "Only hunches, speculation."

"Don't give me that," Bird replied. "This guy should've been put away years ago. We've all fucked up on this one."

"There's more, Captain," Eric said. "Atlanta Vice says he's long been suspected of supplying photos to kiddie porn magazines and Internet sites. A set of nude photos of one of the kids was spotted by a relative. They were traced back to Potter, who apparently took them with the father's consent. But there was no hard evidence proving that Potter supplied them to the magazine. The matter was investigated, then dropped."

"Jesus H. Christ." Bird shook his head. "Any complaints or suspicions since he moved to town?"

"None. Maybe he's been scared into going straight. Maybe he's a Born-again Christian. I don't know. What I do know is that he no longer takes pictures of kids. It even states in his ad that no subject under eighteen will be accepted."

"Yeah, now he's going after more well-developed game." Bird looked at Dantzler, who had listened to Eric's debriefing with his eyes closed. "What do you think, Jack?"

"Probably not our boy," Dantzler said. "But definitely worth a look."

Bird nodded. "You and Eric find out all you can about this hands-on shutterbug. You come up with one small piece of dirt and I'll see to it that the bastard is strung up by his thumbs."

Bird stormed out of the room, slamming the door behind him. Laurie and Eric sat with heads lowered, eyes fixed straight ahead.

"Think maybe the big guy is a little bit pissed?" Dantzler said, almost cheerfully.

Laurie and Eric looked at him and offered meek smiles.

"I'd say so," Laurie said. "What got under his skin?"

"You're a cop. You tell me."

Laurie thought for a few seconds, then said, "He has children. Right?"

"Two girls. Twelve and nine."

"Then I can see why it would hit home."

Dantzler tapped Eric on the arm and pointed at the notepad. "Nice work on this, Eric."

"Thanks."

CHAPTER 13

Thirty minutes later, Dantzler spied Laurie in the break room and decided to join her. She was sitting alone reading a magazine. After grabbing a bottle of Evian, he ambled over to her table. "Learning anything new?" he said.

Laurie held up the magazine she was reading. "Johnny Depp is the Most Handsome Man in the World," she said. "Says so right here in *People* magazine."

"Well, who would dare challenge such a definitive authority as *People* magazine?"

"Speaking from a woman's perspective, I'd say Johnny is a fine choice."

Dantzler shook his head. "Depp's okay—a Kentucky boy, by the way—but if I were a woman, I'd prefer Brad Pitt."

"Is that a closet door I hear opening somewhere, Detective Dantzler?"

"I didn't say I lusted for Brad Pitt, only that I think he's more handsome than Johnny Depp."

"Defensive—always a telling sign."

"Nah, a life-long practicing heterosexual. And I have the scars to prove it."

"Denial—another telling sign."

"Where are you originally from, Laurie?"

"What makes you think I'm not a 'Kentucky girl'?"

"Accent. It's got a midwestern sound to it. I'd bet on Chicago."

"You've looked at my personnel file, haven't you?"

"Only a nosy bastard would do such a thing." Dantzler shrugged. "Chicago? Right?"

"Yep. Oak Park, to be exact." Laurie closed the magazine, rolled it up, and put it in her purse. "My accent's that pronounced?"

"Not really. Just enough to locate you on the map." Dantzler took a drink of water. "How did a Chicago girl wind up living in Lexington, Kentucky?"

"Good question. I don't know—I just kinda ended up here. I certainly never planned it. But things happened, choices were made, and here I am."

"You go to the University of Kentucky?"

"Northwestern."

"Good school. What'd you study? Wait...let me guess. Psychology."

"Nope. Criminology, with the aim of becoming a lawyer. By the time I graduated, I knew I wanted to work in law enforcement. You know, catch the bad guys rather than find loopholes to get them off. I did some checking around, found several cities that were recruiting police officers, and decided that Lexington was the best location for me. I applied, got accepted, went to the academy, and, presto, I was a cop."

"A career choice that surely must've thrilled your parents," Dantzler said.

"Actually, they were pleased. See, my folks were sixties' radicals. Ex-hippies, extremely liberal. Hell, what do I mean *ex*. Essentially, they're still hippies, only with shorter hair and no tie-dye clothes. But they've still got that sixties spirit. You know—that fuck-the-establishment mentality. They still cling to the notion that the world can be changed for the better."

"What do your parents do?" Dantzler said.

"Dad's a lawyer. With the ACLU, of course. Mom's a social worker." Laurie took a drink of Dantzler's water. "I'll give my parents credit—they didn't just talk the talk. They walked the walk. They constantly preached to us—my sister Emily and me––that we could be anything we wanted to be. All we had to do was dream high, set our sights on a goal, work hard, and those dreams would come true. And they meant it, too. They offered no resistance when Emily told them she wanted to join the FBI. They only encouraged her, and you know how difficult that had to be for them, given their past history with old J. Edgar and his band of jack-booted thugs. Same with me. When I told them I had enrolled at the police academy and would be moving to

Lexington, they couldn't have been more positive or supportive. They're really cool parents."

"Sounds like it. But what made you want to be a cop?"

"Now, here's where I could bullshit you and say things like, 'Because it's such a noble profession,' or "Because I want to protect the honest citizens of our country.' But the truth is, I think it was because of all those great old TV shows that keep rerunning forever. You know, 'Hawaii Five-O,''Kojak,' 'Mod Squad.' Those cops were really smart, really hip. And they said the coolest things. 'Who loves ya, baby?' and 'Book 'em, Dan-O.' I just loved that stuff."

Dantzler stood. "So, we have Telly Savalas and Jack Lord to thank for you being here."

"Makes about as much sense as anything else, I suppose." Laurie pointed at Dantzler. "Why'd you become a cop?"

He was silent for several seconds, then said, "Fate."

"Kind of an evasive answer, isn't it?"

"Who loves ya, baby?" he said, turning and walking away.

CHAPTER 14

Dantzler pivoted to his left, drew his right arm back and cut loose with a vicious swing, bringing the racket from low to high, just like he'd been taught when he was a kid. The yellow ball shot off the racket, a perfect topspin bullet that whizzed past an overmatched—and fatigued—Randall Dennis, hitting just inside the right corner of the court before crashing into the backstop. Dennis bent over and put both elbows on the net. He gulped hard to refill his lungs. Sweat dripped from his face. "That's it, Ace," he wheezed. "I'm finished, through, retired. A man can only suffer so much humiliation in one day."

Dantzler picked up his towel and slowly walked toward the net. After wiping his face, he stuck out his right hand, which Dennis quickly accepted. "What were those scores again?"

"You know damn well what they were, you heartless prick. Love, love, and love. Hell, if you were a true friend, you'd at least allow me one courtesy game."

"You gotta pay the price if you want to reap the glory."

"Spare me that damn Vince Lombardi crap, will you? You know, you'd be a helluva lot easier to deal with if you had more Mother Teresa in you and less Johnny Mac. Hey, you played him once, didn't you?"

"Who? McEnroe?"

"Who? No—Johnny Mack Brown, you *putz*. Yeah, John McEnroe. The Brat. You two guys played, right? "

"When we were in juniors. A tournament in Miami."

Dantzler stuffed his towel into his duffel bag, opened a bottle of water, and drained it. He then slid his racket into the cover, zipped it, and slung it over his shoulder.

"Judging by your lack of interest in pursuing this matter further, I can only assume that young Johnny Mac cleaned young Jackie boy's arse. Am I right?"

"Not even close," Dantzler said.

"You beat him? Nah, I'm not believing that."

"McEnroe won. Beat me six-four in the third set."

Dennis shook his head. "Damn, Jack. Why'd you become a cop when you could've been a tennis pro?"

That was a question Dantzler had been asked on more than a few occasions. He'd certainly had the talent to turn pro—everyone agreed with that. He also had the dedication, smarts, and focus to make it to the top. His style helped too. He was a serve and volleyer during an era when most youngsters, influenced by Borg and Chrissie Evert, preferred to hit heavy topspin shots from the baseline. He and McEnroe were exceptions to the rule. They couldn't get to the net fast enough. That's why their match had been so exciting to watch.

When asked, Dantzler had a standard stable of answers to choose from. There was the age factor—he was only fifteen when he graduated high school, twenty when he earned his master's. He wanted to pursue his doctorate. He wasn't up to the daily grind of being a high-level professional tennis player. Too much travel, too many nights spent in hotels, too many strange cities.

But those were nothing more than diversionary tactics. Bullshit, really. Age was never a factor—he won the state singles title when he was fourteen and fifteen, and he was a two–time all-America and all-conference player in college, which proved that he could compete successfully against older players. As for the grind, it never really entered his mind. The travel, the cities, the hotels—he would've loved that life.

No, Jack Dantzler knew the reason he became a cop. More specifically, he knew why he became a homicide detective. He also knew the exact moment that decision was made.

The night his mother was murdered. He didn't need any two-bit shrink to help him figure that out.

Three sets of tennis weren't enough for Dantzler. He needed more punishment, more pain. Forty-five minutes on the Stairmaster and another thirty on the treadmill did the trick. After a steam and sauna and a shower, he dressed and headed up to the club bar.

Randall Dennis spied Dantzler and waved him over. Dennis was sitting at a table with David Bloom. Dantzler ordered a Diet Pepsi from the bar, then joined the two men at the table.

"The boy wonder," Bloom said, "beating up on a helpless *shmuck* like Randy. Tell me, Jack, you reasserting your tennis manhood or taking out your frustrations?" Dantzler chewed on a piece of ice. "You're the C-note-an-hour shrink. You tell me."

"I'd say you're lashing out at some faceless *meshuggeneh* who has killed three women and who has managed to elude your grasp."

"That's it? That's the best you've got to offer? I can hear shit like that on any street corner."

"Yeah, but not from someone with my wit and charm."

"Let me tell you something, Bloom. If your wit and charm were money, you wouldn't have enough to buy an extra-small jock strap for that circumcised pickle of yours."

"You kidding, Jack. This tool of mine is a fearsome weapon."

"Small arms, small caliber is what I heard."

"Rumors, Jack. Nothing but vicious rumors and lies." Bloom chuckled, then picked up his vodka and cranberry juice and took a drink. "Captain Bird shared some of the details with me. You've got a problem on your hands."

"Richard talks too much."

Bloom took the hint. Having worked with the police in the past, he understood Dantzler's reluctance to discuss an ongoing case in front of strangers. His attempt to do so had been a breach of professional discretion, and he knew it. Bloom quickly changed the subject, and for the next few minutes the talk centered on the current steroid controversy that was circling like vultures around Major League Baseball.

After half an hour of chit chat, Dantzler, feeling restless and bored, excused himself and walked outside. It was late afternoon; the sun was beginning its descent and the air felt cool and crisp. Dantzler closed his eyes and took several deep breaths, drinking in the air like it was liquid. The evening—this moment——was perfect.

Except…

"You'll catch him, Jack," Bloom said, standing at the club's front door. "Of that, I have no doubt. It's just a matter of time."

"It's just a matter of time until he kills again," Dantzler answered. "Of that, *I* have no doubt."

"Yes, he'll kill again. And sooner rather than later, I'm afraid."

"Did Rich tell you about the decorations our killer leaves on the victims?"

"Yes, he did."

"What do you make of that?"

"I'm a Hebrew, Jack. The whole Catholic thing mystifies me."

"Give me your best guess."

"With Saint Jude, the obvious answer is the killer is looking to let you know that catching him is a hopeless cause," Bloom said. "However, in my opinion, I doubt that's the case. That would be giving him too much credit. A more plausible answer is that it reflects his hatred for the Catholic Church."

"You suspect he's Catholic?"

"Raised one, probably, but fallen away from it long ago."

"The *Pietà*—what about that? It's Catholic *and* Christian."

"That's a mother issue, I think. I would venture to say that your killer hates his mother intensely. At the same time, he envies Jesus for having a loving, caring mother. Jack, you are after one seriously disturbed individual. In everyday parlance, he's one fucked-up dude."

Bloom waited until two female club members hurried past and entered the building before continuing. "The cutting of the victim is far more difficult to understand, especially since he does it post-mortem. Here's a guy who selects very beautiful women—almost physically perfect, in fact—and yet he willingly destroys that beauty. I'm stumped by that."

"It's an attempt at misdirection," Dantzler said. "Sleight of hand, if you will."

"I'm not following you."

"It's like Nietzsche's pale criminal. The judge wonders why the criminal committed murder when he really wanted to commit a robbery. But Nietzsche says the judge has it wrong, that it was blood, not robbery that the criminal was after. 'The bliss of the knife.' But the criminal's reasoning couldn't comprehend the madness, so in his own head, he's thinking, 'What matters blood? Don't you want to commit robbery with your crime?' And that's what he does—he robs when he murders. Why? Because he doesn't want to be ashamed of his madness."

"You think he's trying to divert attention away from the sexual aspect of what he does?" Bloom shook his head. "Then why leave them naked and in such an exposed, sexual position?"

"Madness *after* the deed, Nietzsche calls it. Maybe he's trying to come off as more macho, using a knife rather than his dick. Maybe he can't get it up. Maybe the sexual angle masks his thirst for blood. Maybe he really thinks he's fooling us. Maybe it's the only way he can live with himself."

"Lot of maybes, Jack."

"Look, I'm just rambling, okay? Tossing out theories."

"Here's something that's not a theory. This guy has a real taste for it now, a real...hunger. He's killed at least three women and he's still walking free. His confidence level is probably off the charts right now. He's feeling invincible."

Dantzler nodded. "I once played a guy in college who hadn't lost a match all season. Unbeaten, ranked number one in the country. He was feeling pretty invincible, too. Know what? I smoked the guy. Know why? Not because I was a better tennis player, or because I had more talent. I won because he was so damn sure he was invincible. He was absolutely positive that he couldn't lose. Once you start believing that, you immediately become beatable. And I'm gonna beat this guy, too. And for the same reason—because he thinks he can't lose."

CHAPTER 15

Dynamite Darleen McCormick took one final drag on her cigarette before smashing it into the ashtray. She ground it out, looking up at Laurie Dunn and smiling conspiratorially. "Nothing I like better than firing one up in a no-smoking area. You smoke?"

Laurie shook her head. "Never had one in my mouth," she said, unzipping the top of her Reebok sweatsuit.

"You are talking about a cigarette, aren't you?" Darleen said, chuckling.

Laurie grinned and nodded.

"Good." Darleen picked up two menus and handed one to Laurie. "What are you having?"

"Soup and salad."

"That's it? Soup and salad? That's no meal."

"I'm going jogging in a couple of hours, so I need to keep it light." Laurie closed the menu and laid it on the table. "Thanks for meeting me on such short notice."

"Hell, girl, I'm known as Miss Spontaneity," Dynamite said. "Always ready to go. Pack light, take the next flight. That's my motto. All I need is an invitation."

After the waitress took their order and left, Laurie unfolded her napkin and placed it neatly on her lap. "How much longer do you plan to work before calling it quits?"

"I'll never quit, not if I have anything to say about it. I want to go out in style—just fall over dead one day sitting at my desk. Anyway, what else would I do?"

"Move to Florida. Hang out at the beach. Just kick back and take it easy."

"Boring." Dynamite grinned. "Nah, they'll have to run me off if they want me gone. I'll never quit voluntarily. I've been there so long the damn job is part of me."

"You just like being around all those good-looking guys."

"What girl doesn't? But let's face it—there ain't but one real looker in the bunch. Jack."

"He's your favorite, isn't he?"

"Yep. Has been from the first moment I laid eyes on him."

"Why?"

"Hell, I don't know. We just clicked right from the start."

"Happens sometimes."

"What do you know about him?"

"Professionally, I know he's considered a great detective. Personally, I know nothing about him."

"Well, let me fill you in on a few things," Dynamite said. "For starters, Jack is a very intelligent man. And the best damn detective this department has ever had. *Ever.* Has been from the first day he got his shield. This town's lucky to still have him. Damn lucky. And believe me, he could've been long gone years ago. He's been approached by all the big boys—FBI, DEA, Treasury Department—all begging him to come work for them."

"That doesn't surprise me."

"Back in the late eighties, early nineties, we had this double murder. Two prominent business executives found shot to death in their office two blocks down Main Street. Happened late at night, no one else in the building. Dale Larraby was the lead investigator on the case. Dale and Bill Mallory. Bill's dead— cancer got him. Anyway, Dale, who everybody knows couldn't find his dick with a spotlight, became convinced that one of the wives committed the murder. Brought her in for questioning two or three times, really beat up on her. Bill, God rest his soul, felt that Dale was swimming in the wrong pool. So he asked Jack to take a look at the evidence, which, of course, Jack did. And, remember, Jack's only, what, twenty-four, twenty-five at the time. Well, right from the get-go, Jack sees gigantic doughnut holes in Dale's theory of how the murder went down. No way the wife could've done it. How Jack knew that, I don't know. Instincts, I suppose. Bottom line, Jack nailed the killer in three days. Turned out to be the nephew of one of the dead men."

Dynamite laughed. "Think that didn't piss off Larraby."

"That's the genesis of their animosity?"

"There are a million reasons why they don't get along. That's just one of them."

"They certainly make no effort to conceal it."

Dynamite said, "Bet you didn't know that Jack practically has a doctorate in philosophy, did you?"

"No."

"All he lacks is the dissertation. He keeps promising me that he'll write it, but he won't. I keep saying, 'Jack, you've got to get after it. You've got to kick the Big D's ass.' He just ignores me. Says the dissertation isn't going to make him a damn bit smarter, just more of a snob. Naturally, I tell him he's already a snobbish prick and that doing the damned dissertation won't change that one way or the other. But the real point is that it isn't about being smarter; it's about accomplishment. Completing something you started. Like a marathon runner. Winning isn't important to a person who runs twenty-six miles. Finishing is. But Jack just laughs at me. Says I'm crazy."

Laurie watched as the waitress placed their food on the table. After she walked away, Laurie picked up her fork and stabbed indifferently at her salad.

Dynamite took a bite of her tuna salad sandwich and chewed it slowly. "Jack's life has been shaped by the death of his parents," she said. "How could it not be?"

"I know about his mother. That she was murdered. But what happened to his father?"

"Bought it in Nam. Jack was five or six at the time."

"I didn't know."

"Yep, lost both parents when he was still just a kid. Something like that happens, you grow up fast. Can make you bitter, too. But Jack was lucky."

"How so?"

"His grandparents were solid, loving people. So was his uncle Tommy. Back then, anyway. Tommy's had his share of problems as an adult. They raised Jack—really got him through what must've been difficult times. And, of course, he had tennis as a diversion. Did you know Jack was state champ when he was only fourteen? Could've been a pro if he'd wanted to."

"Did you know his parents?"

"His dad, I didn't know at all. His mom, Sarah, was a couple of years behind me in school, so I knew her enough to say hello." Dynamite took another bite of her sandwich, then washed it down with some Coke. "Sarah...God, what a beautiful woman. Tall, built like a brick shithouse, smart as a whip. If I were gay, I'd be on the prowl for a woman just like Sarah..." Dynamite looked away.

"What happened to her?"

"No one knows for sure. One minute she's alive, the next day they find her body in a dumpster behind the junior high school."

"Her killer, was he caught?"

"Nope. You can just imagine how much that gnaws at Jack. The one case he can't solve is the one dealing with his mother's death. That has to drive him mad."

Laurie continued to pick at her salad. "You really care for him, don't you?"

"Jack and me go back a long way," Dynamite said. "We've been tight from the beginning. I'll tell you one thing, there's not much I wouldn't do for that man."

"Did you ever..."

"Ever what? Sleep with him? No, Jack's still a kid to me. Always will be." Dynamite threw her head back and cackled. Her eyes glowed with warmth. "Now, under different circumstances, my answer might be yes."

Laurie pushed her plate away and waved for the waitress. She dug into her purse, pulled out a twenty, and laid it on the table. "My treat," she said.

"You shouldn't have to pay," Dynamite said, pointing at Laurie's plate. "You didn't take two bites."

"I wasn't very hungry. Mostly, I just wanted to talk."

Laurie started to stand, but hesitated when she felt Dynamite's hand on her arm."Honey, take this bit of advice from a hardened old broad who's been through the ringer more times than you can count," Dynamite said. "Working for Jack Dantzler is a double-edged sword. There'll be times when you'll admire him and times when you'll hate him. That's only natural. But if the moment comes—and I'm betting it will—when you start to feel something else for him, be wise enough to back away. You don't want to get caught in his darkness."

Laurie stood, zipped her sweatsuit, and picked up her purse. "I only want to work for the man, not fall in love with him."

They walked toward the front entrance. Dynamite lit a cigarette, took a deep drag, and exhaled. Her eyes followed the cloud of smoke as it rose toward the ceiling, broke up, then disappeared completely. She looked at Laurie. There was a smile on her lips. "Honey, where have I heard those words before?" she said.

CHAPTER 16

After reading the Saturday morning paper, Eldon Wessell's mind was bombarded by a crisscrossing tangle of thoughts and messages. For the better part of two hours, his mind shifted back and forth, one moment providing confidence, the next moment stealing it away, leaving him without direction, without a clear understanding of which path to follow.

If he was nothing else, Eldon was a man of clear focus. Indecision was simply inexcusable to him. No one in any field of endeavor could succeed if burdened by indecision. A successful person must be straight, unwavering, and confident. That was especially true in his chosen field.

You simply can't be a weak killer.

Eldon lived those two hours in hellish agony. He spent the first hour driving aimlessly through downtown Lexington. The second hour was spent in his room, pacing, thinking, debating with himself, his thoughts and feelings bouncing back and forth like a ping pong ball.

This was not acceptable.

Why the doubting in the first place? he asked himself over and over. What reason for it? It couldn't be because of the newspaper article. After all, hadn't Captain Richard Bird been quoted as saying the police were "still out in left field" on this one? And hadn't Richard Bird told a television interviewer that "the department was no closer to apprehending a suspect now than it was eighteen months ago?"

Yes to both questions.

Yet, for those two hours the doubts persisted. They lingered like a bad odor. And always that single, disturbing question: Why?

Of course, Eldon knew perfectly well why. It was simply a matter of admitting it to himself. It had to do with Jack Dantzler. That's what this was really all about, anyway. Him versus the legendary Jack Dantzler. One on one, with the highest stakes imaginable. Yes, now that Jack Dantzler was involved, the ante *had* been upped considerably. No denying that. Yet, that's what he'd always wanted.

But...

"No buts," he whispered to himself. No more chastising himself. It was only natural to have concerns, to feel butterflies in the stomach. Any formidable opponent must be taken seriously. And Jack Dantzler was, indeed, a formidable opponent.

Eldon lay on his bed, his head propped against two pillows. He felt spent, used, betrayed by his own courage. He had finally gotten what he wanted most, and now that he had, his nerves were melting faster than ice in a microwave.

Pitiful.

Eldon forced himself out of bed and out of the big house. He needed a change of scenery. He needed to move, to get out of this funk that had overtaken him.

He walked two miles from his house to Woodland Park. After stopping at a water fountain, he went to the tennis courts, where two teenage girls traded deadly passing shots with professional accuracy. Watching them, seeing their long tanned legs stretching down from white panties exposed by their every move, he could feel his penis begin to harden. Turning, he walked away and sat on a bench beneath a large tree.

Discipline. In all matters, discipline.

He sat on the bench for close to an hour, watching the evening shadows creep toward him. It had been a long and eventful day. A turbulent day. Seldom in his life had he felt such turbulence. Confidence and self-doubt had been bitter rivals for his soul. The result of this inner war had left him feeling battered and beleaguered.

Sitting there, lost within his own thoughts and the lengthening shadows, he was certain he would prevail. In the end he would get the best of Jack Dantzler. No doubting that. He would prevail because the game was his. He called the shots. He was in complete control. He could halt the game at any moment. Dantzler *had* to play it out until the end. What if there was no end? What if he stopped? What if there were no more killings?

What if he left Dantzler with nothing but a list of victims? Living every moment in anticipation of when it would happen again. Only it wouldn't happen again. The killings would simply stop. Surely, that would be enough to drive Dantzler insane.

As Eldon stood and turned to his left, a jogger sprang from behind the tree and crashed into him. The impact sent him sprawling to the ground.

"Sorry, I didn't see you."

"That's quite all right," Eldon said, slowly picking himself up. "I don't think any serious damage was done."

It was only after getting to his feet that Eldon realized the jogger was a female. When she stepped out of the shadows and into the fading sunlight, he realized something else as well: she bore a strong resemblance to Rose.

And to Allison Parker, Becky Adams, and Abby Kaplan.

Tall, well-built, dark hair, full breasts, strong facial features...this woman was sculpted from the same model. Maybe a little too old for his taste, but the physical similarities were definitely there. If she were younger, and if the circumstances were different, she could easily be the next Chosen One.

"Are you absolutely positive you're okay?" she said, running in place. "I won't leave until you're sure."

"I'm sure," Eldon said. "Take my word, I'm not as delicate as I look."

She adjusted the top of her Reebok sweatsuit, looked at her watch, and winked at him. "Beware of runaway joggers," she said, laughing. "They're killers."

As Eldon watched her jog off into the growing darkness of night, he felt his penis begin to stiffen. This time he made no attempt to divert his thoughts. He was satisfied to let nature take its course.

He closed his eyes and gave in to his excitement.

Under cover of darkness, Eldon put his right hand into his pants pocket and touched himself. He looked up at the clear, starry sky and was suddenly overwhelmed with a renewed sense of purpose. His nerve had been rediscovered, his courage brought out of exile.

He giggled at the prospects of what lay ahead. Jack Dantzler, be damned. The game had begun.

CHAPTER 17

It was just after dark when Dantzler and Eric Gamble found Photos Par Excellance. Traffic was a nightmare, finding a parking space virtually impossible. Dantzler pulled the Forester into a tow-away zone, took his Official Police parking pass out of the glove box and placed it on the dashboard. He and Eric got out of the vehicle, waited for a break in the busy Saturday night traffic, and darted across the street.

Photos Par Excellance was located on Limestone, on the top floor of a two-story brick building less than a mile from the University campus. It was an ancient building situated in the middle of several older houses, many of which had been renovated and converted into small apartments that were usually rented to students.

The bottom half of the building was home to a used bicycle shop. Out front, lined like soldiers, were two dozen display bikes of various styles and quality. As Dantzler and Eric approached, a college-age male came out and began moving the bikes inside, two at a time.

"Can we get upstairs through your place?" Dantzler said.

The kid shook his head. "Nah. You gotta take the steps around in the alley. That's the only entrance."

"Thanks."

Dantzler and Eric went to the right side of the building and started down the alley. The metal steps, thick and rust-covered from years of neglect, were located near the back of the building. Beneath the steps were two large trash cans. Several empty paint cans and paint brushes lay scattered on the ground beneath the stairs. Behind the building there was a parking space big enough for two vehicles. Only one was there—a red Honda Civic.

Dantzler began climbing the stairs. Eric trailed behind.

"Detective Dantzler, you…"

"Can the formalities," Dantzler said. "Call me Jack."

"Why did you say Casey Potter isn't our man?" Eric said.

"Hunch, mostly. A feeling. Potter is a sleaze, but not a killer. That's not his pathology. Our boy is a different breed of cat altogether, I'm afraid."

When they reached the top of the stairs, Dantzler opened the door without knocking and went inside. A tall wiry man with a goatee and long white hair tied in a ponytail was sitting alone at the receptionist's desk working the daily crossword puzzle. He wore leather cowboy boots, jeans, and a black shirt that was open halfway down his chest. Two gold chains dangled from his neck, and a single diamond stud gleamed from each ear. His eyes were cold, like a reptile's; his lips were thin and narrow, his teeth stained brown from years of smoking.

He looked up and smiled. It was anything but a warm smile. "Come in, gentlemen," he said, standing. "I don't normally work past six on a Saturday, but tonight I'll make an exception. What can I do for you? Individual portraits, passport photos, anything …I do it all."

"Are you Casey Potter?" Dantzler asked.

"The one and only," Potter said, looking down at the puzzle.

"We're with the police," Dantzler said. He took out his ID badge and held it up. "We would like to ask you a few questions. That is, if you can tear yourself away from the crossword puzzle for a few minutes."

"Gladly," Potter said, taking his seat. "This one's too tough for me. Can't come up with a nine-letter word for sycophant."

"How about ass-kisser?" Dantzler said.

"Very good, Detective, very quick. But wrong, I'm afraid. The word I'm looking for begins with an F."

"An F opens a world of possibilities, but flatterer is probably what you're looking for."

"Flatterer, hmm." Casey spoke each letter out loud as he filled in the squares. "Why, yes, I think that fits."

"Wasn't so tough after all, was it, Casey? Now, about those questions."

Potter leaned back in his chair and put his feet on the desk. "Questions?" he said, the smile still on his face. "Go right ahead. You'll find that I'm a well-spring of delightful information."

"Where were you on the night of Thursday, April nineteenth and the early morning hours of April twentieth?" Dantzler said.

"That's almost two weeks ago," Potter replied. "I'd have to give it some thought."

"You look like a thinker, so why don't you do just that?"

"To the best of my recollection, I was right here. Sober until around eight, completely plastered by eleven. That's my standard routine."

"Can that be corroborated by anyone?"

"Most certainly," Potter said. "Let's see…yes, I do believe I shared the evening with Jack Daniels and Johnnie Walker. Red, if I'm not mistaken. Yeah, they were with me from start to finish. We were a wonderful trio."

"You might want to do better than that," Dantzler said.

"Why should I do better, Detective?"

"Because this is serious and you might need a better alibi before this is finished."

"Let's cut to the chase, Detective," Potter said. "What misguided cunt of a mother filed a complaint against me this time?"

"What makes you think someone filed a complaint against you?"

"Because that's the way it always is, everywhere I go. Some poor mother isn't happy with little Nancy's pictures, says I charge too much, or that I didn't take the time to get a perfect smile from the precious little angel. So what does she do? She gets her vengeance by claiming that I felt up the kid. That's an old story…been beaten to death. But this time, Detective, I can assure you that she's barking up the wrong tree. I haven't photographed a child in years. So why don't you and your fellow Vice officer here go do something useful, like ridding the streets of prostitution."

"We're not with Vice," Dantzler said.

"Who are you with?"

"Homicide."

"Ah, Homicide." Potter laughed. "For a second there, I thought I was in real trouble."

Dantzler grabbed Potter's feet and in a single move swept them off the desk. He leaned in close enough to see the cluster of acne scars covering both of Potter's cheeks. He was also hit with the sour smell of alcohol. "Don't get cute," Dantzler said. "I'm in no mood for cute."

"Well, well, aren't we a bit touchy this evening. I do declare, that might have been an example of police brutality." Potter looked at Eric. "You being a Negro, you surely know all about police brutality. What do you think about your partner's conduct?"

"Must've blinked, cause I didn't see a thing," Eric said.

"Ah, so you've sold out to The Man. Such a pity. What would Malcolm X think?"

"That you're a redneck loser."

Dantzler jerked Potter around and moved even closer. He held Potter's stare for almost a full minute. Finally, he slowly backed away. "Eric, let Mr. Potter see his artistry."

Eric opened the folder, took out two 8x10 photos, and held them in front of Potter. "Recognize these?"

Potter put on a pair of reading glasses and looked at the two pictures. He nodded, pointing to the picture of Becky Adams. "I remember her. I don't recall the other one at all."

"You remember Becky Adams?" Eric said.

"Vaguely. She had a series of photos done for a portfolio. Wanted to be a model, an actress...something along those lines. Just another pretty face with stars in her eyes. Seen a million of them like that." Potter took the second photo from Gamble and looked at it more closely. "You're sure I took this photo?" he said.

"Says Sunshine Photography on the back," Gamble said.

"Hell, man, no wonder I can't remember her. That was almost six years ago." Potter handed the photos back to Gamble. "I've photographed hundreds of women since then."

Eric removed a third photo, one of Abby Kaplan, and held it up. "What about her? She look familiar?"

Potter studied it closely, then shook his head. "Nah, never saw her before in my life. Hey, why are you so interested in these women?"

"Don't you read the paper?" Dantzler said.

"Only the sports and the comics."

"These three women were murdered," Eric said. The smile left Potter's face. "You're implicating me?" he said, taking off the reading glasses. "Are you telling me I'm a suspect in the murder of these three women?"

"Right now, our only suspect," Dantzler said.

"You've got to be kidding."

"Joke time is over, Casey. Like I told you, this is serious." Potter moved between Dantzler and Eric, pushed the glasses onto his forehead, and clasped both hands together. "Look, fellows," he said. "I'm a second-rate, drunken photographer who's maybe done a thing or two that's not quite *kosher*. I'll cop to that. But kill someone? No way. I'm not a murderer. You have to believe that."

"We'll see," Dantzler said. He opened the door. "But until we do, don't let your wanderlust get the better of you. Stay close."

"Yes, yes, by all means, I will," Potter said.

"Jack, Jack, please save me!"

Dantzler's eyes snapped open and confronted the immense darkness of his bedroom. He lay perfectly still, unable to move, his heart racing. The ticking of the clock next to the bed intermingled with the lingering sound of his mother's eternal plea.

"Jack, Jack...!"

Dantzler sat up and tried to get control over his breathing. Sweat dripped from his body. He thought about the dream. There was something troubling about it, something disturbing...different. But how? In what way? After twenty-five years of seeing the same scenes, how was tonight's dream different? What had changed?

He sat there in the darkness, forcing himself back into the nightmare he always wanted to escape. Back into the awful blackness of memory.

He sees his father running toward his mother, past the blurred faces of unrecognizable people—dead souls?—and toward the riverbank. He hears his naked mother call out to him as the black cloud begins to sweep down around her. He sees his father standing on the riverbank, preparing to leap into the murky waters. He hears the blast, sees the bullet crash into his father, watches as the mortally wounded man falls to the ground. There he is, watching helplessly as the black cloud engulfs his mother, lifts her up and carries her off into eternity. He sees himself on his knees, hands over his ears in a futile attempt to keep out the sound of his mother's distant cries.

"Jack, Jack, please save me!"

Like a movie editor searching for a glitch, Dantzler replayed the dream a hundred times. Each time he played it more slowly. Finally, he was able to see the dream in slow motion. Only then, just seconds from drifting off to another troubled sleep, was he able to see the difference.

It was because of the presence of a second woman standing safely behind the black cloud of death. A tall, pretty woman with long dark hair, round eyes, and a wonderful smile.

Laurie Dunn.

CHAPTER 18

Deborah Tucker awoke with the all-too-familiar symptoms of a hangover. Headache, queasy stomach, eyes unable to focus...the paybacks for overindulgence were all present in full force. She closed her eyes, groaned, and tried to raise herself up to a sitting position. Realizing her tired body was unwilling to cooperate, she let her head fall back onto the pillow and groaned louder. Never again, she vowed. Never that many frozen margaritas in a single night. How many did she have? She wasn't sure, but the number eleven kept swimming around inside her throbbing head. Holy shit, she thought, how many brain cells were permanently laid to rest by last night's binge? Probably enough to genetically manufacture a Rhodes Scholar or two.

An hour later, having decided that her head wasn't going to miraculously heal itself, she struggled out of bed and plopped down two Advil. She undressed, and on unsteady legs, climbed into the shower. The hot water felt like spikes being driven into her skull.

Deborah and her friends spent much of the previous evening in Louisville, attending a new play at the Actors' Theatre. Later, they hooked up with two of the actors in the play, one of whom had played Brick opposite her Maggie the Cat, and toured a string of popular watering holes. The group closed two taverns and kept another open thirty minutes past closing time. It was only when the owner spotted a patrol car cruising the area that he shepherded them out the back door and sent them on their way home. Deborah walked into her apartment at 4:10 in the morning.

She loved the play, the first by a black female playwright from South Carolina. The play, *Chitlins and Ice Cream,* was the powerful story of two high school girls—one black, one white—and their struggle to remain friends during the racially divided 1950s.

Deborah adored the young black actress who played the role of Junnie, whom she felt had touches of real brilliance. A quiet strength and dignity radiated throughout her performance. She displayed a depth that came from real life rather than something learned in an acting class.

Deborah was much less impressed with the performance turned in by the white actress. It lacked subtleties, nuance, and character shading. Deborah found it to be a straightforward, stereotypical rendering of a well-to-do Southern white girl who defies the times—and her family—in an effort to keep alive her friendship with a poor black girl.

It was a role Deborah could have—should have!—played. She would have been more daring, taken more chances, opened the character up more. The part demanded an actress with enormous range, especially in the third act, when the character—Nellie—begins to realize that her friendship with Junnie is being changed forever by the new and growing civil rights struggle. The actress who played Nellie never succeeded in sweeping the audience into the inevitable pain and loss that often accompanies life-altering change.

Deborah would have connected with the audience. Made them share the pain, the sense of loss. She was right for the part, and the part was right for her. It would be a perfect pairing. She made a promise to follow the play's progress, and to do whatever it took to get an audition for the role of Nellie should the play move to New York. It could be the breakthrough role she needed.

After checking her answering machine for messages—there was one from David—she dressed, quickly downed a large tumbler of orange juice, and headed downstairs. She fed ravenous Sylvia, watered the plants, then left for an 11 a.m. mass at Christ the King Church. Although she was still feeling rocky, missing mass would only make her feel worse. A hangover topped off by guilt. She didn't need that.

At 4:10 a.m., when a very drunk Deborah Tucker had been going to bed, Jack Dantzler had been sitting in the darkness of his den. He had a half-empty bottle of Pernod in his hands and a troubling dream in his head. He sat Indian-style on the floor, naked except for a blanket draped over his shoulders, eyes unfocused. With increasing regularity, Dantzler brought the bottle to his mouth and sucked down the fiery liquid. His insides were an incinerator.

Dantzler reached up and took the framed picture of his parents off the desk. Bringing it close to his face, he looked deep into his mother's wild and wonderful eyes. His own eyes began to fill with tears.

Sarah Dantzler. Gone.

How could that be?

He put the picture on the floor and told himself that the aching had to stop. Twenty-five years of mourning was long enough. His parents were gone, and nothing was going to bring them back. It was time to move on.

He took another drink and felt his insides burn. Taking the manilla folder from the end table, he opened it and removed the photos of the three dead women. He lined them in reverse order of their death—Abby Kaplan, Becky Adams, Allison Parker—and studied them closely. Once again he was struck by their physical similarities. These women could have come from the same family. And Laurie Dunn could have been their older sister.

Incredible.

Dantzler downed another shot of flames.

This maniac, whoever he is, has a clear preference for a certain look: tall, dark hair, dark eyes, strong facial features, large breasts—beauty in an almost-classic way.

Dantzler leaned against the couch, turned the bottle up, and drained the final drops. A liquid fireball rushed down his throat.

Outside, a blast of thunder rocked the night. A second blast was followed by a rapid series of lightning flashes that illuminated the night sky. Within minutes the downpour began, as though the heavens were weeping.

His head nodded, his thoughts drifting in and out of consciousness. Voices and pictures flashed in his head, faded, only to be replaced by new sounds and images. A twenty-five-year-old newsreel running through a projector that no switch could possibly turn off.

Jack, Jack, please save me...the cloud closing in...his mother naked...his father running...Jack, Jack, please save me...his father running hard but going nowhere...run, Dad, run harder, mother needs you...Jack, Jack, please save me...dark cloud getting closer...a blast...his father falling...his mother being lifted up and carried away...forever...Jack, Jack, please save me...Laurie, why are you here? Why are you in my dream? You have no right to be in this dream...it's private...please leave...please....

Dantzler rolled to the floor and curled into a fetal position. He cradled the empty bottle against his chest. For the rest of the night, he alternated between uneasy sleep and troubled wakefulness. When asleep, he had the dream; when awake, he replayed the dream in his head. In both versions, the pretty dark-haired woman moved away from the shadows and became a clearer image.

Laurie Dunn. She was now a permanent fixture in his dream.

CHAPTER 19

It wasn't by accident that he worked in a bookstore. The written word had always been Eldon Wessell's passion. He loved to read, and had from the time he was a very small boy. Books of any type, any subject. Fiction, non-fiction...it mattered not. Famous author or first-time writer...he didn't care. If Eldon saw a new book that intrigued him he would wolf down the words the way a starving dog wolfs down scraps of food.

In the darkest recesses of his mind, Eldon had always fancied himself a writer. Dostoyevsky was his favorite among the dead guys, Mailer his preference among the living. Indeed, writing was the occupation Eldon most wanted to pursue. He had, in fact, been published—a small New England publisher had put out a collection of Eldon's short stories back in the late 1980s. He hadn't made a nickel on the book, but that didn't matter. He was a published author. In print, just like Mailer and Updike and Bellow and the rest of those wonderful writers whose works lined the shelves of his bookcase. Since then Eldon had written two novels, neither of which were deemed worthy of publication by the many publishing companies he had contacted over the years.

The failure to have a novel published was the great frustration of his life.

Eldon spent much of Sunday sitting at his computer, composing a letter to be sent to the great detective. Writing was a slow and painful process for Eldon. Words—the proper words—didn't come easily for him. Each one was an impacted wisdom tooth that had to be cut loose from its roots. It had taken him six years to write his first novel, seven to write the second.

But that wasn't the case today. On this gray, overcast Sunday, the words flew out of Eldon's brain and onto the computer screen. Unlike most days, when the blinking cursor sat motionless for hours flashing its mocking Morse code testament to writer's block, the words poured out of his head faster than his fingers could translate them onto the screen. Within an hour he had three full pages. By two that afternoon he was up to seven.

He printed out a copy and read it slowly. Not bad for a first draft. Too long, in need of editing and polishing, but all in all, pretty good.

Eldon spent the next two hours editing and rewriting the letter. The final version came in at just under three pages. That was plenty. No need to say everything in one letter. Dantzler deserved many, and he would get them.

Eldon read the letter aloud. He was pleased with the way the words sounded as they rolled off his tongue. Then he read it into a tape recorder and played it back. Hearing it, he was even more pleased. He had said what he wanted to say and nothing more. Every word fit perfectly. "The common word exact without vulgarity, the formal word precise but not pedantic." Isn't that what the incomparable Eliot said? What Eldon liked best, though, was the language he had used. It was altogether new to him. Unlike any he'd used in his past writings. More experimental, less traditional. Burroughs rather than Steinbeck.

He turned off the computer, stood, and smiled. He should have felt tired, but he didn't. Nothing energized him more than doing good work. And this was his best. A wave of joy swept through his heart.

Jack Dantzler's descent into hell was about to begin, and Eldon's words would send him on that journey.

Eldon checked his appearance in the large mirror and liked what he saw. Black turtle neck sweater, black trousers, black shoes, black sports coat. Very European, very artistic.

He reached into his inside coat pocket; the post card was there. Next, he stuck his hand down into his right coat pocket; the blue scarf and knife were there. Finally, he dug into his right pants pocket; St. Jude was there.

Hail, hail, the gang's all here, he said to himself.

He looked at the digital radio clock. Almost 7:30. Perfect. Plenty of time to swing by the bookstore and pick up the book.

At 7:40, he pulled out of the driveway and found his place in the after-church traffic.

He felt like a shadow moving silently in the darkness.

CHAPTER 20

It was 8:20 when Deborah Tucker heard the car pull into the driveway. She was sitting on the sofa, alternately catching bits and pieces of "Cold Case" on TV and reading the latest Patricia Cornwell novel. Her initial thought was that the judge had cut his vacation short and returned home. That wasn't unusual—she could remember at least three occasions when he had been called back to town because of some emergency. He had often lamented that being on constant call was one of the negatives of being a judge.

Deborah laid Patricia on the coffee table, muted the TV, and got up off the sofa. When she looked out the window and saw that it wasn't the judge's car, she felt a brief moment of unease. Three of her fellow college students, all female, all close to her age, had been murdered within the past two years. It paid for everyone to be on guard.

Deborah thought about punching in the judge's security code, then realized that the numbers panel was in the main house. Her other option was to call the police and let them know that an unidentified person had pulled into the judge Malcolm Peterson's driveway. Hearing the judge's name would get the police here in seconds. There was yet another option—do nothing. Wait and see who the visitor was. No, she quickly decided, given what has been happening lately, waiting was not an option.

Better safe than sorry, she told herself. No, make that better safe than dead.

But just as Deborah picked up the phone and started to dial the police, she recognized the man getting out of the car. She was surprised to see him—what could *he* possibly want?—but she had no reason to be fearful.

She could relax. It was, after all, only Eldon Wessell. The chubby little faggot from the bookstore.

"I know it's late, but I thought you might like this." Eldon stepped inside the apartment and handed the book to Deborah. "It arrived yesterday, and as soon as I saw it, I thought of you."

Deborah opened the book, *A History of the Actors Studio*, and began leafing through the pages. She was dressed in yellow pajamas and a white housecoat. Her hair was pulled back into a ponytail. "Thank you very much," she said. "But how did you know where I live?"

"Professor Gardner is a friend of mine. He told me. I hope you don't mind."

"No, not at all. But you didn't have to bring it tonight. You could've given it to me at the bookstore. Coming out here has to be out of your way."

"Nonsense. It's not out of my way at all."

"The Actors Studio certainly has a great history. This should be an interesting read."

"All the great ones have been there," Eldon said, moving into the living room. "Brando, Clift, Dean, Newman, Pacino, Jane Fonda. The Actors Studio's influence on American acting can't be overestimated. You mind if I sit? I'm worn out."

"Oh, no, not at all. The place is a mess, but I wasn't expecting company."

Eldon moved two pillows off the couch and sat down. Looking at Deborah, the front of her housecoat unfastened, he could see the outline of her nipples against the cotton pajama top. They were long and hard. He crossed his legs in an effort to conceal his growing erection.

"Did you know that the Actors Studio grew out of the Group Theatre of the late thirties and forties?" Eldon said. "They were very leftist, very open to new ideas. Odets, Kazan, Strasberg, Stella Adler. It was their fervent desire to create a new American theatre, one that espoused ideas and realities rather than those phony plays being produced at the time. Substance was more important to them than entertainment. They may not have succeeded fully, but they did create something that's had a lasting effect."

"Yes, that's certainly true." Deborah closed the book and sat in the chair across from Eldon. "How is it you know so much about the theatre?"

"I love the theatre," Eldon answered. "I was going to plays long before you were born. I saw my first Broadway play while I was still in my teens. You know, I've attended virtually every play the University has put on in the past twenty years, and I must say you're the finest actress I've seen here. You're really quite wonderful."

Deborah blushed and lowered her head. "Thank you," she said. "That's a very kind thing to say."

"Who's your favorite actress?" Eldon said.

"Vanessa Redgrave."

"Yes, yes, just a marvelous actress," Eldon said. "I don't agree one bit with her politics, but when she's on stage or in front of a camera, she's remarkable."

Eldon let his left hand slide into his coat pocket and touch the blue silk scarf. His eyes lifted and met hers. "As for me, I like Meryl Streep and Jessica Lange among today's crop of actresses," he said. "But my all-time favorite is Barbara Stanwyck. She was tremendous. People talk about Bette Davis and Joan Crawford. They were nothing compared to Stanwyck. She had ten times the range of those two."

"To be perfectly honest with you, I'm not all that familiar with Barbara Stanwyck," Deborah said. "I guess I should make it a point to watch some of her movies."

"By all means do," Eldon said. "I'm sure you'll like her as much as I do." He stood, walked to the television, and picked up a picture. It showed Deborah holding hands with a sandy-haired man. "Your boyfriend?" he asked.

"Yes. That's David."

"An actor?"

"Oh, no. David is far too intelligent to try something as uncertain as acting. He's finishing his Ph.D in clinical psychology at Ohio State."

"You're in love with him?"

"That's a rather personal question."

"Oh, you can share that with me."

"I think so," Deborah said, feeling uneasy. "Yes."

"Must be difficult being in love with someone that far away."

"That's why God invented telephones, e-mail, and airplanes."

Eldon laughed out loud. "A delightful answer," he said, easing his hand into his coat pocket again. "What do your friends say about me?"

The question caught Deborah by surprise. "What?"

"Your friends. When they talk about Eldon Wessell, what do they say?"

"I don't know what you mean."

"Do they speak of me in a kind way? Or do they say unkind things about me? Please, I would like to know."

"Most of my friends probably don't know who you are."

"Come, come, Deborah. Everyone on campus knows me. Especially your crowd. I'm quite a supporter of the arts. You know that."

"Yes, well..." Deborah closed her housecoat and tied the belt into a knot. "My friends, I haven't heard..."

"Do they think I'm gay?"

"I, uh..."

"Do you think I'm gay? Please, Deborah, be honest."

"Really, I've never given it much thought."

"Of course, you haven't. You're the artistic type. You deal with gays on a regular basis, don't you?"

"Being gay or being straight has no bearing on talent, and talent is all that matters. That, and how you treat others."

"Another wonderful answer, my child. You're absolutely correct, too. A person should be judged on ability, not sexual preference."

Deborah stood and went to the door. "It's getting late," she said. "I have a busy day tomorrow. I really need to hit the sack. But maybe we can continue this discussion some other time? I would really like that. I do love hearing about the theatre."

"You still haven't answered my question. Do your friends think I'm gay? Do you think I'm gay? Please, it's important that I know."

"I don't know…I think it's generally assumed that you are gay."

"There, now, that wasn't so hard to say, was it?"

"I just don't see what difference it makes," Deborah said, opening the door. "A person's character, not whether he's gay or straight, is all that matters."

"So open-minded for one so young. What a rare and wonderful trait," Eldon said. "That comes from your background in the arts. Artistic people are more liberal, more worldly in their views. That's why they become artists in the first place."

"Do I owe you anything for the book?" Deborah said. "I can write you a check if I do."

"The cost is nineteen ninety-five. I hope you understand that I would let you have it for free if I could."

Deborah closed the door and went into her bedroom. She returned seconds later with her checkbook and pen. She went to the kitchen table, put on her glasses, and began filling out the check. "Do I make this out to the university bookstore?" she said.

"Yes." Eldon moved behind her. He took out the blue scarf and held it tightly in both hands. "Do you think I'm gay?" he said.

"What difference does it make?" Deborah said, still writing.

"Makes all the difference in the world to me." Eldon tightened his grip on the scarf. "I'd like to know what others think about me. What *you* think about me."

"I hate to disappoint you, but I *don't* think about you."

"You should."

As Deborah finished scribbling her name and turned to hand him the check, Eldon closed in behind her, wrapped the scarf around her neck, and began to pull tightly with both hands. Here's where his weightlifting came into play. Here's where those—like Deborah—who viewed him as a softy would be surprised. His strength, especially in his forearms and hands, was such that Deborah Tucker's windpipe was destroyed within seconds after he began his attack. From start to finish, it took him less than a minute to end Deborah's life. No softy in the world could do that.

Eldon locked the door, carried Deborah's lifeless body to the couch, and began undressing her. When she was completely naked, he unzipped his pants and took out his erect penis. After taking a handkerchief from his pocket, he sat in a chair and began masturbating. As he did, he kept his eyes on the dark triangle between her legs. On that soft tuft of hair that covered the most mysterious region of all—a woman's vagina.

As the flood of orgasm overtook him, Eldon closed his eyes and thought of his mother and sister. Of their bodies and their mysteries. Of the dark forest between their legs. Of the many times he had spied on them.

Of the hatred he felt toward them.

Of the countless times he had killed them in his mind.

After wiping away the evidence of his orgasm, he carefully folded the handkerchief and put it in a small plastic bag he found in the kitchen. Next to discipline, neatness counts the most. If you leave the cops nothing, there's nothing for them to find. And if they have nothing, they'll never have you.

Eldon spread Deborah Tucker's legs, lifting one to the back of the couch, then dropping the other to the floor. He took the St. Jude medal from his pocket and carefully inserted it into her vagina, leaving the gold chain dangling from her dark pubic jungle. This was the part that excited him the most…seeing the gold chain snake its way through that black forest of pleasure.

Next, he took out the postcard and laid it on her stomach. The bottom of the card was perfectly aligned with the top of her pubic triangle. Now Mary had a second body to minister to.

Eldon stepped back a few paces and viewed his handiwork. He was pleased with the results, yet in some odd way, he felt a certain degree of sadness. To kill a creature with such potential went against his basic nature. He adored good actresses, and he hadn't been lying when he told Deborah that she had a terrific gift for the theatre. Killing her meant that he had robbed this nation's theatre goers of an actress who would surely have left her mark on Broadway for years to come. But she had been chosen for her role in this drama just as surely as she'd been chosen to play Maggie the Cat. She had to die. Why? Because she looked like Gee and Rose. Because she possessed a certain arrogance. Because she was tall and thin and regal looking. Because she had a wit and a charm that were the envy of those around her.

Because no one doubted her sexuality. Her sexual preference.

Eldon moved closer to Deborah. Now came the distasteful part—mutilating a flawless body. Such a violent, course act marred beauty, and beauty, in all its forms, was meant to be appreciated, not destroyed.

He knelt beside the body, took out the small knife, opened it, and placed it against Deborah's neck. Closing his eyes, he forced himself to plunge the blade into her skin. Standing quickly, so as to not get any blood on his hands or clothes, he opened his eyes and looked down. A steady stream of blood trickled from the wound onto the couch. He closed the knife and dropped it into the plastic bag.

Eldon looked one last time at Deborah Tucker's naked body. He smiled knowingly. "Gay?" he muttered under his breath. "You think I'm gay? How dare you think such a thing? How dare *anyone* think such a thing?"

He picked the check up off the floor, grabbed the plastic bag, turned out the lights, and stepped out into the night. It had just begun to sprinkle, which he saw as a sign of safe deliverance. No one was likely to see him on such a dark overcast night. He got into his car, cranked up the motor, and giggled.

Four. Count 'em, four.

And the real fun was just beginning.

The mind games, with Jack Dantzler.

Eldon couldn't wait.

CHAPTER 21

For the second time in less two weeks, Laurie Dunn felt an almost uncontrollable fury rise inside her. Looking down at Deborah Tucker's lifeless body and then up at the five men standing in the apartment, Laurie's anger rose like volcanic lava inside her. So did the feeling of embarrassment for poor Deborah Tucker, dead on the sofa, naked and totally exposed.

Laurie felt like an unwanted guest at a peep show. She wanted to cover Deborah. To provide the dead woman with at least a certain degree of modesty. But she couldn't. She was a cop investigating what was an obvious homicide. Personal feelings, no matter how strong, had to be checked at the door. Professionalism was essential.

As the first task force member to arrive, it was her responsibility to preserve the integrity of the crime scene. Five cops wandering around, no matter how careful they were, was a recipe for disaster. She had to take charge, to do what Jack Dantzler would do—scatter this flock like wild geese.

She looked at her watch. 2:20 p.m. Where was Dantzler, anyway? Why wasn't he here already? Surely, he'd been notified by now. Dynamite would've kept trying until she reached him. Laurie felt a sudden churning in her gut. Something had to be wrong. Jack Dantzler is *never* late.

Laurie had received word of Deborah Tucker's death at a little past one Monday afternoon. She had just finished having lunch and was standing outside next to her car when the call came from Dynamite.

"Honey, it looks like our *Pietà* boy has done it again," she said. "Judge Malcolm Peterson's place. Hartland Estates. Two-twelve, Linkwood Drive. They found her in a garage apartment, as I understand it. Two unnies are on the scene, and others are on the way, including the crime scene folks and Mac Tinsley. I'm still trying to round up Jack and Eric, but so far I've had no luck.

You'd better get over there and take charge of things until Jack arrives."

Take charge. Laurie moved closer to the sofa, turned and faced the five men. She took a deep breath. "Gentlemen, I think it might be best if you waited outside." She motioned toward the door. "I don't think anything should be touched or disturbed in any way until Detective Dantzler or the crime scene techs get here."

Despite her show of strength, Laurie knew she wasn't about to get off without a challenge. One of the detectives was certain to call her bluff. To test her, see if she had a pair of balls. She knew which one of them it would most likely be.

Dale Larraby came around from behind the sofa, moving quickly and with purpose. His round eyes were set hard, his face red with indignation. It was obvious that he wasn't impressed with the idea of a female usurping his authority, and he was about to let her know it.

"This is a special situation, sir," she said. "I think it's best if we wait and let Detective Dantzler handle it."

Her preemptive strike might have caught Larraby off guard, but it didn't change his demeanor. His eyes squinted and his nostrils flared. For a moment, Laurie feared that he might take a swing at her.

"Look, young lady, I…"

"*Sergeant* Laurie Dunn. Not young lady."

"Okay, *Sergeant* Dunn, for your information, I'm *Lieutenant* Larraby, and I was working homicide cases when you were still clinging to your mother's tit. So I don't give one good goddamn what you think. As long as I'm on this police force, as long as I'm the ranking officer at a crime scene, I'll run the show. I don't take orders from fresh-face rookie sergeants. You got that?"

Take charge.

"I stand by what I said, Lieutenant Larraby. I certainly do respect your rank. But I think everyone should wait outside until Detective Dantzler gets here. If you're adamant about remaining inside with me, that's fine. The others need to leave."

"I don't think you understood what I just said to you. I'm not..."

Dantzler pushed the door open and came inside. "Shut up, Dale."

Laurie blinked with shock when she saw him. He was a wreck. Dressed in a denim shirt, faded Levis that were torn at the knees and white Nike sneakers, he looked like a refugee from the nearest homeless shelter. His eyes were sunken and bloodshot, his hair was uncombed, and his face was covered with three days worth of dark stubble. He looked, Laurie thought, like a crazy man.

Dantzler looked down at Deborah Tucker's body, scratched his beard, and then moved between Laurie and Larraby. "Got a problem, Dale?" His voice was rough as sandpaper.

"You bet," Larraby shot back. "I don't like virgins giving me orders."

"Feeling a little threatened, Dale?" Dantzler said.

"Not at all."

"Why so hostile then?"

"Don't care for the situation."

"What's wrong with the situation?"

"It's not by the book."

"Know what I say? I say fuck the book."

"Sorry, Jack, but sergeants don't give orders to lieutenants."

Dantzler looked at Laurie. "This one does," he said. "And if you've got a problem with that, feel free to take it up with the brass."

"Lot of good that would do me," Larraby scoffed.

Dantzler walked to the door and opened it wide. "As always, it's been nice chatting with you, Dale. Conversation with you is always stimulating and interesting. But I'm afraid the party's over. We'll take it from here."

For an instant Laurie was certain the two men were going to come to blows. Larraby's jaw looked like it was set in concrete. His right hand doubled into a fist, and his eyes were filled with hate. He held Dantzler's stare for several tense seconds, then abruptly spun on his heels and marched out the door, quickly followed by the other four men.

Dantzler and Laurie were now alone with Deborah Tucker. Laurie breathed a sigh of relief. "What's his problem?" she said.

"Dale's a little too anal retentive for his own good," Dantzler said, closing the door. "Always has been. Must be a Republican."

"He's a dick," Laurie said.

"Exactly. He also hasn't solved a case in fifteen years. Been sucking on the department tit for ages."

Laurie shook her head, said, "What's with you guys and your obsession with female breasts? Is that all you think about?"

"Pretty much."

Dantzler knelt next to Deborah Tucker's body. One of her eyes was open slightly. He closed it. As he was standing, Richard Bird and Eric Gamble came into the apartment.

"What the hell happened to piss off Larraby?" Bird said. "He stormed past me like a damn rampaging bull."

"You know Dale," Dantzler said. "His feelings are easily hurt."

Bird moved a couple of steps closer to Dantzler and looked him up and down. "Jesus Christ, Jack, you look like a walking disaster. A goddamn bum. What's going on?"

"Rough night."

"I've seen you after rough nights before. You never looked like this."

"*Very* rough night."

"The last thing I need is some trigger-happy photographer snapping a picture of you looking like this. People might get the strange notion that I brought in a tramp to work a serial murder case. Do we need to talk?"

"It was just a rough night, Rich," Dantzler said. "Nothing else. Don't make it into a catastrophe."

"That's pretty hard not to do when I'm looking at a major catastrophe." Bird turned to Eric. "Tell BR to come in."

"Beth's here?" Dantzler said.

"Yeah, I picked her up at the airport about an hour ago." He pointed at Deborah Tucker. "How's that for perfect timing?"

"I didn't know she was coming in. When did you hatch this plan?"

"I didn't—she did. She called me yesterday afternoon, said she had some free time on her hands and wondered if we could use her help. No way I turn down that offer."

"Who's this BR?" Laurie asked.

"Beth Robinson. The best damn crime scene investigator I've ever known," Bird said. "If there's a fingerprint, a drop of blood, a hair, or anything else, she'll find it. She's terrific. Worked for us until the FBI snatched her away. I've never understood why she left us to work for that bunch of turds."

"Better pay, better hours," Beth said. She stood in the doorway, a big smile covering her face. "Of course, the quality of turds is much lower."

She winked at Laurie.

"Jack, I've never seen you look so dapper," Beth chuckled. "You in a grunge band now?"

"It's my new look," Dantzler said. "What do you think?"

"I think Neil Young would be proud of you."

"Nice seeing you again, BR," Dantzler said, hugging her. "You've met Eric. This is Laurie Dunn."

"Pleased to meet you," Laurie said.

"My pleasure," Beth said. She put her bag on the floor and went to the sofa. "Choice work. Whoever did this is a real winner."

"A four-time winner, I'm sorry to report," Bird said.

"Well, let's see if we can't put him out of the game."

Beth removed the camera from her bag and spent the next ten minutes photographing Deborah Tucker. As she did, Laurie again felt that familiar feeling of humiliation for the victim. And a terrible sadness. No one should die like this.

When Beth finished, she rewound the film and handed the camera to Laurie. After putting on surgical gloves she knelt beside the body. With a pair of tweezers, she carefully removed the St. Jude medal from Deborah's vagina. She dropped it into a plastic bag, lifted the postcard off Deborah's abdomen, and stood up.

"The *Pietà*," she said, flipping the card over. "Mike L. Angelo? How lame is that?"

"Lame or not, the bastard's one step ahead of us," Bird said.

Beth turned to Dantzler. "What is it you always say, Jack? All killers screw up?"

"Fuck up."

"Yes, well, I was trying to be polite. It's the new me."

"How long do you need the place to yourself?" Bird asked.

"What's been done?"

"Nothing."

"Has Walters been called?"

Bird nodded. "Should be here any minute now."

"Give us a couple of hours if you can. That should be plenty of time for us to do our thing. Then Mac can have the body."

"You get what you need," Bird said. "Count on it."

"Thanks," Beth said. "When they do take the body, make sure nothing else is touched."

Bird nodded again. "I'll leave Eric with you. He'll drive you to the hotel when you're finished."

"Sounds good to me. I'll see you guys sometime tomorrow."

"Try to bring us some good news," Bird said. "God knows we need it."

"If it's here, I'll find it," Beth said. "And you'll get it first, Rich. But only because I've always been hot for your bod." She again winked at Laurie.

"Jesus, I don't need this," Bird said as he stalked toward the door. Laurie and Dantzler, both grinning, followed him out.

By mid-afternoon the rumors had begun to swirl around campus: Something terrible had happened to Deborah Tucker. Eldon first got wind of it when he overheard snippets of conversation between a grossly overweight female student and one of the bookstore employees.

"Deborah Tucker..."

"The actress?"

"Yeah, her..."

"Dead?"

"Murdered."

"For sure...?"

"That's what I heard."

By five o'clock the rumor had become fact. It was official now—Deborah Tucker had been been strangled to death in her apartment. Eldon heard it from a teary-eyed drama instructor who barely spit out the words before breaking down and sobbing hysterically.

Eldon went into his office, closed the door, and turned on the television. With any luck at all, the story might make the 5:30 newscast. He leaned back in his chair, his eyes glued to the screen. It was past the time when he usually left for home, but today he was in no hurry. No sense missing the story while en route to his house. And if it wasn't covered in this segment, he would stick around for another hour or so. Catch it at 6 or 6:30.

But Eldon didn't have to wait—the Channel 27 folks not only had the story, they led with it. He listened as the two anchors briefly discussed the murder. After finishing their lead-in, they cut away to a video taped shot from the driveway of the judge's house. The reporter, a toothy young brunette, gave only the barest of details, then promised to have more during the evening newscast.

Eldon giggled. "Not likely, my young reporter," he whispered under his breath.

Film ran of two men coming down the steps from the apartment. They were well behind the reporter and slightly out of focus, which gave them the appearance of two figures in a misty landscape. Eldon recognized both men, but only after several seconds had passed. Real recognition didn't hit him until they had moved out of the camera's view.

The identity of the man in front, the taller one, came to Eldon first. It was Richard Bird, the man who headed the Homicide Department.

The second man was more difficult for Eldon to pin down. The ragged clothes, the stubble, the uncombed hair…the man didn't look like any cop Eldon had seen in the past. Maybe on TV or in the movies, but certainly not in real life. Then slowly, almost by degrees, recognition came to Eldon. And when it did, his heart jumped with joy and amusement.

Jack Dantzler.

How could he have failed to recognize him? How was that possible? Identifying this man should have been as easy as identifying his own face.

But it hadn't been easy. Why?

He closed his eyes and tried to picture the Dantzler he had just glimpsed on the TV screen. What he saw was the image of someone crumbling under the weight of failure. The man was gaunt, tired-looking, unkempt. No wonder he hadn't recognized Dantzler. How does anyone recognize a ghost?

Eldon switched off the TV. Overpowered by a blast of energy, he stood and paced the office, circling like an animal around its prey. He paused and looked out his office window down into the bookstore. His eyes were filled with tears of joy.

He felt his pulse. It was racing. He leaned over, pounded the desk with both fists, then raised both arms high into the air. He had reason to be this thrilled, this excited. His confrontation with the great detective was going to be an easy victory.

He knew this with absolute certainty. The way he knew for certain the name of the next Chosen One.

Dantzler already had the look of an insane man.

And he didn't even have the first letter yet.

It wasn't until Laurie Dunn was alone in her bed that she had time to review the day's events. She closed the paperback—a bad murder mystery—pitched it onto the floor, and turned off the light. In the darkness, she let her thoughts wander uninterrupted through the day. She found herself placing the major events into three distinct moments, each accompanied by her emotional response.

Watching Beth Robinson remove the St. Jude medal from Deborah Tucker's vagina.

Anger.

Standing toe to toe with Dale Larraby and holding her own.

Pride.

Seeing Jack Dantzler.

Concern.

A chill ran through her body. Laurie felt something else as well—jealousy. She knew from the moment Dantzler and Beth Robinson looked at each other that they had a history together. She didn't have to be an A-1 detective to pick up those vibes.

Wide-eyed, unable to sleep, Laurie lay quietly in the dark.

CHAPTER 22

After refilling his glass with Pernod and orange juice, Dantzler sat at the kitchen table and opened the murder book for the Allison Parker case. He waded through almost two-hundred pages, but found precious little in the way of hard evidence. He reread everything three times, hoping against hope that he might stumble onto something that had been overlooked. Something that would put him in the same ballpark as the killer. Something that would give him the edge.

Dantzler closed the book and took another drink. Reaching to his right, he picked up a stack of unopened mail and began sorting through it. The two bills (electric and phone) went into a basket on the counter, while the others (sales coupons, an offer for yet another low interest Visa Gold Card, *The Watchtower* magazine) found a home in the garbage can.

At the bottom of the stack, Dantzler saw a white 9x12 envelope. He picked it off the table and looked at both sides. His name was printed with blue ink on one side, but his address was missing and there was no return address. And no stamps.

Dantzler carefully opened it, looked inside, then lifted out three pieces of paper.

He began reading.

Dear Jack:

Let me begin by saying that I am mad. Not insane, but mad. Stark, raving mad.

You may be asking yourself: What is the difference between those two mental states? This: Insanity is darkness, madness is illumination.

Insanity is midnight, black, cold, unending, filled with terror at every turn. Madness, like mine, is a series of bright flashes that light the path leading to ultimate understanding, to a higher truth. There is serenity—a peacefulness—that accompanies madness.

The prophets of old, the great visionaries, were men who dwelled inside those illuminating flashes. It was home to them. That's why so many of their tribe were judged to be insane. But they weren't insane. Oh, no, far from it. They lived safely inside the illumination, far removed from insanity's horrible darkness. They were dwellers in the cave of enlightenment.

I have known that darkness, been swept into that midnight of the soul. It surrounded me for many years, suffocating me just as surely as if a pillow was being pressed against my face. I desperately longed for the light, the brightness. Still, my soul remained a prisoner to an endless black.

The shackles of midnight held me firmly in their clutches.

But the powers of darkness, cruel and merciless as they might be, could not continue their hold over me. I was slippery and sly, like a magician or the best of criminals. I waited patiently, silently, until the proper moment presented itself. Then I escaped to freedom. I entered into the cave.

I discovered the light that would lead me away from the darkness of insanity.

"Hell has no power over pagans." Wasn't it the great and mysterious Rimbaud who wrote that? Yes, it was. And he was correct, too. Hell is the domain for the insane, not for the mad. Quite naturally, when I discovered the light, I had no trouble freeing myself from the shackles of hell's burning chains, thus proving that Rimbaud was, indeed, a most-enlightened fellow.

My illumination, my flash of brightness, happened...no, I shan't get into that right now. Later for sure, but not today. No need to be impatient. There is plenty of time, and in time all things shall be revealed. You may be assured of that.

Kafka once entered a darkened room where an elderly man was sleeping. Realizing that he had disturbed the older gentleman, Kafka backed into the shadows and said, "Please, consider me a dream."

Given Kafka's temperament and personality, that was a wonderfully appropriate utterance. Very enlightening. After all, Kafka was a dreamy short of chap. In fact, he often said he dreamed while awake. Most interesting.

It's not by accident that I mention Kafka's statement now. Quite the contrary. I mention it because it is absolutely appropriate to the situation between us. You see, Jack, if I were to inadvertently awaken you, I would back away into the darkness and say, "Please, consider me your nightmare."

I am, you know. Your worst nightmare—if you don't mind allowing me a bit of conceit. (Jack, I detest boasting, and rarely indulge myself. However, on this occasion, I do so without guilt or shame.)

You are, no doubt, puzzled by the above remark concerning "the situation between us." Situation? What situation? How could we, complete strangers, share a situation?

By our respective occupations, that's how. You are a homicide detective; I provide you work. You investigate death; I give you the dead. I give you a reason to get up each morning.

In the words of the immortal Bard, "Misery acquaints a man with strange bedfellows."

However, dear Jack, our relationship isn't restricted to daylight hours. I am also with you at night. You aren't aware of this, but when you dream, as you often do, I am the reason why. It is I who provides you with your nightmares. It is I who gives you the lifeless bodies that torment you so.

And it is I who knows about the heavy cross you bear.

Are you somewhat perplexed by this letter? Are you wondering if it should be tossed into that file of letters sent to you by every poor soul who wishes to confess for even the smallest crime? Don't do that, Jack. Don't be so foolish as to write this off as another crank letter from some miserable wretch claiming to have committed this murder, or killed that poor young woman. I promise you, Jack, this letter is the real thing. I am the real thing.

But why should you believe me? Why is this letter different? Where is the evidence proving that this isn't coming from a raving lunatic? Thought you'd never get around to asking, Jack.

Here's why it's different: those countless other crackpots can't provide certain necessary details known only to you.

And to me.

St. Jude. The Pietà.

Do I have your undivided attention now, Jack? I'm betting heavily that I do.

Poor Deborah Tucker...such a lovely young creature. So talented, too. Did you have the chance to see her perform on the stage, Jack? What a shame if you didn't. Dynamite, pure dynamite. Deborah had that special gift. She could reach into the deepest recesses of our hearts and touch us in a most profound way. Few actors at any level possess such extraordinary power. She could have become a star.

But, alas, she is gone. Like the others. How many unsolved murders are there, Jack? Five? Why, yes, I believe that's the current tally. My, my, what a naughty boy I've been.

Tell me, Jack. How do you feel reading this? Can you adequately put into words the anger that is simmering within you at this very moment? How does it feel to be taunted by the person who's keeping you on the move these days? Must be devastating to someone with your massive ego.

I am that person, Jack. I am the man you're looking for. "That individual," as Kierkegaard might say. (I mention the Melancholy Dane out of respect for your advanced education in the subject of philosophy. Any scribe worth his salt will make every effort to connect with his readers. That is what I'm trying to do. Above all else, Jack, I'm a considerate little fellow.)

Isn't this thrilling, Jack? Hunter and hunted, both men of superb intellect, standing in their respective corners, waiting for the bell to ring, waiting for the dance to begin in earnest. Oh, I can't express to you how delighted I am to be pursued by the best. You are the best, Jack. No one can deny that. I know, for I have followed your exploits for more than a decade. Time after time, I have seen you solve riddles that none of your fellow detectives could solve.

You deserve your status as a legend.

I am going to enjoy this little one-on-one dance you and I will perform over the next few months. This "Waltz of Death" as I refer to it. The stage is lit, Jack, and the curtain has been raised. All that remains is for you and I—the leading characters—to move to center stage. This promises to be a joyous piece of work. A masterpiece.

But please understand this, Jack: When the final curtain has been lowered, it will be you who is left standing alone on the dark stage with only your nightmares and your insanity, while it will be I who will bow to my own brilliant performance. (Dear, dear, how vulgar. Boasting doesn't become the true artist, does it? Olivier didn't tell the world how great he was; he let his work speak for him. I promise that in the future, I will do the same.)

Oh, Jack, I do wish I could continue, but I shan't. Verbosity is one of the dangers I must guard against. Therefore, I will close rather than risk the chance of boring you. But don't be alarmed...there will be future correspondences. Even as I write this letter (incidentally, Ms. Tucker is alive as I'm writing it) my next victim has already been selected. When I'm done with her, I'll get back in touch with you.

Until that time, do try and enjoy your days. They belong to you, Jack, and you should never take them for granted. Days hurry by faster than a bullet fired from a high-powered rifle. Life is so short, so fleeting. And as that old possum T.S. Eliot said, "All time is unredeemable."

Actually, Jack, you don't have to wait until my next letter. I'm with you every night. You can find me in those nightmares you've been having. Yes, Jack, I stalk your nocturnal landscape like a shadow. I prowl your dreamscape like a wolf. Always, Jack, I am always with you.

Sincerely,
Mike L. Angelo
PS: "Fancy thinking the Beast was something you could hunt and kill. You knew, didn't you? I'm part of you. Close, close, close! I'm the reason why it's no go. Why things are what they are."
—The Lord of the Flies

CHAPTER 23

"What do you make of it?" Richard Bird asked, handing the letter to Dynamite. "Sounds legit to me."

"Definitely our boy," Dantzler answered.

"Pretty goddamn arrogant, if you want my opinion," Bird said, "sending a letter to your house."

"He didn't send it, Rich. He *put* it in the mailbox."

"Now, *that* is arrogant," Dynamite said.

"I'll have Beth go over it again for prints," Bird said. "In case the lab folks missed something."

"She won't come up with anything," Dantzler said. "This guy's too smart to leave prints."

Dantzler, Laurie, and Dynamite were seated at a table in the break room. Eric stood next to Laurie, a can of Diet Coke in his hand. Bird, more agitated than usual, leaned against the wall. After several seconds, he pushed himself away, dropped four quarters into the soda machine, and pushed the Pepsi button. He popped open the can, took a drink, and leaned back against the wall.

Laurie took the letter from Dynamite. "And there's nothing special about this paper, either," she said. "Standard stuff...used by a gazillion computer users."

Dynamite picked her cigarette out of the ashtray, flicked the long stem of ashes, and took a drag. "This guy seems to know you pretty well, doesn't he, Jack?" she said, sending a cloud of smoke toward the ceiling. "Either that, or he's coming up with a string of incredibly lucky guesses."

"I don't think luck's involved," Dantzler said.

"You think you know this guy?" Bird asked.

"It's possible."

"Nothing personal, Jack, but I wish the bastard had told us less about you and more about himself," Bird chuckled.

"Read it again, Rich." Dantzler held the letter in front of Bird. "He did tell us a few things about himself."

"Oh, yeah?" Bird's eyes narrowed into a squint. "Such as?"

"He's followed my exploits for a decade, which means he definitely local."

"Okay, so he's president of your fan club. What else does he tell us?"

"He's short."

"Short? What the fuck does that mean, short?" Bird said, his eyes scanning the letter.

"Short, as in not very tall."

"Why do you say that?" Eric asked.

"I'm not saying it. I'm only repeating what he said." Dantzler took the letter from Richard Bird, flipped to the third page, and pointed. "Right here, where he says, 'Above all else, Jack, I'm a considerate little fellow.' He's telling us he isn't very tall. My hunch is it's something that has gnawed at him all his life."

"You don't think that's just an expression?" Laurie said. "Something he said in an off-hand way?"

"When people speak of themselves, when they describe themselves to others, even in off-hand remarks, they almost always tell the truth as they perceive it. Human beings are incredibly honest when it comes to painting pictures of themselves. Take my word for it, this guy is no taller than five-five. Five-six max."

"So he kills people because he's a dwarf, is that what you're saying?" Bird said.

"No, not at all," Dantzler replied. "He kills because he's filled with hate and rage. And judging by the physical similarities of his victims, I would say he's killing the same person over and over again. It's an old story, Rich."

"Yeah, he also says there are five victims," Bird said. "Is his math off, or have we missed something along the way?"

Dantzler shrugged. "Don't know, but we need to find out."

"Have Larraby check every missing persons case within the past five years that involves a female. Have him double-check with the University folks to see if they know of any female students that have gone unexpectedly missing. Tell Milt and Dan to go nationwide. See if they come up with anything that might interest us."

"Eric, you help Larraby if he needs it," Dantzler said.

"Okay."

Laurie finished scribbling in her notepad and looked up at Dantzler. "What else did he tell us in the letter?" she said.

"He's intelligent, well-read," Dantzler said. "Rimbaud, Kafka, Kierkegaard, Eliot, Shakespeare, Golding...not your average Joe Six-pack's standard reading fare. This guy's spent some time with his nose buried in books."

"Gotta be a teacher, writer, editor, maybe a newspaper guy," Bird said.

"That's a start," Dantzler answered.

"I'll visit the English department over at the University," Laurie said. "And the library. Maybe I can find out something there."

"Good idea." Dantzler gave the letter back to Dynamite. "It's a long shot, but right now, long shots are about all we have."

Richard Bird snapped his fingers. "What about Connie Alexander?" he said. "She still teaching?"

Dantzler nodded.

"Jeez, I haven't seen Connie in years," Bird said. "Wonder if she's still as pretty as she was back then."

"Who's Connie Alexander?" Laurie asked.

"One of Rich's many ex's," Dantzler said.

"Yeah, one of the many who got wise and sent him packing," Dynamite said, laughing.

"Anyone ever tell you that you're a real comedian, Dynamite?" Bird turned to Dantzler. "You going to talk to her, Jack?"

"Already have a call in."

"Good. Connie's okay." Bird opened the door to his office. The hint of a smile danced across his face. "Give her a kiss for me, Jack," he said. "Tell her I...just tell her I said hello."

Laurie waited until Bird, Eric, and Dynamite left the break room. When she and Dantzler were alone, she said, "Wouldn't we be lucky if this Connie Alexander was able to help us?"

"More than lucky." Dantzler leaned back and crossed his legs. "But who knows? Maybe she'll detect some element in the letter—writing style, specific words or phrases, anything—that she can match with someone in the English department. Remember, that's how they caught the Unabomber. His brother recognized certain words and phrases. It's a stretch, no doubt about it. But it's something at least. You want to go with me?"

"Can't," Laurie said. "After I hit the English department, I have to get with Grace Kinkade. She wants me to bring the sketch artist again."

"What prompted this visit?"

"She called yesterday. Said she'd been replaying the scene in her head and that she felt like she could come up with a better description this time."

"Her age, this many years later—*that* would be luck."

Laurie picked up her purse and went to the door. She hesitated, then turned back toward Dantzler. "Do you really believe it?" she asked.

"What?"

"That all killers eventually fuck up?"

"Yeah. And this one will, too. It's only a matter of time."

"I hope you're right."

"I am."

"If there's nothing else...." Laurie said.

"No, that's it."

"Then I'm off."

Dantzler sat at the table, his stare deep and far away.

CHAPTER 24

"Busy?" Beth Robinson said as she opened the door to Bird's office.

"Never too busy for you, BR," Bird answered. "Come in." Beth went into the office and sat on the couch. She hadn't slept for twenty-four hours and her raccoon eyes showed it. So did a lengthy yawn. "Bad news, Rich," she said, rubbing her eyes.

"Break it to me gently, if you don't mind."

"Plenty of prints on the letter," she said. "Good ones, too. The kind you die for. They also match the ones we found on the postcard and the Saint Jude medal. Only trouble is, the prints aren't on file."

"Nowhere?"

"The FBI is still checking, but it doesn't look promising."

"What about military records?"

"The person who wrote this letter was never in the armed services," Beth said.

"A job, maybe? Lots of employers require a potential employee to be fingerprinted before hiring them."

Beth shook her head.

"Never fingerprinted—Jesus, can you believe that?"

"It happens, Rich. Fortunately, it doesn't happen as often these days as in the past. That tells us our killer has some age on him. He's no kid."

"Thanks to you and Jack, we know the killer is a short guy who's a little long of tooth," Bird said, shaking his head. "We're really rolling now."

"The beard's a nice touch, Charlie," Laurie said. "Makes you look distinguished

Charlie Bolton ran his fingers through the beard. "Always wanted to grow one, but department rules said facial hair was *verboten.* Except for mustaches—some of the guys were allowed to have them. Now that I'm finally free to grow one, look how it turns out. Solid white. Hell, I look like a skinny Santa Claus."

"A handsome, sophisticated Santa Claus," Laurie said.

"Stop flirting, Dunn. You know I'm too old for you."

Laurie chuckled. "Can't fault a girl for trying."

She picked up a photo off the mantel. It showed her and Charlie, both in uniform, receiving an accommodation for a case they handled successfully while working in the Missing and Exploited Children's Unit. "This seems like a long time ago," she said, putting the photo back on the shelf.

"Time has a way of playing tricks on people, especially when you get older. To me, that seems like yesterday."

"I wouldn't know anything about being old."

"Give it time. You will."

Laurie's expression suddenly turned serious. "Have you seen Jack lately?"

Charlie took a drink from a bottle of beer, then said, "Caught a glimpse of him on the tube a couple of nights ago. Why do you ask?"

"I don't know. What'd you think?"

"Well, I'd say he looked a little frazzled."

"Yeah...frazzled. That's a perfect description. And he is. Frazzled and kind of out of it."

"Well, no wonder. Jack's an arrogant, narcissistic guy. He's also not used to failing. I mean, look at his record. He had a perfect solve rate until two years ago. Now he's suddenly got a pile of dead bodies stacking up and no one to hang it on. I'm sure he's having a tough time dealing with that."

"I think there's more to it than that. I think somehow all these murders have triggered memories of his mother's death."

"I doubt that memory ever leaves him."

"You worked that case, didn't you?"

"Not originally. I was working Vice back when she was killed. Sam Harper and Lee Hutchinson were the original investigators, if I remember correctly...Yep, that's right. Sam and Lee. Hard asses but good cops. Both are dead now. I got involved about twelve years later. Had some time on my hands, so I started looking into a couple of cold cases. One of them was Sarah Dantzler's."

"What do you remember about it?"

Charlie frowned and leaned forward. "Why this interest in ancient history? From where I'm sitting, I'd say you have more than enough on your plate right now to keep your ass firmly planted in the present."

"I'm a cop, Charlie. I'm naturally curious."

"Curious or nosy?"

"What's the difference? Come on, Charlie. What do you remember about Sarah Dantzler's murder?"

"Not much, really. Just that it was one of those puzzles that never got solved. One where the bad guys won."

"Don't bullshit a bullshitter, Charlie. I know you better than that. You remember everything about every case you ever worked. So come on, tell me. What do you remember most about that case?"

"Snowed like hell the night she died."

"What else?"

"A window we could never close."

"Translate, please."

"There was a two-hour window of time where we couldn't account for Sarah's whereabouts. Between eight and ten that night, if I remember accurately. From the time she was last seen until her body was discovered. There is absolutely no trace of her movements or who she was with. But sometime in that time frame she was killed. Whether she knew the killer, met him, ran into him, was abducted by him—we simply don't know. That damn case nearly drove Sam and Lee crazy. After working it myself, I can see why."

Charlie lifted the bottle and finished off the beer. He set it on the table, stared blankly at it for a few seconds, then looked back up at Laurie. "Jack was fourteen, fifteen at the time," he said. "Still just a kid. Something like that happens, it's tough on a youngster. Had to be doubly hard for him, especially after what happened to his father. Jack—he blamed himself for her death."

"Why?"

"Hell, who knows? Jack always was smarter and more mature than most kids his age. Maybe he felt responsible for her, being the only male in the house. I don't know. I'm no shrink. I just remember talking to Sam about it once. He said Jack was really down on himself."

Charlie stood. "Want a brewski?"

"No, thanks."

Charlie pulled a new bottle of Budweiser from the refrigerator and returned to his chair. He twisted off the cap and took a long drink. "I take it you've studied the murder book," he said.

"I've looked at it."

"Well, good luck finding something. I wouldn't hold my breath if I were you. Sam and Lee studied that goddamn thing like a pair of repentant sinners studying the Bible. So did I. Didn't find a thing they missed or overlooked."

"What's your theory of what happened to her?"

"Child, I'm answering no more questions about that case. You want to look into it, go ahead. You're a cop and you have every right to do so. Just don't let anyone see you do it, at least until you catch this guy who's killing these college girls. For now, your attention and energy need to be on that, not on something that happened twenty-five years ago. Ain't nothing about that case is gonna change now, so you just focus on helping Jack. You can look into the Sarah Dantzler case later on."

Laurie grinned. "Okay, Santa. Hey, I think I will have one of those beers if you don't mind."

"Mind?" Charlie said, standing. "It's the first intelligent thing you've said all night."

Dantzler stood in his den and pushed the playback button on his answering machine. A metallic voice informed him that there were three messages. There was one from a telemarketer offering a great deal on a cell phone, one from his uncle Tommy, and one from Connie Alexander.

He ignored the first two, then listened closely to the one from Connie.

"Jack, it was good to hear from you. Surprising, too. Yes, I can meet with you tomorrow. How about three thirty in my office? Unless I hear otherwise, I'll expect to see you then. Ciao."

Dantzler went into the kitchen and fixed himself a Pernod and orange juice. He went back into the den, thought about turning on a light, but decided he preferred the darkness. Stretching out on the couch, he took a drink and closed his eyes. His insides were instantly engulfed in flames. It was a fire he liked.

Leaning his head back against the sofa, he thought about the letter. He also thought about the things he hadn't told them in the break room. The words and insights the killer mentioned. Particularly the insights. How did the killer know about the dreams? And he *did* know about them—this wasn't a lucky guess. What about the advanced degree in philosophy? How could the killer possibly be aware of that?

Dantzler gulped down his drink, felt his insides overcome by fire.

How did the man know...?

Dantzler resisted the thought, tried to force it out of his mind. He couldn't. It broke through his barriers and came at him with a violent intensity.

The heavy cross—how did the man know about that? "It is I who knows about the heavy cross you bear." How could *anyone* know? Not even Rich or Dynamite knew that. That was top secret, locked away in the memory vault, untouchable. But the killer knew. He *knew.*

And...

If the killer knew that, then he also had to know...

Dantzler opened his eyes, terrified by the realization that loomed within him like cancer.

The killer had known Sarah Dantzler.

CHAPTER 25

It was mid-morning and Eldon Wessell wasn't feeling well. He felt weak, feverish, achy. An early morning coughing attack had left him feeling especially rough in the upper chest. He was coming down with something, probably the same damn flu that had hit many of the bookstore employees. He didn't need this. Not now, not when things were going so well.

After spending a perfectly dreadful hour with the representative of a book company, Eldon decided a glass of orange juice and a pastry or sandwich of some sort might help fight off the attacking bug. A mid-morning snack wasn't standard practice for him—snacks at any time are a killer in the constant war against an expanding waistline—but he chose to make an exception on the grounds that a *nosh* might make him feel better.

The University bookstore was located on the first floor in the Student Center. The main cafeteria, where he normally had lunch, was one floor above. But Eldon had no taste for cafeteria food, and since this was something of an adventure for him, he decided to walk down Euclid Avenue, past the Coliseum, to a Hardee's in a small shopping center at the end of the block. Hardee's was by no means his favorite eating place, but at least it was different. It also had a reputation for being above average for a fast-food joint. That was especially true of the breakfast menu. Everybody just raved about the egg and cheese biscuit, which sounded good to Eldon. And, he reasoned, the walk would do him good. It was a glorious spring day, the air warm and breezy. Just what a doctor might order for someone with clogged-up lungs.

After making a quick phone call, Eldon told an employee that he was taking a break. She was stunned...he *never* left during the day. He put on a sweater, and walked out of the bookstore and into the Student Center hallway. Just as he was about to open the door, he heard someone call his name. Eldon turned and saw the tall, dark-haired woman coming toward him. Standing there, watching the woman's breasts bounce with her every step, he felt the blood surging downward, felt his penis begin to stiffen.

Beverly Diaz.

She rushed toward him, a smile on her face. She was, he quickly decided, one of the most beautiful and most sensual-looking women on campus. The reason: her skin, which was darker than any of the previous four victims. This was only natural, given her nationality. She had been born in Mexico City and lived there until she was fifteen. Then, after her parents parted ways, she and her mother moved to Houston. Now a senior, she had come to the University of Kentucky on a tennis scholarship. She was currently ranked among the best singles players in college tennis.

"I was wondering if you'd filled the position I inquired about two weeks ago," she said. "I really do hate to be a pest, but my scholarship runs out at the end of the semester. So I need to know something one way or the other. As soon as possible."

"I understand," Eldon said. "Money is tight these days, isn't it?"

"Money has been tight all my life," she answered.

"To be perfectly honest with you, I haven't made a final decision yet," Eldon said. "And I shan't do so for another week or so. Can you hold off that long?"

Beverly kept her smile, but her disappointment was obvious. "Well, I guess...it's just..."

"Not to worry, my dear. I feel quite confident you'll get the job," Eldon said, reaching out and touching her sleeveless arm. Caressing her smooth, muscular skin, feeling the soft black hair on her forearm, brought him to the edge of orgasm. He removed his hand and looked away.

Discipline, he reminded himself. *Above all else, discipline.*

"Can I chalk that up as a sure thing?" she said. "If I can, then I can go ahead and keep my apartment."

"You have my word," Eldon said.

"Terrific," she said, her coal-black eyes wide and gleaming. "I'm on my own this summer, and I was afraid that I'd have to move to some cheaper place. This will really ease the pressure."

"No roommate?" Eldon asked.

"Not until this fall," Beverly said. "She's playing on the satellite circuit in Europe. Lucky thing."

"Let's see, if I remember correctly, you live in the Park Place Apartments, don't you? On Commonwealth Avenue?"

"That's right," she said. "Hey, you've got a great memory."

"My mind is a veritable repository of information, trivia, and, hopefully, some knowledge." Eldon said. "You check back with me near the end of next week. Friday morning might be the best time. We'll finalize everything, get you to fill out all those nasty forms. If there are no glitches or surprises, we should have you working by the following Monday. How does that sound?"

"Terrific," she said. "The NCAA finals are this weekend, so I'll be finished with tennis and ready to start work. And boy, do I need the bucks."

"Good luck in the tournament."

"Thanks, I'll need it," she said, turning to leave.

"Okay, I'll see you a week from Friday," Eldon said.

He kept his eyes on her until she bounced onto the elevator and the doors closed behind her. His heart was pounding like a timpani drum.

"Or sooner," he whispered.

CHAPTER 26

Dan Matthews and Milt Costello stood when Paul Miller walked into the office. Miller, the head of the University's theatre department, was slim, maybe six-one, elegantly dressed in a pin-striped three-piece suit and wearing a very somber look. He had a neatly trimmed mustache and wore wire-rim glasses. He eased behind the big mahogany desk and motioned for the detectives to sit.

"As you can imagine, gentlemen, things are in an upheaval around here these days," Miller said. "Not only was Deborah Tucker an extraordinarily talented actress, she was also extremely well liked by everyone. Her death is a stunning blow to her friends, colleagues, and teachers. To lose Deborah *and* Abby Kaplan within a period of four weeks is more than many of us can bear. They were two of our brightest stars."

"We certainly appreciate your taking the time to speak with us, Doctor Miller," Matthews said. "I know your time is limited, but…"

"I'll *make* time if it can possibly help you find the person responsible for Deborah's death. And Abby's." His eyes went from Matthews to Costello. "What can I do to help, Detectives?"

"How well did you know Deborah?" Matthews asked.

"Very well. I had her in two classes, and I directed her in her first play here."

"Isn't it unusual for a department head to still teach and direct?"

"It's probably more rare now than it was ten or fifteen years ago. Being the head of a department is time-consuming and burdened with quite a bit of politics, which I care very little about. However, those things go with the territory. I knew that when I accepted the position."

Miller leaned back and put his hands behind his head. A slight smile crossed his face. "I may be an administrator in fact, but in my heart I'll always be a teacher first," he said. "Teaching is my calling, my first love. I prefer dealing with students than with budgets or departmental politics."

Costello said, "Did Deborah have any problems that you were aware of?"

"Not to my knowledge. Deborah was a perfectly normal college student who just happened to possess an extraordinary gift for the craft of acting. Her future in that profession was unlimited."

"What about jealous competitors?" Matthews asked. "Maybe someone who might want to eliminate a rival?"

"Come on, Detective, that's an absurd notion. The majority of students in the theatre department have no desire to become professional actors. Maybe they have the dream, but not the fire inside—the drive and determination it takes to even have a chance to make it big. For most of them, it's a fun thing, something interesting to do. Those who are serious—most of them, anyway—will end up as teachers. Like me. I wanted to be a great actor—the next Brando—but I didn't have the goods. Far more will become writers, teachers, and directors than actors."

"But Deborah—she was different?" Matthews said.

"What she had was rare, indeed," Miller said, again smiling. "A true talent. So did Abby Kaplan, for that matter. Both women were very, very talented."

"Were they friends?" Matthews said.

"Friends? Not to my knowledge. I suspect they knew each other, but there was an age difference of three or four years, which is considerable at this stage of life. Also, Abby was a graduate student, Deborah an undergrad. They moved in different worlds."

"Doctor Miller," Costello said, "we're convinced that Deborah knew her killer. Can you think of anyone, in or out of the department, who might want to harm her?"

"No, I can't. Sorry."

"What can you tell us about James Winstead?" Matthews said.

Miller's eyes came alive. "Jim? Why would you inquire about him?"

"Please, Doctor Miller, just answer the question."

"Well, Jim's primary area of expertise is theatre history. He's quite sharp, too. Really knows his subject. He also teaches a beginning acting class. I still don't understand why..."

"Did he ever have Deborah Tucker in class?" Costello said.

"He very well may have, but I'd have to check the records to be certain."

"What about Abby Kaplan?" Costello asked. "Did he ever have her in class?"

"Well, Abby's focus was dance and movement, so the odds are higher that he didn't. Maybe she was in his theatre history class, but once again, I can't say for certain until I look at the records."

"We'll need to take a look at those records," Matthews said.

"Yes, I'll get them for you before you leave."

"Are you aware that Abby Kaplan rented from James Winstead?" Costello said.

"Really? No, I had no idea."

"Lived in his house."

"I knew Jim moved into an apartment once his divorce was final. But I didn't know he rented the house to Abby. That comes as a complete surprise."

Matthews said, "Word is, James Winstead has a pretty bad temper. Is that true?"

Miller frowned and shook his head. "Detective, why are you asking about Jim's temper?"

"Because he used to beat up his wife?"

"I don't believe that. Not for a second." Miller again shook his head. "If such an incident had..."

"Incidents," Costello interjected. "At least four that we're aware of."

"As head of this department, as Jim Winstead's ultimate superior, don't you think I would have heard about those incidents if indeed they had occurred?"

"Sometimes the top dog is kept out of the yard," Costello said.

"And sometimes the top dog doesn't want to know," Matthews said.

"What are you insinuating, Detective?"

"Inquiring minds want to know, Doctor Miller," Matthews said, grinning. "Where do the theatre students usually hang out when they're away from this building?"

"Socially, off-campus, I have no idea what they do. Typical college things, I would imagine. Date, flirt, study, drink. Same things we all did when we were in college, I suppose."

"Someone like Deborah—where would she be likely to spend her time on campus?"

"Well, of course, most of her time would be spent in this building," Miller said. "Studying, rehearsing, *kibbitzing* with her colleagues. But away from here, I'd say she spent time in the library, the bookstore, the Student Center, the cafeteria."

"Did you know her boyfriend?" Costello said.

"I met him a few times, but didn't really know him."

"What was your impression of him?"

"Smart, likeable, very fond of Deborah. Why? Is he a suspect?"

Costello shrugged.

"If you're looking at him, I'd say you're tap dancing on the wrong stage," Miller said.

"Why do you say that?" Costello asked.

"Let me just say that if I were directing a murder mystery," Miller said, "I wouldn't cast him as the killer."

Matthews and Costello simultaneously rose from their chairs. "That's the thing about real life murder mysteries," Matthews said, closing his notepad. "They rarely follow the script."

CHAPTER 27

At 3:10 that afternoon, Eldon's thoughts were still on Beverly Diaz. He remembered everything about their brief encounter. Her smile, the natural beauty of her face, the texture of her skin, the soft down on her arms. It was a moment frozen in his memory. Then he was struck by a sudden realization—none of the others had affected him this way. This was, he knew, cause for concern. Cause for caution. He needed to marshal his intellectual forces, think, evaluate, plan wisely.

Twice during the day, he had toyed with the idea of killing Beverly Diaz before she left for the tennis tournament in Georgia rather than early next week as originally planned. But he quickly rejected that plan on the grounds that it showed a lack of discipline, and that it was the kind of impetuous act that might lead to a blunder. There was another issue that needed to be factored in. She was a tennis star—her death would draw extra attention. That would mean even more heat from the police. Because of that, it was a risk not worth taking.

Another thought had come to him: let her live. If he was having this much internal debate, perhaps he should forget the whole thing. Just drop it. Wait until later. Find another Chosen One. There was certainly no shortage of women to choose from. He'd just put it off, just wait.

But that idea vanished as quickly as it had arrived. Eldon wasn't about to wait, to put off his rendezvous with victim number five. There was no reason to delay, to change plans. He would overcome his doubts, force these unwanted thoughts from his head. He would use his great discipline.

Eldon admitted to himself that Beverly Diaz was different from all the others. He knew why, too. She triggered his imagination more than they had. Her dark skin, her jet-black hair…he couldn't wait to see the forest between her long and lovely legs. But there was another reason as well. He had physically touched her. That had never happened with the others, at least not until he killed them. But with Beverly, he had been intimate. He had connected. Because of that, he felt closer to—and more sexually aroused by—the wonderful Beverly Diaz.

He was going to take his time with her, to enjoy the experience to the fullest. And perhaps make her his final one. He wouldn't know that until later—and he had his doubts—but it was something that needed to be considered. Every professional has to call it quits sometime. Better early than late. Hang on too long and you risk becoming a has-been. Or in his case, a prisoner on death row.

Eldon sat behind his desk and let his eyes lazily wander through the bookstore. Two male students, both dressed in sweatsuits and sneakers, were standing at the magazine rack, flipping through the new *Sports Illustrated* swimsuit edition. Two tight-lipped, serious-looking female professors were debating the merits of a book in the women's studies section. A group of students, male and female, drifted indifferently through the aisles, looking more bored than interested in making a purchase. A thin, bearded, dark-haired man wearing a blue shirt, leather sports coat, Levis, and white Nikes sifted through the books in the philosophy section.

Eldon closed his eyes and was about to nod off when recognition hit him with the force of a steamroller. His eyes snapped open. He had to look again, had to make sure…Yes, it was him. It was the great detective himself, here, right in front of him.

On my turf, goodgodalmighty, right before my very eyes.

How breathtaking, Eldon thought. How very *right*. The unsuspecting hunter being watched by the all-knowing hunted. Role reversal at its best. Satan watching God.

Given the situation, Eldon was surprisingly calm. He stood, took a single breath, and walked out into the bookstore. He had to get a closer look at the hunter, to smell the hunter, to stare into the hunter's eyes. He wanted to get the hunter's attention, to be acknowledged by the hunter. Oh, if the hunter only knew. If the hunter had any inkling that his prey stood just inches away. If the hunter only knew that the two key players in this Waltz of Death were now sharing the stage together, perhaps for the first and last time.

Eldon was alive with the excitement that belongs to the person who possesses knowledge unknown to others. Secret knowledge hidden from the blind and the ignorant. The kind of knowledge revealed only to the mystics.

Eldon moved into the psychology section, one row away from Plato and Descartes and Kant and Nietzsche and Sartre.

And Jack Dantzler.

Eldon felt the goose bumps rise along his spine. He felt the perspiration drip from his armpits, felt the buzz of nervous electricity in the pit of his gut. He was completely alive, on sensory overload, just as he was when glorifying a Chosen One.

Now, because of whatever twist of fate, decreed by whatever all-powerful being, hunter and hunted were standing virtually shoulder to shoulder. The distance between them was less than three feet. Eldon had never felt more in control of a situation, never been surer of himself than at this moment.

Standing inches away from the hunter, Eldon knew with the certainty of a true believer that he would prevail in this Waltz of Death with Dantzler.

There could be no other outcome.

Eldon half-turned and faced Dantzler, who was looking though a copy of Spinoza's *Ethics*. "Were you looking for something in particular?" he said, his voice strong and steady.

Dantzler closed the book and replaced it on the shelf. "Just browsing," he said, turning away. "Thanks."

"If I can be of assistance, don't hesitate to let me know," Eldon said.

"I'll do that," Dantzler said, stopping to remove a book from the shelf. It was a critical study of the existentialists.

So arrogant, Eldon said to himself. *Just like before.*

Eldon worked his way down a parallel aisle, eventually positioning himself in front of Dantzler. It was a perfect position—the hunted, hidden behind a row of books, could see the hunter without fear of being seen. He watched for two minutes, hardly breathing, taking in every move Dantzler made.

Oh, if you only knew. Eldon chuckled silently. He had never felt more satisfied. More in control. More certain that the hunter, the arrogant Jack Dantzler, was doomed to failure.

CHAPTER 28

Dantzler tapped on the door to Connie Alexander's office, opened it, and stuck his head inside. Connie motioned for him to enter, which he did, leaning back against the door. She was sitting at her desk, surrounded by a trio of students who sat listening to her in rapt attention. Occasionally one would ask a question, but for the most part she did the talking.

After nearly five minutes, she peered around one of the students and caught Dantzler's eye. She smiled and held up an open hand, indicating that she would be finished in five minutes. Dantzler returned her smile, picked up a copy of *All The King's Men*, sat on the couch, and began reading.

Nearly fifteen minutes passed before Connie's meeting began to break up. Two of the students left together. The third, a male, stayed a few minutes longer discussing nothing of relevance or real importance. Dantzler knew the kid either had the hots for Connie or he was kissing ass for a better grade.

Dantzler stood as she ushered the young man out of the office. When he was gone, she closed the door and let out a loud groan. "Damn, damn, damn, when am I ever going to learn?" she said.

"Undergraduate pups?"

"Yes. And not a terribly bright threesome, if I may say so. Earnest but lacking." She hugged Dantzler. "Jack, it's really good to see you. It's been too long."

"You know me—always trying to keep a low profile."

"Hate to tell you, but whatever you're doing, it ain't working."

"Yeah, I've noticed," he answered.

She ran her hand through his beard. "I like the whiskers," she said. "Makes you look distinguished. Like a tortured poet or a revolutionary. One of those foolish romantic stereotypes."

"Tell that to Rich. He says I look like a bum."

"Rich never did appreciate the romantic types."

Dantzler laughed. "No, I guess not."

"Jack, you look tired," Connie said. "And you've lost too much weight. Are you okay?"

"I'm fine."

"You sure about that?"

"Connie, believe me. I'm fine. There's just a lot of shit going on right now that's keeping me on the run."

"Regardless of what's going on, will you at least try to take better care of yourself?"

"Yes, mother. I'll take my vitamins and get eight hours of sack time every night."

"I only wish I could believe that." Connie returned to her desk and sat down. "So, what is it I can do for you?"

Dantzler sat in the chair across from her, reached into his coat pocket, and took out the letter. "I'd like you to read this and tell me what you think," he said, handing the letter to her.

"What is it, a crackpot note?" She took the letter from him and opened it.

"No, it's the real thing."

She put on her glasses, laid the letter flat on her desk, hunched forward, and began reading. When she was finished, she took off her glasses, looked at Dantzler, and frowned. "This man knows you, Jack," she said.

"A lot of people know me."

"No, this man *knows* you."

Dantzler nodded. "Okay, so he knows me. What else do you see?"

"Nothing you haven't already seen, probably," she said. "Intelligent, well-read, a name-dropper. One of those assholes who wants you to know how smart he is. An unmarried man, probably on the boring side."

"Why do you say that?"

"Just a guess, really. But my experience is that men who read extensively are often single."

"Can't get laid, so they read a book. Is that it?"

"You said that, I didn't."

"Anything else?"

Connie smiled knowingly. "What you're really asking me is, do I know anyone in the department who might have written this letter."

"I always said you should have been a cop," Dantzler said.

Connie her chair back, closed her eyes, and frowned. She was silent for almost a minute. "There is one thing that did catch my attention," she finally said. "The word 'shan't.'"

"Why? Do you know someone who uses that word?"

"God, Jack, I hate this. I mean, what if I'm wrong, which I probably am. What if I cause unnecessary trouble for an innocent man?"

"Flip that over, Connie. What if you choose to remain silent and he turns out to be guilty? Which sin is worse?"

"Did you have to word it like that, Jack? Why couldn't you make it easy for me?"

"I just did. If you feel it in your gut, Connie, then you have to tell me. You have no other choice."

"I know, I know," Connie said, shaking her head. "It's just that I don't want to cause waves for someone who doesn't deserve it."

"Tell me, and I'll handle it so the guy won't know he's being investigated," Dantzler said. "You have my word."

"I don't see how that's possible," Connie said. "I mean, he's not stupid. If you show up asking questions, he's gonna figure out pretty quick that it's not because you're interested in literature."

"I'll handle it."

"James Roper. He teaches American lit."

"He have an office in this building?"

"Four doors down, other side of the hall. You probably passed it on the way here." Connie sighed. "I feel like a ten-year-old who just snitched on a friend."

"Tell me about this James Roper. What kind of guy is he?"

"Extremely bright, extremely talented. One of the finest instructors in the department, in my opinion. But that opinion isn't one that's universally shared within the department."

"Why?"

"Because he's a very reclusive, off-the-wall kind of man."

"Explain 'off-the-wall.'"

"Oh, just different…peculiar," Connie said. "An oddball in some ways."

"Come on, Connie. Stop treading around the edges. Tell me what you're thinking."

"Jim is very anti-social," she answered. "Very anti-people, even. He doesn't care for crowds, seldom joins in with group things, just stays to himself. I've often wondered how a man like that becomes a teacher. Seems to me he's more cut out to do research, or maybe work on computers. But Jim's big dream is to write The Great American Novel. He's written several, all pretty good from what I hear, but he hasn't had any luck getting published. I think that's made him even more remote. I know he's very frustrated."

"And the word 'shan't' is part of his vocabulary?"

Connie nodded. "Yes. He uses the term quite often. When he first began teaching here, I…"

"How long ago was that?"

"Eight years ago, maybe. Let me think—yeah, that would be about right. He just came off sabbatical in December, and you have to put seven years in before you're eligible."

"Finish what you were saying."

"When Jim first came here, I thought he used certain terms simply for effect, to make an impression. He seemed pompous, pretentious. But he isn't. That's just his normal vocabulary. He's not being pretentious—he's just being himself."

"Do you like him?"

"I've never had a problem with him. Never. He's always been straight with me."

"You're dodging the question, Connie. Do you like him?"

"Certain things about him, yes. Certain things about him, no."

"What do you not like?"

"He has a thing for younger women," Connie said.

"How young?"

"Students."

"Here?"

"Yes. And I have a problem with that. It's dangerous and uncalled for."

"He dates his own students?"

Connie nodded. "Sometimes, yes. He's been advised against it, but he still does. I'm no prude; you know that. For God's sake, I've had some male students who were so delicious they made me salivate. Under different circumstances, I'd jump their bones in a heartbeat. But I just don't happen to agree with that kind of behavior. To me, there's something unethical about it."

"Has there ever been a problem with Jim?" Dantzler said.

"Once, a couple of years ago, one of the girls felt like she had been jilted by him. She was pretty upset, tried to make a big stink about it. Nothing came of it. Things quieted down in a week or so. That's when Jim was *advised* against continuing such practices."

"But he hasn't stopped?"

"No. Word is, he's heavily involved with one of his undergraduate pups."

"How old is Roper?"

"Oh, late thirties, early forties maybe. Close to our age, I'd say."

"Give me your honest opinion—is he capable of killing four college women?"

"Jack, I just don't think so," Connie said, shaking her head. "Sure, he's weird and off the beaten path, and perhaps a little shy in the ethics department, but a cold-blooded murderer? No way."

Dantzler stood, went to the bookcase behind Connie's desk, and took down a copy of *Moby Dick*. He opened it and smiled. "*This* is The Great American Novel," he said. "You can tell your strange friend to stop wasting his time. Melville got there first."

"I'm sure that'll work wonders for his spirit," Connie said, swiveling her chair to face Dantzler. "Are you going to talk to him?"

"Have to."

"Jeez, Jack, keep me out of it, will you?"

"He'll never know I spoke with you. That's a promise."

Connie rose from her chair and took the book from Dantzler. "Hate to disagree with you, Jack, but this isn't The Great American Novel." She put the book back on the shelf and kissed Dantzler on the cheek. "Don't be a stranger."

Dantzler eased past her and walked slowly to the door. "One last question, Connie," he said. "How tall is Jim Roper?"

"How tall?"

"Yes. Approximately."

"Not much taller than me," she said, a puzzled look on her face. "Five-five, five-six maybe. Why?"

"Just wondering, that's all."

CHAPTER 29

For three straight days Eldon performed a task that was completely alien to him—he read the sports section in the local newspaper. Eldon hated sports. Hated the athletes, the coaches—both groups grossly overpaid and spoiled beyond belief—and the stupid fans who lived vicariously through the exploits of their jock heroes and whose state of happiness or despair depended on their team winning or losing.

Once, while riding to a sales convention with the representative of a book publisher, Eldon had been subjected to almost two hours of the non-stop chatter of a radio call-in sports show. He had been disgusted, felt like a prisoner. Surely, this was what hell must be like. Satan as a radio host, taking calls from ignorant middle-age men who had nothing better to do with their lives than to bitch about whether this coach should be fired or that player should be traded.

It was all so…so lacking in culture.

Yet, for three days Eldon scoured the sports section, searching for news about Beverly Diaz. About how she was doing in the NCAA Tournament. On Wednesday, the first day of team competition, Eldon had no clue where to look for the results. He had resigned himself to asking one of the bookstore employees—a true jock in every sense—where the tennis scores could be found, but was spared that embarrassment when he chanced upon a brief story on page 3 detailing the team's first-round results. They won, beating Michigan four matches to three. Eldon was greatly pleased when he read that it was Beverly Diaz's victory that clinched the match. She won 6-2, 6-4, which, of course, meant nothing to Eldon. But numbers didn't matter. What did matter was the whereabouts of the next Chosen One. Beverly Diaz was still in Athens, Georgia.

No doubt celebrating her victory.

CHAPTER 30

Laurie Dunn took two quick gulps of water from the Evian bottle and opened the file on the table. She was alone in the War Room, thankful for the time to herself. The past week had been disappointing. No new leads had surfaced, and she, like the others, was growing weary of retracing old steps, covering old territory. They needed something new to sink their teeth into, something to get them re-energized. She silently prayed that it wouldn't take another murder to kick-start the engines.

God, what an awful proposition, she thought. Death as stimulus.

As a way of looking at the present—and quite probably the future—Laurie chose to revisit the past. Or perhaps she was seeking, at least for a brief period, to escape the present. She wasn't sure. It didn't matter, really, because in the end all roads led back to now.

Laurie's tour guide into the past lay spread out before her on the table. It was thick, filled with reports, interviews, sketches, photos. The murder book on Sarah Anne (Blake) Dantzler.

Born: June 18, 1941, Boston, Mass.

Died: February 5, 1978, Lexington, Ky.

Cause of Death: Asphyxiation.

In the very front of the file were two photos of Sarah Dantzler. Color shots, high quality. One was a close-up of her face, the second one taken at the death scene. One showed a beautiful, vivacious young woman in the prime of her life; one showed a woman lying face up in a trash dumpster, most of her body covered by a blanket of fresh snow.

Laurie spent the next two hours poring over the details of Sarah's death and the subsequent investigation. Sam Harper and Lee Hutchinson had been the lead detectives, and from all indications they'd done everything they could to crack the case. No investigative procedure had been overlooked, no road untraveled. Yet, everywhere they had turned, they'd run into a brick wall. One dead end after another.

It became clear to Laurie why the two detectives had come up empty: despite the mountain of collected material, there was little in the way of solid evidence. No witnesses, no leads. Not even a semi-educated hunch.

Charlie Bolton was right when he said she wasn't likely to find much in the file. The entire mass of this particular volume could be boiled down to a single fact: after so much effort, no one knew anything. Except the killer.

Laurie read all the interviews. There was a common thread, but not one that led anywhere. Neighbors, friends, and her co-workers were unified in their love for Sarah and in their sorrow that she was gone. The parents praised her as a mother and daughter. Her younger brother Tommy lamented the loss of a terrific big sister and a woman with such a rare and wonderful outlook on life.

When Laurie finished reading and closed the file, she had written but a single name in her notepad. David Langley. The last person to see Sarah Dantzler alive.

Just as Laurie stood, the door opened and Dantzler came in. He saw the murder book on the table, moved closer, and opened it. The two color photos of his dead mother stared up at him.

Laurie expected…she didn't really know what to expect from him. Sorrow? Anger? What? But there was nothing. His face was stone, his eyes cold as a cobra's.

He closed the file. "Find anything?" he said.

"No." She picked up the folder. "I hope you don't mind that I went through it."

"You're a cop. It's an unsolved case. You have every right to look into it." He smiled. "Just don't let it interfere with what's really important—catching our active killer."

"May I ask you a question?" she said.

"About my mother's case, I presume."

"Yes."

"Fire away, Sergeant."

"Do you think your mother knew her killer?"

"Yes. She would never have accepted a ride with a total stranger."

"Maybe she was abducted."

"Possible. But I don't think so."

"Why? It happens all the time."

"That's true. It just doesn't fit in this instance."

"Is that sound detective thinking, or denial?"

"I don't know. You tell me."

"I think she was abducted," Laurie said. "I think the killer saw her alone, abducted her—he probably had a gun or a knife—drove her to the school and murdered her."

"You're assuming she was killed where she was found."

"You don't think she was?"

"I think she was killed in the car, then put in the dumpster. And I believe the murder took place long before they got to the school. That was just a convenient place to get rid of the body."

"Did Harper and Hutchinson look at the abduction angle?"

"They looked at *all* angles. So did Charlie Bolton."

"And?"

"They came away with the same conclusion I have. That your abduction theory just doesn't hold up."

"Why?"

"A couple of reasons. First, my mother wore no expensive jewelry or carried a lot of cash, so that rules out robbery as a motive. And second, there was no sexual assault, which eliminates rape. Scrap them and what are you left with? Certainly no sound motive for abduction. It doesn't make sense."

"Does murder ever make sense?"

"Always. If it didn't, we'd never catch a killer. It's the 'sense' part that gives us a chance."

CHAPTER 31

Eldon lay on his bed editing the first draft of his next letter to Dantzler. He wasn't at all pleased with what he had written. Too clumsy, too wordy, and lacking the smooth flow of the first letter. More work had to be done before this one would be ready for the public domain.

He got out of the bed and saw a piece of paper that had been slipped under the door. He knew instantly that it was from his mother. Only she would choose paper with such a gaudy design. Bright red, with white harp-playing cherubs floating across the top.

Elmer Donald:

Would you be kind enough to take a break from your busy schedule and grace us with your presence at an important family meeting? A matter of some urgency has arisen, one that demands our immediate attention. Eight thirty, in the kitchen. Your sister and I will be eagerly awaiting your prompt arrival. If you are more than five minutes late, we will assume you have elected not to come and will therefore proceed without you.

Mother

Seething, Eldon crushed the paper in his hand and threw it hard against the wall. *Would you be so kind...*He could hear the sarcasm in her voice...*Will therefore proceed without you.* The arrogance of that woman. God, how he hated her.

He stormed down the steps. "Ah, Lilith and Jezabel...what a lovely sight," he said as he entered the kitchen.

Rose, already seated, looked at her brother and smiled. Gee moved away from the sink, pulled a chair back, sat down and opened a manilla folder. She picked up a pen and began writing.

Rose pointed at Eldon's waist. "I do believe you've put on a few pounds, little brother," she said. "You're beginning to look rather thick around the middle. Maybe you need to get out more. Stop staying holed up in that dungeon of yours. What do you do in there, anyway?"

"Plot your demise."

"You're hopeless, you know that?"

"Let's get this over with." Eldon turned to Gee. "What's this all about?"

"A firm offer has been made on the house," Gee said, putting the pen down. "And I think we should take it."

"When did this happen?" Eldon yelled. "Why haven't I been consulted?"

"Because you're always in abstentia," Rose said. "Because you never want to be bothered by anything."

"I refuse to consent to the sale of this house," Eldon said. "I absolutely don't want to discuss it."

"You haven't heard the offer," Gee said.

"I don't care what the offer is. This house will not be sold. Not while I'm still breathing."

"Three hundred thousand dollars," Gee said.

Eldon leaned forward. "It could be three million. I don't care. We will not sell this house."

"Why?" Rose asked. "What's your obsession with this place? It's old. It's too big. The utility bills are outrageously high. And three hundred thousand dollars? Get real, will you. Offers like that don't come around very often."

"With that money, you could buy your own place," Gee said. "And be rid of us once and for all."

"I will not sell it." Eldon stood and started for the stairs.

"*You* will not sell it?" Gee said, rising. "Let me remind you that it's not your decision to make. It's mine. Legally, this house belongs to me. But for the sake of fairness I will abide by a majority vote. I suggest we mull it over privately, then get back together Sunday morning. We can vote then."

Eldon looked first at his Mother, then at Rose. "Yeah, right. Like the deck hasn't been stacked."

Eldon was almost in tears when he got back to his room. He closed the door, locked it, and fell onto the bed. The thoughts were racing so fast inside his head that he could barely make them out. He shut his eyes, listened, hoping to catch bits and pieces.

Sell the house...No way...Too many memories...Beverly Diaz...Discipline...The old elm tree...Three hundred thousand...Who gives a damn...Jack Dantzler...I'll win...Hell has no power over pagans...You've put on a few pounds...Rose and Gee must die...Keep the house, no matter what it takes...Rose and Gee must die.

That was Eldon's last thought before he drifted off to a troubled sleep.

CHAPTER 32

Death in combat is almost always shrouded in mystery. Relatives and family members only get the barest details of what happened and how. *We are sorry to inform you that your son was killed in action...*The rest of the message offers little in the way of specifics. And it shouldn't. No one wants to learn that their loved one had his head ripped apart by a machine gun bullet, or his body blown into tiny pieces by a mortar shell. Some details are better left as a mystery.

When Dantzler was a young boy he yearned to know the details of his father's death, but neither his mother nor his uncle would talk with him about what happened. Later, when a combat buddy of his father's came by the house, Dantzler bombarded the man with questions, only to be answered with silence. *Your old man was brave*, the man told Dantzler. After he had gone to bed, he could hear his mother and uncle talking with their visitor, speaking in voices so low he couldn't make out what was being said. Dantzler had known in his heart what they were talking about—the details.

Time and his mother's murder quelled his desire for those details. Somewhere between his mother's death and his own career as a detective, questions surrounding the death of Staff Sergeant John David Dantzler got lost in the shuffle. Now Dantzler aimed to find them.

Maybe he would never solve the mystery of what happened to Sarah Dantzler. Maybe those questions were destined to go unanswered. In the case of his father, however, there were answers, and he knew where to find them.

Dantzler parked, hopped out of the Forester, and headed toward Apartment 14-A in The Fountains, a swank complex on Todds Road. He was here to see his uncle Tommy, who had lived alone since his wife Judy left him for another man more than a decade ago.

Tommy Blake had been Dantzler's idol, his hero, his mentor. It was Tommy who had taught him how to play tennis and baseball. It was Tommy who had instilled in him a love for learning. Tommy Blake was of those charmed individuals who had star written all over him. Graceful, strong, quick, fearless, and intelligent, he was seen as a can't-miss Major League shortstop or a Rhodes Scholar. All doors were open to him. All he had to do was pick the one he wanted to enter. A career-ending knee injury and the death of his sister, whom he was especially close to, slammed those doors shut. An addictive personality emerged, and Tommy Blake, disillusioned and lost, traded his dreams of glory for drugs, alcohol, and a string of unsuccessful relationships with women. He was, Dantzler knew, a haunted, tragic figure. The classic Magnificent Maybe. Still, he was a man Dantzler loved and respected.

Dantzler knocked, heard Tommy's deep voice from inside inviting him in, and opened the door. Tommy was sitting on the sofa, a glass filled with Chivas Regal and ice in his right hand. He was drunk, or rapidly on his way to getting there. Not unusual for 11 p.m. He looked up at Dantzler through azure eyes that contained both the sparkle of life and the specter of death. A smile creased his still-handsome, thin face.

"Jackie, come in. Sit, take a load off." Tommy motioned to a chair with his free hand while taking another drink. "Unlike Mr. E.A. Poe, I knew exactly who was rapping at my door. Those great powers of deduction of mine at work, you see. The lateness of the hour was the first clue. Also, I knew that no bill collector would be here at this time, nor would a beautiful damsel. And I have few compatriots anymore. Given all that, I could only deduce that it had to be my favorite nephew."

"Your *only* nephew."

"Oh, Jack, if I had legions, you would still be my favorite." He took another drink, his expression turning serious. "As joyous as I am at being graced by your presence, I must inquire—what prompted this visit at such a dreadful hour?"

"I want to know what happened to my father."

Tommy frowned. "You already know. He was killed in Vietnam. Shot by a sniper while on patrol."

"I want details."

"What makes you think I have the details? Why would I? Hell, I wasn't there when he died."

"The man who came by the house that night—he must've told you what happened."

"What man?"

"Dad's combat buddy."

"Jack, that was more than thirty years ago." Tommy held up the glass of Scotch. "How many brain cells do you estimate that I've killed during that time?"

"He didn't just drop by to chat, Tommy. He was here for a purpose—to tell you and mom about dad's death. Come on, Tommy. Think."

"Why do you need to know this now?"

"I just do. I want to know what that guy said to you and mom. I want to know the details of how my father died."

"I honestly don't recall him talking about that at all. What I do remember is that he told us Johnny was a hero, that your dad saved his life."

"How?"

"The guy was wounded, lying out in the open with bullets zipping all around him. Your dad ran out and dragged him back to safety."

Tommy took another drink, his thoughts locked somewhere in the past. "One other thing I remember him telling us," he finally said. "Their squad was ambushed and that Johnny took out all four snipers by himself. Funny how I just remembered that…."

"What else do you remember?"

Tommy shrugged. "That's it. Sorry."

Seeing the look of disappointment on Dantzler's face, Tommy put his glass down and stood. "Wait here for a second," he said. "I have something I want to give you."

Dantzler's eyes wandered around the room, finally settling on three photos lined across the entertainment center. The one on the left showed a uniformed Tommy when he played for the Dodgers' Double-A San Antonio club. On the right, there was a photo of Tommy and Dantzler standing at the net after a tennis match. The center photo, the largest of the three, showed Tommy and Sarah, around the ages of thirteen and ten.

"Here," Tommy said, snapping Dantzler out of his reverie. "Take this and read it." He handed a yellowing envelope to Dantzler. "It's a letter from your dad. The only one he sent me while he was over there. He sent dozens to your mother, just that one to me. I was going to dog his ass about that when he got home."

"Where are the letters he wrote to mom?"

"I have no idea. They weren't in her things, and they aren't here, so I can't tell you where they are. Maybe she burned them or threw them away. Maybe they were too painful to keep."

"She never would have done that."

"No, she wouldn't."

The two men sat in silence for several minutes. Tommy slowly sipped at his Scotch, his eyes hazy from too much alcohol and too many painful memories. Dantzler stared at the envelope, turning it over and over in his hands.

"You know, I got that letter from Johnny about a month before he died." Tommy finished his drink and set the glass on the table. "It's a crazy fuckin' world we live in. You know that, Jackie-boy? My boss at the plant is from fuckin' Vietnam. Shit, he may have fought against your dad—maybe even fired the bullet that killed him—and now I'm working for him. Tell me there's not absurdity in the world."

"No, what's absurd, Tommy, is that my father is dead and I don't really know the circumstances of his death."

"It was a goddamn war. That's all you need to know. Circumstances don't mean a fucking thing."

CHAPTER 33

Dantzler was awakened by a loud knock on the door. He drew himself up to a sitting position and looked at the clock on the stereo. 7:20 a.m. His head was pounding. The empty Pernod bottle lying on the floor by the couch reminded him why. For a split second, he was sure he was going to throw up. But after taking several deep gulps of air, the wave of nausea passed.

He unlocked the door and opened it. "Come in," Dantzler said, his voice coarse as sandpaper.

Eric Gamble entered the house, followed by a man Dantzler didn't recognize. He was medium height, early- to mid-twenties, dressed in khaki pants, a white polo shirt, and loafers. He was, Dantzler quickly concluded, a child of wealth and privilege.

"What's up?" Dantzler said to Eric.

Eric looked at the Pernod bottle, then at Dantzler. "You all right?" he asked.

"I'm fine. I repeat, what's up?"

Eric turned to the man standing beside him. "Russ, this is Detective Dantzler. Tell him what—"

"You sure you're okay?" the man said, looking first at Dantzler, then at Eric.

"Don't I look okay?"

The man chuckled. "Actually, you look like you could use a shower and a shave."

"Happy to hear you say that," Dantzler said. "I'm working undercover. You know, like Serpico. I guess this means my disguise is working."

Eric looked away and fought hard not to laugh.

"And you are?" Dantzler ask.

"Russ Steinberg."

"Abby Kaplan's fiancé."

"Yes."

"Sorry for your loss." Dantzler motioned to the chair across from him. "Please, Russ, make yourself comfortable."

Dantzler looked at Eric and gave a what's-up shrug.
"Russ came by the station this morning looking for you,"
Eric said. "Since I was the only detective there, Dynamite had
him speak with me. I think you should hear what he has to say."
"Didn't Detective Larraby interview you a couple of weeks
ago?" Dantzler asked.
"He did, yes. And I was totally honest with him." Russ
looked away. "But there are some things I left out."
"That's not smart, Russ."
"I know. And I'm sorry."
Dantzler nodded toward Russ. "Let's hear it," he said. "*All*
of it."
"Well, Abby's father, Doctor Kaplan, told me that he had
spoken with you," Russ said. "He told me what you asked and
what he'd said. What Doctor Kaplan told you was the truth…to a
certain degree. But there were some facts that he wasn't aware
of. Things he didn't know."
"Things Abby hadn't told him?"
"Yes. She kept them from him so that he wouldn't worry."
"She was having trouble with an instructor, wasn't she?"
Dantzler said.
"That's right," Russ answered. "How'd you know that?"
"Which instructor?"
"James Roper. In the English department."
"We checked all of Abby's courses and her instructors,"
Dantzler said. "She never had Jim Roper in class."
"No, she didn't. But…let me explain. Before Abby moved
into Jim Winstead's house, she was a dorm director—"
"In Blazer Hall."
Russ nodded. "Well, about six weeks before the murder,
one of the girls in Blazer Hall came to see Abby. Her name is
Deanna Sanders. She had pledged Abby's sorority, and had
become a pretty close friend. Anyway, Deanna had gotten
herself all tangled up with this Doctor Roper."
"An affair?" Dantzler said.
"I don't know if affair is the right word for it," Russ said.
"It was very brief, maybe three weeks. Just a fling, really. Then
Deanna met someone else. A student. Someone more her age.

But when she tried to end it with Roper, he went ballistic. Roughed her up pretty good. Hit her a couple of times, banged her around the room. From the way Abby described it to me, it must have been an ugly scene."

"Did she report it to the police? Or to campus security?"

Russ shook his head. "No. Abby urged her to, but she refused. It's the old story. She didn't want her parents to know about it. Or the administration. Well, Abby was pissed to the max. And being a New Yorker, you know, she wasn't afraid to speak her piece. She went to see Roper. Just stormed into his office one day and read him the riot act. Know what the bastard did? He hit on her. Abby said he just sat there like a boulder, listening with his eyes shut, a smug look on his face. Then when she had finished, he asked her if she'd like to go to dinner and a movie sometime. Said he admired her spunk. Can you believe that? Talk about *chutzpah*."

"Then what happened?" Dantzler said.

"Then it got really bad. Roper began calling Abby a couple of times a day. When she threatened to tell the University officials, he just laughed. Told her to go ahead and do it. He didn't care. Then Abby became convinced that he was stalking her. Maybe he was, or maybe she was just paranoid, I don't know. But she was really scared. That's when I came down and had a little one-on-one session with Doctor Roper."

"When was this?" Dantzler asked.

"Eight days before Abby was murdered."

"Why are you just now telling us this?"

"I don't know. I didn't want Doctor Kaplan to know about it. And I've been pretty fucked up—excuse the language—since Abby was killed. I know I should have."

"What happened when you talked to Roper?"

"Nothing. I laid down the law and he sat there like the chickenshit coward that he is. I told him that if I heard one more complaint from Abby, I'd beat him to within an inch of his life. I swear, I thought the guy was going to break down and cry. You know, I think maybe that's one of the reasons I didn't come forward and tell you guys about him."

"I don't understand. Because he almost cried?"

"No. Because the guy just doesn't look like a murderer. I mean, not someone capable of killing in cold blood. Personally, I don't think the cocky little prick could whip his own shadow." "I've got news for you, Russ. Not every killer looks like Al Capone."

An hour after Eric and Russ had gone, Richard Bird showed up at Dantzler's house. He entered without knocking and went straight to the kitchen, where he found Dantzler standing with a glass of orange juice in his hand.

"That's straight OJ, I hope," Bird said.

"Freshly squeezed and pure as your soul, Rich," Dantzler said. "Says so right on the carton."

"That's the only fresh thing I see." He looked around the kitchen and shook his head in disgust. "Jesus, God, Jack…look at this place. Look at you. What are you trying to be, the world's last dirty hippie? Because if you are, you're succeeding."

"Okay, Rich. Why the buzz saw up your ass?"

"Because I just came from a very unpleasant meeting, that's why. No, let me correct myself. A very unpleasant inquisition. Trust me when I say that I now know how a fish feels when he's about to be gutted and filleted."

"The chief?"

"Along with the mayor, the deputy chief, three city council members, and Ford and Edwards from the FBI—who, as you might've guessed, would be only too happy to step in and give us, and I'm quoting Ford now, 'the lift we need to get the case solved,' unquote."

"I don't want Ford and Edwards anywhere near this case," Dantzler said. "They'd only fuck it up. You know that. Edwards couldn't find his dick without a flashlight, and Ford isn't much better. So, how did you leave it?"

"How did *I* leave it? That's hilarious, Jack. *I* didn't leave it…*I* was told how it's gonna be. We have two weeks to catch our killer or the Feds are taking over. In the meantime, we have to meet with Glenn Rigby—"

"We don't need a profiler, Rich."

"Sorry, Jack, it wasn't a request. The only reason we got those two weeks is because of you. Apparently, his honor and the chief still have faith in the great Dantzler legend."

Bird picked up a stale piece of pizza off the kitchen table. After studying it closely for several seconds, he let it fall back into the box. "If only they could see the great 'legend' now. They'd give the case to the Feds ASAP." He smiled, but only briefly. "Clean yourself up, Jack. The ninth inning is here and we're getting shut out. I need you. At your best."

CHAPTER 34

Dantzler liked Glenn Rigby, always had. He saw the veteran FBI profiler as a stand-up guy, a solid pro and a man dedicated to putting away the bad guys. Rigby, a Medal of Honor recipient for heroism in Vietnam, was tough, fair, and in the minds of many law enforcement officials, the absolute best at his job. Rigby was fine—it was the job part Dantzler didn't care for. Profiling.

In the past two decades, thanks to FBI agents who interviewed notorious serial killers like Bundy, Gacy, and Ramirez, profiling had gained respect and acceptance. Movies and books extolled the virtues and achievements of profilers. Many of them even wrote their own books, offering their unique insights into the twisted minds of men and women who killed.

Dantzler simply didn't buy it. To him, profiling was a high-class voodoo science that offered few, if any, genuine insights into the killer's mind. As Dantzler saw it, most killers weren't all that intelligent to begin with. A few planned their activities carefully, but most killed spontaneously, without a lot of strategy or careful thought. Most killers, serial or otherwise, were little more than jungle predators driven by some primal urge to savage their victims.

What bothered Dantzler most about the notion of profiling was the after-that-fact aspect of it. It had nothing to do with investigative talent or skill. Nothing to do with real insight. He considered profiling as nothing more than glorified Monday-morning quarterbacking. The gathering of questionable information by looking in the rear-view mirror. Dantzler couldn't remember the last time a profiler actually prevented a murder from taking place. That happened about as often as snow in Miami. He had watched profilers interview killers who had already been caught and were behind bars. Men and women who had lied, cheated, deceived, and been world-class bullshitters virtually all their lives. And now, just because a hot-shot profiler sticks a microphone in some scumbag's face, we're supposed to believe what they say? That they have genuinely helpful insights to offer? That they are going to enlighten us? That now, after a lifetime of lying, they are suddenly going to speak the truth?

Talk about bullshit.

To make his case against those who bought into this profiling nonsense, Dantzler pointed to Ted Bundy, one of the rare examples of a serial killer with a legitimately high intelligence level. The FBI profiled Bundy to death, interviewed him dozens of times, yet never once even contemplated pornography as a cause for his murderous rampage or the root of his abnormal personality. But when Bundy was awaiting execution, when his time had finally run out, he blamed pornography for shaping him into the killer he became.

Was he telling the truth? Dantzler doubted it. So did most law enforcement officials. Their take on the matter was simple: Bundy was continuing his steady stream of bullshit, running one last con. Of course, there were those in the psychiatric field who bought into Bundy's con, arguing that he was seeking absolution in his final moments. No one will ever know. But either way, the FBI profilers got it wrong.

Seeing the scowl on Dantzler's face prompted Laurie to work her way to his desk. She walked past, brushing her arm against his neck, and sat across from him. "You hate this, don't you?" she asked.

"Hate's too strong a word. Annoyed is closer."

"Give it a chance, Jack. Some of these guys have done good work, put away some bad people. And Rigby certainly has a glowing rep."

"Rigby's a good guy and I like him. I just think my time would be better spent outside *looking* for this guy rather than stuck here listening to Rigby *talking* about the guy."

Matthews, sitting at the desk next to Dantzler, closed a folder and stood. "She's right, Ace," he said. "Look, I'm an old-school cop, been around a decade or so longer than you, so I'm plenty skeptical about a lot of this modern, new-age stuff. But

I'm not close-minded about it. Maybe it works, maybe it doesn't. Right about now, with four murders unsolved, I'm willing to give anything a chance. Hell, I'd call Miss Cleo if I thought it would help."

Dantzler ripped off a sheet of paper from a legal pad, picked up a pen, and began writing. When he finished, he handed the paper to Laurie, who read it quickly and then handed it to Matthews.

Male, Caucasian, single, early-30s to mid-40s, educated, short, overweight, lifetime of suppressed rage now surfacing, white collar employment, local, probably lives alone, likely a homosexual or has homosexual tendencies, physical similarity of victims means the victims represent a single person.

Matthews finished reading, handed the piece of paper back to Dantzler, and shrugged. "So, what's your point, Ace?" he said.

"That Rigby is only going to tell us stuff we've known all along."

Matthews snickered. "You've always been the ace of aces around here—Mr. Perfect—so whatever methods you used in the past obviously worked for you. Well, you ain't perfect anymore, Ace. And you won't be again unless we catch this joker. So welcome to my world, where ordinary, hard-working cops are happy to accept help anytime they can get it."

"Jeez, Dan, I haven't heard a lecture like that since grad school." Dantzler glanced at Laurie. "People pay big bucks for advice like that."

"I happen to think he's right," Laurie said.

Dantzler grabbed his notepad and stood. "He usually is."

CHAPTER 35

Rose Wessel took a tissue from her purse and dabbed at the tears in her eyes. She looked across the table at Laurie Dunn and shrugged. "Sorry," she said. "It's just that I haven't been in here since…Sitting here now brings back a flood of memories. Abby and I used to eat lunch here two or three times a week. Salads, mostly." She sipped at her water. "I'm sure you know that I own the dance studio five doors down from here," she said. "Been there for almost twelve years now."

"That's why I wanted to meet here. To maybe get more familiar with this area." Laurie touched Rose's arm. "Are you okay with this? If you're not, we can go some place else."

"No, no, I'm fine."

"Thanks for taking the time to meet with me," Laurie said. "I apologize for the short notice."

"It was no trouble at all," Rose said. "I wasn't much help when that Detective Larraby talked to me. Maybe this time I will…" Rose paused, took a deep breath, and gazed out the window. "How long will you continue to look for Abby's murderer?"

"Technically, all unsolved homicide cases remain open forever. Or at least until they're solved. I'm certain this one will remain active until we catch the person responsible."

"I pray to God that you find him," said Rose. "And when you do, I hope…I know I shouldn't say this, but lethal injection is too light a punishment for what he did. His death should be slow and painful."

"I can assure you that we're doing everything we can." Laurie folded her hands together and leaned forward, elbows on the table. "Tell me about Abby."

A smile flashed across Rose's face. "Oh, I could go on for hours about her. She was a truly special human being. An angel. I just adored her."

"How did you meet her?"

"Well...Are you aware that I was once a high school teacher? That I left the profession after being attacked by two former students?"

"No, I wasn't aware of that," Laurie said.

"I taught music and theatre at Lafayette High School. I'd stayed late one night, and as I was leaving these two young men grabbed me and tried to rape me. Fortunately, the basketball team had just finished practicing. When they heard me screaming, coaches and players ran into the parking lot and scared my attackers off before they could do any real harm. Physical harm, that is. Psychologically, I'm not sure I'll ever really get over it."

"Were the two young men caught and punished?"

"Oh, sure. Everybody in the parking lot knew them. They'd just graduated the year before. They were drunk, or stoned. Maybe both. Who knows anymore? They were both sentenced to seven years in prison. Got out in less than three. Funny thing is, one of the boys called to apologize. I told him to forget his apology, that if I had my way he'd spend the rest of his life behind bars. I agonize over my inability to forgive. You'd think that if the pope can forgive the man who shot him, I should find it in my heart to forgive my attackers. But I can't, God forgive me. I suppose that sounds hypocritical. Me asking God's forgiveness when I can't find forgiveness in my own heart."

"And you met Abby after that? After you stopped teaching?"

"Yes, almost five years ago," Rose said. "The high school drama department was doing a production of *West Side Story* and they had asked me to do the music. I play piano. Anyway, it became obvious early in the rehearsals that we needed help with the choreography. The dancing, the movement, they just weren't working. Nothing was really coming together like it should. One of the parents knew Abby, knew about her training as a professional dancer, so we asked her if she'd work with us. Abby was only a freshman or sophomore at the University of Kentucky then. She made that play a success. And the kids...they worshipped her. Then one day, about three years ago, I called her. Right out of the blue. Said I wanted her to come and join the staff at the academy. It was the smartest thing I ever did. That girl was a genuine talent."

"It must give you a great sense of pride to just start up something like that and see it become a success."

Rose nodded. "I had found a vacant space in a ratty old building over on Palumbo. That's where I started the studio. But we didn't have enough room to really do what we had in mind, so when I got a few dollars ahead, I bought the place here. It had once been one of those places where they teach judo, karate, whatever. So it was plenty large enough to accommodate a dance studio. I told Abby to go out and buy a piano that she liked, which she did. A Baldwin, of course. So Abby taught dancing and movement and I provided the music. It was a wonderful time in my life."

"How many students do you have?" Laurie asked.

"Oh, maybe sixty altogether. It's fairly restrictive. I mean, you have to audition to get in. There are classes for different age groups, beginning with the very young. Abby gave private lessons as well. The students who showed real potential were put in an advanced group with her."

"So you guys stayed pretty busy?"

"Yes. But we were having such a good time we never considered it work. We would get here at six in the morning for the early birds and before you knew it, it was dark. Time just flew by."

"Tell me about the night Abby was killed."

Rose took another sip of water and stared down at the table. Tears came into her eyes again. "The thing I remember most is the rain. It was a real flood. Just a very nasty night. High winds, tornado threats—an ugly, ugly night. The beauty salon next door had closed early. And this restaurant, which generally has good evening crowds, was empty. My car was the only one in the entire parking lot. It was a little before eight, and all the students were gone. Except for two—Monica McKendrick and Susan Wallin. They were both waiting for their fathers to pick them up. Abby insisted that I go ahead and leave, but I said I'd stay as long as the girls were there. It must've been about eight when Dan Wallin showed up. He volunteered to give Monica a ride home. Since the Wallins and McKendricks are friends and live in the same neighborhood, we had no problem with that. Parents are always picking up and dropping off kids other than their own."

"So, it's eight. You and Abby are alone."

"I pleaded with her to let me give her a ride home, but she said no, she'd wait for her ride."

"Did she mention the name of the person picking her up?"

"No. I didn't even think to ask. God, how I wish I had."

"Did Abby often rely on others for a ride home?"

"Lord, no," Rose said quickly. "I can't recall it happening more than once or twice previously. No, Abby always drove to work. She was independent as hell. But on that day, if I recall correctly, her car was in the shop being worked on. That's the only reason she was riding with someone else."

"So it was approximately eight, maybe a little after, when you left?" Laurie said.

"Yes. After I became convinced that Abby was going to stay, I decided to go ahead and leave. I've cursed myself a million times for not staying with her. If I had, she'd still be alive."

"Or both of you might be dead."

"I'd prefer to think that things would have turned out differently," Rose said, shaking her head. "There was an old umbrella—I think maybe it had been left there by one of the karate students—and Abby insisted that I take it. That's the kind of person she was, always putting the well being of others ahead of her own. I said goodbye, told her I'd see her in the morning, and walked out into the rain. It was the last time I saw her alive."

"And as far as you know, Monica McKendrick's father never showed up."

"I don't know," Rose said. "I never heard one way or the other."

"What's his name?"

"Mike. Mike McKendrick. He lives in Heritage Estates."

"When you left the parking lot, did you see anyone, or anything, that might seem suspicious?"

"No, not that I recall," Rose said. "I didn't see anyone."

"Is there anything else you can remember about that night? Anything at all?"

"Just the rain. And that it was the last time I saw Abby alive." Her lips quivered. "I just pray that you get a lucky break somewhere along the way and find the person who murdered Abby."

"We'll get him," Laurie said. "Lucky break or not. That's a promise."

CHAPTER 36

When Eldon Wessel learned that Stanford had ousted the women's tennis team from the NCAA Tournament, he made the decision to visit Beverly Diaz on Sunday night. This wasn't an easy decision for him. He was distracted. His thoughts were a jumbled mess. To act now, while his concentration was less than pure, was a questionable choice at best, a stupid one at worse. It could even turn out to be a lethal one.

But Eldon overcame his fears by reminding himself that he had the confidence of a true madman, a true genius. He also possessed the will to silence the swirling winds of insecurity and doubt that tormented him. When those two unwelcome guests paid a visit, he had the weapons to drive them away.

Will, discipline, and patience—the three paths to success.

Eldon was confident that by Sunday evening, he would be his usual calm, focused self.

Eldon had made another decision as well, one that would have monumental repercussions. Beverly Diaz would be his last Chosen One. But not the last of his victims.

That honor would go to Gee and Rose.

CHAPTER 37

No sooner had Dantzler parked in the lot adjacent to the Fine Arts building than a heavy-set campus rent-a-cop came ambling in his direction. Dantzler locked the Forester door and began walking toward the building.

"Hey there, big fella!" the officer yelled. "Unless you've got a permit, you gotta put money in that machine to park in this lot. If you don't, I'm gonna have to ticket you." He took his ticket book from his back pocket and flipped it open. "University rules, you understand?"

Dantzler flashed his gold shield. The officer studied it closely, then shook his head. "That don't get you out of payin' if you ain't here on official police business," he said. "Is this an official visit?"

"Very official," Dantzler said. "Top secret, in fact."

The officer's eyes widened. "Oh, yeah. What's up?"

"Officer..." Dantzler eyed the man's name tag. "Officer Downing, is it?"

"Yeah, Chuck Downing."

"Can you keep a closed mouth, Chuck?" Dantzler looked left and right. "I'm talking hush, hush."

"You bet."

Dantzler leaned close to Downing and whispered in his ear. "I'm here to bang the dean's wife," he said.

Downing quickly pulled back, a look of disgust on his reddened face. "That's just what we need around here, another goddamn clown." He snapped the top of his ballpoint pen. "Official or not, you're gettin' a ticket."

Dantzler smiled and headed up the steps. When he reached the big glass door, Officer Downing was still writing.

Jim Roper's office was located at the far right end of the second floor hallway. The door was slightly ajar, and Dantzler could hear a female voice coming from inside. He knocked twice, then pushed the door open. Roper was standing behind his desk. Sitting across from him was a chubby blonde, obviously a student, who appeared to be extremely agitated and angry. The first thing Dantzler noticed about the young woman were her breasts, which he guessed would easily top out at size 42D.

"Sorry to interrupt, Doctor Roper, but I need to speak with you," Dantzler said. "It's…"

"You will have to wait until later," Roper said. "As you can see, I'm in the middle of a teacher-student conference."

"Sorry," Dantzler said, holding up his shield. "But a teacher-police conference rates a notch higher on the importance scale."

"Police…what…what's this about?" Roper stuttered.

Dantzler looked at the young woman. She stood without saying a word, took her backpack from the floor, and started for the door.

"I have some free time this afternoon," Roper said. "Around three. Come by then and we'll discuss this further."

"Yes, Professor." She left without looking at Dantzler.

Roper sat down and lifted a pipe off his desk. "Mind if I smoke?" he said.

"It's your castle, Professor." Dantzler studied the two large Grateful Dead posters that virtually blanketed one of the walls. "You a Dead Head?"

"An original. In fact, Jerry Garcia was a friend. I knew him for nearly thirty years."

"Never much cared for them."

"That's your problem, Officer…"

"Detective Dantzler. From Homicide"

"How could anyone who wasn't a Grateful Dead fan ever rise to the rank of homicide detective?"

"Amazing, isn't it? Must've been a goof on someone's part."

"Surely." Roper clenched the pipe between his teeth as he spoke. "So, Detective, what on earth brings you to my office?"

"Abby Kaplan."

"Ah, yes, one of our recent murder victims. Dreadful what's happening around here these days. Just dreadful. One can't help but wonder about the impotency of our police department. What with so many unsolved murders."

"I can tell you're really torn up about it," Dantzler said. He sat in the chair once occupied by Miss 42D. "Did you know Abby Kaplan?"

"Obviously, Detective Dantzler, you wouldn't be here if you didn't already know the answer to that question." Roper lit a match and buried the flame in the pipe's bowl. "Yes, I knew her. But only in passing."

"That's not the way I heard it."

"Then you heard wrong." Roper puffed on his pipe until he was satisfied that it was lit. "The version you heard must have come from Russ Steinberg, that gorilla fiancé of the late Miss Kaplan. Pure fiction."

"Suppose you tell me your version, Professor."

"The young lady came on to me and I spurned her. She got extremely angry. Apparently, rejection wasn't something she was used to. One afternoon, she burst in here and began screaming at me. You wouldn't believe the language that came out of her mouth. Vile, filthy language. I threatened to physically remove her if she didn't leave, which she finally did. End of story."

"Until Russ Steinberg paid you a visit?"

"Oh, sure, big macho Russ came in and tried to act real tough," Roper said. "He was here maybe five minutes tops. Said his piece and left. What a jerk. You want my opinion? He probably murdered her. He probably found out she wasn't Miss Purity, that she was banging half the professors on campus, and he was none too happy about it. He goes berserk and kills her."

"You have any evidence that she was sexually involved with other teachers?"

"Not firsthand. But I've heard some things."

"From who?"

"The grapevine."

"What about Deanna Sanders? What was your relationship with her?"

"An easy piece of tail, that's all. I knocked it off a couple of times, then called it quits. You can guess what happened when I ended it. She went nutso on me."

"You must be a real Don Juan, Professor."

"These young women today...such a helpless, pathetic group. Nothing but whiners and crybabies. If this is what the feminist movement has spawned, then I say to hell with Gloria Steinem, Betty Friedan, and the whole lot of them. Their movement failed miserably and I don't mind saying so. What I see is a generation of women who demand equality, who bark their desire to be on equal footing with men, then can't handle it when things don't go to suit them. You know, you can't have it both ways."

"A middle-age college professor having sex with a student doesn't strike me as 'equal footing.' It's kind of like a president and an intern."

"Let me assure you, Detective, Deanna Sanders came on to me. I didn't go after her."

"Why did you beat her up?"

"I didn't."

"She had bruises when she went to see Abby Kaplan."

"That's because she tried to hit me. I was forced to restrain her and to physically carry her from my office. It is highly likely that she was bruised during that encounter. I make no apologies for my actions in that particular instance."

"Tell me, Professor. Where were you on the night of April nineteenth?"

"Get real, Detective. I can't remember where I was three days ago, much less three weeks ago."

"I need a better answer than that, Professor."

"I'll have to check my journal," Roper said. "It's at home. I can call you tomorrow."

"How about I call you tonight? Say around eight?"

Roper shook his head. "Impossible," he said. "I'm tied up tonight from six until midnight."

"With your lady friend?"

"Who? You mean Janie? The woman who was here when you came in?"

Dantzler nodded.

"You've got to be kidding." Roper emptied the pipe's bowl into his hand and dumped the ashes into a trash can. "Tell me, Detective Dantzler, what do you estimate Janie's bra cup size to be?"

"D."

"Exactly," Roper said. "Which matches perfectly her current grade in English lit. Janie's only reason for being here was to plead for a better grade. Believe me, Detective, if I can't do better than that, I'll join a monastery."

Dantzler stood and handed Roper a card. "Call me at that number," he said. "No later than nine tomorrow morning."

"By all means, Detective," Roper said. "No matter what happens, I shan't let you down. We must all do our part to ensure that justice prevails."

CHAPTER 38

"Come up with anything?" Laurie said. She handed Eric a can of Diet Coke.

Eric rolled his chair away from the computer desk and closer to Laurie. "Yes and no," he answered.

"Ah, a man who knows how to cover his ass." She laughed. "Who's yes and who's no?"

"There's nothing on David Langley," Eric said. "I mean, not a thing. No priors, no complaints, not even a single traffic ticket. Zero. The man is seventy-two years old and squeaky clean."

He popped open the can and took a drink. "The same can't be said of Mike McKendrick, though. He's bad news." Eric rolled back around to his computer and punched a key. The screen lit up. "Michael Lee McKendrick. Born July tenth, 1954 in Dothan, Alabama. Served three years in the marines, with one hitch in Vietnam. Honorable discharge. Moved to…"

"Fast forward, please," Laurie said. "Get to the juicy parts."

"McKendrick has been arrested four times," Eric said. "Once for slicing a guy in a bar brawl, and three times for domestic violence. He likes to beat up his wife."

"Ever serve time?"

"Not a day. The bar thing turned out to be self-defense— seems the other guy had the knife. McKendrick took it away from him and sliced off the poor bastard's ear. As for the domestic shit, you can imagine how that played out."

"Yeah, the bruised and battered wife refused to press charges."

"You got it," Eric said. "Counseling was ordered, and they went a few times, but it didn't work. After the third beating, the wife must've figured that enough is enough and decided to find a less-violent spouse. They divorced in seventy nine, and he moved here later that same year. Went to work selling used cars."

"How does a used car salesman afford a place in Heritage Estates?" Laurie asked. "That's pricey turf."

"That's where wife number two comes in," Eric said. "Marsha Lynn McKendrick, nee Marsha Lynn Stocker. First born child of Mary and John Robert Stocker."

"John Stocker, huh?" Laurie snorted. "That certainly explains a lot. It's easy to get a million-dollar house in an expensive subdivision when your father-in-law developed it."

"Did I ever tell you that my old man developed the projects on Charlotte Court?" Eric said. "He did. That's the only way me and mom got in."

"Lucky you." Laurie took the Diet Coke can out of Eric's hand and had a drink. "How long have the McKendricks been married?"

Eric scanned the monitor. "Let's see. They were married on June fifteenth, 1982. In Christ the King Church."

"Hard to believe that a man with Mike McKendrick's past could go this long without reverting to form," Laurie said.

"He has. You can bet money on it. But we're talking high society here. At least, the Stockers are. Those folks don't go public with dirty secrets. They've got too much pride for that. They also have ways of making things like that go away."

"Money is the great cleanser."

"You got that right."

"Thanks for looking this stuff up for me, Eric."

"My pleasure." He turned off the computer, stood, and stretched his arms above his head. "You mind telling me what this is all about? The David Langley thing, I mean?"

"Sarah Dantzler's murder."

"Jack's mother?"

"Yep."

"Is he a suspect?"

"I don't know what he is. All I can tell you is that when I finished going through the file, David Langley was the one name I kept coming back to."

"Wow..."

"Do me a favor, Eric, and don't mention this to anyone. Captain Bird will kill me if he finds out I've spent two minutes away from our investigation."

"Does Jack know?" Eric said.

"He saw me looking at the murder book, but he doesn't know about any of this."

"Are you going to see McKendrick?"

"Yeah. Probably tomorrow."

"Want me to go with you?"

Laurie shook her head. "Nah, I can handle it."

"Watch your step, Laurie. Mike McKendrick isn't someone to take lightly."

CHAPTER 39

A gentle evening breeze, cool for this time of year, kissed Dantzler's face. He breathed deeply, held it for almost a minute, savoring the sweet smell of honeysuckle and pine. The sun, now far to the west, glowed bright orange through the row of trees that lined the narrow street where Jim Roper lived, casting a series of dark shadows across the pavement. Dantzler watched as the shadows were slowly swallowed up by the night's invading darkness. He fought the need for sleep that now engulfed him, fought it the only way he knew how—by forcing his mind to focus on the investigation.

And, more precisely, on James Roper.

Dantzler liked Roper for the killings. Liked him for the oldest of cop reasons—intuition. Dantzler felt it the first moment he laid eyes on Roper. He saw it in Roper's arrogance, in his intense hatred of women, in the way he constantly shifted the blame to others, in the fact that he had access to all four victims. But intuition, which was more often right than wrong, didn't count for much in a courtroom. To prevail on that battlefield, Dantzler would need more than a gut feeling.

The facts and evidence that would get Roper a date with the executioner were buried in the details, waiting to be uncovered. And, Dantzler knew, they eventually would be.

At 9 p.m., exactly to the minute, Dantzler's cell phone rang. He smiled. When Connie Alexander said 9, she didn't mean 8:59 or 9:01.

"Did I wake you, Jack?" she asked.

"Arroused me," he answered.

"Yeah, right." She laughed. "Did you have any trouble finding Jim Roper's place?"

"With your directions, Connie, I could find the Fountain of Youth." He could hear noise in the background. "Sounds like a big party's going on. I always heard those shindigs were dreadfully boring."

"Tell me, how much excitement can you have when two hundred zombies get together? None, that's how much. Save me, Jack. I've landed in the dead zone."

"Is our boy still hanging in?"

"So far, yes. But he looks as bored as I am."

"How much longer do you figure the party will last?"

"I wish you would stop referring to it as a party. It's not. It's the night of the living dead."

"Okay. So how much longer will the morgue meeting last?"

"We just finished dinner. With the speeches and awards, I'd say at least another two hours."

"Good. That gives me plenty of time," Dantzler said.

"Jack, are you sure this is legal?"

"Not exactly. But you didn't hear that from me." Dantzler looked at the clock on his dashboard. "It's two past nine," he said. "I'll be inside for exactly an hour. If Roper decides to check out early, call me. Got it?"

"Yes."

"Don't let him sneak out on you, Connie. It wouldn't be good for me to get caught inside his house."

"I can't believe I'm a co-conspirator in a misdemeanor."

"You're not. This is a felony."

"Jesus. Did you have to tell me that?"

"Relax, Connie. You'll never serve a day over two years."

"That's comforting, Jack."

Jim Roper lived in a small, nondescript two bedroom house at the end of King Street in what was once a grand neighborhood that now had a distinctly lower middle class look to it. To the left was a larger house with a fenced-in yard that was home to a Jungle Jim, a slide, and a sandbox. A sign in the yard said Daley's Day Care Center. To the right, a fence separated Roper's house from an open field, upon which several soon-to-be houses in the next grand neighborhood were in various stages of construction.

Dantzler had no qualms about breaking into Roper's house or any illusions about possible consequences. He had often skirted the law in the name of the law, and if he remained a detective, he would doubtless do it again in the future. He did it with the full understanding that if he got caught, his ass would be hung out to dry. No one would defend him, not in today's ACLU world, where the criminals often seemed to have it better than the victims. And everyone had it better than the cops. It was a risk he was willing to take. When four young women had been brutally murdered, and when it's a virtual certainty that more were going to die, you operated by necessity, not by the law. Rules, the law…that can be sorted out later by the suits in a courtroom. All that mattered now was finding and stopping a murderer.

Dantzler wasn't looking for evidence. Anyway, evidence found during an illegal search, no matter how incriminating, wasn't worth a penny in court. What he wanted was confirmation that his hunch about Jim Roper was correct.

Something. Anything.

He walked slowly between the fence and Roper's house, dodging the overhanging tree limbs that threatened to decapitate him. When he reached the back of the house, he bent down, picked up a small rock, and tossed it into the yard. He wanted to make sure an angry dog wasn't planning a surprise attack, although he doubted that Roper was the pet-owning type. Hearing no sound other than the rock hitting the ground, he went onto the back porch and checked to see if the door was locked. It was. Holding the small flashlight in his teeth, he pulled up on a window and it slid open. He crawled through the opening, scooted across the kitchen counter, and dropped to the floor.

Once he got accustomed to the darkness, he realized that the house was a slightly refurbished old shotgun shack with small rooms on either side of the narrow hallway. Dantzler made a quick trip down the hall, double checking to make certain he was alone. His recon mission revealed that he did indeed have the place to himself, and that the house consisted of two bedrooms, a kitchen, one bathroom, a living room, and a tent-size den. In the smaller of the two bedrooms, a laptop computer lay open on a wooden table in one corner, and a universal workout station, which appeared to be brand new, stood like a shining iron robot in the opposite corner.

Dantzler decided to concentrate on that room. It was obvious from the clutter that Roper spent the majority of his time there, most likely at the computer. Dozens of manuscripts, each with several rejection letters clipped to them, lay on the floor around the desk. Connie was right—Roper was a frustrated writer. Dantzler picked up a manuscript titled *The Fires of Hell* and began leafing through it. On Page 21, one of the characters—a college professor named Ripley—while speaking to a colleague, says, "You remember what Rimbaud said, don't you? How hell has no power over pagans? Well, I happen to believe that. I believe it down to my very soul. It is the pagans who rule the fires of hell."

A cold snake began to slither up Dantzler's spine.

This was precisely what he was looking for.

He searched the desk drawers and the closet but found nothing of interest. Plenty of clothes, papers, and books, but little else. It was only by accident, only when he was on his way out of the room, that he saw the stack of books on the floor behind the universal machine. There were six altogether, oversize hardcover picture books featuring the works of Renoir, Rembrandt, Raphael, Blake, Picasso, and Michelangelo.

The Michelangelo book lay on top. Two pages near the front had been dog eared. He opened to the marked pages. And saw the body of dead Jesus lying across Mary's lap. The *Pietà* seen from different perspectives. One photo showed a close-up of the wound on Christ's hand. One showed the agony on Mary's beautiful face. Still another showed Michelangelo's sculpted name on the cloth worn by Mary.

Dantzler closed the book.

"Gotcha."

On his way home, Dantzler stopped off at a liquor store and bought a bottle of Pernod and some fresh orange juice. The discoveries at Roper's place had made him almost delirious with excitement, and he knew the Pernod would help calm him down.

He needed to be calm now, to think things through, to plan the best way to go after Jim Roper.

When he got home, he quickly slipped off his socks and sneakers, mixed a drink, and turned on the CD player. Sitting on the floor with his back against the sofa, he took a sip of Pernod, laid his head back, and closed his eyes.

Leonard Cohen's words mixed with Russ Steinberg's.

*He was just some Joseph looking for a manger...*the guy just doesn't look like a murderer...*he'll say, I told you when I came I was a stranger...*not someone capable of killing in cold blood... *please understand I never had a secret chart to get me to the heart of this, or any other matter...*the cocky little prick...*and it comes to you, he never was a stranger.*

Not anymore, Dantzler thought, taking another drink of Pernod.

He saw Laurie Dunn several seconds before she knocked on the door. She'd hesitated, he knew, unsure of whether to follow through or leave. She knocked. He was pleased that she did.

"I hope you don't mind," she muttered. "I didn't realize it was past midnight until I was on the porch."

"It's a pleasant surprise," he said, leading her into the living room. "Care for a drink?"

She eyed his glass suspiciously. "What is that concoction?"

"Pernod and orange juice. Rather tasty, I must say."

She picked up the glass and sniffed. "I think I'll pass on this," she said, grimacing. "Got any beer?"

"Check the fridge," he said. "You may find a leftover from the last time Rich was here."

A moment later she came back into the living room, holding a bottle of Bud Light in her hand. She plopped down on the floor next to him. "Who are we listening to?" she asked.

"Leonard Cohen."

"Never heard of him."

He chuckled. "That doesn't surprise me. He's a little ahead of your time."

"So was Jesus Christ, but I've heard of him."

"Yeah, well, only because Jesus had a better publicist."

"Proving once again that PR is everything." She looked at a photo of Sarah Dantzler on the bookcase, then back at him.

"May I ask you a question about the night your mother was killed?"

"No."

"Why?"

"Because I know what you're going to ask and I don't want to go there."

"How can you possibly know what I'm going to ask?"

"I just know, that's all."

"I like this song," she said. "What's it called?"

"Hey, That's No Way to Say Goodbye."

She closed her eyes and listened. A smile came across her face. "I'm not looking for another as I wander in my time," she said, quoting the lyrics. "That could be about you, couldn't it?"

"It could be about a lot of people."

"I've decided that I like Leonard Cohen," she said. "Even if…"

Dantzler leaned across and kissed her softly on the lips. "Even if what?" he said, holding her close.

"Even if his songs aren't about you."

He kissed her again. "Are you okay with this?"

"Yes."

"You sure?"

Laurie nodded, got to her feet, then began walking toward the bedroom.

Dantzler turned off the CD player and followed her into the bedroom.

At 4:45 a.m., as Dantzler lay close to Laurie, Eldon Wessell was putting a large manilla envelope into Dantzler's mailbox. Off to the east, Eldon could see the first tracings of sunrise, his favorite time of the day. As he drove home, he wondered if the lovely Beverly Diaz would rise early enough to see the sunrise.

He hoped she would.

CHAPTER 40

Dear Jack:

Pardon my audacity, but I must tell you how terribly concerned I am about your health. I saw you on television a few days ago and you looked awful. You must take better care of yourself. More rest, better diet, a consistent exercise program...all the things that give us good health and longer lives.

Good health is, beyond a shadow of a doubt, our most-treasured possession. Without it we cannot reach our full potential as human beings. And you do have so much potential, Jack. So, please, take better care of yourself.

There, now, having preached my sermon, I will come down out of the pulpit. It's not my nature to be preachy—I'm much more of a listener—but in this instance, where your health and well-being are concerned, I felt a strong need to warn you of impending doom should you continue to neglect yourself.

Of course, it hasn't escaped me that I am the reason you're looking so run-down. I feel somewhat guilty about that, but given the nature of our disparate roles in this little drama, it's a problem that can't be avoided. We are intertwined, you and I, which means we'll each have to make certain concessions. Above all, though, my concerns for your health are very genuine. Self-serving, perhaps, but definitely genuine. After all, you are my adversary, and I want you to be at the top of your game. When I win—and I will win—I don't want the sweet taste of victory diluted because the challenger was unfit for combat. No hollow victories for me.

So, Jack, moving on.

What did you think of my latest choice? Deborah Tucker? Quite delicious, don't you agree? I selected her from among thousands of candidates. So many faces pass me every day, so many young, taut, evocative bodies stroll past, unaware that they are auditioning for the role of victim. Oh, Jack, what a wonderful parade it is!

How do I make my final choice? Who knows? Instinct, mainly. That's the basis for most of our really tough decisions, wouldn't you agree? We pound things out in our head, trying to be rational or intellectual, then throw everything out the window and go with what we feel in our gut. I dare say you've solved many cases by going with your gut-level instincts rather than your intellect, which I know is prodigious. So you know what I'm talking about, Jack. We aren't so different, you and I, not as far apart as our respective roles might lead one to believe. In some ways, perhaps, we are simply flip sides of the same coin.

Jack, let me ask you...where is the newspaper coming up with its information? Did you read yesterday's story? Pure, unadulterated fiction. Absolutely sloppy investigative reporting. The young lady who wrote the story quoted some buffoon from the police department who continues to say, "The perpetrator of these hideous crimes is your classic night stalker."

Night stalker? Me? Hardly. I'm almost always home by 8:30 and safely tucked into bed by 11. No night owl, I.

Where do these people come up with such empty information? Doesn't anyone have a checks and balances system when it comes to disseminating information? What about facts? Shouldn't people in such important positions—law enforcement officials, politicians, reporters, etc.—have some inkling that what is being stated has some validity and isn't grounded in rumors and innuendo? Responsibility, my friend; people need to be more responsible. It's a character trait that has all but been lost in this country. A sad commentary, but a true one.

Of course, I'm well aware that it wasn't you who called me a "classic night stalker." You're far too wise and insightful to make such a boneheaded statement. Much too good a detective to ever come up with such an asinine conclusion. Already, you've learned much about my character habits, haven't you? You know I don't need to stalk anyone, that these poor wenches know me and that they gracefully accept me into their place of residence. I'll clue you to something else, Jack: They all had a smile on their face when they opened the door and bade me entrance.

Oh, how that must infuriate you, knowing that these lovely young women, not yet in full bloom, are being sent to their graves by a trusted acquaintance. Killing someone you know is the ultimate breech of trust, isn't it? I regret this appalling conduct—normally, I'm a person you can trust with your life (an odd choice of words)—but once again, this situation forces us to alter our usual standards of behavior.

I am hungry, Jack. Ravenous. My appetite must be satisfied. And it will be. Soon. I promise.

Enough of my self-indulgence... let's talk about you. Are the nightmares getting worse? I would imagine they are, judging by your appearance these days. It's obvious you're not getting enough restful sleep, which is one of the real cornerstones of good health. You simply must take better care of yourself. I cannot stress that enough.

Oh, Jack, how I wish we could sit down together and discuss your nightmares. I'd love to hear about them. Why my interest? Because I created your nightmares. I am the author of your dreams, the architect of your agony, the alpha and omega of your torment. I was there at the beginning, Jack, and I will be with you until the end. I am in your head, just as surely as blood is in your heart.

But how can this be, since we've never met? (Or have we?) Because...no, Jack, not now, not yet. You must wait for that apocalyptic split-second of enlightenment when the secrets of your nightmares are unlocked and revealed. It shan't be long, either. Promise.

The question begs: Do you really want to learn the secrets of your nightmares? Not many of us do, though we say otherwise. Fear is a frightening thing, isn't it, Jack? Fear of the unknown (in this case, the unknown being the mysteries lurking within) is even more frightening. Can you handle what you might find? Are you prepared to deal head-on with the demonic forces that are haunting you?

Do you believe in demonic forces, Jack? The devil as an entity of pure evil? Tell me, I'd love to know. You being a *philosophy wizard, I doubt that you believe in things like the devil or God. (Forgive me if I'm overstepping my bounds. I don't want to make a fool of myself, but I am curious.) Down through the ages, philosophers are divided on such concepts as God and Satan. Kierkegaard, for one, was a firm believer in God; Sartre wasn't. Yet both are considered existentialists. Peculiar, isn't it?*

(I know this may come as a surprise to you, Jack, but I do not believe in the devil. Personally, I don't think the human species has much need for dear old Lucifer. We do plenty well without him.)

How presumptuous of me to lecture you on anything dealing with the subject of philosophy. After all, it is you, not I, who has a Ph. D in the subject. You have completed that pesky dissertation by now, haven't you? If you haven't, you should. I don't want to come off as a nagging mother (like mine), but you should always complete what you start. Leaving a task unfinished is unforgivable. Consider what the world would have missed had Leonardo not completed the Mona Lisa or Michelangelo the Sistine Chapel ceiling (or the Pietà). How appalling.

Jack, are you now beginning to understand how much I know about you? How very inside your life I am? I'm the stigma inside the flower. The explosive inside the bomb. May I be so brazen as to borrow a line from Christ…"I am with you always, even until the end of the world."

Sleep well, Jack.

Sincerely,

Mike L. Angelo

PS: "Mais ou sont les neiges d'antan?"

CHAPTER 41

"Any idea what that PS shit means?" Richard Bird said.

"Do I look like Charles DeGaulle?" Dantzler said.

"More like Charles Manson, I'd say." Bird poured coffee into a cup. "So, am I correct in assuming that it is French?"

"You assume correctly."

"Know what it says?"

"My French is a little rusty, but I think it says, 'where are the snows of bygone years.' Or maybe it's the 'snows of yesteryear.' Either way, that's fairly close."

"Who wrote it?"

"Don't know. More Rimbaud would be my first guess."

"Take it to Connie," Bird said. "Have her identify the author."

They were sitting alone at the kitchen table in Dantzler's house. Bird had showed up unannounced with his youngest daughter Nicole, who had discovered the manilla envelope when Dantzler sent her to get the Saturday newspaper and the mail. They arrived no more than five minutes after Laurie had pulled out of the driveway. *"Thank you, lord,"* Dantzler muttered when he saw Bird and Nicole standing on the porch. He knew that Bird would have been one pissed-off boss if Laurie had been there. That was a battle Dantzler wasn't ready to fight.

"He's ready to kill again, Jack," Bird said, sipping at his coffee. "And soon is my guess."

"I think I know who he is," Dantzler said.

Bird set the cup down, spilling coffee onto the table. "I'm all ears, Jack," he said. "Give me a name, please."

"Jim Roper."

"Connie's weird teacher friend?"

"He's our guy, Rich. I'm convinced of it."

"Oh, yeah. Why do you like him so much?"

"Last night, I made a visit to his house. I found—"

"Oh, shit," Bird groaned. "Do I really want to hear this?"

"I found a book on the works of Michelangelo. It was earmarked at pages related to the *Pietà*. Also, in one of his manuscripts, he quoted Rimbaud. 'Hell has no power over pagans.' It's the same line he used in the first letter."

"Coincidences."

"Too obscure, too esoteric to be mere coincidences. Come on, Rich, think about it. There just aren't that many people running around quoting Rimbaud. And the same line at that. What are the odds?"

"Connie says he can't be our man."

"Connie's wrong."

"Even if you're right, there's not much we can do about it," Bird said. "Not now, at least. Your little visit to his house was illegal, so we obviously have no grounds for a search warrant. You really screwed us there, Jack."

"I did what I had to do."

"Next time, try to play within the rules. You know, just in case we do get lucky and catch him."

"You seldom catch guys like this by living inside the rules, Rich. You know that."

Bird shook his head and let out a deep breath. "Jesus, Jack, one of these times you're gonna fuck up so bad that no one's gonna be able to save your ass. You know that?"

"It's worth the risk."

"Let's see if you feel that way when you get caught."

"He's our guy, Rich. We've got to find a way to bring him down."

"Okay, I'll play along. We'll set up around-the-clock surveillance on him. Starting right now."

"He's a night predator, so I don't expect anything to happen until after dark," Dantzler said. "Put a couple of uniforms on him until then. If he goes mobile, tell them to make sure they don't get made. I don't want this guy to even suspect that we're on to him."

"What about night surveillance?"

"I'll put Laurie and Eric on him tonight. They can flip a coin to see who gets the midnight watch. Tomorrow, I'll inform the others, let them work out a rotation system."

"And you?" Bird asked. "Where will you be?"

"Trying to come up with a plan, in case he doesn't try anything this weekend."

"I'm not even going ask what that plan might be," Bird said. "However, if it is at all possible, please make it a plan that will help our side, and not one that is so shady that it will be bounced out of court should we ever get that far. I do not want to see some slick shyster get this man off because of the dreaded technicality, otherwise known as a police fuckup. Is that clear?"

"Let's catch him first, Rich. Then we'll worry about technicalities."

"That is not the answer I wanted to hear," Bird said.

When Dantzler arrived at the police station, he found Andy Waters sitting in the first floor lobby, reading the newspaper. "Andy Waters," he said. "My favorite newspaper scribe."

Waters folded his paper, stood, and extended his right hand.

Dantzler took it. "Anything worth reading in that rag of yours?" he said.

"Oh, yeah. Martha Stewart is adapting well to life as a convicted felon," Waters answered. "Says so right here, in 'Names in the News.' Now that's important shit, Jack. Martha Stewart's personal welfare. I mean, we all want to know about that, don't we?"

"It tops my list of interests."

"How could it not?"

"What's a heavyweight scribe like you doing out on a Saturday morning?" Dantzler said. "Must be something big in the works."

"What's the matter, Jack? Can't a guy drop by to check on an old friend without having his motives questioned?"

"You never 'drop by' unless you want something? What is it this time?"

"To share information," Waters said.

"About?"

"The on-going search for a serial killer, what else?"

"I don't have anything to share," Dantzler said.

"You sure about that?"

"Yeah. Listen, Andy, we've told you guys everything we can afford to tell you. And we'll continue to do so in the future. You know how the game is played. Some things have to be kept under wraps."

"Mind answering a few questions for me? Just to see if I'm on the right track?"

"On or off the record?"

"Let's start with on."

"Okay, shoot."

"True or false. You're one-hundred percent certain that all the women were killed by the same man."

"False?"

"Really?"

"I'd say, more like ninety percent."

"Why the ten-percent hedge?"

"Because the killer used a belt to strangle the first victim. The last three were strangled with a silk scarf."

"True or false. All the women were sexually assaulted."

"False."

"Were any of them?"

"The evidence doesn't indicate any sexual activity at all."

"True or false. You're close to making an arrest."

"Let's cut the bullshit, Andy. You know the answer to these questions as well as I do. What are you really here for?"

"I have a source who's clued me into a few things, Jack. And you know what? Everything he told me has been corroborated by two other sources. Now, I'm here as a courtesy to you, Jack. Out of respect for our friendship and for the fact that you've always been square with me in the past. There's a story running in tomorrow's edition based on the information provided by my source. It's gonna be a bombshell. I'm here to give you a chance to respond, to put your spin on it."

"Who's the source?"

"Come on, Jack. I'm offended that you'd even ask such a question."

"What did your source tell you?"

"Little ditties about postcards with a picture of the *Pietà* on it. Signed Mike L. Angelo. A Saint Jude medal in the victim's vagina. Laceration of the jugular—post-mortem. How's my source doing so far, Jack?"

"Off the record?"

"Sure."

"All that stuff is true. But you can't run it. Not tomorrow, anyway. Hold off for a week. Until next Sunday. If nothing has happened by then, you have my blessing to print it. And if something does break, you get it first. Exclusively. You have my word on it."

"It's too late for deals, Jack. The story's running tomorrow. With or without your comments."

"You know what this will do?"

"Yeah. Give the readers certain facts that you've withheld."

"Withheld for a reason. To separate the crazies who confess from the real killer. Right now, he's the only one who knows all the details. You print that story tomorrow and everybody knows everything. Nut cases will burn up the phone lines confessing. It could even trigger copycat killings. Some fruitcake will start offing young women just for the chance to stuff Saint Jude up their pussy."

"Sorry, Jack, but it's out of my hands. My editors are on this one Barry Bonds on a fastball."

"That's bullshit and you know it. You carry weight in that place. If you make a strong enough case to hold onto the story for a couple of days, they'll listen."

"And then my source goes to another rag. Or to the TV guys. We get burned. *I* get burned. No, Jack, it's not worth the risk."

"Then withhold one of the details. Leave out the stuff about the Saint Jude medal. That'll at least give us one fact known only to the killer and to us."

Waters looked away.

"I need that name, Andy. I *want* that name."

"Can't do it. Sorry. You know the rules."

"Off the record. You tell me. I'll say I found out from another cop. One of the uniforms or techs at the crime scene. Your name will never come up."

"Nice try, Jack. But professional ethics being what they are, I simply cannot do it."

Waters started walking toward the front entrance, stopped, and turned back toward Dantzler. "About the other thing...I'll plead your case for that. I can't make any promises, but I will make the pitch."

"Pitch hard," Dantzler said.

CHAPTER 42

Eldon Wessell allowed himself the rare luxury of sleeping in. Normally, he didn't distinguish between weekdays or the weekend, preferring instead to keep to his standard routine of rising early enough to watch the sun climb over the eastern skyline. To remain in bed, or "sleep in" as it was most-often referred to these days, was anathema to Eldon. Only young children, the aged, the sick, or the infirm should be allowed to sleep late. Everyone else should rise early, face the day with vigor and make the most of it. After all, as T.S. Eliot reminded us, all time is unredeemable. The clock is ticking; better make time count while we have it.

When Eldon rolled over and looked at the digital clock on the table next to his bed, the green numbers read 11:47 a.m. Under normal circumstances, Eldon would have been appalled by such sloth-like behavior. But on this rapidly vanishing morning, he wasn't bothered in the least. He'd been out until almost five in the morning performing his postal duties—What'd you think of this letter, Jack?—and hadn't gotten to bed until a few minutes before six. The extra sack time was necessary for him to regain his own strength and vigor.

Eldon knew without looking out at the driveway that his car would be the only one there. Gee and Rose followed ancient Saturday rituals that never changed. Gee went shopping at the downtown fruit and vegetable market every Saturday, where she hooked up with two friends. Then, after finishing with their shopping, the three old battleaxes headed off to the Cracker Barrel for a late breakfast. Rose spent her Saturday mornings giving piano lessons to Glenda Farmer, a sixteen-year-old paraplegic who was confined to a wheelchair.

Eldon had the house to himself.

He filled the tub with water, tested to make sure it wasn't too hot, and, after concluding that the temperature was perfect, he climbed in.

Almost instantly, his thoughts were on Beverly Diaz. Just as quickly, he was fully erect. Taking his penis in his hand, he began to slowly masturbate. He closed his eyes, thinking, drifting into a world only he was allowed to visit.

He could hardly wait until tomorrow night when, at last, he would see her in all her glory. He would, once again, touch her arm, feel the skin's smoothness, the soft down that delighted him so. Caress her breasts, her well-muscled legs. See the dark forest between her legs. He made himself a promise to spend extra time with her. To savor every detail, to fully appreciate the time he spent with her.

Beverly Diaz was his finest Chosen One.

And his last.

Eldon felt the wave of pleasure surging toward him. He squeezed his penis hard, like he'd done hundreds of times in the past, but this time something went wrong. The pleasure overtook him, sending shock waves of orgasmic pleasure coursing through his body. Semen shot from his penis like lava from a volcano, falling back onto the bath water, then drifting like a float toward the side of the tub.

Eldon was stunned, virtually in tears, upset by his lack of discipline. Never…never before had this happened to him. Never had he been unable to control the pleasure when it threatened to overtake him. He had always controlled his own destiny, mastered his own body. This was the ultimate sign of weakness.

Eldon believed in omens, good and bad. This was a bad omen. He had to take stock, try to figure out what it meant, what went wrong. Maybe it meant he should forget about Beverly Diaz. Find another Chosen One. There were plenty to choose from, no question about it, so why not do so? No reason to act unwisely.

"Calm down," Eldon whispered. *Think logically. Accidents happen. Look for reasons. It's because I was out late, because I slept in. My body clock is out of whack. There…that's it. Nothing to get alarmed about. Accidents happen. Everything will be fine. I'll get to bed early tonight, get up at the usual time. Get back into my natural patterns, my natural rhythm. What happened just now is an aberration. Tomorrow, I'll be back to my old self.*

His breathing once again under control, Eldon looked at the clumps of semen that floated on the water between his legs. As he started to get out of the tub, he was suddenly overwhelmed with a tremendous feeling of excitement. He stood frozen, paralyzed by a realization that was at once both thrilling and terrifying.

Tomorrow night, he was going to do something he'd never done before.

He was going to fuck the Chosen One.

CHAPTER 43

By early afternoon the gray cloud cover had lifted and given way to a clear sky and blazing sun. The expected high of seventy five had been passed an hour ago. The weather folks were now predicting the temperatures to reach the mid-eighties, with, of course, the ever-present codicil "and the chance of a thunderstorm."

Laurie rolled up the window and turned on the AC. She was driving to Heritage Estates, located on the western edge of the city. The land had once been part of a horse farm that had gone belly-up in the early eighties. John Stocker purchased the land at auction for almost nothing, then developed it into what was now the most exclusive property in town. The most expensive houses, none of which were assessed at less than three million dollars, circled a large lake. Others, ranging in price from $900,000 to two million, were scattered at various intervals throughout a wooded area where a great Civil War battle had been fought. A private eighteen-hole golf course, with clubhouse, tennis courts, and swimming pool, was also part of the package.

Thanks to Heritage Estates, John Stocker had gone from being rich to being filthy rich.

Laurie drove her VW Jetta up to the guard shack, rolled down the window, and flashed her shield. The attendant, a sandy-haired man with a nametag that said Simon, took the shield, brought it close to his face, and studied it with great intensity. To Laurie, the old codger looked like a grandfather who'd just been handed his first porn magazine and was hell bent on memorizing every detail.

Finally, after almost a minute, he handed the shield back to Laurie. "Who you here to see?" he asked.

"Mike McKendrick," she answered, putting the shield back into her purse.

"Mad Mike," he said, chuckling. "He lives on the lake. Fifth house on the left. The second biggest house on the property. Second only to John Stocker."

"His father-in-law, right?"

"Right."

"Why do you call him Mad Mike?" Laurie said.

"Because of his temper, that's why."

"Mike's a hot head?"

"You better believe it."

"Have you had trouble with him?"

"Yeah, me and just about everyone who lives here. Well, I ought to say, they've had trouble with him. Me, he just bitches at, 'cause I'm nothing but hired help, which makes me a nobody in his eyes. I need the job, so I can't say much when he goes off on me. He cussed me out once just for taking a bathroom break. Like he never has to answer nature's call."

"Sounds like an unpleasant man," Laurie said. "The others, the ones who live here, he's clashed with some of them?"

"Some? Make that virtually all of 'em. 'Specially on the golf course. See, Mike cheats like a son of a bitch. People out here take their golf seriously, know what I mean? And they don't cotton to cheaters. But when they call Mike's hand on it, he just goes off. Says they're all crazy, that he don't have to cheat to beat those bums. Things like that. Last summer, he beat the daylights out of Marv Simmons. Sent him to the hospital for a week."

"Did Marv press charges?" Laurie asked.

"Nope. It's easier, and more advantageous financially, to keep some things quiet."

"John Stocker paid for his silence, right?"

"Hundred thou, from what I hear. But you didn't get that from me."

"I guess it pays to turn the other cheek."

"Does for some people, that's for certain."

"Thanks for the info," Laurie said. "And if I catch Mad Mike cheating at golf, I'll look the other way."

"That'd be the prudent thing to do," Simon said, waving her past the gate.

Mike McKendrick was on the front lawn playing catch with a young boy Laurie figured to be about ten. The boy wore a pinstripe baseball uniform that had Yankees scripted across the front. Number 2. Must be a Derek Jeter fan, Laurie thought.

Laurie pulled into the driveway and got out of the car. McKendrick pounded the ball into his glove as he watched her coming toward him. The expression on his face was not one of warmth or welcome.

"Come on, Dad, throw me the ball," the boy pleaded.

McKendrick tossed the ball to his son, who caught it smoothly. "Throw some against the steps," he said. "You need to work on fielding grounders."

"But I want to pitch some, Dad. Come on. Please."

"Do what I said," McKendrick ordered, pointing toward the steps, "while I see what this pretty little lady wants."

The boy did as he was told, throwing the ball against the concrete steps, then scooping up the grounders that came shooting back at him.

McKendrick walked over to Laurie, the grim expression on his face unchanged.

"Your son's pretty good," Laurie said. "Bet he plays shortstop."

"And pitcher," McKendrick said.

"How is he with the bat?"

"What are you, a scout?"

"No. Just interested, that's all."

"If I were a betting man, I'd lay down a bundle that you're a cop."

"You'd be a wealthy man."

"You mean, a *wealthier* man," he corrected. "I'm already wealthy."

"Must be nice. Me, a lowly civil servant, I wouldn't know."

McKendrick shrugged indifferently. "What's on your mind, cop lady? Why'd you drive all the way out here to see me?"

"I'm investigating a murder that—"

"Seems like a lot of that's going around here these days. Makes me wonder about the efficiency of our police department. Makes me think that maybe you cop folks are spendin' too much time at the Dunkin' Donuts."

"Don't much care for doughnuts. Too many calories."

McKendrick eyed her up and down. "You could stand to put on a pound or two," he said. "Man likes a woman to have some meat on her bones."

"I appreciate the concern, Mike, I really do. But I'm not here to discuss my weight."

"What are you here for?"

"I need to ask you a few questions, if you don't mind."

"Fire away, lady. Ask me anything. Wouldn't want you wasting gas driving all the way out here for nothing."

"I'm investigating the murder of Abby Kaplan. Your daughter's dance instructor. Can you recall—?"

"Hell, lady, you're a little behind the times, aren't you? That was what, three, four weeks ago? You've got fresher cases you ought to be looking into. Like that Tucker girl who got whacked."

"Whacked? You've been watching too many episodes of 'The Sopranos.'"

"Why in the hell are you talking to me? I got nothing to tell you."

"On the night Abby Kaplan was murdered, you were on your way to pick up your daughter. But Monica got a ride home with Dan Wallin and his daughter."

"So what? That's no big deal."

"What time did you get to the dance studio?"

"You gotta be fuckin' kidding, right? How am I supposed to remember that?"

"You did get there at some point during the night, correct?"

"Well, I suppose so…" McKendrick shook his head. "No, come to think of it, on the night that chick bought it, I didn't get there. It was raining like hell that night, right? Yeah, now I remember. I passed Dan on the way in. I saw the two girls in the front seat, so I turned around and came on home. Never made it to the studio."

"You're positive?"

"Damn straight. So scratch my name off your list of suspects."

"Dan Wallin will corroborate this if I ask him about it?"

"I don't know what Dan will say. He and I ain't exactly friendly these days."

"Why? Did he catch your shenanigans on the golf course?" Laurie said.

McKendrick's eyes became slits. "What the hell's that supposed to mean?" he growled. "What's that rat bastard been sayin' about me?"

"I've never spoken to the man," Laurie said. "It's just that, well, you don't have a glowing reputation around here. I doubt that you'll be voted Mr. Heritage Estates anytime soon."

"Like I could give a fuck. Let me tell you something, little lady. These highbrow humps out here don't mean dick to me. I can buy out all of them, I don't care how uppity-up they are."

Laurie got in the car, closed the door, and rolled down the window. She looked up at McKendrick and gave him a big smile. "I'm sure you can," she said, adding, "as long as dear old J.R. keeps slipping the cabbage your way."

"What's that supposed to mean?" McKendrick said through clenched teeth.

"That it's easy being rich with someone else's money."

She gunned the motor and squealed away, leaving him standing red-faced and fuming in the driveway.

CHAPTER 44

Dantzler used his cell phone to call Eric and tell him to take the first shift watching Roper. Eric offered a mild protest, arguing in favor of Laurie on the grounds that he had a hot date with a woman he'd been pursuing for months.

"Hate to do it to you, pal," Dantzler said, "but this guy's an after-dark killer who prefers the weekend. If he goes prowling tonight, I want you on him."

"You really think this Roper dude is our man?" Eric asked.

"He looks good to me," Dantzler answered. "We got another letter from him today. He put it in my mailbox sometime last night."

"The man does have some rather large testicles," Eric said. "What time do you want me on him?"

"Say about eight. A couple of unnies have him until then. I'll have Laurie relieve you around two. Or if I'm feeling up to it, maybe I'll take a shift."

"I'm not familiar with that neighborhood," Eric said. "Anybody gonna get upset seeing a black guy sitting in a car at midnight?"

"In that neighborhood, you'll be the best-dressed, richest guy on the block."

"Hell, that can be more dangerous than being black and poor," Eric laughed.

"Just keep this guy on your radar," Dantzler said. "And if he does go out, and if problems should arise, do what you gotta do."

"With pleasure."

After punching off with Eric, Dantzler drove over to Connie Alexander's condo just off Nicholasville Road. She wasn't home, so he wrote out the French phrase and his translation on a small yellow Post-it and put it on her front door. On a second Post-it, he wrote a brief note asking her to come up with an author's name and get back to him ASAP. He signed it, "Love, Mike L. Angelo."

It was closing in on three p.m. when Dantzler left Connie's place. He got back on Nicholasville Road and headed downtown. Traffic was unusually light for a Saturday afternoon, so he made the trip in less than fifteen minutes. Once downtown, he quickly found a parking spot on West Short Street, across from Coyle's All-Night Diner.

His cell phone rang just as he was about to get out of his car. It was Connie.

"Have you suddenly developed an interest in French poetry, or did your new pen pal strike again?" Connie said.

"I'll give you two guesses."

"Mr. Pompous Wordsmith."

"You got it."

"Well, I'll give him credit, he's one eclectic son of a bitch."

"More Rimbaud?"

"No. You have to go back about three centuries before Rimbaud to find this guy."

"I give up, teacher. Who are we talking about?"

"Villon."

"Francois?"

"Very good, Jack. You can now move to the head of the class. How'd you know that?"

"I've read some of his stuff. Like him a lot, actually. What grade do I get for my translation?"

"An A-plus," Connie said. "It's Medieval French, which is a little different from what they speak nowadays. But you nailed it. 'Where are the snows of bygone years?' It's from his poem *Le Testament.* Or The Testament to us English speakers."

"Can you get me a copy of the entire poem? In English, of course."

"No problem. Pete DeMoisey teaches Villon. He'll have all kinds of books on him. I'll get one of his."

"Thanks, Connie. One more deed and you're on the payroll."

"Do I get a badge?"

"Yep. Just like the one Elvis got when Nixon made him an honorary cop."

"Me and The King. Oh, boy, I can't wait."

"Thanks again, Connie. No kidding."

"Hey, Jack."

"Yeah?"

"You still think it's Jim Roper?"

"Nothing's happened to make me change my mind. Sorry."

"I don't know how to feel about all this, Jack. Whether I hope it's him or someone else. I'm twisted up inside. I mean, if it's not him then I've put an innocent man through hell. But if it is him, that means an end to the killing."

"You did the only thing you could do, Connie. Regardless of the final outcome."

"I know. It's just that…it's not a comfortable position to be in."

"I've got to run, Connie. Get me that Villon poem as soon as you can."

"Will do."

Dantzler picked up the large package lying in the front seat, got out of his car, and locked the door. He had to wait until two cars passed, then slowly crossed the one-way street to Coyle's.

The late-afternoon crowd was small, mainly made up of regulars looking to taste one of Lacy Coyle's legendary Saturday night specials before the "outsiders" began pouring in. Tonight's special was country fried steak, mashed potatoes, green beans, and a fresh garden salad. The dessert list, always a favorite with regulars, was topped by banana pudding and chocolate pie.

Dantzler went to one of the booths and slid in, placing the package in the space to his right. Almost immediately, Marcy Coleman arrived and set a glass of water in front of him.

"You're Jack Dantzler, aren't you?" she asked.

"Yes. How'd you know?"

"I've seen your picture in the newspaper. And on TV. You're the cop who's after that serial killer."

"That's me."

"What would you like to drink?"

"Pepsi's fine."

"Regular or diet?"

"Let's break the rules. Make it regular."

"Care to see a menu?" she said.

"Actually, Marcy, I need to talk to you. What time do you get off?"

"Four."

Dantzler looked at his watch. "Fifteen minutes. Good. We can talk then."

Marcy's face flushed crimson. "Am I in any kind of trouble?"

"No, no, not at all. Quite the contrary, in fact. I'm here to ask for your help in a certain matter." He touched her hand. "Sorry if I frightened you. I didn't mean to. I should've sounded more like a guy in need of a favor and less like a hard-ass cop."

"Why do you need my help?" Marcy asked.

"Tell you what, Marcy. Bring me my Pepsi. Do what you have to do to finish up here, then we'll talk. Okay?"

"Sure. If you say so."

Dantzler had timed his arrival to coincide with the end of Marcy's shift, which he guessed would be 4 p.m. But with no traffic to fight, he'd gotten there earlier than expected. He had fifteen minutes to kill, so he opened the package and lifted out the contents: a book manuscript, 271 typed pages, double spaced, bound on the left side by three gold fasteners. It was not unlike the thousands of other manuscripts that landed daily on the desks of literary agents and editors around the world.

After Marcy put his Pepsi on the table and had gone back into the kitchen, he slowly leafed through the manuscript, paying particular attention to the numbers at the bottom of each page, making sure they were in order. Satisfied that nothing was out of place, and that Dynamite had done her usual excellent work, he closed the manuscript and took a drink of Pepsi.

Then he looked at the manuscript's title page.

The Darkness of Forever by Marcy Coleman

Of course, Marcy Coleman had not written *The Darkness of Forever*. The book's true author was Bryce Shanklin, a bony-faced, stern-looking man with gray beard and glasses who looked more like a rabbi than the "master of psychological terror" proclaimed on the book's jacket.

Over the years, Dantzler had read several of Shanklin's books, including *The Darkness of Forever*, which was, he felt, the author's best. It was also his least successful from a sales standpoint, although none of Shanklin's books was ever going to squeeze Stephen King or Anne Rice off the best-seller lists. No Shanklin book had ever been published in hardback, and none had ever gone beyond a second printing. He was doomed to forever be a first-rate talent with third-rate sales.

Dantzler had given his paperback copy of *Forever* to Dynamite late last week and asked her to transcribe it into manuscript form. He also forbade her to disclose to anyone, including Richard Bird, what she was doing. As always, Dynamite grumbled mightily, then did extraordinary work. Pleased, Dantzler put the manuscript on the seat next to him.

At precisely 4 o'clock, Marcy Coleman scooted into the booth across from Dantzler. She opened a fresh pack of Juicy Fruit gum, took out a piece, unwrapped it, and put it into her mouth. After wadding the wrapper into a ball and putting it in an ashtray, she looked at Dantzler and shrugged her shoulders. "Okay, so why do you need my help?" she said.

"Before I answer that, I need to know if I can trust you," Dantzler said. "Completely. Can I?"

"Well…sure. I guess so."

"Guess won't get it. Yes or no?"

"Wow, this sounds serious."

"Yes or no, Marcy. If your answer is no, we have nothing to talk about."

"Yeah, you can trust me. Sure."

"Good." Dantzler drained the last drops of Pepsi. "You're still in college, aren't you?"

"Not this term," Marcy said.

"Why? You flunk out?"

"No, I did not flunk out. I'm an A student. In pre-med, thank you."

"So why aren't you in school?"

"Mom and Dad thought it would be best for me to sit out this term. Because of what's been going on, you know. They felt that because I resemble those murdered girls, it would be wise to stay out. I'll go back after the killer is caught."

"Did you ever take a lit class with Doctor James Roper?" Dantzler said.

"I haven't had lit yet."

"Do you know him?"

"No, I'm not familiar with him."

"You're sure you've never met him?"

"Positive. Why?"

"Because if you know him, then we can't do this."

"Well, I don't know him."

"Okay. Here's what I want you to do. You're gonna call him tonight and tell him that you've written a novel. You'll tell him it's your first work, and that you would like to have it evaluated by someone with a sharp eye for literary merit. Should he ask why you picked him, you'll say that after asking around for guidance, someone—you can't remember who—mentioned that he was an excellent writer with several novels to his credit. You'll say that you can drop the manuscript off first thing Monday morning, and that he can get back to you whenever he finishes reading it. How does that sound?"

"Like one helluva bullshit story, that's what."

"Will you do it?"

"Sure. Sounds like a hoot. But…"

Anticipating her question, Dantzler picked up the manuscript and placed it on the table in front of her. She saw the title page and began laughing.

"Man, you must've been awfully sure that I'd go along with you on this." She picked up the manuscript and read the title and her name out loud. "Marcy Coleman…author. I like the sound of that."

Dantzler handed her an index card. "That's his phone number," he said. "Call him tonight, say, around eight. If you get his answering machine, give him your number and tell him why you need to speak to him. Got it?"

She nodded. "Shouldn't I read this before I give it to him? I mean, just in case he quizzes me on it?"

"By all means."

"Why am I doing this?" Marcy said. "Does it have something to do with the murder investigation?"

"Nothing that clandestine or exciting, I'm sorry to say."

"Then why? Don't I deserve to know why I'm helping you in something that is obviously a lie?"

Dantzler smiled and nodded. "Point well taken. Truth is, it involves a bet I made with a friend of mine. Another detective on the force. If this plays out like I hope it will, we'll settle the bet and I'll win five hundred smackers."

"What kind of bet?"

"Have you ever heard of a writer named Jerzy Kozinski?"

Marcy shook her head.

"Well, he was quite an excellent writer. He wrote *Being There*, which was made into a terrific movie with Peter Sellers. Anyway, after Kozinski died, a friend of his wanted to prove that it's almost impossible to get a novel published these days. So, what he did was, he took one of Kozinski's earlier novels, one that had been universally praised by critics, had it typed into manuscript form like this, and then he submitted it to several different publishing houses. It was rejected by every one of them. What we're doing is similar to what Kozinski's friend did."

"But you're not sending this to a publisher."

"No, we're not that serious about it. Also, we don't want to wait that long to find out. So a friend of ours, a woman who teaches at the college, suggested that we send it to Doctor Roper. I'm betting he'll say it stinks. My buddy says Roper will like it."

"And I'm betting that that's the most bogus story I've ever heard in my life," Marcy said. "I don't believe a word of it. You didn't go to all this trouble to settle a bet about a book getting published."

Dantzler crossed his heart and held up his right hand. "Swear," he said. "Crazy as it may sound, it's God's truth."

She looked at the index card, then put it into her bag. "After I call him, then what? Call you?"

"Yes. Let me have the card." She handed it to him. "This is my number. Give me a call tonight, no matter how late."

"What if he tells me to get lost?" she said. "What if he has no interest in reading it?"

"He will," Dantzler said, giving the index card back to her. She stood, picked up the manuscript, and tucked it under her arm. "Looks like I've got a phone call to make and a book to read," she said. "And all because you want to settle some silly bet that I'm convinced is pure fantasy. Thanks a lot, Detective."

CHAPTER 45

After making a quick stop at headquarters to pick up copies of the two letters the killer had sent, Dantzler drove to his house, arriving at a little before 6:30. As he went inside, he could hear his own voice on the machine, instructing the caller to leave name, number, and a brief message.

He picked up the receiver. "Hello."

"Jack?"

"Hold on a second, Eric, until this thing plays through." He waited. "Okay, what's up?"

"I just wanted to let you know that I'm babysitting Roper. I relieved the uniforms about thirty minutes ago."

"You bucking for a promotion, or what?"

"Nah. I figured since my Saturday night activities had been derailed, I might as well be here. If I stayed home thinking about what I'm missing tonight, I might quit the force altogether."

"*Lieutenant* Gamble," Dantzler said. "Has a nice ring to it, don't you think?"

"I think you're bullshitting me, is what I think."

"Never," Dantzler said. "Any sign of Roper?"

"Caught a glimpse of him when he came outside to check his mail. That was just before I called you."

"Watch him closely, Eric. Whatever you do, don't let him know you're watching."

"Roger."

"Have you spoken to Laurie today?" Dantzler asked.

"No. I called a couple of times, but her cell phone must be off. I tried to leave a message at her house, but that was a no-go. She said her answering machine's been on the blink for the past week or so."

"If she calls, tell her to get in touch with me."

"Okay."

"Call me if anything happens."

"Jack?"

"Yeah?"

"Roper's not our killer."

"On what basis do you say that?"

"Just a gut feeling, really," Eric said. "I know my gut's not as experienced as yours, but...that's just my feeling."

"Laurie agrees with you, doesn't she?"

"Yes."

"Well, you may be right. Who knows? This isn't an exact science, and God knows I've been wrong before. But humor me for a night or two, will you? Let's see how it plays out."

"You got it."

Dantzler hung up, then pushed the rewind button. He had one message. It was from Andy Waters.

"Jack. Just wanted to let you know that I bought you some time. Got you a temporary injunction, you might say. Saint Jude will be absent from tomorrow's story. My bosses aren't happy, and should someone else break that piece of news, my ass is cooked."

Dantzler erased the message, then went into the kitchen and mixed a Pernod and orange juice. After taking a drink, he opened the manilla envelope and laid the two letters on the table, side by side. He leaned over the table and began reading the first letter. Before he was halfway through the first page, he heard the front door open. He quickly put the letters back into the envelope and stashed it in a drawer.

Richard Bird came into the kitchen, followed by his daughter Nicole. She nonchalantly came over to Dantzler, gave him a hug, did a sharp about-face, then went into the den and turned on the TV.

"Wish I could train the wife to behave like that," Bird said. He noticed Dantzler's drink. "What's that?"

"Vitamin C."

"Jack..."

"It's one drink, for crying out loud. Don't make a big deal out of it. Okay?"

Dantzler opened the drawer, took out the envelope, and put the letters on the table. "It's all in here, Rich," he said. "Everything we need to know. I've just got to find it."

"Listen, Jack. I spoke with Laurie and she—"

The phone rang. "Nicole, honey, can you get that for me?" Dantzler said.

"Sure." Nicole scrambled off the floor, ran to the phone, and answered. After listening for several seconds, she held the phone out at arm's length and said, "It's for you, Jack. Some woman."

Dantzler took the phone from her and gave her a quick kiss on the cheek. She made an awful face, wiped her cheek, and went back to watching TV.

"Hello," Dantzler said. "Oh, Marcy. How'd it go?"

Bird came out of his chair and moved closer to Dantzler.

"Great," Dantzler said. "I knew he'd go for it."

He listened.

"When? One-thirty, Monday afternoon? Have you read it yet?"

More listening.

"Finish it before you go. Remember, he has to believe you're the author."

Listening.

"You'll do fine. Give me a call as soon as you leave his office. And, Marcy. Thanks for helping out."

He put the phone back on the cradle, turned and faced a scowling Richard Bird.

"Marcy?" Bird said, an edge to his voice. "From the restaurant?"

"Yes."

"What kind of game are you playing, Jack? I want to know. *Everything.*"

"She's just…"

"Wait a minute," Bird said. "You're using her as bait, aren't you? You're sending her out to meet…who? Roper?"

Dantzler nodded. "We've got to flush this guy out, Rich," he said. "Force his hand. Right now, he's dictating the pace. I'm tired of playing by his rules."

"So am I, Jack. But I'm not going to let you play by your own set of rules. Not when it means putting a civilian's life in harm's way."

"What, you think I'm going to let something happen to her? Come on, Rich, give me some credit. At no time will she be in any danger."

"You can't say that with certainty. Things happen. Plans unravel. Even the best plans can fail. You know that." He pointed a finger at Dantzler. "Call it off, Jack. Whatever it is, call it off. It's not worth risking Marcy's life."

"There's no risk involved, Rich."

"End it now, Jack. That's an order. If you don't, I'll take you off the case."

Bird walked down the hallway and into the den. "Come on, pumpkin. Time to hit the highway."

Nicole bounded up, gave Dantzler another hug, and sprinted toward the front door. "See ya, Jack," she said, not looking back.

"Wouldn't wanna be ya," Dantzler called.

Bird opened the front door, paused, and turned back toward Dantzler. "Laurie says you're wasting your time on Roper. Says you've got a hard-on so big for him that you're not even considering other possibilities."

"That seems to be the consensus," Dantzler said.

"I happen to agree with her."

Dantzler shrugged.

"Maybe you should step back, explore other avenues."

"Maybe I'll do that."

"Good. Just leave Marcy out of it."

Less than an hour later, Laurie walked into Dantzler's house carrying a large brown paper bag under each arm. Dantzler closed the door, then took one of the bags from her. She leaned up and gave him a kiss on the lips.

"Vittles," she said, smiling. "You look like a man who hasn't had a home-cooked meal in ages, and I've come to rectify that problem."

"Really?"

Dantzler followed her into the kitchen. After she put her bag on the counter, she took the one from him, planted another kiss on his lips, then placed the second bag next to its partner.

"You probably don't know this," Laurie said, "but along with being a top-flight movie buff and a brilliant up-and-coming homicide detective, I'm also a superb chef."

"Not a shabby braggart, either." Dantzler pulled her close and kissed her hard on the mouth. "But you are beautiful, and that's not open for debate."

She stepped back and did a slight bow. "A compliment from the great Dantzler. My life is now complete."

"So, what's on the menu?" he asked.

"My specialty. Spaghetti, meatballs, salad—and this." She pulled a bottle from one of the sacks. "Bowing to our mutual love for movies, I give you this lovely concoction, Cabernet Franc, from the California vineyards of Niebaum and Coppola. That would be Francis Coppola of *Godfather* fame. Open, please." She handed him the bottle.

He opened it, filled two glasses with the dark red wine, and handed one to her. "To movies and meatballs," he said, holding his glass out. "The stuff of life."

"Here, here." She clinked her glass against his and took a sip. "Now, please vacate the area and let me work my culinary magic. Much as I enjoy gazing into your dark eyes, I prefer being alone in the kitchen. So, vamoose, please."

Two hours later, having finished dinner, Dantzler stood alone on the deck. Feeling slightly buzzed from the wine, he gazed out at the lake and listened to the evening sounds of crickets chirping, frogs bellowing, and gentle waves slapping against the wooden dock. Standing there, he realized that he felt an inner peace, a happiness, that he hadn't experienced in months. Maybe even years.

He also realized that for the past two hours he hadn't thought of, or spoken about, the four unsolved murder cases that hung over him like death's black shadow. The break, he knew, was welcomed and much needed. Tomorrow would get there soon enough. *The black shadow hovers, always. So, enjoy tonight, enjoy the sights and sounds, enjoy being with Laurie.*
Enjoy life.

Laurie came out of the kitchen and stood next to him. She took his wine glass from him and finished off the last drops. "Okay, cowboy," she said. "How do you rate the spaghetti and meatballs?"

"What you're really asking is, how do I rate you as a chef?"

"Of course."

"Somewhere between me and Wolfgang Puck."

"That's not exactly an unqualified endorsement."

"You're cocky enough as it is. An unqualified endorsement would send you over the edge, make you unbearable."

"You didn't like the meal. You were disappointed."

"Laurie, if I didn't like the meal, if I were disappointed, I wouldn't have made such a pig of myself. The meal was terrific. And sharing it with you made it even more terrific."

"Stop before this gets sappy." She kissed him on the cheek. "I know you liked the meal. I cooked it—how could you not like it?"

They stood in silence and listened to the night sounds. A chilly breeze had kicked up, quickly dropping the temperature several degrees. Dantzler put his arm around Laurie and drew her close. She snuggled next to him, resting her head on his shoulder.

"Tell me about Beth Robinson," she whispered.

"BR? She's the best, just one terrific lady."

"Do you still love her?"

"I'll always love BR. She was a big part of my life for almost ten years. But if you're asking me if I'm still *in* love with her, the answer is no."

"Good."

"Why the sudden interest in Beth Robinson?"

"Because maybe I would like to be a big part of your life someday. To be where she once was. But if you still have feelings for her, then I'm intelligent enough to back away before I get in too deep."

Dantzler brushed her hair back and kissed the top of her head. "You are already a part of my life, Laurie," he said. "How big, I can't say right now. I guess only time will answer that."

"Are you sleepy?" she asked.

"No. But I am ready for bed."
"Good answer."

CHAPTER 46

Dantzler eased out of bed, careful not to wake Laurie, slipped on a robe, and went into the kitchen. He opened a can of Diet Pepsi, sat at the table, removed the two letters from the drawer, placed them side by side and began reading. He read them slowly, deliberately, like a monk poring over an ancient text. Fifteen minutes into it, he found a yellow legal pad and began making notes. Tedious as the task was, Dantzler enjoyed doing it. He liked it because there was no bullshit. Here, alone in this room, it was *mano a mano*, his mind against the killer's. No rules, no regulations, no Richard Bird barking orders. *It's just me and him locked in our "one-on-one dance."*

There was much about the killer's ramblings that Dantzler discarded immediately. The references to famous people, the literary quotes—that was meaningless bunk vomited up by a man trying to make himself sound more intelligent than he really was. Dantzler also gave little merit to anything the killer wrote about himself. For the most part, it was, Dantzler felt, self-absorbed and self-aggrandizing. Virtually all letters written by murderers were little more than love poems to themselves.

At 2, bleary-eyed and still feeling the effects of the wine, Dantzler undressed, went into the guest bathroom, and took a quick shower. Refreshed, he slipped on the robe and turned on the TV. Thirty minutes later, after catching a rerun of Larry King interviewing Don Imus, he was back at the kitchen table reading. This time he focused only on those comments that he had written down.

- *There is plenty of time, and in time all things shall be revealed.*
- *I am also with you at night. You aren't aware of this, but when you dream, as you often do, I am the reason why.*
- *Five.*
- *Like that heavy cross you must forever bear.*

- *I am the author of your dreams, the architect of your agony, the alpha and omega of your torment.*
- *But how can this be, since we've never met? (Or have we?)*
- *You must wait for that apocalyptic split-second of enlightenment when the secrets of your nightmares are unlocked and revealed.*
- *The question begs, Do you really want to learn the secrets of your nightmares?*

Dantzler went over his list several times. When he finished, he circled one word—*five.*

Dantzler smiled, recalling a story he had once read. A student challenged the famous Rabbi Hillel to teach him the entire *Torah* while the student stood on one foot. Hillel said, "That which is hateful to you, do not do to your neighbor. The rest is commentary."

The killer's message—his confession—was somehow wrapped up in that single word. *Five.* Everything else was commentary.

Deborah Tucker had been the killer's *fourth* victim, not his fifth.

There had been an earlier murder.

Dantzler picked up the phone and dialed Tommy Blake's number. Tommy answered on the fourth ring. His voice was scratchy, dry, tentative.

"Do you know what time it is, Jack?" he mumbled.

"Sorry about the lateness, but I need to know something. Did you ever know a guy named Jim Roper?"

"What?"

"Did you know Jim Roper? Come on, Tommy, try to remember. It's important."

"I vaguely recall a Stan Roper. He was a grade behind me at school. But Jim Roper…can't help you there. Why are you asking?"

"Because I believe he's the one who killed those college girls. I also think he murdered Mom."

"Jack, have you gone completely out of your mind? Are you saying—"

"I'm not saying anything. Roper is. In his letters. That's why they were addressed directly to me. It's personal. Otherwise, he'd have sent them to headquarters, or to one of the newspapers."

"I don't know, Jack. I just…"

"And he knows things, Tommy. Stuff only the killer would know. Personal things about me."

"Jack, your mom was killed twenty-five years ago. That's a long time. This Roper guy would've been a kid."

"Roper is forty-six now. That would've made him twenty-one then. The prisons are filled with twenty-one-year-olds who committed murder."

"Give it a rest, Jack. You have to. And stop blaming yourself for what happened to your mom. She got a shitty deal, okay. It happens sometimes. The bastard who killed her got away with it. That happens sometimes, too. Life doesn't always deal us a winning hand. When it doesn't, you have to fold and wait for the next deal. You can't keep playing a losing hand."

"He did it, Tommy. Jim Roper is our guy. And I'm going to prove it."

Laurie was standing in the kitchen doorway when Dantzler hung up the phone. She went to the refrigerator, opened it, took out a bottle of water, and sat at the table across from him. "Hope you don't mind me wearing one of your shirts." She took a drink and smiled. "Don't most guys think this is a sexy look?"

Dantzler didn't answer.

Laurie put her hand on his arm. "About Roper—I'm just not convinced…"

"I was supposed to be with her that night. The night she was killed."

"Who…your mother?"

"We were supposed to go into town. Have dinner, see a movie. She made a big deal of it, saying we'd both been so busy that we hadn't spent enough time together. I was all involved with my tennis, she was working hard as a realtor—we just kept missing each other. So, she laid down the law. 'We're going out, just the two of us, and we're gonna have a fun time.' Those were her exact words. I can still hear them..."

"But you didn't go."

Dantzler shook his head. "Before she left for work that morning, she told me to be at the house around five-thirty, that she would pick me up then. She gave me a hug, then left, this huge smile on her face. It was the last time I saw her alive."

"What happened?"

"A girl. Cindy Knight. I had the hots for her like you wouldn't believe. Kept asking her to go out with me, but she always turned me down. Until that day...Of all days, she picked that one. And I got so swept up in it, I said okay. I went home and called Mom at work. Told her Coach Barnett had called a special late practice for the tennis team. I told her Coach wanted us to practice under the lights because we might have to play at night during the regional finals. Of course, Mom believed me. She told me to practice hard, and that we would go out tomorrow night. So...the last thing I said to my Mother was a lie."

"You can't blame yourself for what happened to her," Laurie said. "That's being unfair to yourself."

Dantzler shrugged. "If I'd been with her like I was supposed to be, who knows? She probably wouldn't have crossed paths with whoever killed her."

Laurie squeezed his hand. "There's only one person to blame, Jack. The person who murdered her. Deep down in your heart, you know that."

"Deep down in my heart, I'll always wonder."

CHAPTER 47

Eldon Wessell read Andy Waters's lengthy piece in the Sunday paper with great delight. According to Waters, the investigators were outwardly putting a positive spin on the situation, but, he writes, "sources within the department tell me homicide detectives are extremely frustrated, and that the investigation is virtually at a standstill."

Eldon was especially taken with Richard Bird's assessment: "Clearly, we are dealing with a clever, cunning killer. He doesn't make mistakes, and that makes it far more difficult for us."

At last, Eldon thought, a reporter who gets it right, and a cop who is honest enough to admit the truth, no matter how unflattering it may be. Maybe there's hope after all.

Despite the glowing praise found in the article, Eldon did have a couple of quibbles, minor though they were: the comments concerning him didn't appear until the seventh paragraph, and they had been given by Bird rather than Dantzler.

Eldon wanted to know what Dantzler thought. To hell with Richard Bird. Who was he, anyway, but a lousy paper-shuffling bureaucrat with his nose buried up the mayor's ass? Eldon wanted to hear Dantzler use words like cunning and clever. Praise from a legend was always more meaningful. Norman Mailer proclaiming your greatness would carry far more weight than the same praise coming from Barbara Cartland.

Eldon wasn't about to let it get him down. Not today. Not on the day he had such big plans for Beverly Diaz. And for himself, for that matter.

Let the detectives and reporters say and write whatever they wanted. Let them spin it in whatever direction suited them best. It didn't matter. It was all drivel, anyway. Guesswork. Speculation and postulation born of desperation. Only one person knew the real truth. Only one person knew what had happened. Knew how things went down.

And he was that person.

He was the only one on the inside looking out. The rest, all of them—that fucking legend Jack Dantzler included—were like pitiful, bumbling scientists floundering in their attempts to crack the deepest secrets of the universe. Or puzzled mystics trying to prove God's existence.

Eldon smiled at that last thought. Although he had never given much credence to the existence of an actual god, he had always embraced the idea of God as a tool to be used by poets and writers. Anyway, there were so many gods to choose from, where did one begin? Certainly, the god that Gee and Rose knelt before was far removed from the god of Dante and Dostoyevsky. Those two wonderful scribes believed in the god of scripture; Gee and Rose believed in the god of dogma.

In fact, Eldon concluded, Dostoyevsky's Grand Inquisitor was their god.

Feeling inspired by thoughts of Dante and Dostoyevsky, Eldon went to his computer and began writing a letter to Dantzler. It was, he knew, the final one he would send. After tonight, after Beverly Diaz had been properly enshrined as a Chosen One, and this last letter was on its way, there would be no further need for correspondence with Jack Dantzler.

He would be useless, like a penis on a corpse.

Eldon laughed out loud at that thought. Limp dick Jack Dantzler…impotent…frustrated…angry.

Defeated.

It took Eldon two hours to write, edit, and polish the letter, less than a third of the time it had taken to get either of the first two into good enough shape to send out. For this letter, Eldon was less concerned about form and structure and flow and language, and more interested in getting his message across in the simplest, least-cluttered manner. He did not fight and struggle this time; rather, he allowed his stream-of-conscious thoughts to take him in whatever direction they dictated. He was a passenger along for the ride.

After printing out a copy and giving it one last read—he had to make sure his stream of words had not led him to disclose clues—he spent the next hour soaking in the tub, his thoughts centered on tonight.

This was going to be his crowning achievement, personally and professionally. His most glorious moment. Beverly Diaz was destined to be sacrificed on the altar of his virginity. Secretly, he had always wondered which of the Chosen Ones would be worthy of such an honor. Abby Kaplan and Deborah Tucker had come the closest. Physically, he judged them to be almost perfect. Virtually above improvement in any way. But their arrogance, their high-brow I'm-somehow-better-than-you attitude, their condescension, was the sin that kept them from entering into his paradise.

Eldon wasn't going to settle for almost perfect; he wanted total perfection.

Isn't that the goal of all the truly great ones?

And he was more than willing to keep going until he found it. Body count was a non-issue; getting what he desired was. Eldon reasoned that if the biblical God could wipe out every man, woman, child, and beast except for righteous Noah and his pitiful gang, then he had a right to continue his quest to find the perfect Chosen One, no matter how long it took, or how high the bodies piled up.

If God was a useful tool for poets and writers, then why can't he be a useful tool for killers? Why shouldn't God be used as a shining example? After all, in all of recorded history, no one had murdered more innocent people than God. Given that, Eldon viewed his actions as being those of a loyal servant.

Who could take issue with that?

And, Eldon reasoned, murder is murder, whether the butcher be God or me. But there was, Eldon felt, a difference between him and God, and it was an important difference: God was a coward, he wasn't. God sent floods and angels and devils to do his dirty work; Eldon allowed his victims to look their executioner in the eye.

Eldon suddenly recalled the words of another great— Leonardo: *The student who does not surpass his Master, fails his Master.*

In Eldon's mind, he had more than met Leonardo's challenge.

Eldon slipped on a robe, went down into the kitchen, and poured a glass of apple juice. He sat at the table and looked out the big kitchen window. The sky was gray, the slow-moving clouds heavy with the possibility of an afternoon shower. Two robins drank from the bird bath in the backyard, then flew away. A slight breeze whispered its presence by gently weaving through the grass and trees.

The note posted to the refrigerator was succinct and to the point:

> Elmer Donald: We are off to visit CeCe. Try not
> to destroy the house while we are away.
> Mother

Eldon smiled as he crumpled the note and tossed it into the wastebasket. CeCe was Cecilia, Gee's younger sister. She lived in Sarasota, Florida, in a condo on the Siesta Key beach. A visit to CeCe's never lasted less than two weeks. Of course, Gee never told him how long they would be gone, or gave a specific return time. Uncertainty had always been her weapon, her way to keep him in line. He marveled at how, after all these years, she tried to intimidate, threaten, and, ultimately, control him as if he were still a helpless child.

God, how he despised that woman.

He took his time drinking the juice. With that despicable duo out of his hair, having debunked before sunrise, there was no need to rush. With them absent, time belonged to him. He owned it. He was truly free, and the man who was truly free had no need for the concept of time, that greatest of all slave makers. Time was surely man's most-destructive notion.

Eldon closed his eyes and thought of Beverly Diaz. He tried to imagine what she would look like naked, this most beautiful and perfect work of art, this—

A thought jolted through him like a current of electricity, causing the hairs on the back of his neck to stand up.

It was something he had never before considered: Should he make love to Beverly Diaz before or after killing her?

He stood and began to pace furiously around the kitchen, rubbing his hands together, shaking like an old Jew at the Wailing Wall. He bolted up the stairs, went into his room, and flung himself onto the bed. Less than five seconds later he was back up, pacing around the room, asking himself a single question over and over again:

How is it possible that I had never addressed such a crucial detail?

Eldon undressed, filled the tub with hot water, and got in. He leaned back and put a washcloth over his face. He needed to think, to calm down, to collect himself. He had to sort through the possibilities, the options, choose the one that had the most appeal—and the least danger—then act on it with total conviction.

Like he had always done in the past.

After mentally rummaging through all options, he concluded that both scenarios held a certain appeal for him. The idea of fucking Beverly Diaz while she was still alive, spread-eagle on the bed, was especially thrilling. Alive, she would feel him inside her, look into his eyes when his orgasm swept through his body, hear his sounds of pleasure.

Alive, Beverly Diaz would be an active participant.

However...

That scenario carried within it the potential for disaster. Every situation did, no matter how carefully planned in advance. Eldon had always acknowledged that with any mission, the possibility of failure always exists.

Tonight's mission posed much more risks and danger than any of the others.

Beverly Diaz wasn't only the most beautiful Chosen One, she was also the strongest and most athletic. Subduing her could prove to be a handful for any man, even one with his obvious size and strength advantage. Therefore, his initial strike had to be well timed and perfectly executed.

That meant he had to be more cunning tonight than he'd ever been in the past. To succeed tonight, he had to be quick, and he had to be true. There would be no margin for error or slip-up. One mistake would be fatal.

What manner of strike should he unleash? A punch that rendered her unconscious, or nearly so, would be the optimum choice. The safest. Then he could tie her to the bed and wait until she regained consciousness before having sex with her. A blow of knockout force would, in all probability, mar her absolute beauty, and that thought didn't appeal to him in the least.

Above all else, Eldon wanted to fuck perfection.

He ran through a list of other possible options—drugs, chloroform, stun gun, pistol, knife. All were quickly rejected. Too dangerous, too uncertain, too much chance for failure.

In the end, Eldon knew, there was but one option—he would do what he always did.

He would strangle Beverly Diaz.

Only this time he wouldn't kill her. He would cut off the flow of blood and oxygen to the brain long enough for her to pass out, then he would take her to the bed, bind her hands and feet, cover her mouth, and wait until she regained consciousness.

That way she would experience the glory of the moment. Her last living moment on this earth.

CHAPTER 48

Eldon parked across the street from Beverly Diaz's apartment, waited until two youngster-packed SUVs zipped past, then exited his car. Standing alone in the night, again dressed in his black ensemble, he was engulfed by excitement and anticipation. This was the moment, *the* night, the one all the others had been pointing toward.

Everything else had been a prelude to tonight.

Bolstered by feelings of power and sexual hunger, Eldon all but ran across the street. He caught his breath, rang the doorbell, then stepped back several feet. Inside, Billy Joel was singing "New York State of Mind." As Eldon heard footsteps nearing the door, he reminded himself to take his time, to savor this night like no others, to experience Beverly Diaz to the fullest.

And to be disciplined.

When Beverly Diaz pulled the door open and saw Eldon standing there, the look on her face was one of surprise and confusion. She tilted her head back and squinted.

"Mr. Wessell, what…?"

"I brought papers for you to sign." He held up a white manilla folder. "To expedite the hiring process. I hope you don't mind."

"Well…"

"I know you said you wanted to get started ASAP, and the faster we get the paperwork out of the way, the sooner you can begin. If now is not a good time, we can figure out a Plan B."

Beverly thought for a moment. "No…no, since you're already here, we might as well get it over with." She stepped back and opened the door further. "Come on in. Make yourself comfortable."

Eldon walked straight to the sofa, put the folder on the coffee table, turned and—he couldn't believe the vision that now stood before him. This, he thought, was absolute perfection. Men gladly went to war and died for women who looked exactly like the one standing in front of him. Poets wrote sonnets, balladeers penned songs. Surely, the angels in heaven sang their praises to this level of beauty and perfection.

Beverly Diaz was dressed in a pair of white gym shorts and a blue sleeveless cotton T-shirt that had been cut at mid-waist. Her thick black hair was combed back and still wet from a recent shower. She wore no shoes, no makeup, no jewelry. This was beauty stripped of accessories, of superficiality. This was beauty at its most natural.

It was her skin, bronze and flawless, that most captivated Eldon. Beverly Diaz looked like a figure in a painting by one of the masters. Could any of the great masters truly capture and do justice to this beauty? He seriously doubted it.

Eldon sat on the couch and crossed his legs. He was already fully erect, and feeling the initial stirrings of orgasm rumbling inside him. Closing his eyes, taking several slow, deep breaths, he again reminded himself that this was going to be his grand night, that there was no need to rush or hurry, and that discipline was his greatest strength.

"Are you all right?" Beverly asked. "You look a little shaky."

"I'm fine, my dear." Eldon picked up the folder, opened it, and took out a small stack of papers. "Here is your official application, your W-2, and the insurance forms. You need only fill out those areas that I have highlighted in yellow."

"Wow, this could take a while. You sure you wouldn't rather leave them, let me bring them to you tomorrow?"

"It won't take as long as you think. And I don't mind waiting."

"It's your time." Beverly held out a hand. "Got a pen?"

Eldon fished one from his coat pocket and handed it to her. She knelt across from him, leaned over, and began filling out the W-2. As she did, her T-shirt momentarily fell away, revealing her breasts. When Eldon saw her dark brown nipples, he was immediately seized by a rapidly encroaching sense of helplessness. He looked away, closed his eyes, dispatching his thoughts in other directions. He dug deep, reminding himself that the great ones don't crumble under extreme pressure.

But his discipline *was* crumbling. He knew it, could feel it happening, knew he was powerless to prevent it. He fought hard, called upon a lifetime of pleasure-denying tricks, but nothing worked.

He was losing control.

The tide of orgasm overwhelmed him, sending wave after wave of pleasure rocketing through his body. He kept his eyes closed, straining with all the strength inside him to muffle the sounds of pleasure that normally accompany such moments. Squeezing his legs together, the pleasure so intense it was almost painful, he felt the warm semen spurt from his penis.

Eldon was outraged by this turn of events. How could this have happened? How could his discipline desert him at such a moment? *His* moment, the night of his crowning achievement? How could he be such a…failure? There was no other word to use. He had failed.

Opening his eyes, he looked at Beverly Diaz to see if she was aware of what had just transpired. Thankfully, she wasn't. The Piano Man had seen to that. Beverly continued to fill out the forms, oblivious to his failure. Next, he uncrossed his legs and checked to see if any tell-tale signs of his orgasm were visible on his pants. They weren't.

Thank God.

Eldon realized he had a decision to make—abort or continue. Leave now, accept failure, plan for the future. Or stay, regain his composure, follow through with his original plan. The two notions echoed inside his head like alternating bolts of thunder.

"Are you positive you're okay?" Beverly Diaz said, looking up. "Can I get you something to drink? You look weak."

In that instant, Eldon made his decision.

Rather, his decision was made for him. By her words.

He smiled, feeling his penis begin to stiffen.

Weak? Not me. He was going to fuck her.

"Yes, if it's no trouble, I would like a glass of water," he said. "I haven't quite been up to par lately. A touch of the flu, I think."

Beverly stood up and went into the kitchen. Eldon got to his feet and walked over to a case filled with tennis trophies. He let his hands drop into his coat pocket, touching the various icons that would help consecrate this glorious event. Removing the silk scarf, he brought it up and wiped perspiration from his brow. A clock on the walk chimed. It was 8:30. He needed to move, to get on with it, to glorify Beverly Diaz.

She returned and gave him the glass of water. He took a long drink, then set the glass on an end table.

"Thank you," he said. "I'm feeling better already."

"I'm almost done here," Beverly said, kneeling at the coffee table. "Five minutes at the most."

"Accuracy is more important than speed," Eldon said, moving behind her. "So don't feel the need to rush."

He twisted the scarf until it was taut, holding it in both hands as he eased closer to her. His senses were overloaded with excitement, anticipation and, yes, fear. Eldon was scared, there was no getting around it. But wasn't that normal? What great warrior, at the supreme moment of battle, could honestly say that fear wasn't present? Those who did deny it weren't being honest with themselves. Fear was part of the equation. It's the fear, the apprehension, that kept you alert, kept you from being reckless, kept you from making unnecessary blunders.

He could afford no blunders.

Eldon moved directly behind and closer to Beverly. He was now virtually hovering above her. The next five seconds, he knew, were critical. Beverly Diaz was strong, athletic, and quick—she wouldn't go down without a struggle. To subdue her, he had to be in peak form. He had to be better than he'd ever been in the past.

He took a deep breath, let it out slowly. He felt good now, confident, disciplined, in control. The old Eldon was back.

It was time to glorify Beverly Diaz.

But just then he heard a noise coming from his right. He jerked upright as if stabbed from behind, turned, and saw the blonde man standing in the doorway. He was tall, well-built, deeply tanned, and around the same age as Beverly. A large

white towel was wrapped around his torso, and he used a second
towel to dry his hair.
He looked at Eldon, then down at Beverly. "What's up?" he
asked.
"Paperwork for the job at the bookstore. I'm almost done."
She stopped writing and looked up. "Oh, Mr. Wessell, this is
Bobby Flemming. Bobby, Mr. Wessell."
Bobby nodded and sat on the sofa, making no attempt to
shake hands with Eldon. He reached out his right hand and
stroked Beverly's hair. "Still want me to order a pizza?" he said.
"Yeah."
"What do you want on it?"
"The usual."
Bobby rose and went into the kitchen, again without
acknowledging Eldon's presence.
Beverly finished filling out the papers, stood, and handed
them to Eldon. "Sorry it took so long," she said. "I'm better at
tennis than I am at writing."
"That's quite all right," Eldon answered. "I...I thought you
told me you lived alone. That you had no roommate."
"Bobby's my boyfriend. My roommate is in Europe this
month, playing in several tournaments."
"I see." Eldon took the papers, slipped them into the manilla
folder, then opened the front door. "Well, with this nasty
business out of the way, we should have you gainfully employed
within the next week or so."
"Sounds good to me," Beverly said. "And thanks so much
for bringing the paperwork over here. That was a wonderfully
kind gesture on your part."

Tears rolled down Eldon's face. He had never felt so
humiliated, so broken. So scared. Terror racked his body when
he realized how close he had come to making a fateful mistake.
How could he have been so stupid? How could he have failed so
miserably? How could this have happened?
Eldon sobbed uncontrollably as he steered his car into the
driveway. Blinking the tears away, he couldn't believe what he

saw. Gee's car was parked in the garage. But…how could that be? Why weren't they on the way to Sarasota? Why were they here? What had happened?

Eldon cut the engine and scrambled out of the car. All the way to the house, he fought the urge to scream at the top of his lungs, to ask whatever supreme being that might exist why this nightmare was continuing.

"Back already," he growled as he walked into the kitchen. "What happened—the folks in the Sunshine State deny you entrance?"

"Car trouble," Gee said. "It was more prudent to turn back than continue forward."

"Have it repaired tomorrow and tell them to send the bill to me. I'll happily pay any price to get you two queens back on the road."

Rose eyed Eldon up and down. "I like that ensemble, Elmer. It's very arty, very European, very…pretentious. Yes, that's the word I'm looking for."

Eldon smoldered with hatred and anger. *"Je n'ai pas le sens moral, je suis une brute: vous vous trompez."*

"Yes, pretentious was indeed the correct word," Rose said.

Eldon let out a cry of exasperation, then pivoted on his heels and started to leave.

"Oh, Eldon, dear," Gee called out. "We need to vote on whether or not to sell the house. So, please, would you grace us with your presence for a few more minutes?"

"Okay, let's vote," Eldon said, coming back into the kitchen. "I vote no. What about you two?"

"Yes," Rose quickly said. "I say sell and good riddance."

Eldon looked at his mother. "And what about you, dear Mumsy? How say ye?"

"Yes."

"What a surprise. Two against one, you two against me. Who'd a thunk it?"

"I'll begin the proceedings when we get back from Sarasota," Gee said. "In the meantime, you might want to start looking for a new place to live."

"This house will not be sold," Eldon said. "Not next week, not next year, not ten years from now. I will make sure that it's not sold."

"And how might you do that, Elmer?" Rose asked.

"I have my ways," Eldon said, leaving the room.

CHAPTER 49

Milt Costello chomped down on a jelly doughnut, then washed it down with a swig of Diet Dr. Pepper. Dan Matthews sat next to Costello, doodling. Dale Larraby, the familiar scowl on his face, sat with his arms crossed and head bowed. Eric Gamble, notepad in hand, stood next to the chalkboard, his eyes scanning the names and dates of death of the four victims. Glenn Rigby, the FBI profiler, sat at the table, hunched over, reading his own list of notes. Except for an occasional cough—and Costello's munching and drinking—the small room was dominated by silence.

At a few minutes past nine Dantzler and Richard Bird entered the room. When they did, Gamble fell into the empty chair at the far end of the table. Bird maneuvered his way to the chalkboard and scanned the room, his eyes finally settling on Rigby.

"Thanks for joining us, Glenn," Bird said.

"Happy to help in any way I can," Rigby answered.

Bird looked down at Gamble. "Where's Dunn?"

"She got a call about thirty minutes ago," Eric said. "From Rose Wessell. She said Rose needed to speak with her, and that it sounded important."

Bird nodded. "Okay, gentlemen, I want an update. I want to know exactly where this investigation stands." He looked at Dantzler, who was leaning against the wall. "Let's start with you, Jack."

"I still like Roper," Dantzler said.

"Why?"

"Several reasons. First, as a professor, he had access to all four vics. He—"

"He never had any of them in class," Matthews said.

"No, he didn't. But he did have access."

"So did every instructor on campus," Costello noted.

"Come on, Milt, get real. The English department and the theatre department are first cousins. It's not like he taught animal husbandry."

"Still...that's a stretch," Bird said. "What else you got?"

"He's violent; he dates his students; he has a book earmarked to the page with the *Pietà* on it; he uses the same quote from Rimbaud in his own novel that he used in the first letter to me, and he uses the word *shan't*. Circumstantial, maybe, but tie enough circumstantial evidence together and it begins to look pretty solid."

Bird looked around the room. "What about it, detectives? It does start to add up."

"I'll grant you some solid points, Jack," Matthews finally said, "but I just don't like the guy for this. He just doesn't strike me as having the intestinal fortitude to look four women in the eye, then strangle them to death. Like it or not, that does take some guts. I just don't think Jim Roper has them."

"Plus, he does have an alibi for the night Becky Adams was murdered," Costello said.

"*Partial* alibi," countered Dantzler. "He was at a party, yes, but no one can say for sure when he left. Unless his time of departure can be nailed down, we can't say for certain that he didn't kill Becky Adams."

Glenn Rigby cleared his throat and leaned forward. "Mind if I toss in my nickel's worth, Rich?" he said.

"Absolutely not."

"Jack, I have to side with Dan and Milt on this one," Rigby said. "From what I can make out, James Roper is a classic wannabe in every way. He *wants* to be a famous novelist, he *wants* to make it with every pretty young student who comes his way, he *wants* to come across as sophisticated and intelligent, he *wants*, he *wants*, he *wants*. He's frustrated, angry, empty inside. He is a man who very well may someday put a gun to his head and check himself out, but he's not a man who can kill another human being in cold blood."

"Bullshit," Dantzler said. "Are you telling me it doesn't take some guts to stick a gun against your head, pull the trigger and blow your brains all over the place?"

"Two entirely different situations, Jack. You know that. By the time an individual gets to the point where suicide is the number one option, having or not having guts doesn't factor in."

Matthews said, "Milt and I still think James Winstead needs a closer look."

"Explain," Bird said.

"We know for a fact that Winstead knew at least two of the victims—Tucker and Kaplan. The one, Abby Kaplan, rented from the guy, so he had unlimited access to her. We know that on the night Abby Kaplan was murdered he was supposed to pick her up from the dance academy. He claims to have arrived after she left, but we only have his word on that. We also know he's violent—that he does have the guts to look a woman in the eyes and smack the shit out of her. In my mind, all that adds up to Winstead being a serious suspect."

"Any thoughts on him, Glenn?" Bird said to Rigby.

"I haven't looked at him hard enough yet to render an opinion either way," Rigby said. "But from what Dan says, I certainly don't think I'd be wasting my time if I did."

"Good. Put a rush on it, if you can." Bird nodded to Gamble. "What've you got, Eric?"

"Well, Laurie seems to think we can't rule out Mike McKendrick," Gamble said, flipping through his notepad. " And I tend to agree with her. McKendrick's—"

"John Stocker's son-in-law?" Bird asked.

Eric nodded. "Right. According to Laurie, Mike, or 'Mad Mike,' is one bad-ass dude. A real redneck rowdy. Used to punch out his first wife, and has probably done the same with Stocker's daughter. We'll never know, because the rich tend to hush up dirty shit like that. McKendrick beat up a golf partner with a club, and he once cut a guy's ear off in a fight. So I don't think anyone can doubt his willingness to inflict serious damage."

"All well and good," Larraby said. "But how does Dunn connect him to our murders?"

"McKendrick's daughter is a student at Rose Wessell's dance academy," Gamble said. "And Mad Mike was supposed to pick up his kid on the night Abby Kaplan was murdered. But the kid caught a ride with another parent. McKendrick claims to have seen her in the car, turned around, and gone home. But I did some checking around and found out that Mike didn't go through the gate until well after midnight."

"Any idea where he was?" asked Costello.

"From ten-thirty until around midnight, he was at the Grapevine doing some heavy drinking. Abby Kaplan was last seen alive at eight. That gives him more than two hours that are unaccounted for. That, plus the fact that he lied about going straight home, has to make him a candidate."

"Hook up with Dunn and go pay him a second visit," Bird said. "If he gives you any lip, haul his ass in. We'll interview him here, away from the safety of good old daddy-in-law John Stocker. See how he likes that."

Bird looked around the room. "If there's nothing else, let's get back at it. I'm not going to waste my breath or your time giving a big pep talk. You know the score. We need to stop this guy, and we need to do it yesterday. Let's nail the bastard."

They all stood the leave. Bird pulled Dantzler aside out of hearing range of the others. "About that other situation," he whispered. "The one with Marcy. Is that taken care of?"

"I already called her," Dantzler lied. "It's off."

"Good."

Fifteen minutes later, Dantzler sat at his desk studying names on his computer screen. Eric came over to his desk, picked up a folder, and started to leave.

"Hey, Mr. GQ," Dantzler said. "Hear from Laurie yet?"

"Nah. I tried her cell phone, got no answer. She probably has it turned off again."

"Any idea what Rose Wessell wanted to talk about?"

"Laurie didn't say."

"Where you off to now?"

"The Grapevine. I want to talk to the owner, see if I can begin to piece together a timeline for where Mike McKendrick was—or wasn't—on the night Abby Kaplan died. Then I'll hook up with Laurie and we'll go see why Mad Mike lied to us."

"Sounds like a plan. And tell Laurie to turn her damn phone on. She needs to be accessible."

"I think she's kind of a lone wolf, too."

"Yeah, well, there's only room for one lone wolf and I'm it."

Beth Robinson caught up with Dantzler just as he was leaving the building.

"Hate to break the news to you, Jack," she said. "But Jim Roper isn't your killer."

"You're positive?"

"Yeah. His prints came back and they're not a match for anything at any of the crime scenes, or on the letters and envelopes the killer sent you. He left plenty of prints, Jack. Good ones, too. But I didn't get any hits. Not one. You have to forget Jim Roper and move on."

"You're absolutely certain?"

"You can take it to the bank."

"Fuck."

"Jack—"

"Sorry, BR. I didn't mean to question you." He looked away. "It's not what I wanted to hear, but if you say it, it's gold. But…it's just that I was dead certain he was our guy."

"Sorry." She reached out and took his hand in hers. "I've missed you, Jack. Missed us."

"We had our moments, didn't we?"

"Yes, we did." Tears came into her eyes. "Sometimes I lie awake at night thinking about the time we spent together. How great it was. How great you were. I can't help but wonder if I made the right decision."

"You did. Took me a long time to come to grips with it, but it was the right thing for you to do."

"Who said life's choices were easy?"

"Groucho Marx."

"Damn, I thought it was W.C. Fields." She let go of his hand and wiped away the tears. "You'll always own a big piece of my heart, Jack. I hope you know that."

He gave her a kiss on the cheek, then turned to walk away.

"Hey, Jack. It's okay to be wrong."

"Not when lives are on the line."

Dantzler got in the Forester, took out his cell phone, and dialed Marcy Coleman's number. She answered on the third ring.

"Hello?"

"Marcy, Detective Dantzler."

"Oh, hi. Didn't expect to hear from you so soon. What's up?"

"Where are you right now?"

"On campus. In the Student Center. Why?"

"Have you met with Jim Roper yet?"

"Not till one-thirty."

"Call and cancel the meeting."

"Why?"

"My friend and I have settled our bet. Kinda mutually agreed that it was a silly idea."

"What do I tell Jim Roper?"

"Anything. No, wait. Tell him you found an agent who is willing to read it."

"Are you sure? This was starting to be fun."

"Yes, call him and cancel."

"What about the manuscript? What should I do with it?"

"Toss it."

"Mind if I keep it? I kinda like seeing a manuscript with my name as author. Who knows, maybe it'll inspire me to become a writer."

"Keep the manuscript. But, Marcy…"

"Yeah?"

"Stick with med school."

CHAPTER 50

Eldon Wessell paced.

Although it was nearing noon, the events of last night were still fresh in his mind, like a photo he'd just seen, one whose image refused to fade. He hadn't slept at all last night, not one second. How could he sleep, given what had taken place? The night had been a disaster of epic proportions, a series of events that left him frustrated, rattled, and terrified. What had happened—first at Beverly Diaz's house, then in his own kitchen—was almost beyond his ability to comprehend.

He had come so close to being caught in the act. How dumb and careless was that? And why? Because he hadn't prepared properly, that's why. He hadn't made sure that Beverly Diaz would be alone. He'd always done that in the past. It was a basic. Even a person with a lesser intellect than his knew that. You scoped things out, left nothing to chance. He had not. He had failed. Like some run-of-the-mill amateur.

Pitiful.

Then there was his appalling lack of discipline. What could account for that? How could he have become so weak, so ordinary? And why now, why at the ultimate moment of truth? Thousands of times he'd taken himself to the edge of orgasm only to halt the on-rushing wave of pleasure. He had will, discipline, strength of character. He'd spent a lifetime building and solidifying those crucial traits. Now, after last night's debacle, he could only wonder if those traits were real or only an illusion.

Was *he* real…or just some common fraud?

Then to come home after such a dreadful experience, in need of rest and a place to think, only to be told by those two aging queens that the house was being sold—that was more than any human being should be subjected to.

Eldon paced his office, his thoughts now squarely on Gee and Rose. Regardless of what had happened with Beverly Diaz, or whether or not there would be another Chosen One, he knew with absolute certainty that *he was going to kill them.* He'd always known that; when had been the only question. Well, now he knew. As soon as they returned from Sarasota. And if they bailed on that trip, then within the next week. The sooner those two hags were out of his life, the better. They would trouble him no more.

Tired of pacing and beating himself up, Eldon left his office and went down into the bookstore. In an effort to divert his thoughts away from last night's debacle, he picked up the new Faye Kellerman novel and began leafing through it. He liked Kellerman's stories, her plotting and in particular her two main characters—Decker, the tough cop, and Rina, his complex Jewish wife. Eldon had read everything of Kellerman's, and was eager to get started on her latest effort.

Eldon closed the book, tucked it under his arm, and went to one of the check-out lines. There, a young student, Samantha Durbin, took the book from him, scanned it, and told him the price.

Eldon took out a credit card and handed it to her. "And, Sam, don't forget my ten percent discount," he said, smiling. "A poor man like me needs all the help he can get."

"Will do, Mr. Wessell. Employee lesson number one— never shortchange the boss." Samantha looked at the woman standing behind Eldon. "Right, Marcy?"

Marcy Coleman nodded. "Absolutely." She playfully punched Eldon on the arm. "But I'd keep my eye on her anyway if I were you, sir. Samantha's a notoriously shady character."

"Is that so?" he said.

"Yep." Marcy handed a T-shirt to Samantha, who scanned it and rang it up. "Just ask anyone on campus. They'll tell you she's a legendary thief."

"Thanks for ripping me in front of the boss, Marcy." Samantha crammed the shirt into a yellow plastic bag and handed it to Marcy. "Be gone, evil one."

The two girls laughed out loud.

Marcy reached out, took the book from Eldon, and looked at the cover. "Faye Kellerman," she said. "Any good?"

"Yes, I highly recommend her," Eldon answered. "She's a superb storyteller and a top-notch writer. One of the very best, in my humble opinion."

"Really?"

"I have all of her books, most in hardback, and I would be more than willing to lend them to you. I suggest that you begin with *The Ritual Bath*, since it is the first of a series."

Looking up from the book, Marcy smiled and said, "Thanks, I just may take you up on your offer."

"Since you seem to know Sam, I must assume you are a student at the University," Eldon said.

"Well, I'm sitting out this semester, but I plan to start back in the fall." She handed the book back to him. "If I decide to read the book you mentioned, *The*...what was the title?"

"*The Ritual Bath*."

"Yeah. If I do, how can I get in contact with you?"

"I'm the bookstore manager," Eldon said, extending his right hand. "Eldon Wessell."

"Marcy Coleman," she said, shaking his hand.

"You can find me here anytime," Eldon said, still holding her hand. "Call, let me know when you want to read it, and I'll make sure it's here."

"Maybe I'll do that," Marcy said, touching his arm. "And, hey, thanks."

Eldon bought a can of Dr. Pepper from a vending machine, went back to his office, and lay down on the small brown leather sofa. Over and over in his head he replayed the brief encounter with Marcy Coleman. He remembered everything about the moment, everything about her. She was friendly, charming, warm, genuine. Kindness radiated from her like sunlight. She had been physical with him, too, touching his arm not once but twice, as though they were long-time acquaintances. She had accepted his offer to borrow the Kellerman book without hesitation. She valued his opinion, his wisdom.

Marcy Coleman was someone special...someone to be appreciated. And, of course, there was her resemblance to the others. Tall, dark hair, full breasts, marvelous skin, wonderful smile. She could easily be a sister to any of them. True, her beauty—real as it was—came up short when compared to the others, especially Beverly Diaz. But perhaps that was a blessing. Beverly Diaz and the others possessed an arrogance that sickened him. Marcy Coleman lacked that horrible trait. She was real, down to earth, not condescending. Eldon thought back to when she touched his arm. In that split-second, that moment of contact, Eldon realized two things: his discipline and will were back in full force, and what had transpired with Beverly Diaz was an aberration.

Marcy's warm hand on his arm sent the blood rushing to his loins. Feelings of intense pleasure rumbled through his body like an out-of-control automobile. Aware that another horrible catastrophe was only seconds away from happening, he'd reached deep down inside himself, into an inner reservoir of strength, and summoned the discipline, the will, to halt the tide of pleasure and avert potential disaster.

Instead of yielding to the forces that threatened to overwhelm him, he had assumed control of his body and his mind. He faced the challenge and prevailed. Just like he'd done hundreds of times in the past.

Discipline—above all else, discipline.

He, the Eldon of old, was ready to redeem himself.

CHAPTER 51

"That's just terrific, Jennifer," the young woman said, hugging the child. "You've really had a good session today. You keep improving like this and you may become a great ballet dancer someday."

The young girl's pretty face glowed with pride. "Maybe I'll be as good as you someday, huh, Caitlin?" she said.

"Oh, sweetie, you'll be much better than me," Caitlin answered. She hugged Jennifer again, then kissed her on the forehead. "Now, run along. Your mom's waiting. See you tomorrow."

Jennifer ran to one of the chairs lined up against the wall, grabbed a backpack, and started for the door. "See you tomorrow, Rose," she yelled over her shoulder.

Rose Wessell stood by the piano, a smile on her face. "You were terrific today, Jennifer."

"I know," Jennifer said, opening the big door. "Caitlin told me that already."

Rose laughed, then waved at Laurie Dunn, who was sitting near the front entrance. Laurie had been there for more than thirty minutes, having arrived in the middle of Jennifer's practice session. Watching Caitlin as she worked with young Jennifer made Laurie think about Abby Kaplan. She wondered what kind of a teacher Abby had been. Probably a good one.

The half-hour wait also piqued Laurie's curiosity. What could Rose want to talk about? Did she have something new to add to the investigation? Laurie hoped so, but had her doubts. What *could* Rose possibly have to offer? Nothing, as Laurie saw it. More than likely, she just needed someone to talk to. A friend. Laurie judged Rose to be a person surrounded by many people but having few real friends.

Laurie stood and greeted Rose with a nod. "Hello, Rose. Good to see you again."

Rose hugged Laurie tightly, then stepped back. "I am so sorry that you had to wait this long," she said. "I know how busy you are, and…"

"Don't apologize," Laurie said. "I actually enjoyed watching Jennifer. She seems to have some real talent."

"Exceptional talent," Rose said, smiling. "She knows it, too. As you could no doubt tell."

"The next Margot Fonteyn, maybe?"

"Well, let's not get too far ahead of ourselves," Rose said. "A little thing called puberty looms on the horizon. That's the real test. Most young girls, even those with great potential, are quick to trade the Bolshoi for boys. But…we can dream, can't we?"

"Yes, indeed." Laurie glanced around the vast room. "Where's the best place to talk?"

"If you're up for brunch, we can walk down to the restaurant. If not, we can go to my office."

"The office will be fine."

"Would you care for something to drink?" Rose asked as they entered the small office. "I can brew us a fresh pot of coffee if you like."

"I'm fine. Thanks."

"Water, maybe? It's very stuffy in here."

"No, really, I'm okay."

Rose adjusted the thermostat on the wall, then motioned for Laurie to sit. "That couch must be a hundred years old, but it sure is comfortable," she said, sitting behind her desk. "Sometimes when I'm really tired, and when I'm between students, I just fall down on that old thing and take me a nap."

"It's very comfortable," Laurie said, settling in. She removed her notepad from her jacket and opened it. "So, Rose, how have you been doing?"

Rose sighed and forced a smile. "It's been a difficult time, but I'm starting to come around. At least, I think I am. Being around the students really does wonders for my spirit. Watching them, seeing their enthusiasm, their joy, their willingness to listen and learn—it's hard to feel much darkness when you're surrounded by these wonderful, pure particles of light."

She looked up at a picture of Abby Kaplan on the wall. Her eyes filled with tears. "I miss that girl," she said, pointing to the photo. "I'll always miss Abby."

Laurie waited a few seconds for Rose to continue. When she didn't, Laurie said, "You sounded kinda urgent on the phone. Are you sure you're all right?"

"I remembered something. From that night."

"The night Abby was killed?"

"Yes, yes, and I can't believe I'm just remembering it. In the shock and confusion, it must've slipped my mind. How stupid of me…"

"It's easy to forget things during a stressful time like that. Go on."

"You remember asking me if I saw anyone that night?" Rose asked.

"Sure. You said you didn't."

"Well, I was mistaken. I did see someone."

"Who?"

"My brother."

"Your brother?"

"Yes. As I was turning left out of the Commonwealth Plaza parking lot and onto Lane Allen, his car was stopped at the light. I went right past him. I didn't pay much attention until I was parallel to his car. That's when I looked in and saw him."

"Are you positive it was your brother? With the rain, the darkness, it would be easy to be mistaken."

"Yes, I am absolutely certain. There's a streetlight right at that intersection. It was directly above his car. I saw him plain as day. I remember thinking, what in the world is Eldon doing out on a night like this?"

Rose scribbled the name Eldon Wessell in her notepad and underlined it three times. "Did he see you?" she said, looking up at Rose.

"No, I don't think so."

"Did you ask him about it?"

"My brother and I aren't exactly on speaking terms."

"Does he still live around here?"

"Oh, you couldn't pay Eldon enough to leave this town. He's convinced that the University of Kentucky would crumble if it weren't for him."

"He works there?"

"Manages the bookstore. Been working there since he was a student. Thinks he's indispensable."

Laurie wrote "bookstore" next to Eldon's name. "Where does your brother live?"

"With my mother and me."

"How old is Eldon?"

"Let's see...He's three years younger than me, which makes him thirty-nine."

"Can you think of any reason why Eldon would be in this area of town at that time of night?"

"No, and that's what makes this so unusual."

"Why?"

"Eldon seldom goes out after he gets home from work. He just shuts himself off in his room and does who knows what. Sits at his computer, writing, I would imagine."

"Is he a writer?"

Rose snorted. "He likes to think he is."

"What about reading? Is he a big reader?"

"As a young boy, he devoured books. So I can only assume that he still reads quite a bit."

Laurie wrote *writer/big reader* in her notepad. Looking up, she said, "Does your brother have a woman in his life?"

"I'm not sure he's ever been on a date with a woman."

"Is he gay?"

"He would say no, I'm sure. But personally, I think the jury is still out on that one."

"Did he know Abby Kaplan?"

"If he did, it would come as a complete surprise to me."

"He never met her here at the academy?"

"He has never set foot in this place. Not once."

"Has he ever been in trouble with the law?"

"Good heavens, no! Eldon is a complete ass, but he certainly doesn't have a criminal mentality. He's just a..."

"What?"

"A lousy son and brother. There, I've said it. My mother and I have tried to connect with him, but he won't allow it. He feels that we are always against him, which, I suppose is true, since he never agrees with us on anything. He's quite impossible."

"And you're one-hundred percent certain the man you saw that night was your brother?"

"Absolutely."

"Anything else you think is important?"

Rose shook her head. "No, that's it. And I'm not sure how important it is. I'm just so sorry for not remembering it earlier."

Laurie closed her notepad and put it back in her jacket pocket. "It's probably just a coincidence," she said. "I'll ask your brother about it. Perhaps he saw someone else that night."

"Yes, maybe he did."

"Tell me, Rose, what made you remember seeing your brother?"

"Mother and I were on our way to Florida yesterday when we had car trouble. The gentleman who pulled over to help us bore a slight resemblance to Eldon. He also drove the exact same kind of car. When I saw him pull up next to us, it just came to me. Strange how the mind works, isn't it?"

"Sure is." Laurie opened the door, hesitated, then turned around. "Out of curiosity, Rose, how tall is your brother?"

Rose seemed taken aback by the question.

"You're a tall woman," Laurie said. "Is your brother also a big man?"

Rose laughed. "Hardly. Eldon is quite short. I don't know exactly how tall he is, but he's a good four or five inches shorter than me."

"That would make him...what—five-five or five-six?"

"Yes, I would say that's pretty accurate."

CHAPTER 52

Beth Robinson walked into the War Room at a little past 3 p.m. and set two large travel bags on the table. Dantzler was alone in the room, studying photos from the four crime scenes. He looked up when Beth came in.

"What's up, BR?" He nodded at the two bags on the table. "Looks like you're running out on me again. Keep this up and you'll give me a complex."

"I've been summoned," she said. "Seems the war on terrorism can't be won without me. Hate to leave, but…a higher duty calls."

"What time is your plane?"

"Six. Rich is chauffeuring me. Ridin' with the big dog. Think I don't rate high?"

"Nah, you're only getting a lift because Rich is afraid you'll bill the department for cab fare."

Beth chuckled. "He's right." Her expression turned serious. "How are you doing, Jack? Really doing?"

"You asked me that already."

"I'm asking again."

"Given the circumstances—the fact that some maniac has killed four women and I haven't caught him—I'd say I'm doing fine."

"You don't look fine."

"How *do* I look?"

"Like a wreck, to be honest with you. You've lost too much weight, your hair is too long, you need a shave, and you look like you haven't slept in a month. Those bags under your eyes are big enough to carry five pounds of sand. Rich is concerned that you've been drinking too much."

"Rich is wrong," Dantzler said. "Dead wrong. The other shit I'll cop to. I'm tired, I don't eat enough, and sleep hasn't been a top priority lately. Know what I say about all that? Fuck it. None of that's going to change until I get this guy."

"Listen to yourself, Jack. Until *I* get this guy. *I* haven't caught him. Where does it say that you have to do this by yourself? Look, whether you want to acknowledge it or not, you don't work here alone. You have other detectives here, some that are pretty damn good, and if you'd rely on them a little more, it just might..." She laughed and shook her head.

"What's so funny all of sudden?" he asked.

"I was about to say it just might relieve some of the pressure on you. That would be a waste of breath, wouldn't it? You live for the pressure, don't you, Jack? You thrive on it. The challenge, the intellectual aspect of it, pitting your mind against the killer's. With you, it's as much an intellectual exercise as it is a homicide investigation."

"I—*we*—want to catch this guy, BR. That's it, pure and simple."

She walked over and kissed him on the lips. "You will, Jack. Just don't fall apart on me before you do." She ran her hands through his hair. "You know, the lovely Miss Dunn has quite a thing for you."

"Is that a fact?"

"Solid as a *Jeopardy* answer. I can see it in her eyes. She's in love with you, Jack."

"Jealous?"

"I feel a twinge."

"A twinge? That's all I'm worth?"

She kissed him again, stood, and picked up her two bags. "Sorry I won't be here when you do catch the guy," she said. "Will you send me the newspaper clippings?"

"You got it."

"And, Jack. Do take care of yourself. Laurie's not the only one who loves you."

"Meaning?"

"Dynamite is crazy about you."

Dantzler smiled and nodded.

Beth opened the door, then looked back at him. "I am too, Jack. Always will be."

CHAPTER 53

Eldon turned right off Main onto Broadway, then made another immediate right onto West Short Street. He drove slowly past Cheapside Bar & Grill, hooked a left, and parked in an empty lot next to a bank. The night was clear and exceptionally warm for mid-May, and noise from the Cheapside patio, which was packed, seemed louder to him than usual. Cutting the engine, he picked up the book lying on the seat next to him—a near-perfect hardcopy of Faye Kellerman's *The Ritual Bath*—studied it for several seconds, and then placed it back on the seat.

Now was not the time to be the bearer of gifts. That would come later. In due time, Marcy Coleman would get her book.

Eldon was fully aware of the inherent danger in what he was about to do. He was charting a new course, one that he would never have dared contemplate in the past. Even if he had considered it, his caution radar wouldn't have allowed him to follow through. This was revolutionary, perhaps even reckless, and yet seldom had Eldon felt so excited, so energized, so filled with a sense of daring.

He had always resided in the safety of the bookstore, where the Chosen Ones came to him. But this was different. Now he was about to make himself available to a Chosen One. He was venturing into the outside world, following and observing the prey, a true hunter on the prowl.

See me now, arrogant Jack Dantzler. See how I move in your world.

This was, Eldon acknowledged, an impetuous act, and he was not by any definition an impetuous man. Indeed, he was free at this moment precisely because he refused to take unnecessary risks. He studied and calculated every possible scenario. Like a great battlefield commander, he formulated a game plan that left nothing to chance.

All contingencies were factored in. All options considered.

Eldon got out of his car, locked it, and quickly made the one-block walk to Coyle's All-Night Diner. Once inside, he seated himself in a booth near the front door. He picked up a menu, gave it a perfunctory look, closed it, and put it down. He hadn't come to eat.

When Marcy saw him, she did a quick double-take, smiled, and walked over to his booth. "Mr. Wessell," she said, grinning. "From the bookstore. How are you tonight?"

"Terrific. And you?"

"Hanging in."

"I'm surprised to find you here this late at night."

"Four to midnight this week. Sucky hours, but Cynthia is off on maternity leave, so I'm filling in for her." Marcy filled his glass with water. "Haven't seen you in here before. First time?"

"Oh, no, my dear. I used to eat here regularly. But it has been a long time."

"Know what you want, or do you need some more time to make up your mind?"

"Being a constant calorie watcher, I know I shouldn't do this. But I would like a piece of cheesecake. With strawberries."

"Excellent choice, Mr. Wessell. The cheesecake is great here. Best in town."

"I'm sure it is."

"Care for anything to drink?"

"Water is fine."

"Be back in a sec with your cheesecake."

As Eldon watched her walk toward the counter, he felt a new rush of excitement tear through his body. There was something truly special about her, something…he wasn't quite sure what it was. But it was there, he felt it, a connection, a bond. She touched him, moved him. He would take his time with her, just like he'd planned to do with Beverly Diaz. Marcy Coleman would be the final Chosen One, and he was going to enjoy her to the fullest.

"Here you go," Marcy said, setting the cheesecake on the table. "I sliced it myself. Gave you a little more than usual. Our little secret."

"Not that I need it," he said, touching her hand. "But thanks anyway."

Our little secret. My child, you have no idea.

When Eldon finished his cheesecake, he fished in his back pocket and took out his billfold. He removed a ten-dollar bill and set it on the table along with the check. Sliding out of the booth, he stood and looked around the dining area, hoping to say goodbye to Marcy. She was at one of the tables, her back to him, taking an order. Only a handful of customers were still in the restaurant. One in particular caught his attention. A tall, thin, bearded man sitting alone in a corner booth reading the newspaper. Eldon recognized him from somewhere but he couldn't put face and name together. He stared a few seconds longer, yet a name eluded him.

It wasn't until Eldon got to his car that recognition hit him. How could he have not known? The beard had thrown him off. And the long hair.

Could I be mistaken, Eldon asked himself. *Is it possible that I'm wrong?*

No. It was him.

Eldon giggled.

It was Jack Dantzler.

CHAPTER 54

Dear Jack:
Now let us speak of another victim—Sarah Dantzler.
Yes, Jack, your beloved mother, whom you worshipped above all others. I have always felt great sympathy for you, having lost her while you were still but a child. (And your father when you were even younger; how horrible!) How old was she when death stole her away from you forever? Thirty-four, thirty-five? Tragic. The death of a loved one at such a young age is never easy to accept. And such a horrible way to die, being strangled. (Thank God she wasn't defiled sexually. At least she was spared that indignity.)
How much does your mother's death trouble you, Jack? Does it eat at your soul like crows pecking at a hanged man's eyes? I would imagine it does, you being a man of obvious sensitivity. And does her death make you wonder about the very nature of God? All questions eventually lead to the one big question: Does God even exist? And what about the Messiah? When do you think the Messiah will grace us with his next visit? The world is such a filthy place that you'd think he would have already blessed us with an appearance. If, indeed, the Messiah's mission is to eradicate the evil here on earth, then I would argue that history has never presented him with a more opportune time to begin his work.
It's like Travis Bickle said: What we need is a great rain to come and wash the filth and scum off the streets. Wasn't De Niro superb in that role? I've never forgiven the voters for not awarding him the Academy Award. What a performance! Easily the best of the decade.
Now back to this Messiah mystery. How terrible do things have to get before he returns? How many people like me will it take until he's had enough? How many innocent victims must die at the hands of suicide bombers or terrorist assassins before he gets upset enough to make his next grand entrance? Or perhaps

you agree with Kafka's statement that the Messiah will come only "when he's no longer needed." Interesting twist, don't you agree? Leaving it up to us to straighten out this mess here on earth. Of course, if somber old Franz is correct, then I shan't count on seeing the Messiah for another millennium or two. Incidentally, Kafka was a Jew, which I'm sure you know. Just so you'll know, I am not Jewish. I tell you this because I don't want you reading too much into this talk about the Messiah. I'm just sharing information, nothing more. It dawned on me that you might see these references and assume my Jewishness, then go off to every temple and synagogue, hounding the poor rabbis about "some little Jewish guy who might be capable of brutally murdering five women." (Yes, Jack, victim number five has already been chosen.) To send you on such a wild goose chase would be a waste of your time and the taxpayers' money.

Come to think of it, wasn't the Kaplan girl Jewish? Yes, she was. My, my, wonder what her parents thought when they heard about the Pietà and the St. Jude medal? I would imagine they were terribly offended by such clear Catholic symbols. Had I been a tad more considerate, I wouldn't have tarnished their religion with such tawdry, carnival-like relics.

My religious affiliation? I have none. Organized religion is such a sham, such a shallow entity. Probably the root cause of men such as myself, if you want the truth. Religion inflicts hang-ups the way dentists inflict pain. Me, I believe in a continual search for personal pleasure tempered by discipline. Above all else, Jack, a human being must develop discipline. It is our highest calling and our greatest failing. We take and seek and grab for pleasure with little or no restraint. That's abominable. That's behaving like a wild jungle animal.

Take me, for instance. I've murdered four women (and counting), yet I've been called to murder ten times that many. My appetite for death is voracious; however, unlike the obese individual, I had the discipline to rein in my impulses.

Discipline—above all else, discipline.

Oh, Jack, how disingenuous of me to laud my own discipline when I have allowed my self-absorption to take me away from the subject of your dear, dead mother. I apologize with the utmost sincerity. It was shallow and disrespectful on my part. I promise to do better in the future.

So…let me continue.

You were at home when you first learned that your mother had been murdered. The two detectives informed your uncle Tommy, who had the difficult and unenviable task of breaking the news to you. Did you cry, Jack? Did you curse God for allowing your beautiful young mother to fall victim to such an evil act? Did you ask yourself where the God of love was on that dark, hate-filled night?

I can tell you where that great coward was, Jack. Hiding, of course. Lost within the endless silence that has been his trademark for more than two centuries. How pathetic! And religious leaders wonder why the world is blanketed with such darkness, such hate. They need ponder this no more. The answer is simple: God whispers; Satan screams. Hence the many victories by the Evil One we find so repulsive yet so appealing.

Back to you, Jack. I know that you have always felt suffocating guilt for what happened to your mother. But are you being fair to yourself? You were only a young lad—what could you have possibly done to prevent her death? You can't be held responsible. Therefore, you shouldn't blame yourself. Accept it for what it was, a random act, simply part of the chaos in which we live. That's how the detectives saw it, as random. Two human beings intersected at a precise moment in time and history, absolutely by chance, resulting in an outcome that had been decreed by the cruel gods of fate. Killer and victim—their respective destinies guided by some unseen force. Providence prevails.

(Of course, not all murders are the result of a random act. Take mine, for instance. Each one is calculated with the precision of an algebraic problem.)

Your mother did not know her killer, Jack. The detectives were convinced that she was killed by a complete stranger, and I concur with that assessment. The killer likely used a weapon to get her into his car, strangled her almost instantly, and then drove to the site where he left her body.

Why do you think he killed her, Jack? What was his reasoning? It wasn't for money or jewelry, the two most obvious motives. She had no debts or money problems. She wasn't a substance abuser or an alcoholic. There were no other men in her life at the time. When we rule out those possible motives, we are left with a genuine mystery.

So what's your take on it? After twenty-five years, surely you've come to some conclusions. Me, I tend to think the killer's initial plan was to rape her, then kill her. However, since there was no sexual assault, I'm left to conclude that he struggled with her, killed her, panicked, dumped the body at the first convenient place he could find, and then vanished into thin air.

Have you seen the crime scene photos, Jack? Your mother's twisted corpse lying on top of the garbage, naked, covered by a light blanket of snow. If you have seen them—and I'm almost certain that you have—how did it make you feel? Outraged, heartbroken, melancholic? I doubt I can even begin to understand the depths of your pain and anguish.

Of course, my feelings were quite different when I saw the photos. I must admit to being turned on, excited, sexually aroused. Your mother was an incredibly beautiful woman, Jack. She had the face of a Hollywood movie star and a body to match. With those looks, it's not hard to envision her up there on the silver screen. Even death could not diminish her beauty. I remember everything about her, Jack. The dark hair, the nice full lips, the smooth skin. And most of all I remember the one breast not covered by snow. Oh, I must have stared at that dark nipple for hours. Did she breastfeed you, Jack? Did you suckle at that very nipple I saw in the photo? Oh, how I envy you. How I wish I could have been so fortunate. But, alas, I wasn't. The nipple offered me when I was a child might as well have belonged to a succubus. I would rather drink the pus that drips from open sores than suckle from the scorpion that is my mother.

You loved your mother more than life itself. I hate mine with an equal passion.

Fate, Jack. It always comes back to fate.

By now I'm sure you are asking yourself two questions: How could he possibly know these things about my mother, and, did he murder her?

With all due respect, I can only answer one of those two queries. To reveal my source of information would be an unwise move on my part, so, sadly, I shan't do so. However, the second question, I can answer. And I offer it without hesitation.

No, I am not the one who stole your mother from you.

But I know who did.

Tantalizing, isn't it, Jack? To know that with a dozen or so strokes on the keyboard, I can solve the one mystery that haunts you the most. These ten chubby fingers of mine hold the answer to your life-long puzzle. Shall I begin typing? Shall I spell out the killer's name? Shall I put an end to your agony?

No, I think not. Like God, I choose to remain silent. If you want answers, you'll have to find them without my help. Revelation won't come from me.

I must go now, Jack. Duty calls, and I am not a person who shirks his duties. My next victim awaits her coronation—I shan't delay her moment of glory. Incidentally, Jack, this will be my final outing. After this, there will be no more. Why? Because I choose not to press my luck. I dare not risk being "retired" by you. Instead, I will, like the man who murdered your mother, simply vanish into thin air.

Poof...gone like those snows of bygone years.

But...

What if, at some future date, I decide to pick up where I left off? What if I bring the Beast out of hiding? What if I decide to show you (again) that my cunning is far superior to your intellect?

I can do it, Jack. I hold the power. And I just might. Only time will answer that, won't it?

Do you see the beauty of it all, Jack? Do you see the perfection of my plan? I have killed at will. I have eluded your grasp. I have fed your nightmares. I might kill again at some future date. I know the name of the man who killed your mother.

Add it all up, Jack, and what do you get?

The most beautiful part of all: I have left you damned by
uncertainty.

Sincerely,
Mike L. Angelo
PS —The face of evil is always the face of total need.
—William S. Burroughs

CHAPTER 55

Dan Matthews read the letter for the third time, looked up, and whistled through clenched teeth. Pointing to the letter, he said, "This guy's nuts, Jack. Crazier than a loony bird."

"*Au contraire*," Dantzler answered. "This guy knows exactly what he's talking about. He's anything but crazy."

The two men were alone in Dantzler's den. It was just past 7:00 a.m. and Matthews had already been there for nearly an hour. After finding the letter in his mailbox, Dantzler called Matthews at home, rousted him out of bed, and asked him to come over. The veteran detective was there in less than twenty minutes.

"You do realize what this letter hints at, don't you?" Matthews said.

"That a cop killed my mother."

"Jesus." Matthews quickly read through it again. "I doubt anyone even considered that possibility."

"Maybe someone should have."

"Do you think this son of a bitch killed her?"

Dantzler shook his head. "No. But I believe him when he says he knows who did. He knows details only a cop would know. He's seen the crime scene photos. His theory of the killing is absolutely on target. The only way he could've gotten information like this is from someone extremely familiar with the case."

"A cop."

"How well did you know Hutchinson and Harper?"

"I got to know Sam fairly well later on. After I'd been on the force a few years, right before he retired, he made himself available to me. Helped me out a couple of times when I needed it. Nothing major, just an old cop being nice to a young cop. Hutchinson, I never really knew. He was a tough nut to crack."

"Funny, as a kid, when it happened, I remember Hutchinson being the friendlier of the two."

"You must've caught him during one of his sober periods, which wasn't all that often."

"Think he could've done it?"

"Absolutely not," Matthews said, shaking his head. "No way. I had only been on the force a couple of years when it went down. Maybe three years. But I remember Sam and Hutchinson working their asses off trying to solve that case. I mean, they really busted their humps. Sam was an excellent detective, and like him or not, so was Hutchinson. No, Jack, if the killer really was a cop, it was someone other than Lee Hutchinson. You can take that to the bank."

Matthews handed the letter back to Dantzler. "Get down to personnel, go through the records and pull the files on all the cops on the force when your mother was murdered. It also might not hurt to go back a few years, check the files on cops who had recently retired. That's a place to start, anyway."

"I'll do that," Dantzler said, slipping the letter back into the large manilla folder. "I'll also talk to Charlie Bolton, see what he thinks about it."

Matthews nodded. "Charlie would know if anyone on the force was hinky enough to do something like that. He also worked the case, so he can help you from that angle, too."

Dantzler walked over to the bookcase, picked up a photo of his mother, and studied if for nearly a minute. After replacing it, he turned, went to the front window, and gazed out at the early morning sun.

Matthews picked up his sport coat and put it on. "I'm gonna say something, Jack, and I hope you don't take it the wrong way."

"I'm listening.

"Your mother died twenty-five years ago. That was—"

"Save your breath, Dan. I know the priorities. I'll work on that case once we catch our serial killer."

"Who knows, Ace? We solve one; maybe we solve two. That would be sweet, wouldn't it?"

"Yeah, it would."

"Well, stranger things have happened. We both know that."

"Do you and Milt still like Winstead?"

Matthews shrugged. "We like him, but hell, what we've got on him is pretty damn thin. This fuckin' case is nothing but thin. Four murders and not a single legitimate suspect. Your boy Roper is out, we don't really have turkey shit on Winstead, and John Stocker's son-in-law alibied up. So..."

"Where was Mike McKendrick?"

"With a dame. Seems Mad Mike, upon realizing that his daughter had a ride home, took a detour to see a little chippie named Natalie Black. Lives out on Trent Boulevard. Stayed with her for a little over an hour, then spent the next three hours drinking at The Grapevine. That's all been verified by Gamble and Dunn."

Matthews opened the front door. "Let's face it, Ace," he said. "We're dealing with one slippery dude."

Dantzler nodded but said nothing.

After Matthews drove away, Dantzler stood at the window, looking out at the rising sun. The day was shaping up to be a scorcher, even by early June standards. Excessive heat was no friend to law enforcement. Unlike most of the population, cops didn't welcome summer with open arms. Summer is a bummer, as one old detective put it. Everything seemed to ratchet up a notch or two on hot days, especially tempers. A blistering summer, which the forecasters were predicting, would only make matters worse. Cops hated the heat.

Dantzler turned and saw his reflection in the hall mirror. He stared deep into his own dark eyes, unblinking, but thinking.

I'm smarter than you, goddammit.

CHAPTER 56

Eldon stood at his open window watching that same fiery red sun make its way up toward the heavens. His hand was on his erect penis, his thoughts on Marcy Coleman. Her date with destiny was nearing and the prospect of making love to her was thrilling. And this time there was no ambiguity about how things would go down. Not like there had been with Beverly Diaz. He would perform the act while Marcy Coleman was still alive. To deny her the honor of bearing witness to such a monumental event would be unfair and selfish.

Eldon had slept little last night, kept awake by his letter delivery duties and the growing excitement he felt for the lovely young Miss Coleman. He was also aware that larger forces were at play here. That he was at the epicenter of a truly special drama. He was orchestrating something majestic, something almost Shakespearean in scope, a combination of mind and flesh, a twisted journey that would lead to death and insanity.

I am fucking with Jack Dantzler's sanity and I will soon fuck Marcy Coleman.

Eldon giggled.

Let's talk of games, of worms, of epitaphs.

Eldon lay in the bathtub, a washcloth covering his face, steam rising from the hot water. It was 9:30 and he'd been in the tub for almost an hour. Seldom had he felt more relaxed, more in control. Using his right foot, he turned the nozzle and ran more hot water into the tub. Satisfied, he turned it off, reheated the washcloth, and draped it across his face.

A few minutes before getting into the tub, he had called the bookstore and informed Samantha Durbin that he wouldn't be in until mid-afternoon. He told her he had a dental appointment… which wasn't the truth.

"Elmer Donald, is it beyond the realm of possibility that someone other than you might be allowed in the bathroom?" Gee yelled from outside the door. "I tend to believe that an hour in the tub is more than enough time to cleanse one's body."

"I will be out when I'm finished," Eldon yelled back. "Perhaps within the next ten to fifteen minutes."

"That's breaking news worthy of CNN," Gee said. "And at some point this morning, you need to see me. We have a certain matter that must be discussed."

Eldon pulled the plug, threw his washcloth against the wall, and stood. "I won't allow this house to be sold out from under my feet!" he screamed, tears filling his eyes. "That will *not* happen!"

CHAPTER 57

When Charlie Bolton opened his front door and saw Dantzler standing there, he smiled sadly and shook his head. Without saying anything, he shoved the door open wider and motioned Dantzler in.

"You look awful, Jack," Charlie said. "Like a goddamn bum."

"I think a cop killed my mother," Dantzler said.

Charlie snickered. "And I think you've officially lost your mind."

"Maybe, maybe not."

"Exactly what brought you to this conclusion?"

"It's not a conclusion, only a theory."

"Oh, pardon me, Einstein. What brought you to this theory?"

"I got another letter from our serial killer. In it, he claims to know who killed my mother. And he provides some details that only a cop could know. It's pretty convincing stuff, Charlie."

"Are you sure of that? Or is it that you *want* to be convinced?"

"Listen, contrary to popular opinion, I haven't gone off the deep end. Not just yet, anyway. I wouldn't say shit like this unless I believed it's possible."

Charlie thought for a moment, then shook his head. "No, you haven't gone off the deep end." He laughed. "You're one of those lucky fucks who would never allow that to happen."

"So?"

"So—do I know of anyone on the force back then who might've been capable of killing your mother? My initial response is, no, I don't. Out of fairness to you, and because I'm a good cop, I will give the matter some thought. Give me a day or two."

"You got it. And, Charlie, thanks."

"Don't thank me yet, Jack, 'cause I think you're pissing in the wind on this one."

"You know something? I hope you're right."

CHAPTER 58

Eldon observed a smiling Marcy Coleman interact with the clerk inside the jewelry store, and it suddenly hit him that his plans for her were incomplete. In the swirl of excitement, he'd overlooked one critical element: a suitable location. It was a detail—and not a minor one—that had simply slipped through the cracks.

Eldon knew why, too. He'd become so accustomed to executing his plan in the victim's own home that he'd just taken for granted that this would be no different. Things had to be different this time. The situation demanded it. Marcy lived at home with her parents, which meant he had no choice but to come up with an alternate plan.

He mulled this over, carefully running through a list of possible alternatives, giving equal weight to each one. There were obvious choices—his house, his car, the bookstore—that were worth considering. He could phone her, tell her he had the Kellerman book, and set up a time and place to meet. But that was too dangerous; phone calls were easily traceable. It would also likely mean being outside somewhere, and he wasn't inclined to leave his handiwork to the mercy of the elements. That was especially true with Marcy Coleman. She had to be immortalized properly, in the context of absolute perfection.

St. Jude and weeping Mary would expect nothing less.

In the end, Eldon knew that his only option was to wait outside Coyle's until Marcy got off work, tell her he had the book, then...what? Where did he go from there? Eldon pondered this, and quickly realized that he had no answer. He was back where he started, having to *overpower* her outside, in public, which was far too risky. And even if he did, where could he take her? Where would...

The answer hit him like a blast of arctic air.

Rose's Dance Academy.

Jesus, yes—that's it. I'll take her to Rose's place.

It was so obvious he wondered why he hadn't thought of it earlier. He would go there—to the place where virgin sister Rose had set up shop in an effort to escape the memories of that night she was almost raped—and he would lose his own virginity.

It was pure genius.

Unbeknownst to Rose, he had a key to the building; so entrance was no problem. It would be well past midnight, past closing time for the restaurant, which meant no one was likely to be in the vicinity. And if, per chance, someone did see him going inside, well, after all, he could say in all honesty that he was the owner's brother. He would say that he was there at her direction, retrieving some important papers that she left behind and that Marcy was his date.

The plan was flawless. It had a built-in safety net. It had an inherent believability. It would be an easy sell to Marcy. He would tell her that that's where the book was, and that they could zip over, get it, and be back in fifteen minutes. There was no way she wouldn't go for it.

Equally important, it was an exceptionally devious plan. There was a symmetry to it that Eldon appreciated. Pure and chaste Rose would arrive at six in the morning, smiling and happy, as if she were a character in a children's book, only to find Marcy's lifeless body. To know that Rose would confront such pure evil—that she would see the end results of the very act that *almost* happened to her—would only make the night even more memorable.

Rose would be in for the shock of a lifetime.

Oh, if he could only be there to see the horror on her face.

At 4 o'clock, following a stop at the bakery for a French creme horn and a glass of milk, Eldon sat at his office desk going over weekly reports and next week's work schedule. It was tedious work that demanded concentration, something he found difficult. Too many other thoughts bombarded his brain for him to be able to think about such mundane matters as the bookstore's finances and personnel concerns.

He'd given serious thought to blowing off the entire day,
but decided against it. Now was not the time to begin exhibiting
uncharacteristic behavior; and for steady, dependable Eldon
Wessell to miss a full day's work, well, that would certainly rate
as uncharacteristic. He *never* missed work. He was the
consummate professional, a man who could always be counted
on.

Sitting there, waiting for 5 o'clock to roll around, Eldon
reflected on what had happened last week in the bathtub. His
"accident." When his wall of discipline had crumbled faster than
an imploded building. Given the luxury of time and distance, he
was able to examine the events in a clinical way. To place them
in perspective. It had happened, it was over and done with, it was
time to move on. That's precisely what he had done—moved
forward. The anger and apprehension that overwhelmed him
then had all but dissipated, having been replaced by the old
confidence that he carried with the pride of a saber scar. What
had happened earlier was an aberration, a freak occurrence.
Helping to ease his anxiety was the knowledge that even the
great ones experience momentary lapses. The secret, though—
and this was what elevated the great ones to a plateau above the
common person—was to never make the same mistake twice.
And above all else, Eldon ranked himself among the great ones.
He had failed while in the solitude of his own bathroom—he had
dismissed his "accident" with Beverly Diaz; that resulted from ill
health and lack of sleep—he would not fail when face to face
with Marcy Coleman.

Drowsiness overtook Eldon. He yawned and flexed his arms
in an effort to stimulate his blood flow. The bookstore was all
but deserted, save for the two students sitting behind cash
registers and the young woman who had just walked in. She was
tall and extremely attractive, with long dark hair that fell onto
her shoulders. She was dressed in white slacks, a blue cotton
shirt, and brown Topsiders. A pair of expensive sunglasses were
pushed up onto her head.

Eldon studied her face, certain that he'd seen her before.
Where, he couldn't recall. But it hadn't been in the bookstore,

that much he did know. If he'd seen her there, he would remember.

The woman said something to the young man at the cash register, then let her eyes follow his arm as he pointed in Eldon's direction. She smiled, nodded her thanks, and began walking toward the steps leading up to Eldon's office.

Eldon felt his heartbeat speed up when he heard the woman's footsteps on the stairs. A nerve in his neck began to twitch uncontrollably. Who was she? What could she want? And why now, just as he was preparing to leave? It was an unwanted invasion of his precious time, a distraction neither needed nor wanted. Not now, not with so many things going on and so much to do.

Upon hearing the woman's knock at the door, he closed his eyes, took a deep breath, and slowly exhaled. With eyes still closed, he performed a quick inner-evaluation, searching for flaws, for possible chinks in his armor. There were none.

He opened his eyes. "The door is open," he said. "Please, come in."

The woman pushed the door open. "Mr. Wessell?" she said, smiling.

"Yes, I'm Eldon Wessell," he replied. "What can I do for you?"

"I'd like to ask you a few questions, if you don't mind," she said. "Do you have some time you can spare me?"

"Well, we normally close at five during the summer sessions," Eldon said, looking at his watch.

"No problem. This'll only take a couple of minutes."

"Questions, you say? About what?"

"Mind if I sit?" she said.

He motioned to an empty chair across from his desk. "Are you with the media?" he said.

"Why would you ask that?"

"It's not unusual for one of the TV stations to send a reporter to do interviews at the bookstore. Talk to the students— or to me—about what's going on here on campus. And to be honest, you do have the face of a television reporter."

"I'm not sure that's a compliment, but, no, I'm not with the media." She sat in the chair, set her purse in her lap, and opened it, taking out her shield. "My name is Laurie Dunn. I'm with Homicide."

Eldon felt a surge of blood rush to his head. Icy fingers danced along his spine. "Homicide? Really?" He forced a smile. "What on earth brings a homicide detective here?"

"As you know, four University of Kentucky students have been murdered and—"

"It's tragic what happened to those young women. To die so young, so senselessly. Such a waste." Eldon glanced at his watch. "However, if you are here to speak with me about those murders, I'm afraid you've come to the wrong place. I can't help you at all. I didn't know any of them, although I'm quite certain that I've seen them in here at one time or the other. Virtually every student on campus passes through these doors at some point."

"Are you positive you never met any of them?"

"Well, let me think. The one girl, the actress…"

"Deborah Tucker."

"Yes. A marvelous talent. I saw every play she was in and she was extraordinary. I may have met her at a post-production party, but I can't say that with any degree of certainty."

"And the others? Allison Parker, Becky Adams, and Abby Kaplan?"

Eldon shook his head. "Like I said, it's possible I met them here. But if I did, it was only to sell them a book or answer their questions."

"Are you positive you never met Abby Kaplan?"

"I'm fairly positive, yes."

"That's interesting."

"Why?"

"Because Abby Kaplan worked for your sister Rose at the dance studio. She was the top dance instructor."

Eldon thought for a few seconds, then said, "Yes, now that you mention it, that name does ring a bell. Sorry I didn't make an immediate connection."

"Your sister never spoke to you about Abby Kaplan's death?"

"Rose and I don't often communicate with one another. You might say we've taken a vow of silence with each other."

"The reason I'm here is because Rose may have been the last person to see Abby Kaplan alive. Except, of course, for her killer."

"I wouldn't know about that."

"Rose said that when she was leaving the parking lot that night she saw your car at a stoplight. What I was wondering is—"

"You spoke with Rose?"

"Yes."

"And she claims to have seen me that night?"

"She does."

"Where...exactly?"

"On Lane Allen."

"That's absolutely preposterous. No way that was me. No way I would be out in that kind of downpour."

"Funny that you recall the rain."

"There's nothing funny about murder, Detective Dunn."

"No, there isn't. Is it possible that you were on Lane Allen that night and you've forgotten it? If you were, and if you saw another car, you might help us catch the killer."

"I was not there that night. I wish I could be of some assistance in this matter, but I can't. Sorry. My sister is mistaken."

"You're certain of that?"

"One hundred percent positive," Eldon said. "Either my sister's eyesight betrayed her that evening, or she had, as Rimbaud said, 'drunk of the untaxed liquor of Satan's still.'"

"You like Rimbaud?"

"Very much. Do you?"

"To be honest, I've only begun reading him recently. What I've read, I like." She stood. "Thanks for your time, Mr. Wessell. You've been very cooperative."

"Cooperative, yes. But of little help, I'm afraid." He opened the door. "Let me lock up, then I'll walk you out."

When they were back in the bookstore, Laurie picked up a book by Camille Paglia and began leafing through it. After a few seconds, she replaced it and slowly walked toward the front, where Eldon was putting a new roll of paper into the cash register.

"Must be nice being surrounded by so much information and wisdom," she said. "I tend to see bookstores as large houses, and all the authors as part of one big family."

"I never looked at it in that light," Eldon said. "But you are absolutely right."

"Are you aware that we've met before?" Laurie asked. "Crossed paths, to put it more accurately."

"I sensed the moment I saw you that we've met. But for the life of me I can't pin down the time or place."

"Woodland Park. I was jogging and I…"

"Ran over me like a steamroller."

"That's me…Steamroller Laurie."

The young man who had been at the cash register came out of the rest room, went to a locker, and retrieved his backpack. After slipping it on, he held out his arm and pointed to his watch. "It's ten past five, Mr. Wessell," he said. "Time to close shop."

"Relax, Tim," Eldon said, closing the top of the cash register. "We shan't be much longer."

He looked at Laurie and smiled.

She smiled back, her eyes locked into his.

CHAPTER 59

Laurie took the address book from her purse and looked up Rose Wessell's phone number. After finding it, she flipped open her cell phone, punched in the numbers, dropped the book back into her purse, and waited. Seconds later, she heard the familiar busy signal. She punched off, thought about trying again in a few minutes, but decided against it.

She would go see Rose.

It was late—a little before 9:00 p.m.—so she needed an excuse for making the house call. Laurie thought about this for a while, tossing around several ideas before finally settling on telling Rose that this was a personal visit and not part of the murder investigation. She would invite Rose and her mother out for a drink at one of the nearby neighborhood bars. That was a safe plan and one that might have some appeal for the two Wessell women, whom she considered lonely and rather sad. Then at some point in the evening, after the ice had been broken, she would steer the conversation toward Eldon. She would have to be subtle, not set off any alarm signals, but if she played her cards right, she could finesse them into giving her more insight into little brother Eldon.

He was the killer, Laurie knew, and she was going to prove it. But in order to do so, to convince herself that she was a hundred percent right, she had to ask Rose and her mother a few more questions. She wanted to get a better read on his personality, background, and habits. Once those questions were answered to her satisfaction, once any lingering doubts were laid to rest, she would call Jack, tell him what she had, and wait for further instructions.

Maybe Jack would want to bring Eldon in for questioning tonight. Or he might opt to wait until tomorrow. Either way was okay with her, just as long as they put the bastard away.

Laurie was stuck in traffic less than two miles from 431 Sycamore Street. A tractor-trailer had overturned on Tates Creek

Road, closing both lanes heading into town. She'd already been sitting there for ten minutes, and the prospects of moving anytime soon didn't look promising. Normally, the delay would have had her steaming, cursing like a standup comedian, and chomping at the bit to get going. But she wasn't upset; in fact, she welcomed it. It gave her time to think, to piece together the questions that had to be asked and how best to pose them in a friendly, un-investigation-like manner.

She saw one of the uniformed patrolmen walking in her direction. He had obviously been dispatched to walk down the line of stalled cars and let the drivers know what was happening. It was a task she'd performed plenty of times in the past, and it wasn't fun, because usually the drivers were pretty pissed. When he got to Laurie's car, he immediately recognized her and waved.

She rolled down her window. "Hey, Jeremy, rough night, huh?" she asked, smiling.

"Yeah, it is. Fortunately, no one was injured. But it's a real mess, traffic-wise."

"How much longer you think it'll be?"

"Shit, I'd say at least another thirty minutes. The tow truck's not even here yet. I'd say more like an hour, maybe even longer."

"Jeez, I can't sit here that long. Any way I can turn around?"

"Sure, if you need to, we can manage it."

Jeremy stepped away from Laurie's car and looked around. After thinking about it a few seconds, he nodded and said, "If you take it real slow, I think you can turn around right here. The median is kinda low, so keep your car angled a bit. If you do that, you'll be okay."

"Thanks, Jeremy, I appreciate it."

Laurie backed up as far as she could, then slipped out from between cars. She slowly cut across the grassy medium, following Jeremy's directions. When she traversed the medium and was clear to enter the opposite lane, Jeremy moved to the center and waved his flashlight, stopping traffic long enough for her to pull out.

It was now ten past nine, and if she wasn't there within the next fifteen minutes she figured it would be impossible to get the Wessell girls to venture out. She didn't see them as night owls. In truth, it was probably wishful thinking on her part to believe that they would go to a bar at any hour, never mind this late at night. The plan was a long shot at best, but one she had to try.

At 9:23, Laurie pulled into the Wessell driveway. There were two cars parked side by side. The white Honda Accord, she knew, belonged to Rose. As for the black Lincoln LS, she assumed it was Eldon's. Just in case, she scribbled the license plate numbers of both vehicles into her notepad.

Laurie climbed the steps to the front porch, rang the doorbell, and listened. Not hearing anything, she rang it again, then knocked. After waiting for close to a minute, she knocked on the door once again, much harder this time. She could see the glow of a light from inside, and she thought she heard music being played, but there was no activity and no sign of the Wessells.

Stepping down from the porch, she walked around to the side of the house, next to where the cars were parked. From there, she could tell that the light was coming from the kitchen. She could also hear the music much clearer, and she immediately recognized the song "Memory" from the soundtrack for *Cats*.

Laurie went back around to the porch and knocked on the door again. She waited, then turned the doorknob, and pushed. To her surprise, it was unlocked. Stepping into the foyer, she was hit by the smell of something harsh coming from inside the house. Her first thought was wood lacquer. Or perhaps paint. Maybe one of the Wessells was doing some late-night painting or shellacking.

After closing the door, Laurie called out for Rose. Getting no response troubled her, even though she knew that the music was likely the reason she hadn't been heard. The music was coming from somewhere upstairs, so Laurie went to the bottom of the stairs and called out Rose's name again, this time louder. Nothing. She unsnapped the strap on her Glock and started to remove it, but didn't. She decided that the last thing the Wessell women needed was to see an armed person coming toward them. Still, she felt no need to secure her weapon. She left the holster unsnapped.

Laurie walked toward the light coming from the kitchen. She flipped on an overhead light in the dining room and another one in the large hallway leading to the den. As she proceeded down the hall, the odor became stronger, causing her eyes to water and her nose to run. She set her purse on a table, took out a Kleenex, wiped her eyes, and blew her nose. After tossing the tissue into a wastebasket, she continued down the hall, cautiously, her fingers gently touching the handle of her weapon.

On the right, near the end of the hallway, a heavy wooden door was slightly ajar. Laurie opened it and saw steps leading down to the basement. She called out Rose's name, again getting no response. Halfway down the steps, the smell became so overwhelming that Laurie gave serious thought to retreating back up the stairs. As she started to turn around, she spied an old cloth rag hanging on the wall, lifted it off the nail, gave it a couple of hard shakes to get rid of the dust, then placed it over her mouth and nose.

At the bottom of the steps, the smell was so powerful that Laurie felt for an instant that she might throw up. She took a couple of slow, deep breaths, pressing the old rag firmly against her face. The wave of nausea passed, but not the burning sensation in her eyes. She tried to blink the tears away, and when that didn't work, she wiped her eyes with the rag. Deciding that she'd had enough, she started up the stairs again when an object in the corner of the basement caught her eye. It was an old metal tub, very large, sitting against the far wall. What intrigued her was the cloud of steam rising from it. Whatever was in that tub, Laurie knew, was the source of the horrible odor permeating the house.

Fighting off a crushing, choking feeling in her lungs and a horrible burning sensation in her eyes, she slowly made her way toward the tub. With each step she took, the smell became more pronounced. Laurie reached the edge of the tub and looked inside.

And froze.

Lying in the tub were the nude bodies of Rose Wessell and an older woman that Laurie assumed was Rose's mother. They lay facing each other, with the older woman slightly above Rose. What Laurie saw was unlike anything she'd seen before—grisly, repugnant, sickening. The flesh on the two women's bodies was being burned away by the solution that filled the tub. Pieces of flesh and gristle, some surprisingly large, floated inside the tub like little islands, bubbling from the heat.

Laurie guessed the solution to be some form of acid, or possibly lye. Maybe a mixture of several types of acid. Whatever it was, it was no slow-acting compound. Rose was immersed slightly deeper in the tub than her mother, and well over half of her flesh was already gone. Her mother had more flesh, but most of her face had been burned away. One eye hung suspended on her right cheek, and the skin around her mouth was gone completely, revealing a perfect set of teeth.

Laurie reeled backward, sure now that she was going to vomit. She bent over and retched, but nothing came up. She coughed and retched, again producing only dry heaves. When the nausea passed, she wiped her eyes with the rag, took one more look at the two dead women, and turned to head upstairs.

Then everything went black.

CHAPTER 60

Dantzler was pissed. He'd spent the past hour trying to get in touch with Laurie, phoning her at least a dozen times. There was no answer, either on her cell phone or her home phone. Even the damn answering machine failed to respond. As a last resort, on the off-chance that she might be working late, he phoned the police station. Bruce Rawlinson picked up before the first ring had ended. At least someone was alive.

"Bruce, this is Dantzler."

"Hey, Ace, what's up? Caught any killers lately?"

"Not today. Listen, Bruce, you seen Dunn tonight?"

"Ah, Ace, you're supposed to be chasin' murderers, not poontang."

"Funny, Bruce. You should do a gig at Comedy Off Broadway, you know that?"

"I'd wow 'em, no doubt about it."

"What about Dunn? You seen her?"

"Yeah, she was here a couple hours ago."

"She still there?"

"I didn't see her leave, so, yeah, she could be. Want me to check?"

"Nah, I'll come by, see for myself."

"You don't trust me with her, do you? Scared I'll steal her from you?"

"That's it, Bruce. I've heard you're The Man when it comes to satisfying the babes. That you really set off the sexual pyrotechnics in the boudoir."

"Damn, Ace, I don't know what that shit means, but I think I like what you're saying."

Ten minutes later, Dantzler walked into the station and went past the front desk. Rawlinson wasn't there, and Dantzler was thankful for that. He liked Rawlinson, but he was in no mood for more inane chit-chat with the always-talky sergeant. Dantzler bounded up the stairs, went through Dynamite's office, Bird's office, and into the War Room. The only person there was a Vice detective named Fuller, who was draining the last drops from the coffee pot.

"Seen Dunn around?" Dantzler asked.

"'Bout two hours ago," Fuller answered. "She was at her desk."

"Did she leave?"

"Can't say, really. If she did, I didn't see her go."

"But it's been two hours since you last saw her?"

"At least."

"Thanks."

"No problem."

Dantzler went into the Homicide squad room, stopping at his desk. He picked up the phone and dialed Laurie's cell phone number again. After listening to ten rings, he hung up, stood, and went to Laurie's desk. He didn't like the cold, helpless feeling that was beginning to stir in his gut. That churning he felt when every instinct in his body told him something was wrong.

Laurie wouldn't remain incommunicado this long unless she was in trouble.

Now Dantzler was pissed *and* worried, with worried taking a slight lead.

He picked up the phone again, intending to dial Eric's number, when he saw the piece of scrap paper lying on Laurie's desk. It was partially hidden beneath a yellow legal pad, and it would've escaped his notice had he not seen the words "OUR MAN!!!" underlined several times. Sitting in Laurie's chair, he slipped the paper out and studied it.

Eldon Wessell/bookstore/writer/big reader/5'5"/chubby
OUR MAN!!!

Dantzler had no clue who Eldon Wessell was. He'd never run across the name at any stage of the investigation, and Laurie had never mentioned him during any of the briefings. Nor had any of the other detectives, for that matter. So, who was this Eldon Wessell, Dantzler wondered. What did Laurie know about him that no one else did? And why hadn't she shared her feelings with the task force? Dantzler realized that pissed had edged back in front of worried.

He knew there had to be a connection between Eldon and Rose Wessell. That much was a given. But what exactly was the connection? And how did it relate to this case? Did it relate? Dantzler closed his eyes, thinking. What he knew for certain was that Laurie had spoken with Rose on two occasions, once at the request of Rose. What Laurie *hadn't* done was share with him the information gleaned in those two interviews.

Eldon had to be Rose's husband, Dantzler figured. No, that wasn't right. He remembered Larraby telling the group that Rose had never been married. Okay, that meant Eldon was probably Rose's brother or father. Maybe an uncle or cousin. Definitely kin, though.

Dantzler picked up the phone book and thumbed through until he got to the W's. Running his forefinger quickly down the page, he found two listings for Wessell:

WESSELL, Eldon 431 Sycamore St.   273-9599
WESSELL, G & R 431 Sycamore St.   273-9628

Same address but different numbers offered further confirmation that Eldon was related to Rose in some way. Dantzler zeroed in on the address. Sycamore Street was in the Chevy Chase neighborhood, probably off Fontaine. Nice place, upscale, solid old-fashion houses, safe.

Sycamore Street.

Dantzler pushed his fingers through his hair, a frown covering his face. *Sycamore Street.* Some crumb of ancient information had broken free and was bouncing around inside his head. He tried to make sense of it, to make a logical connection, but he couldn't. It had to do with Sycamore Street, but...whatever he was looking for eluded him.

"Fuck," he grunted out loud.

He glanced at his watch—almost midnight. Under normal circumstances, too late to phone the Wessell household. However, given the situation, he had no other choice. He had to find Laurie. He wanted to make sure she was safe. He wanted to hear her voice.

Most of all, he wanted to bust her ass for being so irresponsible.

As he began punching in the numbers for G & R Wessell, the loose assemblage of information bits inside his head finally connected.

Sycamore Street.

He knew.

Dantzler punched the button to cut off his call, then began punching in a new set of numbers. On the third ring, Charlie Bolton answered.

"Charlie, Jack Dantzler. I've got—"

"Damn, Jack, do you ever make a phone call at a decent hour of the night?"

"Charlie, where did Lee Hutchinson live?"

"What?"

"Hutchinson—where did he live?"

"Goddamn, Jack, have you gone off your rocker?"

"Answer the question, Charlie. Then you can go back to bed."

"I wasn't in bed."

"Hutchinson, Charlie. Where did he live?"

"Jesus Christ, Jack, let me think about that for a minute."

"I don't have a minute to spare. Where did he live?"

"Several places, best I remember. I know he had a house on Third Street. That was when he was still married to Lois. After they called it quits, he lived down in Wellington Arms for a while. Not long after he retired, he bought a house somewhere in Chevy Chase. I'm not exactly sure where."

"Sycamore Street?"

"Yeah, that sounds right. Hell, pull his jacket and you'll know for sure."

"I don't need to. He lived at 433 Sycamore Street. I was there a couple of times, talked to him about my mother's case. It's the second house on the right."

"Yep, I remember now. It's right next to a huge old house on the corner of Fontaine and Sycamore. That's where old Lee drank himself to death. Poor bastard. Tell me, why you so interested in where Lee lived?"

"Gotta go, Charlie. But thanks."

"Sure thing. Hey, Jack, how's Dunn doing?"

"I'm about to find out."

CHAPTER 61

Laurie awoke to the sounds of shuffling feet and a loud ringing in her head. Her throat was dry and there was a dull ache at the back of her neck. She tried to recall what had happened, why she was lying in a soft bed beneath a single silk sheet, but her mind refused to cooperate. Neither would her eyes, which still stung from the harsh odor in the basement. Everything she saw appeared fuzzy, like the blurred images of an out-of-focus photograph. Tilting her head to the right, she tried to read the green numbers on the digital clock. She couldn't—they looked like a green snake. Even the person in the room with her looked more like a moving cloud than a human being. Closing her eyes, thinking of Jack Dantzler, she immediately fell asleep.

When Laurie came to the second time, it was due more to nausea than the pain at the base of her skull. She knew she was about to toss her cookies, and that she needed to get out of bed and into the bathroom. If she threw up now, while lying on her back, she could easily choke to death. She tried to get up, but couldn't. Her arms and legs seemed to be cooperating, yet nothing was happening. She tugged with both arms, then tried to move her legs. There was some give when she gave a hard pull, but she still couldn't get them free.

What the fuck is happening to me?

Tilting her head back and to the right, squinting like a drunk trying to get some focus, she soon had her answer.

Her arm, bound at the wrist by a nylon stocking, was tied to the bedpost. In fact, both arms and both legs were bound, leaving her spread eagle on the bed. Laurie tugged harder with both arms, but to no avail. She thrashed her body on the bed, hoping one of the stockings might rip or come undone. After nearly a minute of trying, exhausted, she gave up, lying back and breathing deeply.

She forced her mind to penetrate the haze, to try and remember what had happened. To recall exactly how she'd gotten into this situation. The images came, slowly, in bits and pieces, like a jigsaw puzzle being solved.

The Wessell house...a horrible stench...Rose and her mother...burning flesh... blacking out...

Fear.

Laurie had never been more terrified in her life. Or more angry with herself. How could she have been so stupid, so careless? How could she have allowed herself to get in such a predicament? How could she have been such an...

Idiot.

Okay, she thought, *stop crucifying yourself and start thinking of a way out of this mess. Work your arms and legs, keep pulling, and just maybe one of these nylon suckers will break. Most of all, though, keep calm. Look for options, strategies. And...*

Laurie heard the door open and saw Eldon come into the room. At first, given his all-black attire, she thought he might be a preacher. Or perhaps a mortician. He came closer to the bed, and she noticed that he was holding something in his hand. It was, she immediately realized, a syringe.

"Tsk, tsk, tsk, such an inquisitive young maiden," he said, smiling. "You do know what they say about curiosity and the cat, don't you? The same principle applies to humans, too, I'm afraid."

"You know you'll never get away with this," Laurie blurted out, fully aware of just how ludicrous that sounded.

And judging by Eldon's reaction, a loud pig-like snort of a giggle, he had sensed the absurdity of the statement as well.

Eldon placed the syringe on the table next to the bed, dug both hands into his pockets, fished around for a few seconds, then brought them out and held them in front of Laurie. There were two items in each hand.

"Familiar?" he said, displaying the St. Jude medal, the *Pietà* postcard, the silk scarf, and the small knife. "They should be—I know you've run across them before. Except, of course, for the knife. You might say the knife is making its debut performance."

Eldon put the four objects back in his pockets. "I'm somewhat disappointed that I won't be adorning you with these wonderful gifts in the customary way. You certainly are deserving. However, things being what they are, I'm forced to break with tradition and do a little bit of improvising. But worry not, Miss Dunn, you won't be cheated."

One lone thought cascaded through Laurie's head: *Keep the bastard talking.*

"Why are you doing this?" she said.

"Because you're here and you are worthy."

"The four women—why did you kill them?"

"Why? Why do birds chirp, Miss Dunn? Why do volcanoes erupt? Why do predators hunt and kill their prey? Because it's what they're wired to do. It's the same with people like me. We are programmed to hunt and kill. It's in our nature. If you are looking to place the blame on someone, I suggest you point a finger at that great deity in the sky. 'Our Beloved Father' is how my recently departed mother and sister referred to him. No doubt, he and the 'Blessed Virgin Mother' have already welcomed that horrible pair to the safety of their bosom." Eldon burst out laughing. "I give God two weeks before he'll start trying to pass them off to his old buddy Lucifer. Maybe he'll suggest a trade—Mother and Rose for Hitler and Stalin. Lucifer is far too sharp to fall for a sucker deal like that. God will be stuck with them, I'm afraid. And he'll tire of them rather quickly, you can count on that. Just like I tired of them."

"Why do you hate them so much?" Laurie asked.

"*Did* hate them."

"Why did you hate them?"

"Miss Dunn, you are no more interested in hearing that sad tale than I am in recounting it. I understand your desire to keep me chatting away—you are no doubt thinking that it's going to somehow delay the outcome of this night. But, I can assure you it is not. Nothing is."

Eldon looked at his wristwatch. "You have approximately thirty minutes of life left, Miss Dunn. Within that time span, I am going to remove that sheet, then remove your clothes, then my clothes, and then I am going to fuck you. When I am finished, I will take this scarf, wrap it securely around your lovely neck, and squeeze the life out of you. Then you will join

Mother and Rose for a nice little dip in the hot tub. That, my dear, is your fate, and I'm afraid there is little you can do to alter it."

"Do you really think I'm going to just lay here and allow that to happen?"

"That would be 'lie' here, Miss Dunn. If you are going to converse with me, please try to use proper grammar. Otherwise, you will come off as common and uneducated."

"I'm not going to be a passive victim. I will fight you."

"You have two options, Miss Dunn. You can cooperate and make this as painless and trouble-free as possible for both of us. That would certainly show courage and character on your part. Or you can make this difficult, in which case I will simply inject a dose of this serum into you, thus making you passive and easy to handle. Of course, if I am forced to resort to that measure, it will rob you of the joy and pleasure that awaits you."

Keep him talking.

"What's in the syringe?"

"A little cocktail of my own making. And a particularly nasty one, I might add. I learned how to mix it from information gleaned from the Internet. Amazing, the things you can pick up there. Of course, I must be extremely careful when applying the dosage. Just enough will make you docile, too much will make you dead."

"Jack Dantzler knows about you."

Eldon chuckled. "My dear, if Jack Dantzler knew about me, he would've already been here."

"I told him about you."

"One would think that a seasoned detective like yourself, having listened to countless criminals telling nothing but lies and falsehoods, would become very skilled at the art of prevarication. Sadly, that skill has thus far eluded you."

"How do you know so much about Jack?"

"*Jack?* First name basis with a superior? That can only mean one thing—you are having sexual relations with him. Is he a skillful lover?"

"Jack—*Detective* Dantzler—is impressed that you know so much about his mother's death. Your depth of knowledge is quite amazing."

"Oh, it's much more than amazing. It's complete and total."

"Did you kill Sarah Dantzler?"

"My dear, you know the answer to that question. I gave it to you in my last letter, and I do not lie. No, I did not kill her. However, I know who did."

"How do you know? How *could* you know?"

"I know—and that's what matters."

"But how?"

"This conversation is becoming rather tiresome. I do think it's time to move on to other matters."

Laurie tugged with her right leg and felt some give. She pulled harder, twisting her leg. She felt more give, but the nylon didn't snap or come untied.

Keep him talking.

"Please, Eldon, tell me how you learned so much about Sarah Dantzler's death. I'm a detective, I'd like to know. Surely, you're a decent enough man to grant me that request."

"Playing on my ego—what a sly move on your part. I'm impressed." He smiled and patted her shoulder. "As a tribute to your cunning, I will indeed grant your request. I learned it from a cop."

"Did a cop murder her?"

"Not quite. However…no, I shan't go there. My dear, if you must know, I was told the whole story by one of the original detectives who worked the case. He—"

"Sam Harper?"

"No, it was the other half of the team. You see, when I was a young lad, Lee Hutchinson lived next door. Sadly, Lee was by that time a bona fide drunk. The man drank Jack Daniels like you and I drink water. Drunks tend to fall into one of two categories: somber and silent, or excessively chatty. In Lee's case, the more he drank, the more talkative he became. He loved to regale me with stories about his days on the police force. I'm quite positive he greatly enhanced his own exploits, making himself out to be a better cop than he really was. But that didn't matter to me in the least. To a kid of twelve or thirteen, hearing heroic stuff was exciting. That was especially true in my case. Here I was, living a mundane, tortured life with two people who dismissed me as some sort of freakish clown. I was a captive in their horrible prison. To escape that existence, all I had to do was go to Lee's backyard and let him take me into another world. No kid can have had a better fantasy source than an alcoholic cop, especially one who worked Homicide."

"And Lee told you all about the Sarah Dantzler case?"

"Not only told me, he showed me. He still had a copy of the murder book, which he constantly studied. See, Lee was convinced that he knew who killed Sarah Dantzler. He even said they had interviewed the guy once, then let him go because he had a solid alibi. Well, Lee didn't believe the guy's alibi. Said there was something not right about it. But Lee's drinking finally got the best of him and he was 'retired' from the force. Anyway, one day he let me see the murder book. The crime scene photos, the witness statements, interviews, everything. About a month later, when Lee was passed out, I took the book to the library and copied it. That's when I really began to study it in earnest. Know what? I came to the same conclusion Lee did concerning the identity of the killer. I told Lee, and he was impressed."

Laurie tugged, felt more give.

"Look, Eldon, you could use that information to work out some kind of deal with Detective Dantzler. He's desperate to know who killed his mother. He'll listen, work with you."

"Like he listened that time we met?"

"You met Jack Dantzler?"

"Once, briefly, in Lee Hutchinson's backyard. That was more than twenty years ago. At the time, I expressed an interest in becoming a policeman. I mentioned that to Dantzler. Know what he did? He laughed. The smug bastard dismissed me as if I were no more significant than a fleeting thought. So, no, I think I'll pass on sharing information with Jack Dantzler."

"But this is different. You have the answer to the one question that haunts him day and night. He'd have to listen, make a deal."

"And do what, my dear? Let me trade the needle for life in prison with no chance of parole? Do you have any concept of what life behind bars would be like for someone like me? It would not be pretty, that I can assure you. No, Miss Dunn, that's a trade I'm not willing to make."

"You certainly don't expect to get away with this, do you? You can't be that arrogant."

"Oh, but I am—and I will. You see, once I've concluded my business with you, I will baptize you in the same solution that I baptized Mother and Rose. While you are slowly dissolving, I will move your car to one of the lots on campus. I will then walk home, remove some items that I treasure deeply, get into my car, and go for a little drive. I'm thinking maybe an excursion to Knoxville. At approximately eight o'clock tomorrow evening, a series of fires will break out at various locations inside the house. Arson is another subject I've studied quite extensively on the Internet. Within minutes, this place will be reduced to a heap of ashes. It will break my heart to see this old house burned to the ground, but it's a sacrifice that I must make."

"It won't work."

"Oh? And why not?"

"A third body in the house. How will you explain that?"

"My dear, I will have no explanation. I'll be as dumbfounded and perplexed as the police. How could I possibly know what happened? I will be out of town when this terrible tragedy occurs. In Knoxville, or maybe Atlanta. Far, far away. And when I do return, and when I am questioned, as I surely will be, I will inform the police that dear sister Rose had recently received a series of disturbing correspondences from an unknown admirer, and that these letters contained threats of a violent and sexual nature. Of course, the police will have no way of checking this, since said letters will have been burned to ashes by the fire."

"You don't really believe Jack Dantzler will buy that story, do you? It's ludicrous."

"Enough chit-chat, my dear. Time is fleeting."

Eldon moved suddenly to the bed and yanked the silk sheet off Laurie's body. He stepped back, looked down at her, and

took a deep breath. Before him lay a woman every bit the equal
to the other Chosen Ones. Even more important, before him lay
Jack Dantzler's chosen one. Fucking, then killing her—that
would be his ultimate victory over Dantzler. That thought
brought a smile to Eldon's face.

"Now it begins, Miss Dunn."

Eldon grabbed her blouse and ripped it down the middle,
exposing Laurie's bra. Leaning forward, he cupped her right
breast in his hand. Despite her fierce struggling, Eldon kept his
hand on her breast for several seconds, then began moving it
down between her legs. Toward what he knew would be a dark
jungle of pleasure. He couldn't wait to touch, then enter that
sacred region.

Eldon was proud of himself. His discipline tonight was
extraordinary, much stronger than it had ever been in the past.
He could say this without equivocation. And the facts would
back him up. Despite being so close to such a lovely creature,
one who lay semi-nude and spread-eagle before him, he felt no
threat of an impending orgasm. His will was...

Then it hit him—something was terribly wrong.

He wasn't erect.

His penis was as limp as a hanged man.

Feeling overwhelmed by a sense of panic, Eldon reached
inside his pants pocket and stroked his penis. No response. He
pulled at Laurie's bra, exposing one breast. Still, his penis
remained flaccid. He was stunned, flabbergasted. Never before
had this happened to him. Never had the thought of impotence
even crossed his mind. Never had he failed to produce an
erection. Why was it happening now? What had caused his
body's failure to respond? What was wrong with him?

Eldon fought off the panic and willed himself to act. He
leaned over and kissed her nipple. When he did, Laurie lifted her
head and managed to bite his left earlobe.

Eldon squealed, snapped back, and put his hand to the
wounded ear. "So I can only assume that you've chosen to take
the difficult route," he said, looking at the blood on his hand. "I
am disappointed but not surprised."

"You fucking bastard," Laurie hissed.

Eldon picked up the syringe from the table, held the needle up, and sent a small stream of serum into the air. He then grabbed Laurie's right arm and began searching for a vein.

"Struggling is only going to make this more difficult," Eldon said. "So, please, be a nice little girl and accept your fate willingly."

"Fuck you!"

"Oh, lookie what I found," Eldon said. "A nice big fat vein just begging for the needle. Relax, my dear. In less than a minute, you'll think angels are ministering to you—"

"*Wessell!*"

At first, Eldon thought the sound was coming from inside his own head. It wasn't until a fraction of a second later that he realized the sound had come from behind him. He spun around quickly, keeping the needle poised against Laurie's arm. A smile crept across his face.

"Well, well, Jack Dantzler to the rescue. I might've guessed."

Dantzler stood just inside the door, Glock in hand, crouched in the classic shooter's stance. "Put the needle down, get your hands above your head, and move away from the bed," he ordered. "Slowly. Make one move I don't like and you're dead."

"Well, now, Jack, I just don't see how I can do all that." Eldon moved the needle up and placed it against Laurie's jugular. "In fact, I have an entirely different set of terms. You put the gun on the floor and kick it in my direction, or else I will be forced to inject the lovely Miss Dunn with enough serum to kill her instantly. I understand completely that if I do, you will shoot me dead. You will have that small victory, but only at the cost of her life. Are you willing to sacrifice her on the altar of your legend?"

Laurie gave one hard tug with her right leg and felt the nylon stretch three to four inches. When it did, she looked at Dantzler and cut her eyes upward. On her left hand, she held up three fingers.

Dantzler saw the three fingers, looked at Laurie, and nodded.

"On the count of five, Wessell, if you haven't followed my orders, I'm firing," Dantzler said.

"Oh, really? Well, I think I'll just call that bluff. In fact, I'll even count for you."

"Go."

"One…"

Dantzler looked at Laurie.

"Two…"

Laurie nodded.

"Three…"

On three, Laurie yanked her right leg free and rolled to her left. At the same instant, Dantzler fired, scoring a direct hit in Eldon's chest. Eldon slammed hard against the headboard, slumped, and toppled onto the floor, knocking over the table.

Dantzler rushed to Eldon's body, carefully took the syringe from his hand, and checked for a pulse. There wasn't one. Eldon Wessell had died instantly.

Standing, Dantzler holstered his weapon, looked down at Laurie, and said," Are you okay?"

"I think so, yes."

Dantzler quickly untied her, and when she was free, she wrapped her arms around him and hugged him hard for almost two minutes. It was only then that she realized she was trembling, and that tears were streaming down her face.

"You sure you're okay," he whispered into her ear.

"Yes," she said, although she wasn't sure if she said it out loud or to herself.

CHAPTER 62

"Well, Ace, you're perfect once again," Dan Matthews said, chuckling. "Congratulations."

"Only because of her," Dantzler answered, nodding toward Laurie, who was standing next to the door talking to Richard Bird. "She figured it out before any of us."

"True, and I'll give her credit for that. But she didn't handle certain things particularly well. You have to admit that. In this business, knowing something and sharing it go hand in hand. I hope she learned that lesson."

Matthews gave Dantzler a playful punch on the arm. "She's a damn good *detective*, Ace. A real keeper. She's also one lucky young lady."

The room was a buzz of activity. Costello and Larraby were going through Eldon's closets and dresser drawers. CSI personnel were gathering prints and blood samples. Eric Gamble stood alongside Mac Tinsley, who was kneeling next to Eldon's body.

Finally, Mac stood and turned toward Dantzler. He was grinning like a kid who'd just been given a new bike. "Jack, old James Butler Hickok couldn't have been more accurate than you were with this shot," Mac said. "You scored a direct bull's-eye. Got the sorry prick right in his valentine. Nice shootin', cowboy."

"What about the two vics in the basement? Any guess as to cause of death?"

"That may take a while, if it can be discerned at all. Given the state of deterioration of their bodies, we may never know for sure. But if I had to hazard a guess, I'd say they were strangled."

Costello came over and stood between Dantzler and Mac. He was holding a large cardboard box in his hands.

"No wonder the guy knew so much about you," Costello said. "He's got every article ever written about you in here. There's stuff in here going back for years. Look at this one. It's one from when you won the high school tennis championship. Shit, man, I never realized it, but you've got some serious bird legs."

"And check this out," Eric said, holding up a blue three-ring binder. "This is the murder book on your mother's case. I mean, he's got *everything* in here. How the hell did he manage to get his hands on this?"

"Lee Hutchinson."

"Hutchinson gave it to him?" Eric asked.

"Nah, he took it when Lee was passed out, then had it copied."

"Damn, I hope I never become a drunk."

Matthews came up behind Eric and put an arm on his shoulder. "Way you spend money on clothes, Eric, you won't have any left to buy booze." He looked at Dantzler. "This guy Wessell was one sick fuck, Jack. Porno magazines, porno Web sites, porno videos. Hell, he even had his own peephole into the bathroom. Know what he used to cover it?"

"A picture of the *Pietà*."

"Damn, you're good, Ace. I was sure I had you on that one."

Costello said, "Wessell kept articles about the four dead girls. But in those letters, he alluded to a fifth victim. If there's anything in here about number five, I can't find it."

"My mother—she was the fifth victim," Dantzler said.

"Damn, what a loony fuckin' bird this guy was," Costello said.

"Hey, take a look at this," Eric said, handing a torn piece of newspaper to Dantzler. It was a clipping from the Lexington *Herald* obit page dated February 6, 1978, the day after Sarah Dantzler's death. In the clipping, a red circle had been drawn around Sarah's picture. Outside the circle, near the top of the page, someone had written two names: David Langley and Lucas White. Next to White's name were four stars. "Those names ring a bell, Jack?"

Dantzler pointed at David Langley's name. "This guy, yes. He was interviewed during the investigation." His finger tapped several inches below the second name. "But this guy—Lucas White—I don't know him at all."

"What do you make of the four stars?" Eric said.

"I haven't a clue."

Matthews took the clipping from Dantzler and studied it. "Damn, Ace," he said, looking up. "Think these two guys killed your mother?"

Dantzler shook his head. "I don't know. But at some point, I intend to find out." His cell phone rang. He stepped away from the crowd, put one hand over his ear, and spoke. "Dantzler."

"Jack, Andy Waters."

"What's up, Andy?"

"You tell me."

"We got our killer. He's dead."

"Good to hear that. Now our fair city can sleep peacefully once again."

"What's on your mind, Andy? I'm kinda busy here."

"Just wanted to remind you of our deal. You haven't forgotten, have you?"

"Call me tomorrow morning. Say around ten. I'll give you everything."

"Think there's enough here for a book?"

"Oh, yeah."

"Hot damn, that's music to my ears. Thanks, Jack. You're a man of your word."

Dantzler punched off, turned, looked at Laurie, and winked. Seeing her now, face drawn, eyes weary—*safe*—he admitted to himself for the first time that he was in love with her. Only now did he realize just how true Matthews's words were: *She's also one lucky young lady.*

Richard Bird walked to the center of the room. "Listen up, folks," he said loudly, getting everyone's attention. "When you finish up here, go home and get some rest. Let's all get together Monday afternoon, say around one o'clock. We'll tie up any loose ends then. And I want you to know how proud I am of you. All of you. You did a terrific job. I'm just thankful it worked out like it did."

He put his arm around Laurie and drew her next to his side. "I'd like to offer a special compliment to Sergeant Dunn," he said, hugging her. "While some of her judgments might be questionable, there can be no denying that her detective instincts were outstanding. Good job, Sergeant."

Laurie was too exhausted to acknowledge the compliment.

CHAPTER 63

Dantzler sent a soft volley in the direction of the striking young black woman across the net. She handled it perfectly, smacking a surprisingly hard shot back at him. Dantzler moved deftly to his right, deadened his racket, and dropped the ball just over the net. Eric, caught by surprise, charged toward the ball, getting to it well after it had bounced three times.

"Damn, man, that's not fair," Eric said, catching his breath. "Dink shots shouldn't be allowed."

"Stop whining, Eric," Dantzler said. "Be more like your partner. Gwen hasn't complained once."

"That's because you don't hit her anything *but* dink shots."

Dantzler turned to Laurie. "What's the score, partner?" he said.

"I do believe it's 40-15."

"And I do believe that brings us to match point. Show 'em what you've got, pal."

Laurie tossed the ball into the air and brought her racket through, just the way Dantzler had taught her. She connected dead center, sending a well-placed serve toward the left corner of the court. Eric anticipated the shot and was there waiting for the ball. He drew his arm back and took a hard swing, but the ball hit his racket frame and shot high into the air. As soon as it went skyward, Dantzler moved close to the net, racket drawn, waiting for the ball to come down.

"Get ready, Eric, this one's going right into your family jewels," Dantzler announced loudly.

"Ah, shit," Eric said, bringing his hands and racket down to protect his privates.

As the ball descended, Danzler drew his racket back ever farther, as though he were going to crush the yellow ball. But at the last moment, he barely moved the racket forward, again dropping a dink shot just over the net.

"Match point," he said, putting an arm around Laurie. "Next up for me and Dunn—the U.S. Open."

"Next up for me is golf," Eric said. "Maybe Tiger Woods will treat me better than you do."

"No way. Tiger will hate you."

"Oh, yeah? Why?"

"Because you dress better than he does."

Two hours later, Dantzler and Laurie were on his deck, watching the glorious summer sun nestle into the horizon. On the edge of the lake, a family of ducks battled for the small pieces of bread two young children were tossing into the water. The temperature was in the high sixties, perfect for an early June evening.

Laurie sat in the chair next to Dantzler, a bottle of Coors in her hand. He looked at her, and judged her to be more beautiful at that moment than ever before. Reaching across, he took her left hand in his and gave it a squeeze. She lifted his hand up and kissed it.

In the two weeks since the events at the Wessell house, they had seen each other often but spent relatively little time together. Between the meetings, hearings, debriefings, coroner's inquest, other cases that had to be attended to, and the reams of paperwork that had to be filled out, they had barely been able to snatch a couple of nights for themselves. With things now winding down and a sense of normalcy having returned, Dantzler looked forward to spending more time with Laurie. If all went well, if another serial killer didn't pop up, he planned on spending the next few months defining—and cementing—his relationship with her.

Of course, the weather forecasters were still predicting a blistering summer, which could send even the best-laid plans into the tank. Hot temperatures and homicide were brothers bound by blood.

"Turn this song up," Laurie said. "It's my favorite."

Dantzler did as he was ordered. It was "Master Song" from Leonard Cohen's first album.

"Why do you like this one so much?" Dantzler asked.

"Because there's a lyric in it that could've been written for you."

"Which one?"

"'He was starving in some deep mystery like a man who is sure what is true.' That fits you to a T."

"That's flattering, but I'm not sure I agree."

"Hush. I want to hear this."

Dantzler feigned a wounded look, but inwardly he was pleased. Beautiful, sexy, *and* a Leonard Cohen fan. How could he *not* love this woman?

As the sun dipped over the horizon and darkness blanketed the city, Dantzler stood, leaned over, and kissed Laurie on the lips. "Tired?" he whispered.

"No. But I am ready for bed."

"Good answer."